BROKEN PROMISE

BROKEN PROMISE

--- by ---

Kent Hayes
and
Alex Lazzarino

G. P. PUTNAM'S SONS
NEW YORK

This book is lovingly dedicated to two beautiful wives, Betsy Hayes and Diane Lazzarino, and to our children who helped us through the depressing and painful experiences of reliving the disturbing memories and case histories of the many persons described in this book.

Published simultaneously in Canada by Longman Canada Limited, Toronto.

SBN: 399-12188-9
Library of Congress Cataloguing in Publication Data

Hayes, E. Kent.
    Broken Promise

    I. Lazzarino, Alex, joint author   II. Title

P24.H4168Ab   (PS3558.A8296)   813'.5'4'   78-4832

PROLOGUE

1951–1964

The county courthouse in Newark had seen better days. The limestone exterior was covered with the soot and grime of more than a half-century of industrial pollution. Inside the building, the ancient wood floors creaked, and the plaster ceilings were cracked beyond repair. Only the dark mahogany paneling, spanning the eighteen feet from floor to ceiling, bore its age with dignity and beauty.

"All rise," the bailiff intoned as the judge entered the courtroom. "The Criminal Court Division of the Second Judicial District is now in session. Judge Julius Weinberg presiding."

"Be seated," the judge instructed as he took the bench. "The defendant will come forward for sentencing."

A defiant nineteen-year-old boy was led forward by his court-appointed attorney and stood glaring up into Judge Weinberg's impassive eyes.

"Thomas Calvin Clawson, one month ago you pleaded *nolo contendere* to the charges of aggravated assault upon a law

7

officer, resisting arrest, and drunk and disorderly conduct. We were advised at that time by the Public Defender that you had refused to cooperate in the preparation of your own defense, so we ordered a complete assessment of your personal history in an attempt to uncover any circumstances that might mitigate in your behalf.

"Every piece of information that has come to us tends to reinforce our impression that you are a recalcitrant and bitter young man. Yours has been a long record of truancy, malicious mischief, and vandalism that brought you into official custody for the first time when you were but eight years old.

"The only person willing to step forward in your behalf was your former juvenile parole officer, Mr. Guardino, and, no thanks to you, he was finally able to locate your mother and stepfather."

"He ain't NO kind of goddam father to me," snarled the boy.

". . . Your mother and her husband, then," the judge said, his face beginning to flush. "But the point is that your mother refused to involve herself further in your problems, and we are now left with no one except Mr. Guardino to offer this court some explanation for your behavior.

"Dr. Patton's psychiatric evaluation portrays you as a . . . ," the judge paused and scanned the report. "Here it is," he continued in a sarcastic tone. "He sees you as 'A lost child rebelling against authority and searching for the father he never knew.'"

"That's a bunch of shit, and you know it," mocked the boy.

Judge Weinberg, obviously struggling with his temper, agreed through clenched teeth, "Yes, I know it, and I suspect the policeman that you brutally battered also knows that you are not some child to be pitied."

"Nevertheless," the judge continued as he reined his anger, "Mr. Guardino has urged the court to consider the fact that you were expelled from your home when you were fourteen years old and have been left to your own devices since.

In considering the limited alternatives that are available to this court in the disposition of your case, we nave conferred with the military recruitment officers in this building, and Sergeant Collins is willing to talk with you in a few minutes. If it is true that you are looking for a 'father figure,' young man, this court is now prepared to offer you a choice. Your new 'father' will be either a cellblock commander or a drill sergeant.

"In other words, Thomas Clawson, either you will voluntarily enlist in the United States Army—if they will have you—or you will be remanded to the custody of the county sheriff, to be delivered to the State Prison for a period not less than three nor more than five years."

The year was 1951, and the practice of giving young hoodlums the choice of going to jail or serving in Korea was quite prevalent. The street-wise Tom Clawson had known all along that that option would be made available to him, and he also knew how simple it would be to work a quick discharge from the Army and return to the streets.

He laughed contemptuously and, scanning the courtroom for Sergeant Collins, he announced his decision in a mocking drawl:

"Where's my new daddy?"

Tom spent the night in the holding tank and was driven to Fort Dix the following morning. The deputy who accompanied him goaded him in every way possible, but Tom was careful to respond to the taunts with simple and derisive "Yes, sir," "No, sir," and "Thank you, sir" because he knew that prison could be an unhealthy place for a cop-beater. By the time they reached the reception center, the deputy was livid with anger and frustration, and Tom was flushed with the pleasure of conquest.

Within a week of induction, Tom Clawson was transferred to Camp Gordon, Georgia, for basic training. The entire company was distressed with the rumor that Camp Gordon was the training center for people scheduled for combat in

Korea, but Tom was unconcerned. His plan was to prove himself unworthy of being shot at, and he set out to make his point without delay.

Shortly after arriving at Camp Gordon, Tom received an official reprimand for stealing from other trainees, and when he repeated that offense two weeks later, he was brought up on charges. Only four months after Judge Weinberg had entrusted his care to the United States Army, a military tribunal handed him his undesirable discharge and a ticket to New Jersey.

Savoring the pleasure of having manipulated the system once again, Tom was nonetheless wary of tempting the fates. Rather than risking a confrontation with the policeman he had assaulted, Tom left Newark for Paterson, where he drifted in and out of unskilled jobs for a year, working just enough to keep himself in gambling and drinking money.

He lived alone in one room of a run-down boarding house, and most of his free time was spent in the neighborhood bars where he continued to enjoy the company of people on the fringe: small-time hoodlums, gamblers, bookies, fences, con artists, pimps, and prostitutes. Tom occasionally picked up some loose change by helping to fence burglared jewelry and watches—cheap stuff never amounting to more than five dollars an item.

He was flattered one evening when one of the biggest of the local small-time operators asked him to ice down stolen securities. This entailed nothing more than accepting a locked satchel and taking it to his room for safekeeping until a messenger arrived to transport the stolen securities elsewhere, but to Tom, it was a sacred trust that bespoke his acceptance by the thieves he admired. He was especially comforted by the fact that he had won this recognition with virtually no risk to himself.

But since it was found money that disproportionately exceeded the hazards, Tom's ego was pumped up. He avoided participating in the commission of other crimes, but he became a regular contributor to the local crap games, and his eye for the horses went from bad to disastrous. The gambling debts that he was permitted to accumulate served only to reinforce his self-image as a person to be trusted—a young man on his way up.

Early one morning, he staggered to his room in a drunken stupor; as he reached for the light switch, a hand reached out and locked his wrist in a vice. "Take it easy, Tommy boy, no one wants to hurt you," came the voice from the darkness.

Alarmed into complete and instant sobriety, Tom pleaded for his safety without even asking who was there or why.

"Mr. Piccone thinks you should start paying off your markers."

Terrified that a connected mobster even knew his name, Tom whimpered, "But . . . but I don't owe Mr. Piccone. He doesn't even *know* me."

"That's where you're wrong, kid. Mr. Piccone knows you. He even *likes* you. That's why he's been taking your markers. And now he figures you owe him," the voice continued without releasing Tom's wrist.

"Oh, God," Tom whined.

The vice opened, and Tom almost fell to his knees. "Take it easy, kid. Like I said, Mr. Piccone *likes* you. He figures you might want to show your appreciation by doing him a little favor." The scene was right out of Tom's favorite movies, but he did not enjoy being the star.

"What does he want?"

"Mr. Piccone will call you when you're feeling better," said the gentle voice. Then the door opened, closed, and Tom was again alone in his dark room.

Two days later, Tom listened to his options: first there was the cheerful and optimistic explanation of how simple, safe, and rewarding it would be to advance from cooling securities to delivering them; then there was a horribly graphic description of how painful it would be to have his fingers broken at every joint should he refuse. The decision was an easy one.

Tom was assigned the Philadelphia-to-Paterson route. On

his first couple of trips, he saw Treasury agents under every raincoat and rival mobsters under every fedora, but he soon settled into the routine and began to enjoy not only the financial rewards of his craft but also the peripheral respect that came with associating with connected people. He belatedly celebrated his twenty-first birthday by purchasing his first suit, and many others followed as he began to emulate his aloof benefactors in manner and dress. When Tom Clawson felt he had outgrown his New Jersey associates, he moved to Philadelphia to be closer to the action, but the only thing that changed about him was his clothing. He still rented a one-room hovel and frequented the same sleazy bars, but wherever he went, he was the biggest spender and flashiest dresser there.

June Womack was hustling one of the neighborhood joints when she saw Tom for the first time. She immediately pegged him for what he was: a small-timer who was riding the coattails of others. June noted the flashy clothes and free-spending grandiosity that was the manner of men without influence who needed to have others believe otherwise, but she was attracted to a certain detachment in Tom that was characterized by his reluctance to share barroom bragging with others, and his willingness to listen to the drunken lies of those around him.

June shrewdly decided to hustle Tom without any mention of money, and by the end of that first evening, Tom was flattered by her obvious attraction to him. After the first night together, June knew she had found a meal ticket, so she moved in with him. She intuited Tom's preoccupation with appearances, so she avoided her old haunts except when in Tom's company. She persuaded him to move them into a more respectable apartment, and whenever Tom was traveling to New Jersey, she stayed home to await his calls.

Tom's run was soon expanded to include Toronto, and his income reflected the additional risk of delivering stolen securities across international boundaries. He was away from home more, but the intensity of their nightlife was heightened whenever he returned.

One night in the early summer of 1952, June informed Tom that she was pregnant. She had chosen to break the news in the plush and romantic atmosphere of one of Philadelphia's best supper clubs. The evening had not gone well because of her own apprehensions and Tom's discomfort in that strange and elegant setting.

The cocktails did little to help them unwind, and the atmosphere was tense. They ordered from the strange menu with affected casualness, but when the appetizers were served, and Tom realized that they had ordered snails, his mood darkened further. June decided she could wait no longer.

"Tommy, the doctor told me last week that I'm going to have a baby."

The entire room seemed to grow quiet as Tom stared at her in silence.

June continued nervously, "Nothing has to change, baby. I can get it taken care of if you don't want it. Everything will be the same as always."

There was another moment of silence, then Tom said, with a trace of humor, "Is that why you brought me to this joint? You're knocked up? Is that all? Let's get the hell out of here." He pushed his chair back, and in the grand manner of his favorite movie heroes, peeled off a generous amount of folding money and tossed it on top of the table. He then walked past her on the way to the door.

June scrambled out of her chair and scurried after him. "Baby," she cried as she caught his arm, "it's no big deal. I told you, nothing has to change. I can get it taken care of."

Tom looked down at her as they walked and almost laughed. "You're right, it's no big deal. Matter of fact, it don't make no difference to me at all."

"Does that mean you want me to have the baby or not," June asked.

"It means that I don't give a crap one way or the other. If

it's my kid, I'll take care of it, but I don't care if you have it or not." Neither of them raised the subject again as they spent the remainder of the evening making the rounds of their more familiar haunts.

June agonized over her decision for several weeks before making up her mind to abort. She visited a physician whose license had been revoked ten years earlier, and to assure herself of the best treatment possible, she made the mistake of dropping the names of her "husband's" employers. By the time she got to the name of Vito Piccone, the abortionist was too intimidated to take any risks, so he informed her that she was too far along to have her pregnancy terminated safely.

Left with no alternative, June dedicated herself to having the baby with a minimum of inconvenience to Tom and herself. As she outgrew her wardrobe of tight dresses, she applied herself more diligently to household chores, but her domesticity kept Tom on the road for longer and longer periods.

Aside from the fear of losing Tom, June's uppermost awareness was the embarrassment of having made such a mistake. She'd been on the streets since she was fifteen and should have known how to take care of herself. She fended the derision of her girl friends by pretending that she had planned the pregnancy as a first step in the process of getting married and settling down. At first, it was a shallow ploy, but she began to be obsessed about it, and, ultimately, just to quiet her nagging and badgering, Tom agreed to marry her in November, on the one day he would be in town all month.

June Clawson gave birth to Patricia on January 17, 1953, at Liberty Memorial Hospital, on the last day of a snowstorm that had raged for almost a week. June was oblivious to the pain, to the weather, and to the obligatory ceremony of holding her baby for the first time. She was aware only of her relief in having finally thrown off this impediment to her sleek good looks. Now she would have the chance to win back Tom's attentions. She hadn't seen him for three weeks, and if he would only stay away a while longer, she would be fitting into those tight dresses he used to like so much.

Tom returned to the Philadelphia apartment in late February without fanfare and without a word of explanation for his two months' absence. June was sitting at the kitchen table and was well into a fresh bottle of bourbon when he unlocked the door and walked in. She looked up and rose slowly.

"I heard you had it," he said, pointing to her stomach. "Boy or girl?"

"Girl," June responded without emotion. "Patricia. In the bedroom if you want to look."

"Later," Tom said, appraising her trim figure. "How about us going down for a drink?"

June perked up. "It'd take me a while to get ready," she said as she smoothed the front of her shirt and tucked it into her jeans. "And I'd have to check around for a baby-sitter," she added apprehensively.

"You do that," Tom said. "I'll be down the corner."

Not about to lose this opportunity, June ran to her closet the moment Tom closed the door behind him. She had been planning this for so long, every move seemed rehearsed: the bath, the curlers, the silky new underwear, the cosmetics, the clinging new dress, and the perfume. She completed the transformation in only forty minutes, and, admiring the results in her full-length mirror, she thought herself ready to leave when a short gurgle from the crib snapped her back to reality.

"Oh, no," she said aloud as her mind screamed *THE BABY-SITTER!*

She ran to the telephone and wasted ten precious minutes trying unsuccessfully to find a sitter. To add to her panic and disorientation, Patty started screaming angrily from the crib. June ran to the kitchen and filled a bottle with cold milk, capping it with a nipple that was lying on the counter. Walking quickly to the bedroom, she stuck the nipple into Patty's mouth and propped the bottle in a rolled-up blanket. While Patty sucked voraciously, June took one last look around the room and left the apartment.

"Well," Tom exclaimed in surprise when she walked up to his table. "Wellll . . . ," he repeated in a deeper voice of sensual appreciation as he gazed at her tiny waist and swollen breasts. "We're gonna have us a party!" They resumed their sociality as if the five months since their last fling had passed in less than a day. They hopped from bar to bar, drinking heavily at each, and dancing whenever the music was slow enough to savor each other's bodies.

It was the courtship June had never known, and she was reluctant to end it, but Tom was anxious for the intimacy that could not be afforded in any bar, so they started back to the apartment long before closing time.

Tom and June Clawson proceeded down the street as they had left the bar: arms around each other, tipsy, giggling, and laughing—Tom mischievously grabbing at various parts of June's body, and June playfully slapping at his hand. They stumbled around the last corner, and Tom froze in his tracks. He squinted his eyes in an effort to focus his blurred vision.

June pulled away and looked at him quizzically. Then she glanced down the street and saw a police car parked in front of their building. The red light was revolving lazily, and the car was empty.

Without a word, Tom spun away from her and retraced his steps around the corner as fast as he could run. June instinctively started after him, hissing, "Wait . . . wait . . . it must be someone else. Come back." One hand was outstretched, but after a few steps, she stopped as the thought came through her fuzzy mind . . . *THE BABY!*

June turned and bolted toward the house. She climbed the stairs one at a time because her tight dress would permit no more, but her feet were moving so fast that the sound of her heels gave rapid-fire notice to those who were waiting in her apartment.

One policeman was interviewing Mrs. Greenberg while the other took notes. June ran past them toward the bedroom without saying a word, her face ashen. All three looked up, and Mrs. Greenberg said, "That's the mother, there."

June burst into the bedroom, shouting, "Patty!"

The infant jumped in Mrs. Gargiulio's arms, and frightened by the commotion, she started to cry as June snatched her baby from the arms of her neighbor. Mrs. Gargiulio stepped back with a scowl of angry disapproval as June began to sob uncontrollably. It was perfectly apparent from the gusto of Patty's outburst that she was all right, and even before June brought herself under control, her mind was racing through her predicament, sorting through the excuses and lies that would seem most plausible to the police.

The two policemen approached her mutely and stood a few feet away. Out of the corner of one eye, June saw her two neighbors huddling near the door: the stout Mrs. Gargiulio, with tears in her eyes and anger written all over her face, and the wiry Mrs. Greenberg, standing on her toes, whispering animatedly up into her ear.

With the sure instinct for survival that had always been her strength, June heard herself whisper, "Jenny . . . Where's Jenny? . . . Is she all right? . . . Where is she?"

Sergeant Mullins asked softly, "Mrs. Clawson? Who's Jenny, m'am?"

"The baby-sitter," June answered. "I left her here to take care of Patty. Where is she?"

"There was no baby-sitter, m'am. Your neighbors heard the baby crying and got worried when no one answered. They called us, and when we got here the door was unlocked. That was a half hour ago, and there's been no baby-sitter."

"But what happened to her? How long ago did she leave?" asked June, feigning concern and confusion.

Mrs. Greenberg answered in an accusatory tone, "There was no baby-sitter. That child had been screaming for an hour before we called the police. There never was no baby-sitter."

"If you can swear to that," Sergeant Mullins said to Mrs. Greenberg, "I'd like you to sign a complaint. This could be a serious matter."

The prospect of further involvement, especially at so formal a level as signing a complaint, wilted Mrs. Greenberg's indignant resolve. "I only said that I didn't *see* a baby-sitter. She could have left before the baby started to cry."

June felt the tension draining because she knew she was out of the woods. She fabricated cursory answers to the remaining questions: Her husband was a traveling salesman; Jenny was a high school girl who showed up on a regular basis on the first Thursday of the month; June had been using her for months, and no, she didn't know where the girl lived.

Closure of the entire episode was finally assured when June advised the officers that she and her husband were about to move to Newark, and that she just left him at the train to find housing for them.

From the odor of liquor on her breath, and from the way she was dressed, the policemen doubted that she had been to the train station, but if, indeed, she was about to move herself and her baby out of their jurisdiction, then why ask for trouble?

The two policemen left with rather bland assurances that they would be checking up from time to time, and Mrs. Greenberg followed them through the door. Mrs. Gargiulio, who had raised seven children of her own, remained behind. The anger in her face had not diminished; her lips were trembling, and there were tears in her eyes when she looked at June and hissed, "You are a pig!"

Mrs. Gargiulio left without another word, and the sound of the door slamming behind her was the signal for June to drop Patty back into the crib and forget everything that had transpired. Her only thought was, *He ran away. I may not ever see him again.*

It was three weeks before Tom ventured a telephone call. June assured him that there had been no problem with the police—they were only in the building to remove a couple of drunks from the hallway. Five minutes later, Tom arrived at the apartment, and the two took up where they had left off. Tom remained close to home for more than four months, and it was June's primary task to keep Patty out of her father's way as much as possible. Tom never fed her, held her, or even looked at her unless in passing. Yet he never seemed angry or resentful toward her. It was just as if she did not exist.

By the time June found out she was pregnant again, she had lost some of her urgency to hold on to her husband's affections, so she was completely void of apprehension when she announced one morning in August, "I'm pregnant again . . . the end of February."

When Tom left her this time, June made no pretense about waiting home for his calls. She made the rounds of the neighborhood bars on her own every night, never forgetting to leave Patty in someone's care. The local men avoided picking June up because of some vague recollection of her husband's connection with the mob, but as often as not, June was successful in finding strange men to pick up her tabs.

By early fall, her pregnancy began to show, so June confined herself to solo drinking in the apartment. Tom became little more than a memory. The last time he had popped in, he told her to call when it was all over, and she told him to go to hell.

John was born on February 20th, 1955, and six weeks later, Tom moved back to the apartment. If it was possible for the situation to get worse, it did the following year, when he moved out permanently . . . six months before Sue Anne was born.

June had dreaded the thought of having Patty, and she was angry about having John, but she was resentful about Sue Anne.

Fortunately, there were no great financial problems. Soon after Tom disappeared, June left word with his bookmaker that she would contact the police unless he provided financial support, so he deposited funds with the bookie every month, and when June picked up her money, she in turn left the bills that needed to be paid.

June brought Sue Anne home from the hospital as indifferently as she would have brought in a bag of groceries. But when she arrived, she was puzzled by an uncustomary excitement that was generated by Patty's enthusiasm for the new infant. Patty, who was then three years and nine months old, had been waiting at the upstairs window when June emerged from the taxi. She came bounding down the stairs and met her mother at the front door. Patty locked her arms around June's legs, shouting, "Lemme see! Lemme see!"

June released Patty's hold to keep from falling, then she bent down and lifted the corner of the delivery blanket that covered the baby's face.

Patty was awestruck. "What's her name?" she asked excitedly. "Did you name her after my dollie?"

"Yes," said June. "Sue Anne."

"Then she's mine," Patty exclaimed. "Can I carry her?"

"Okay," June responded indifferently, handing one baby to the other and following both up the stairs.

There was a familiar face at the landing. Mrs. Gargiulio was standing there holding John, who was a lively two-and-a-half-year-old who headed for the stairs every time the apartment door opened. Wiggling in the arms of the robust woman, he pushed against her and yelled, "Momma! Momma!"

June stopped on the staircase and looked questioningly at the older woman. She had arranged for Sherie, an old friend, to stay with the children while she was in the hospital, but Mrs. Gargiulio was now clearly in charge. The older woman answered the question without being asked: "My

Vito found John downstairs on the sidewalk, so when that floozy came back, I told her to get out and stay out."

June nodded imperceptibly and continued to the top of the stairs without acknowledging John's greeting. Patty gently deposited Sue Anne on a blanket she had prepared on the floor, and when Mrs. Gargiulio finally released John, he bounded into the apartment after the others.

June stared listlessly at her neighbor, who was still in the hall. Mrs. Gargiulio reached in to pull the door shut, and as if in response to an unspoken expression of gratitude, she said, "I did it for them, not you."

Patty assumed responsibility for Sue Anne's care from the very beginning. She learned how to prepare her formula and rock her to sleep; and whenever clean diapers were available, it was Patty's job to change them. As June reverted to her custom of spending more time in the bars, Patty made sure that John was fed and went to bed in his pajamas. By the time Patty was four years old, she had become the children's full-time baby-sitter and surrogate mother.

Tom made no attempt to get in touch with June or to see the children, but he continued to provide financial support for another year. Then, in October, 1957, there was no money waiting for June at the regular time and place. She returned every day for a week, and then she learned that Tom had been arrested in Buffalo. By the time he was extradited to Philadelphia, June was desperately in need of cash, so she arranged to visit him in jail.

She hadn't seen him in almost two years, and she was shocked at his appearance. Perhaps it was the way he was dressed, perhaps it was his prison pallor, but his cockiness was gone, and he seemed to have aged by fifteen years. But she was concerned only with her financial problems, and when she asked the question, he laughed and told her there was no money left.

In July, 1958, Tom was sentenced to Lewisburg for a six-to-ten-year term for interstate transportation of stolen securities. June and the children had been evicted from the apartment and placed on the welfare rolls. The separation from Mrs. Gargiulio had been a tearful one for the children, but they looked forward to moving as a new adventure.

The family moved into a third-floor flat in the worst slums of Philadelphia. There were two bedrooms, a living room, and a small kitchen. There was a butcher shop on the ground floor of the building and a neighborhood grocery store adjacent to that. The long hallways and staircases were darkened and unventilated, and the odor of dampness and urine pervaded the entire place.

June was picked up twice for drunk and disorderly conduct, but the children were not removed because the court felt that it was better to keep the children in a marginal home situation than to place them in foster care.

Thirteen months after Tom went to prison, June gave birth to her fourth baby, Karen, on August 9, 1959. The six-and-a-half-year-old Patty accepted the new child into her care without question, and the routine continued until Sue Anne's accident. She broke her leg and lay in pain for four days while Patty and John tried to find June. Sue Anne almost lost her leg and remained hospitalized for months, and the three other children were placed in separate foster homes. June Clawson was arrested for child desertion and criminal neglect, but that was not the sort of thing they really put parents in jail for then, so she was let out on her own recognizance, on condition that she undergo psychiatric treatment.

June's "psychiatric treatment" consisted of four interviews with a young social worker. Her strategy was simple: Be tough and unyielding for the first two interviews, then break down halfway through the third session, sobbing that she had been a victim of a bad home, white slavery, and a rotten husband, and that no one had ever helped her before the social worker had plied her skills. By the end of the fourth interview, three months later, June walked out of the office with a smirk on her face and a paper in her hand that said that she could now reclaim her four children.

The children were generally delighted to be together again. Patricia and Karen had had unhappy foster home placements, but John had been cared for by a loving older couple, and he had mixed feelings about returning home.

In spite of her cynical reaction to the social worker, June was determined to be a better mother, but her resolve lasted all of forty-eight hours before she returned to the neighborhood bars. Four months later, on March 12, 1962, Charlie—the fifth and last child—was born.

June's physical appeal faded, and men no longer gave her those extra gifts that had made life bearable.

She began to look forward to Tom's release. She fantasized about having a husband who would support the family and give them yet another fresh start.

Charlie was fifteen months old when Tom Clawson finished his six-year term at Lewisburg. He had left three children behind when he went to prison, but he was not particularly surprised to find two more when he returned. He knew they couldn't have been his, but no questions were asked.

Things did not go well for the Clawson family. The stigma of being an ex-con made it tough for Tom to find work in Philadelphia, and before long he stopped looking. The welfare checks had provided barely enough for the children to survive and to keep June Clawson in her alcoholic stupor. When Tom returned, however, even the welfare checks were about to stop, and there would be no income unless Tom found work soon, but his heart wasn't in it.

The bills were piling up. The rent and utilities had not been paid in two months, and the grocers were duped into extending credit only because June had the sense to send Sue Anne, now eight years old, who spoke with a cute lisp and walked with a pitiful limp. When that ploy failed, Sue Anne carried Charlie, her eighteen-month-old brother, on her back. As a final ruse, she ordered all five hungry and pathetic children out to beg for bread and peanut butter. Patty, who was eleven, refused to comply, and when the others returned empty-handed, Tom Clawson knew that the string had run out.

By midnight, he had persuaded June that their only hope was to seek a fresh start in California, and an hour later they were ready to leave. They rousted the children out of bed long before dawn, stuffed them and their belongings into the back seat, and left the children's dog behind in their rush to set out for the land of milk and honey. The children were confused and sleepy and didn't realize that their dog was gone until they awakened the next morning in Ohio.

Tom Clawson almost lost control of the car when he reached back to swat indiscriminately at the children who were wailing over the loss of their dog. June Clawson screamed at her husband to watch the road, then angrily warned the eleven-year-old girl, "Patty, you're the oldest— keep those goddam kids quiet."

The pilgrimage to better things went from bad to worse. The August heat was intolerable, they ate peanut butter sandwiches, and they slept in the car, oblivious to the insects feasting on their exposed skin. The parents argued incessantly and clearly conveyed the feeling that disaster was at hand. In spite of Patty's attempts to control the children, the baby cried constantly, expressing the discomfort, frustration, and anxiety they all felt.

The battered car wheezed from gas station to gas station, without rest, across four states. Their money finally ran out when they reached the Corn Belt, and a scheme for supplementing their depleted cash was devised and implemented.

PART I

THE CORNFIELD MYSTERY

It would probably be the hottest day of the year. The August sun blazed down without clouds to shade the ground or breezes to cool the hot and humid air. The lines of the white clapboard houses seemed to oscillate like sound waves through the rising heat vapors.

The old Chevvy slowed when it turned onto Sunflower Drive. Tom Clawson scanned both sides of the street intently. "There's the church on the next corner," he said. "Now, where in hell's the preacher's house?"

"Please, Daddy, I don't want to do it again," Patty pleaded.

June Clawson whirled toward the back seat and swung the back of her open hand as if chasing a fly. "Shut up, Patty. You'll do it, or NONE of us will get to California," she warned.

Patty threw herself backward into the tangled mass of children in the back seat to avoid the blow. Shouting defiantly above the loud protests of her four younger brothers and sis-

25

ters, the eleven-year-old girl retorted, "But Momma, you KNOW I hate to beg for money."

Tom glared an unspoken warning that stifled the four older children, but when Charlie continued to cry, Patty scooped up the infant and tried desperately to quiet him.

"There it is," Tom mumbled as he drove slowly past the church and came to a stop in front of the adjoining house. Flowering shrubs lined the walk leading to the covered porch, and the picket fence surrounding the yard bore the sign, "The REV. JAMES DURWAY."

"You know what to do," Tom said impatiently. "Now put that damned kid down and MOVE."

Heedful of her father's fury, Patty scrambled forward to comply with his orders. "And this time, say what I told you . . . and take her with you," jerking his right thumb toward Sue Anne. "No preacher is gonna say no to a crippled kid."

Sue Anne did not react to Tom's cruelty. She was delighted to be included and welcomed the chance to escape the sweltering confines of the crowded jalopy. The eight-year-old girl swung her bad leg through the open door and jumped nimbly to the sidewalk as her father added, "Especially one who can't even talk right."

The two girls held hands as they walked toward the house: Sue Anne wide-eyed, smiling, and limping, and Patty straight-backed and grim.

"You okay, Suni?" Patty asked her younger sister.

"Oh, thure," Sue Anne lisped.

They climbed the concrete steps and crossed the covered porch slowly and uncertainly. Their footsteps echoed on the hollow wood floor. Patty agonized for a moment, then she reached out and rapped on the screen door. The housekeeper, forewarned by the sound of their cautious footsteps, opened the door and responded quickly, "Yes? What is it?"

"Is the Reverend home?" Patty asked.

"Well . . . yes," she said dubiously, glancing out at the

tired and crowded old car, "But he is very busy. May I help you?"

"Could . . . could we talk to the Reverend, please?" Patty persisted.

At that moment, the front door was pulled open the rest of the way, and Reverend Durway appeared. "What's the problem?"

The words Patty had been forced to memorize spilled out like the worst kind of acting in a bad play and beat a tattoo under the roof of the porch: "We're going to our grandma's funeral and it's two hundred miles away and we run outta gas money so could you kindly help us out?"

The Reverend contemplated the pathetically ragged condition of the two girls, then he glanced toward the car and directly into the eyes of two more children and a woman who was furiously bouncing a screaming child. He knew instinctively that this was a situation that he neither wanted to get involved in nor know more about, so when Sue Anne said, "Pleathe," he quickly reached into his pocket, took out two dollar bills, opened the screen door, and thrust them into Patty's hand. Then he closed the door and walked off before the girls could react.

Mrs. Clarke followed the Reverend through the hall, scolding, "You didn't believe that fairy tale, did you?"

Without looking back, the Reverend Durway said, "If two dollars will get that bunch out of my parish, consider it a good investment."

Patty stared blankly at the door that had been closed in her face, then she turned and said, "Let's go."

She clutched the bills in her fist without looking at them, but Sue Anne's curiosity soon prevailed, and she reached for her sister's hand, snatched the money, and hobbled ahead to the car.

Patty slowed her pace as she saw Sue Anne duck into the back seat and hand the money to her father. She knew that he would be hard to please, and she did not want to be within striking range if the amount of money fell short of his expectations.

She stopped a few steps from the car, heard no outburst, then cautiously proceeded. Now she could see Tom's face. There was no anger. There was nothing. He just stared vacantly at his wife, then said quietly, "That settles it, doesn't it. Get in, Patty."

Patty? she thought. *He doesn't call any of us by name. Something's not right.*

As soon as Patty was in the car and seated, her mother passed the baby to her automatically, without saying a word or even looking back, as if Charlie really belonged more to Patty's care than June's.

Patty took Charlie and comforted him in the same way in which he had been proffered—automatically and without comment, as if nothing were unusual. But if Patty could have seen June's face, she would have seen tears forming in her mother's eyes.

As they drove out of town, Patty noted that the terrain was changing dramatically. The sunbaked countryside was now flat, and tall corn was growing in the fields. The August heat was oppressive, and there was no escaping it. John complained that his mouth was too dry to play his harmonica. Then the ten-year-old boy said, "It feels like I'm burning from the inside out."

However, Patty was not disturbed by the heat. She was more concerned with the change that had come over her parents. Tom and June had stopped screaming. They mostly whispered, then June began to sob. Patty sensed that some new disaster was about to befall them, but soon she was eleven years old again, and she was too hot and too hungry to give it further thought.

Karen climbed over Sue Anne to sit next to Patty. The five-year-old was rarely out of reach of her older sister, and when Patty saw how unhappy she looked, she asked, "What's wrong, Karen?"

"I'm hungry," came the soft reply.

Then, more loudly, "Momma, I'm hungry."

"Me, too," said John. "Thirsty, too."

To the surprise of all, Tom was responsive. "We're not far from a town. I'll pull into the first restaurant I find."

"Tom . . . ," said June in a pleading tone, and all of Patty's earlier concerns came flooding back.

"That looks like a truck stop up ahead. You kids put on your shoes," Tom ordered.

The restaurant was on the edge of a city. They could see the dark silhouettes of tall buildings against the horizon. Tom pulled into the gravel parking lot, kicking up clouds of dust and pebbles behind. The lot was empty except for one diesel, and the shades of the coffee shop were drawn against the afternoon sun.

Tom drove to the far end of the lot, stopped the car, picked up the Reverend Durway's two dollars from the seat, and held the money out to Patty. "Take the kids in and get some hamburgers," he said. "You can all wash up and cool off while you're at it."

Patty didn't take the money. She asked suspiciously, "Why we doin' that? We haven't done that before."

"Because I told you so, goddam it," Tom shouted angrily. Then, in a calmer voice, "Anyway, it's Karen's birthday."

Although puzzled by a mosaic of perceptions, fears, and emotions that she could not quite fathom, Patty took the money and barely avoided being trampled by the younger children, who happily abandoned the muggy discomfort of the back seat. Visions of hamburgers and cold water had them jumping and giggling as they raced across the dusty parking lot and rushed the door of the restaurant.

Patty had not moved more than a few steps from the car. She held Charlie in her arms and backed away slowly. She saw June's swollen eyes, and said, "Momma?"

June lowered her head and shook it quickly from side to side.

Then the commotion of the other three children racing

back toward the car interrupted her thoughts and precluded any further communication. John was in the lead, but the amazingly agile Sue Anne was right behind. "C'mon, Patty," they shouted. "You got the money."

Pat was wary, but she was also a child, and when little Karen finally caught up with the rest, the pleasure of seeing so much rare excitement in her eyes, and the spontaneous enthusiasm of the others pushed all else from her mind. She walked quickly toward the restaurant carrying Charlie while the three other children ran and jumped all around her like "Indians circling the gravy train." Together, they formed an amoebic mass, changing shape while moving forward, until the entire cluster made it through the door of the restaurant as one.

"WowWEE!" John exclaimed as the cool air struck their faces. They were transfixed by the change in temperature, but soon found their way to a nearby booth.

The waitress finished pouring iced tea for the two drivers, then she moved toward the children's table. "What'll it be, kids?" she asked with a smile.

"HAMBURGERS," John shouted.

"You don't have to yell," Patty scolded mildly.

Then, to the waitress, she said, "Whatever hamburgers two dollars will buy, please, with everything on them except onions. And we want to eat them in the car."

The excitement in their faces shone through the grime, and as they squirmed with anticipation, the waitress made up her mind that their two dollars would stretch a lot farther than usual.

In addition to being hungry and thirsty, the children were dirty and covered with the insect bites suffered during many evenings of sleeping in the parked car. Their skin was streaked with perspiration and dirt, and their ragged clothing was caked with grime.

The truck drivers looked at the children and lost some of the gusto with which they had been attacking their rolls and butter. Four other Sunday diners, returning from afternoon church services, first wrinkled their noses in revulsion, then stared in pity. Patty was sensitive to both reactions and comfortable with neither.

The waitress scurried past the table carrying two plates heaped with roast beef, vegetables, and mashed potatoes with gravy. The savory odors wafted toward the children and enveloped them. They stared at one another, but no one spoke until Sue Anne reached for the returning waitress and asked, "Do you have any water?"

"You betcha, sweetie, comin' right up," said the woman, cursing herself for overlooking such an obvious need.

The waitress then ignored her other customers and hovered over the children with a pitcher of ice water, refilling their glasses repeatedly. Finally, their pace slowed, and Patty asked, "Do we have time to wash up before the hamburgers get done?"

"Sure thing, sweetie, there's the bathrooms. I'll make sure your hamburgers don't get cold."

The walk to the washrooms was a long one for Patty as the procession weaved past the staring customers. She was miserable, but the others were too excited to notice. They sprinkled water on their faces, then smeared the roll-up towels with prodigious amounts of grime.

Alone in the men's room, John went one step further to create the illusion of cleanliness—he plastered his hair down with water.

John was the first to emerge and was standing at the cash register inspecting the inviting display of candy bars when Sue Anne returned to the booth with Charlie.

"Where's Patty?" he asked as he approached their table.

"Did the hamburgers come yet?" Sue Anne asked impatiently.

"No. Where's Patty?" he repeated.

"Oh, she's in there hogging the mirror," said Sue Anne disgustedly, ". . . messing with her hair."

"She better not be too long, or Poppa's gonna be mad," John said.

Patty and Karen soon returned, and although their faces had been scrubbed pink, little else could be done to improve their appearance, and Patty's discomfort was obvious. In spite of the air-conditioning and the delicious aromas of the place, she was anxious to get out.

The waitress finally arrived with a bulging sack, and John grabbed it with both hands. Placing the precious bundle in his lap, he opened it and peered in. "Oh, boy!" he exclaimed, "SIX of them."

The waitress smiled and said, "Well, I thought a big guy like you might have room for two."

"Yeah," John said, "but one'll be for our mother."

That reminder of their waiting parents was like pushing the button that deactivated their trance, and all five of them scrambled from the booth en masse.

Patty swung Charlie to her hip in one easy motion and followed the waitress to the cash register holding out the two crumpled dollar bills. The waitress said with a conspiratorial grin, "That'll be two dollars exactly . . . unless you kids would like some gum or something."

"No, thanks," Patty said as she turned to follow the others through the door.

Patty had forgotten how hot it was outside, and the shock of stepping into the parched, dusty parking lot made her gasp for air. She saw John in the middle of the lot turning in silly circles and slipping in the gravel as he flopped his arms in confusion and alarm, his head darting from one side to the other, and his eyes wide with fear.

"John, stop it!" Patty called out.

Then Sue Anne started screaming something from across the lot that Patty could not quite understand. She conveyed only an apprehensiveness that was sufficient cause for Karen to release her usual hold on Patty's dress and take a firmer hold around the leg. She clung to Patty's leg so hard that she almost toppled all three of them to the ground.

"John, what's the matter with you. Quit acting so silly," Patty scolded angrily as she hopped about trying to regain her balance.

It just seemed like the thing to say at that moment. There was really no need to have asked the question, for she knew the answer the instant she saw his frightened expression. Sue Anne's words finally began to sink in to corroborate Patty's conclusion, and the world went into slow-motion.

The images flashed through her consciousness again: her mother sobbing, her father screaming, the whispers, the hamburgers . . . the other clues that something terrible was about to happen. She had felt it for two hundred miles, and now it was here. Tears came to her eyes, and she had to grit her teeth to keep from screaming. In a single motion, she hitched Charlie higher, embraced him more tightly, and buried her head against his stomach.

Her mind raced. She had to come up with a plan. But first she needed time. She had to think of something to say before the kids panicked and did something dumb—some kind of lie that would hide the awful truth that she could no longer hide from herself:

Their parents were gone and would never be back.

It was no longer a maybe-type thing to worry about. It was a by-God-sure thing fact. Patty coughed to clear the lump from her throat and rubbed her face back and forth against Charlie's shirt to wipe away her tears. When she looked up, Sue Anne and John were standing next to her, staring at her as though her expression alone would tell them what to do.

Patty coughed again to test her voice and make certain that her words would come out clearly and confidently. "Like I said, don't be silly. You know Dad's been having trouble with that old car. It probably—they took it somewhere so he could work on it. You heard him say that before—'I gotta find some place that will let me work on this car.'"

John nodded his head in obvious relief, and with a smile said, "Yeah, I did hear him say that. Yeah, I remember."

"If that's so, why didn't he tell us?" demanded Sue Anne. Even though she was younger than John, she was not nearly as gullible as he. With her limp, her lisp, and her silly giggle, most people failed to take Sue Anne seriously, but Patty knew just how quick she was, and she knew also that she would need Sue Anne's help to hold things together until she figured out what to do.

The two girls stared at each other. Patty did not have to wink or move her head—she silently entreated *Please*, from somewhere deep inside herself, and no spoken words were necessary.

John, now anxious again because of Sue Anne's question, squinted from one sister to the other as if waiting for the verdict.

Sue Anne smiled. It wasn't her best smile, but it was good enough. "Yeah, you're right," she said. "I think I even heard him say it just before we got here."

Patty hadn't realized it, but she had been holding her breath, and it came out in a whoosh, along with her instructions: "Let's go over there and sit down and wait for them." Patty then led the group slowly across the lot, toward the railroad ties that separated the parking area from the highway.

Karen's left thumb was in her mouth, and her right hand clung tightly to Patty's dress. Charlie, balanced in his usual position on Patty's hip, held her belt with one hand and wiped the sweat and dust from his eyes with the chubby knuckles of the other.

Sue Anne's limp always got worse when she was upset, and although Patty could not see her, it was obvious from the stumbling sounds that she could hardly walk.

John was the first to reach the bumpers, and he immediately set about to open the bag of hamburgers.

Patty instinctively shouted, "John! Don't you mess with those hamburgers; Momma will skin us good." It was pure reflex, and Patty would have felt embarrassed for herself except that her outburst served to break the ice and might even have convinced Sue Anne that their parents might actually return.

Sue Anne wasn't fooled for a moment. She looked at her older sister as if she had flipped, and in the spirit of the moment, Sue Anne's face contorted into a mask of mock lunacy, and she cracked, "How 'bout if we just suck on those grease spots coming through the bag?"

John guffawed loudly, and even Karen managed to giggle without removing her thumb from her mouth.

The hamburgers were not really at issue, because the children had lost their appetites. The three girls sat in silence. Sue Anne mostly stared at the ground poking at the pebbles between her feet, Karen leaned against Patty, and Charlie dozed in Patty's arms. John was the lookout. He was alert to every approaching vehicle, and whenever a car approached that even faintly resembled theirs, he would jump to his feet, hop up on a railroad tie, and say, "Is that them? Is that them?"

After an hour, John's angry impatience was reflected in such questions as "What's keeping them?" "Which direction did they go in?" "What the heck are they doing?"

As their anxiety level increased, the children seemed to forget the heat. The temperature was close to a hundred, and there was no shade in the parking lot. As the supper hour approached, the restaurant traffic increased significantly. Every car entering or leaving the parking lot kicked up more gravel and dust, and the exhaust fumes lingered about them in the hot air.

The children began to attract attention. People entering the restaurant gave them no more than casually disapproving glances, but those glances turned to morbid curiosity when those same people returned to their cars some time later. After two hours, the waitress walked out to them and said, "Hey, kids, is something wrong? Where's your mother?"

Patty explained quickly that their father was doing some repair work on the car and would be there soon.

"Well, okay," said the skeptical woman. "You let me know if I can do something or call someone, you hear?"

The sound of the strange voice awakened Charlie, and as he stirred in Patty's arms, she was aware of her own discomfort. The sweat streaming from Charlie's face was burning her skin, especially around the insect bites, and there was a painful rash on the side of her neck where Charlie had snuggled his head. By now, they were all covered with white dust, and black dirt streaked their skin whenever they wiped the sweat.

Patty knew they were only biding their time and couldn't stay there much longer. She had a well-developed instinct for survival, cultivated by her mother's propensity for abandoning the children to Patty's care for days at a time without a scrap of food in the house.

She ransacked her brain for a solution, considering the pros and cons of every possibility except one: she would not permit herself to think of asking others for help. The last time their mother had abandoned them—she was gone for more than a week—the kids had to ask for help, and they were picked up and placed in separate foster homes, and Sue Anne wound up in the hospital. They weren't permitted to see one another for months, and by God, that wasn't going to happen again.

Her mind began to wander, and she drifted back to Sue Anne's accident—a painful memory that still haunted Patty. The image of that terribly swollen, hideously purple leg brought new tears to Patty's eyes, and all the guilt came surging back. Her head began to reel, and her alarm bells went off just as she started to lose consciousness. She snapped herself awake, knocking Karen off her perch and almost dropping Charlie from her arms. She found that her legs and arms were too stiff to function, so it fell on John to reinstate the sobbing Karen.

Sue Anne stared at Patty as if to say, "How long do we keep this up?"

Patty got the message. She passed the baby to Sue Anne and stood, for the first time in more than three hours, to get her blood circulating again.

Karen's sobbing moved one of the returning diners to inquire, "Is something wrong? Are you children all right?"

"We're okay, mister," responded Patty. "My dad had car trouble and went down the road to get it fixed. I know where they are, so we'll just go down there and wait." She took Karen's hand, accepted Charlie from Sue Anne, and started toward the road.

John held back. "You don't . . ."

Patty cut him off before he could say anything else. "Momma said where to meet them if it got too late. Now, come on. You're not so lazy you can't walk a little ways."

John was too confused to do anything but shuffle forward a few steps. Then, remembering the sack of hamburgers, he angrily turned, scooped them up, and strode toward the others, who had already reached the blacktop.

"Well, let us give you a lift," came the voice from the parking lot.

John started to turn around when Patty spit instructions at him through clenched jaws, "Don't you turn around—walk!"

John's head snapped forward as instructed, but it was obvious to Patty from the set expression of his face and his rippling jaw muscles that he was about to blow up. She knew that John was gullible but not stupid, and gentle as he was, his temper could be something to behold. Patty prayed that it would hold until their good samaritan lost interest.

Patty was convinced that their only hope was to keep walking—to escape the people with whom they had made contact. If John would keep his mouth shut and no one acted funny, they might have a chance.

A car came up behind and slowed. Their persistent benefactor rolled down the window and offered, "You sure we can't give you a lift?"

"No, thanks, mister," Patty responded. "We might miss our folks if we got in your car."

"Okay," he said. "You take care," and he drove off.

John jumped out ahead of Patty, and walking backward, he asked angrily, "Why did you lie to that man? Why did you tell him you knew where Mom and Dad were?"

Patty didn't answer. She didn't have an answer. Not yet. She just had to keep them moving.

"And anyway," John persisted indignantly, "how're they gonna find us if we're not in the parking lot?

"You better answer me, Patty," he warned ominously.

Patty's determination to press on was unshaken. She knew that there might be screaming, or yelling, or crying when the moment came to tell them the truth, and she wanted to be as far away from that restaurant as possible.

But with each step, the children became more irritable and complained about their thirst. Even though the sun was about to set, it was still miserably hot, and in Patty's tired, hungry condition, every pound of Charlie and every tug from Karen seemed to pull her further into the pavement.

John knew that he was not getting through, so out of frustration, he changed his tactics and whined, "Maybe we're going in the wrong direction. I bet they're looking for us back there at the restaurant right now."

Forward progress stopped, and they all looked to Patty for direction. Her composure began to crack, and the eleven-year-old sobbed angrily, "You're old enough to know what's going on! They DUMPED us! They're not coming back NOW or any OTHER time!"

Karen continued to hold the hem of Patty's skirt, and other than looking up, did not react at all. But for the others, the game was over. Sue Anne's expression did not change, but her eyes filled with tears as she stared at Patty.

John dropped to his knees and pounded the ground beside the highway, sobbing, "Why did you lie to me? Do you think I'm a baby? D'ya think I didn't KNOW something was wrong?"

Patty let her ten-year-old brother vent his emotions without moving or speaking.

John rolled to his side into a fetal position, then sat up with his knees drawn up to his face. He continued to sob, chanting rhetorically, "How do you KNOW they're not coming back? How do you KNOW?"

The deception had been the only reason to continue walking, and now that it was over, each of the children looked around for a place to rest. Karen released her hold on Patty's skirt and flopped down next to John, who had buried his face into his drawn-up knees and was sobbing deeply.

They were sitting on the shoulder of a busy highway, but they were in a world of their own. Sue Anne finally broke the spell in her own impudent way when she said, "Like I was saying, I'm STILL thirsty."

Patty was shaken from her daze, and for the first time, she noticed cars slowing as they passed on the highway. Several came close to stopping, and Patty dreaded the prospect of carrying off the charade one more time. She knew they had to get out of sight. She would cope with the other issues of eating, sleeping, and raising the children later, but first, they had to leave the rest of the world behind them.

Patty's back stiffened and her eyes opened wider as she realized that the immediate solution was directly across the road. A wall of cornstalks, ten feet tall, stretching down the highway as far as she could see, would keep out the rest of the world forever. She jumped to her feet and flipped Charlie onto her hip; she reached for Karen's hand and said, "C'mon you guys, follow me."

The three of them had crossed the macadam road before the wary Sue Anne understood the plan and jumped to follow. Sue Anne hobbled across the road and jumped over the drainage ditch separating the cornfield from the highway as Patty stumbled across it with the two children. By the time they reached the corn, Patty noticed that John had not yet moved. "C'mon, John, you're gonna get lost if you don't keep up."

John looked up with tears streaming down his dust-streaked face. "GET lost! We ARE lost! We gotta find somebody to help us."

Patty was too tired to argue and too confused and frustrated to explain. "It's getting dark," she said. "Right now, let's get in here and eat those hamburgers."

In spite of the uncertainty she was feeling, Patty's voice was firm and sure, and provided all the direction John needed to bring himself to his feet. He snatched at the grease-stained, dirty sack and trudged across the road as the others poked tentatively into the tall, dry cornstalks. "Get outta the way," he grumbled, "I'll do it," and he bent at the waist and opened a path through the thick shafts.

The cornfield offered two advantages: the stalks were seven to ten feet tall and dense enough to hide them, and there was a farmhouse on the western edge of the huge tract that would have an outdoor water spigot.

By the time they had pushed through ten rows of corn, they had effectively entered another world. John pulled up some of the stalks to give them enough room to sit together in a tight circle, and Sue Anne passed out the cold hamburgers. The meal was soggy, cold, and stale, but no one noticed. It was food, and it was good.

The group was almost completely enveloped on four sides, and they greeted the approaching darkness with a kind of security that was new for them: they knew where they would spend the night, and they knew that they would do so without the shouting and arguing of adults to make them uneasy.

"I'm gonna save the rest of this greaseburger till we get some water," Sue Anne said in a relaxed way. They were all thirstier now than before they had eaten, so after the general expressions of agreement, Patty stood and peered up at the halo of light emanating from the farmhouse. She realized that her brothers and sisters had tolerated enough pain and discomfort to last a lifetime, and she knew that they would have to risk finding water before they broke.

"Wait here," she ordered. "I'll be right back." Patty then squirmed her way through a dozen columns of corn until the house lights were visible through the straight rows. She turned to rejoin the others but found them making their way toward her.

Patty reached for Charlie, but John stopped her. "It's okay. I'll take Charlie," he said. "You lead the way." She looked at the ten-year-old, and, even in the shadowy gray light, the remnants of his pain and hurt were evident, but she also saw a new determination in the set of his mouth and somehow, a new toughness. That fleeting insight triggered more anguish for Patty. For her, growing up fast had been no accident—it was a necessity, so she had never known the fun of being a child. Without knowing what she was doing, or why, she had surrendered her own girlhood to the cause of maintaining some essence of childhood for the others, and the tough maturity in John's face was wrong—all wrong.

"Let's go," Sue Anne urged. "I'll hold on to Karen."

"Okay," Patty said softly. "But don't get separated . . . and don't make any noise." She led them single file down the long row toward the shaft of light that would occasionally disappear in the foliage. The house was farther than they had anticipated, and the going was slow and noisy as the dry leaves scratched their skin and crackled against their bodies. Even though they were still too far away to be heard, Patty whispered for effect: "From here on, get down low so you don't hit so many leaves. You sound like . . . like a herd of blind elephants." Someone giggled, and Patty's temper flared. "Now be serious—this corn pops like firecrackers when we hit it, so stay low, and don't say a word."

Patty was certain they were making too much noise to remain unnoticed, but when they finally emerged from the cornfield, all was quiet. They carefully surveyed the open space between themselves and the house—another thirty yards.

Charlie began to squirm and whine, and John's unskilled attempts to placate him were futile. As Patty slipped over to take Charlie, Karen pulled her hand from Sue Anne's and grabbed Patty's skirt. This time, Patty's whisper was necessary and for real: "Walk fast, and watch where you're going."

The fescue lawn had been cut high to retain moisture, but the drought had taken its toll. The grass was brittle and crunched under their feet. The children walked slowly, alert to the night sounds, sensing that the whole world was watching them. They fully expected to be exposed by a barking dog or a howling cat, but miraculously, they made their way undetected to a darkened corner of the house.

They kneeled and squatted in a tight circle while they regained their composure. Minutes later, Patty told them to sit tight while she looked for the water faucet. She passed Charlie to Sue Anne, but Karen was too frightened to let Patty go.

Rather than create any further disturbance, Patty took Karen's hand and proceeded to feel her way along the side of the building. Within seconds, she located a faucet immediately below the lighted bathroom window, and she signaled the others to join them.

Patty turned the water on to a trickle, and, using a cup she had fashioned from the wrap of her hamburger, she attempted to fill it for Karen, but they found it easier to drink directly from the spigot. As the children satisfied their thirst, they sat back and leaned against the building to rest. They were comforted by the light from the window, and, leaning against one another, they began to doze off. Patty decided to let them sleep while she stood watch, but she, too, dropped off a few minutes later.

Her last thoughts were of John, her white-skinned, blond-haired brother. A year younger than Patty, he was so thin that he sometimes looked taller than she. He was her blue-eyed poet and dreamer who had brought music into their lives, and Patty's half-sleep was almost disrupted as the ghost of his angry face flashed before her.

Equating John with toughness and maturity was incongruous, and it filled Patty with a premonition of gloom. He had come out of a dream world. Could he survive? A chill went through her. Patty reached out to touch his face, and even when her own eyes had closed in sleep, a tear rolled down her cheek.

In the upstairs bedroom, Leona Wilson sat stiffly at her dressing table. Her head was cocked as she tried to identify the sounds that had interrupted her nightly hair-brushing ritual. The brush was still poised at the back of her head when she whispered, "Harry! Harry, did you hear that?"

Harry Wilson woke with a start and rolled over to prop himself on his elbow. Not yet fully awake, he asked, "What? What is it?"

Leona lowered the brush from the back of her head, then shook it abruptly to silence him. "Listen! I think someone's out there!" The intensity in her voice and facial expression were enough to force him awake. Neither moved as their eyes darted from each other to the curtained window. Finally, a passing truck broke the tension, and Harry swung his massive body from the bed.

"What did you hear?" he asked, as he walked toward the open window.

"Nothing, actually. I mean, I think the water was running, but I didn't actually notice it until it stopped. Do you know what I mean? Suddenly it was quiet, and I realized that the water had been running, and someone turned it off."

"Did you hear anything else?" Harry asked.

"When I was coming up the stairs, I could have sworn I heard something out in the corn, but I wasn't sure," she answered as she mechanically resumed her brushing. "I guess that murder down the road has me spooked worse than I thought."

The lead story on the six o'clock news had been about a middle-aged farm woman from Nagasaw County—about a hundred miles away—who had been raped and killed that very morning in the fields near her home. There were no clues as to the whereabouts of the sick animal who had done it, but summer brought so many strangers to the open roads and farming communities that it was generally assumed that the criminal was someone passing through and already gone.

Harry listened as the gentle wind in the dry cornfield created a myriad of sounds punctuated by the movement of nocturnal animals ranging from badgers to coyotes. But Leona had lived in the country for all of her fifty-four years, and those sounds were as familiar to her as they were to Harry. Above all, Leona was not the nervous type, and if she heard something, then, by God, he'd better look into it. And if it was that animal from Nagasaw County . . .

Harry's tanned face darkened further, and the white skin on his bald head turned red as he struggled with combined feelings of anger and fear. He clenched his fists and ground his teeth reflexively as he strode toward the closet and withdrew the shotgun. He reached up to the shelf and took several shells from the box, broke the gun, and loaded both chambers.

Leona was alarmed by the intensity of his expression. "Harry, please don't take the gun. You know how I feel about those darned things."

He locked the barrel and started for the door without answering.

"Harry, don't," she pleaded. "It's probably nothing. I'm sorry I woke you up. Don't be mad."

Harry stopped at the door and realized that she had misinterpreted his reaction. He propped the gun against the door jamb and returned to Leona. He gently took the brush from her hand, pulled her to her feet, and held her close. "I'm not mad at you, sweetheart. I just hate to see you scared like this. If someone is sneaking around out there, I'm gonna get him . . . Period!"

"Well, I'm going with you," she insisted, and without further discussion, they walked together toward the bedroom door. Harry picked up the shotgun and led the way down the stairs. She switched on the outside lights as Harry unlocked the kitchen door and stepped out to the back porch; then Leona stood in the doorway as he descended the three steps and walked toward the clothesline.

If Harry had then walked around to the east side of the house, he might have tripped over the sleeping Clawson children. Instead, he returned to the back door, locked it, and walked through the house to inspect the front yard. They listened intently from the porch, and hearing nothing unusual, Harry ventured into the front yard on another perfunctory search.

"At least I feel better," he said when he returned. "If anyone was out there, he's gone now."

Leona proceeded him into the house, and as a final gesture, he asked, "Would you like me to call the sheriff, just in case?"

"Oh, no," she answered quickly. "We've already made too much out of it. Let's go to sleep."

Patricia awoke with a start. It was morning already! Her first thought was to get the children away from the house before they were discovered. She gently shook John's shoulder and placed her index finger over her lips to warn him to remain silent. Sue Anne opened her eyes as soon as she felt John stretch his legs, and the three of them were fully awake and alert to their danger immediately. Patricia passed Charlie to John without waking him, then she picked up Karen. Without a word, they made a dash for the safety of the cornfield as quickly and unceremoniously as their feet would carry them.

By the time they re-entered the cornfield, Karen and Charlie were also awake, so Patricia led the group all the way down one of the rows to the spot they had cleared the evening before. It was good to see that familiar place again, and they all flopped down in nervous laughter.

Sue Anne giggled, "The last time I woke up running like that was when I fell asleep in Momma's bed, and she came home drunk and plopped into the bed with that half-naked cab driver and landed right on top of me. He was laughing, she was screaming, and I was running. Don't you remember?" she asked.

"Yeah," John said, joining the laughter, "by the time Momma staggered into our rooms, we were pretending to be asleep, and she didn't know which one of us had done it."

They all delighted in the comedy without knowing why except that the sun was out, they were out of danger, and they were together.

The roar of a passing diesel snapped them back to the present. It was impossible to see the road through the corn, but it was obviously very close. Patty had been carefully scanning John's face for some reaction to Sue Anne's story about their mother, but she saw no pain or displeasure, and she didn't know whether to be sad or happy. But that would have to wait. Patty's concern now centered upon the loud reminder that their old world was only ten yards away.

"What are we going to do today?" asked John.

"How about a movie?" Sue Anne teased.

"Get serious, Suni," John said impatiently. "I think we ought to get out on the highway before it gets too hot."

Never lost for words, Sue Anne shot back, "Get serious yourself, dummy. You gonna WALK us all the way to California?"

Patty had no answers either, but remembering the stares of the passing motorists, she instinctively decided to lead the group away from the highway and deeper into the dense cornfield. "Let's go this way," she said.

They made their way south, across innumerable rows of corn, and for three hundred yards, the stalks stood like sentinels posted to impede their progress as the brittle leaves cut every part of their exposed skin, and the corn dust adhered to their perspiring bodies.

When they finally emerged from the cornfield, they huddled on the edge in a cluster to clear their eyes and survey the narrow stretch of pasture that led up to a riverbank. No signs of life were visible in any direction. An ancient and majestic cottonwood towered between them and the river.

John was the first to venture into the open, and he headed straight for the shade of the huge tree. The others followed, happy to escape the dusty confines of the cornfield. The sandy loam under the tree was soft and cool, and the children soon discarded their shoes, but the real attraction for all of them was the river. The children of the slums had never been close to a river before, and they delighted in the feel of the sand between their toes as they approached it.

John and Sue Anne bent to roll their trouser legs above their knees before wading cautiously into the water. Giggling nervously about frogs, sharks, and whirlpools, they were careful not to get their clothes wet until Sue Anne playfully pushed her brother from behind.

"Look out," John cried, scrambling back toward shore to avoid getting his pants wet. His reaction caught Sue Anne off guard, and she was unable to avoid the collision that sent her sprawling into the water on her backside.

She sat there sputtering and stunned by the cold water swirling about her chest. Then it dawned on both of them that there was no adult to scold them for getting wet, so when Sue Anne reached for John's leg, he gleefully tumbled into the water on top of her.

"Don't worry, strange lady, I'll save you," he shouted in mock alarm as his weight and momentum submerged her completely.

Sue Anne came up spitting water and gasping for breath, and it was a free-for-all from that point on. They splashed, dunked, and romped in the water with complete abandon, pausing only to try to entice Karen to join them.

Patty had never heard them laugh and shout so joyfully, but before surrendering herself to her own eleven-year-old instincts, she engaged Charlie in the pleasures of digging in the wet sand. Then she gathered up the shoes and socks that had been haphazardly strewn about the sandbar and tossed them into a shallow hole under the tree without realizing that she had just staked out their future home.

She then ran to join the others in the river.

The uninhibited shrieking of the children seemed to reverberate off the wall of cornstalks as John and Sue Anne plowed through the water to jump on Patty. She managed to fend them off one at a time until she was finally pulled laughing into the swirling river. Patty surrendered to the shallow water with an exaggerated flailing and kicking of her arms and legs.

Karen watched from ankle depth and showed no emotion except to jump excitedly in place when Patty finally went down. But when John menacingly turned his attention to her, she turned and, giggling nervously, sprinted to the safety of the sandpile that Charlie was amassing.

The exhausted children staggered out of the river one at a

time to dry themselves in the morning sun. They gravitated toward the place where Patty had tossed their shoes, and they flopped on the ground with their feet dangling over the edge of the large hole. Then Sue Anne and Karen scooted to the bottom of the hole and rested their backs against its sloping sides.

As if by mutual agreement, no one spoke. All five children lay there quietly listening to the sounds of the river, looking up into the tangle of leaves of the huge tree that blocked out the sun and sky. They had never known such peace.

The large depression had probably been fashioned by a large animal burrowing for cool respite from the summer sun. In contrast to the grassy ground above it, the sides and bottom were of sand and dirt, but it too was soft, cool, and comfortable. It wasn't like city dirt or people dirt. It was clean and good, and it smelled fresh.

Sue Anne broke the silence by articulating what Patty was beginning to feel—"let's stay right here!"

No one responded, but Patty let it sink in. It didn't really make sense, but what did make sense? These past few days— no, these past few years—had been a horrible nightmare. Patty knew that it was out of the question to ask grown-ups for help, and that they were now on their own. When the thought flashed into her mind that it was up to her to make the decisions, she snorted derisively because that responsibility had *always* been hers. There had been lots of mistakes, but she had *never* screwed things up as badly as Momma had.

The fleeting thought of her mother brought another twinge of sorrow, but this time her grief was diluted by other emotions—first anger and resentment but finally relief. She understood their predicament, and she knew that things were going to be rough, but for the first time Patty felt in control, and the eleven-year-old relaxed with the knowledge that things would surely get better.

Five children, the oldest eleven, the youngest eighteen months, alone in the world, fifteen hundred miles from home, sitting on a riverbank totally isolated from adults or parental support, and they were consciously trying to keep it that way. Like the ostrich with its head in the sand, they thought they were safe.

"Stay *here?*" John laughed as he sat up on the edge of the hole, staring down at his youngest sister. "Sue Anne, you're crazy. We can't stay here."

John's outburst had interrupted Patty's reverie, and she asked lazily, "Why not?"

John knotted his eyebrows as the grin disappeared from his face. "I'll tell you why not," he answered defensively, jumping to his feet waving his arms. "There's nothin' here. No windows, no doors, roof, or *nothing.*"

He could not tell whether Patty was serious or not, so in his confusion, he managed to be purposeful and funny at the same time, and while the truth of his words struck home, his jumping and gesturing made them all laugh.

"What do you say to that, Miss Smarty Hoot Howl?"

"I say you're a nut factory," intervened Sue Anne.

"And I say we *can* stay here, and we *will* stay here," Patty answered.

John stopped his lunatic antics and stood there with his hands on his hips, his mouth twisted in disgust. "And what d'you think we're gonna eat, stupid? It's breakfast time, you know."

Sue Anne again interrupted, "Look around you, dummy. There's food all over the place," and she scurried up the side of the hole and ran off toward the cornfield.

The first row of corn was no more than twenty yards away, and the others watched Sue Anne cover the distance with only a trace of a limp. She seemed dwarfed by the stalks, which were twice as tall as she, but she reached up and tore off an ear of corn in a single, violent motion. With a quick glance toward her brothers and sisters, she began to peel away the outer covering, and as the golden core emerged, John bolted toward her, shouting in surprise, "Hey, that's real CORN!"

Sue Anne was the first to return to the hole. "If you bite into this stuff and suck on it, it's good."

Patty stood Charlie on his feet, pulled Karen out of the

hole, and took the treasure from Sue Anne's outstretched hand. She tested it, then instructed Karen in the procedure.

John returned, and the three older children sat on the edge of the hole tearing shucks from the raw corn, laughing at Charlie as the milky juices squirted from the ripe kernels and plastered his face.

Eventually, the children had their fill, and Charlie slid off Patty's lap, down the slope of the hole. On his climb back to the top, Charlie stopped to dig at the sides, and Patty said, "That's a good idea, squirt, let's make this hole big enough for all of us."

The other children then jumped to the center of the hole and began to dig at the soft, sandy dirt with their hands, throwing the loose dirt over the edge. No one stopped until they had doubled the size of the original burrow. When Charlie stood up in the middle, he could no longer see over the edge, and it was wide enough for all of them to lie down comfortably, like spokes in a wheel, with their feet at the hub.

Now the children were completely satisfied. Their stomachs were full, and they had a safe and comfortable place to rest. Patty selected her spot, then Karen and Charlie stretched out on either side, leaving John and Sue Anne to spread out across the other half of their new home.

During moments like this—quiet times—Patty could think. She turned her head unobtrusively from one side to the other, and she was able to see the entire family—her family.

The restless Sue Anne soon surrendered to her curiosity and climbed from the lair to explore the surrounding area. It was no accident that brought a minor sandslide down around John's ears, provoking him to scramble out in pursuit.

Charlie sat up to watch them run off, then he flopped down on Pat's stomach and crawled up to her chest. Lying on top of his sister, he turned his head to the side, stuck his thumb in his mouth, and prepared for his morning nap.

Pat rubbed his back with one hand and ran her fingers through his dirty blond hair with the other. Charlie was her baby. Except for the physical aspects of gestation and delivery, Patty had accomplished every task of motherhood. And as she thought back to that snowy night a year and a half ago, she realized that there never would have been a live birth if she hadn't called the cab and half-carried her drunken mother from the apartment and into the hospital.

Patty tenderly rested her cheek against the top of Charlie's head as he began to doze, and she returned to her reverie. When Charlie was awake and alert, and his stomach full, he delighted in making people laugh. His favorite trick was to blow spit bubbles and look at them cross-eyed as they expanded. When the bubbles popped, he would laugh, and when Charlie laughed, everyone laughed. Those were the good moments.

During the bad times, Charlie became morose, clinging to Patty with his arms around her neck and his legs wrapped around her middle, perched on the skinny hip she would thrust out for his convenience. With her arm around his back and his head against her neck, they were as one.

During the long drive from Philadelphia, Charlie had spent most of his time sleeping. When he was awake, he lay curled up in the back seat on Patty's lap, sucking his thumb and crying for something to eat or drink. Back in their old neighborhood, the children could usually scrounge, beg, or steal enough to satisfy the pain, but those long days on the road had taken their toll. Charlie's stomach now stuck out, his pale blue eyes watered constantly, and the shine had gone out of his beautiful blond hair, but what worried Patty most was that her precious baby could no longer stay awake for more than an hour at a time.

Then Karen reached out for Patty's hand, and she was abruptly reminded that her five-year-old sister would require even more of her attention and love than Charlie. Karen had not been the same since the aftermath of Sue Anne's accident, but that was an unhappy experience that Patty was not ready to relive, so she put it from her mind immediately. Besides, John and Sue Anne were returning, and she was eager to hear about their excursion.

"Hey, Karen, look what I found for you," John said, holding out a rusted, beat-up old coffee can.

Karen stared at the empty can, then looked quizzically at her brother without moving.

"Take it," John said. "It's for digging in the sand."

Karen just stared.

"C'mon," John said, "I'll show you."

Karen reluctantly released her grip on Patty's hand as John hoisted her from the hole and led her away to the sandy bank.

Sue Anne dropped down on her stomach and rested on her elbows, with her face out over the edge of the hole. She spoke softly because Charlie was still asleep.

"You won't believe how far away we are," she whispered.

"From what?" Patty asked.

"From *everything*, dammit. You know what I mean," Sue Anne snapped angrily.

"No, I don't. We have to get far away from *people*, but we have to stay close enough for food and stuff."

"Well, how do you plan to buy food? You gonna get a job or something?"

"No, but there's garbage cans and things like that. People throw away good stuff . . . especially at that restaurant, I bet."

"YUCK!" Sue Anne responded. "This corn is plenty good enough for me. I ain't gonna eat somebody else's crap from outta garbage cans."

Patty turned her head to look at her sister. She saw that Sue Anne was genuinely disgusted by the thought of scavenging through garbage cans for food, and Patty turned away again, thinking of the countless evenings she had prowled the back alleys of their old neighborhood searching through the trash cans for anything edible. Sometimes there were chunks of meat and potatoes that she would have to wash off and reheat for her brothers and sisters. Often there were pieces of hard bread—or even soft bread that had green stuff on it that she cut away.

Patty used to look forward to Thursdays and Sundays—spaghetti days at the Gargiulios. Mrs. Gargiulio used to say, "There's only one rule for cooking Italian style: first figure out exactly how much food you'll need, then double it—and add a little extra for unexpected company." And she certainly followed that rule religiously, because there were always lots of leftovers in their trash. Not only that, but Mrs. Gargiulio always wrapped her garbage carefully to discourage flies and rats. As a result, Patty could count on finding heaps of spaghetti stuffed into empty milk cartons or large tomato cans, separated from the coffee grounds and wilted lettuce, ready to be reclaimed for the hungry Clawson children.

Patty winced involuntarily when she recalled the night Mr. Gordon caught her scavenging in back of his butcher shop. At first, he was alarmed to discover someone in the darkness. Then, after recognizing Patty, he was suspicious about her sneaking around in the dark, especially after she was so evasive about her reasons for being there. But when the truth finally hit him, his grasp on her arm changed from that of an apprehending law officer to the caress of a concerned neighbor. He placed his hand around her bony shoulder and gently led her through the back door of the butcher shop. Patty was so frightened that she took no note of the good odors of the store. Mr. Gordon filled a sack with kosher frankfurters, and when he held them out to her, there were tears in his eyes. Patty's fear was replaced at that moment by a heavier emotion—shame. She grabbed the sack and ran through the back door without acknowledging the gift, and after she prepared the meal for the other children, she could not bring herself to partake of the feast.

Two days later, she returned to thank Mr. Gordon, trying in vain to assure him that he had misunderstood her motives, that she was trying to find one of Karen's toys that might have been mistakenly thrown into the garbage. He kindly accepted her explanation, but she knew that he was humoring her. Above all else, Patty resolved never to be caught again . . . and she never was.

"Maybe you're right," she heard herself saying to Sue Anne. "It would be too dangerous. We can't take a chance on being caught."

"Hey, what are you guys talking about?" John asked as he and Karen returned.

"That was quick," Patty said, ignoring his question as Charlie began to stir in her arms.

"Yeah," he said. "Karen wouldn't dig with the can because it's crooked. I'm gonna try to hammer it out," and he began pounding on the inside of the can with a rock.

"We gotta get you cleaned up," Patty said to Charlie as he rolled off her chest, leaving a telltale wet place on the front of her loosely fitting faded dress. "Let's go down to the water."

Thanks to the constant attention Patty had given Charlie over the past several months, she had managed to get him toilet trained at an early age. But accidents were not unusual, and this was one of those times.

Charlie was wearing diapers under his short pants, both of which were stripped from him to be washed in the river. As an afterthought, Patty also removed his T-shirt and permitted him to run naked in the sand.

"Just stay away from the water," John quipped, "or some hungry fish is gonna jump up and bite your worm." Sue Anne laughed, and Patty jokingly slapped at John's head. Charlie thought they were laughing at him, so he went into his act to entertain them further.

The children spent the afternoon of that first day exploring the north bank for almost a mile in each direction. They managed to salvage such items as a wooden chair without legs, a plastic platter, and two more rusty cans.

When they returned to their site, they shucked more corn and once again satisfied their hunger. Later that day, they made sand castles, got into a mud-slinging contest, and again played in the water.

As evening approached, they gathered closer to the hole, and John took out his harmonica to play their favorite songs.

Other than the water they had ingested accidentally from the river, they had had nothing to drink, so their final act of the day was to suck the sweet juices from the corn. Then Patty crawled into the hole with the two younger children.

Holding Charlie in one arm and Karen in the other while they settled in for the night, Patty contentedly listened to John's music, and it occurred to her that this had been the happiest day of their lives.

It was completely dark by the time the deep breathing of the children signaled Patty they were asleep. She carefully extricated herself from them and sat motionless while they shifted around for a comfortable position. As soon as she was assured that they would not awaken, she climbed to the top of the hole.

"Where are those cans?" she asked John.

"Here's one of them," he said.

"There's another one," Sue Anne said. "Why?"

"I better go to that farmhouse for some water," Patty responded. "You guys wait here. I can be more quiet by myself. I won't be long."

John was about to volunteer to make the trip, but the thought of traveling so far—in the darkness—by himself was thoroughly intimidating, so he agreed, "Okay, I'll stay with Sue Anne."

Patty collected two of the "water buckets" and slipped away toward the faint halo of light emanating above the cornfield from the house in the distance. The five of them—products of the city slums–were reluctant to drink water from the fresh river, but they would relish tap water brought to them in rusty cans.

Patty returned to the Wilson house over the same route they had taken earlier. She weaved her way north against the grain of the cornfield until she could see the lights of the second story. Then she stole down one of the rows toward the house until she reached the clearing.

She stopped on the edge of the cornfield to catch her breath and survey the open space in front of her. There were no lights on the ground floor, but the moon illuminated the yard.

Patty advanced cautiously from the cover of the cornfield. She covered the ground tentatively, slipping from one shadow to another. Suddenly, she dropped to her hands and knees, and without knowing why, began to crawl backward toward the protection of the cornfield.

There was no visible reason for alarm. Everything was the same as the night before, but she had learned from experience to trust her instincts. Before the signal had risen to conscious level, though, she had somehow perceived the movement of a shadow near the house. She stopped all movement and quietly flattened herself to the ground. She peered intensely into the darkness, and a human form began to take shape.

Someone was standing there, next to the back porch, looking out into the darkness. Whoever it was had to have seen her. Patty turned cold with terror, but she did not panic. She stopped breathing and lay there motionless.

Suddenly, a deep voice from within the house shattered the silence. "Leona, are you coming to bed?"

"Okay, Harry. I'll be there in a minute."

"What are you doing out there?"

"It's just such a beautiful night I had to take one last look at the moon." Then the form turned, climbed the back steps, and entered the house.

Patty was trembling as she decompressed. She lay motionless for more than thirty minutes after the upstairs light had been extinguished. She had been lucky this time, but next time she would figure things out better before taking such chances.

Patty had lost about a third of the water by the time she found her brothers and sisters. As she approached the clearing, a tremulous voice called out, "Who . . . Who's there?"

Silence.

Then, softer, "Patty? Patty? Is that you?"

"Yes, John, it's me."

"Jeesus Christ," John shrieked as he spun around in reaction to the voice that had come up on his blind side. "Gawd dammit, Patty, you did that on purpose. Where you *been*? You said you'd be right back!"

"I had to wait for the people to go to sleep. You weren't scared, were you?" she teased.

"Not for *me*," he answered. "I was scared something happened to *you*."

"I'm okay. Where's Sue Anne?"

"Asleep."

"Asleep?" came Sue Anne's sarcastic retort. "He was too busy 'protecting' me to let me go to sleep."

Patty thought it best not to threaten John's ego further, so she dropped the teasing and offered him the two cans of water. "Why don't you pick a safe place for this, and let's go to sleep."

The second day passed in much the same way for the Clawson children, but the novelty was beginning to fade. There were fewer mud fights, and the kids didn't laugh at Charlie's messy face any more. The boisterous activity of the first day gave way to a listlessness punctuated by John's harmonica renditions of melancholy tunes.

That night, Patty went to the Wilson house for water again, and she was so weary when she returned that she went to sleep immediately. The route through the cornfield was difficult. Her skin was scratched raw and her muscles ached. She resolved to find a new path. She slept fitfully for several hours, then awoke with a start.

Her unfocused eyes stared up into the darkness as she tried to place herself in time and space. Something was different. Noise—that's what was missing—noise. People yelling—dogs barking—neighbors stomping overhead and up and down the stairs in the hall next to her bed—car noises. All those things were missing. And the smells—the garbage smells—the pee smells—the dirty people smells.

Her arms ached, and a dampness clung to her body like a layer of oil filling the pores of her skin.

Then Patty's eyes focused on the giant cottonwood overhead, and as the fuzzy thoughts of her half-sleep fell into place, she remembered. And as she remembered, she took a deep breath to relieve the pain of abandonment.

For the first time since stepping out of the restaurant, she wanted to scream with all her strength, "MOMMA . . . MOMMA . . . I love you. Come and get me . . . I love you."

Then she was fully awake, and her fear evaporated. The sun was beginning to rise, and she was again in control. It was time to take inventory of her surroundings. She looked to her right and left—Charlie and Karen were asleep on each of her arms . . . as asleep as her arms were. She lifted her head and saw John curled up on the opposite side of the hole with his knees drawn up to his stomach. *Poor John, so impatient to become a man, yet not nearly as strong as his younger sister, Sue Anne . . . Sue Anne . . .*

Sue Anne! Sue Anne is gone!

Patty's arms were devoid of feeling, but she scrambled to her feet, dislodging Charlie and Karen, almost yanking them from their sleep. Patty knew instinctively that there was no need to panic, so she calmed herself and peered into the scant light until she sighted her sister near the river.

Patty started to call out to her, but stopped as Sue Anne began to lower her jeans past her twisted leg in preparation for her private bath.

Karen and Charlie rolled toward each other and returned to a deep sleep only after their bodies touched. Patty looked down at them, then climbed up to sit on the edge of the hole and watch Sue Anne.

Sue Anne was a living paradox. Patty saw her as an eight-year-old fluffy rock. She was innocent and wide-eyed on the one hand, and cynical and pragmatic on the other. She had reddish-blond hair, freckles, and a pug nose that combined to give the first impression of cuteness, an impression corroborated by her captivating lisp and infectious good humor. But beneath the surface was a personality matured and tempered by physical and emotional pain, and there was the budding intellect of a survivor.

Patty and Sue Anne had always been close. They shared thoughts without speaking, they shared pain without crying, they fought without hurting, and their bond went beyond sisterhood.

Without knowing why, tears began to form in Patty's eyes. Then she realized that she was staring at Sue Anne's deformed leg, and the memories came flooding back.

It had happened before Charlie was born. The family had just moved to the third-floor apartment in the old tenement building. The odor of dampness and urine pervaded the place, the hallways were dark, and there were always stray animals nesting on the darkened stairs, along with derelicts and drunks who wandered in off the streets for the night.

June had been gone for more than a week, and there was no money and no food in the house. Patty's late night foraging through the garbage cans had not yielded anything edible, and she had come to the conclusion that people ate more and threw away less food in the winter.

It was bitterly cold that night, and the children were painfully hungry. Patty was only eight years old, but she had been an accomplished surrogate mother for more than half her life. As she weighed the alternatives open to her, her thoughts were controlled by her mother's constant admonition: "Learn to solve your own problems. If you call in outsiders to help, the police will separate you, and you will never see each other again."

Patty was desperate. It was getting late, and the store would close soon. Mr. Casey had already told her to tell her mother there would be no more credit until she paid the grocery bill. Mr. Casey seemed to like Sue Anne best. Maybe she could . . .

"Suni, would you go down to the store and ask Mr. Casey to put some peanut butter and bread on our bill?"

"Thure!" came the quick reply from the five-year-old redhead.

Sue Anne was wrestling with her coat as she bounded down the stairs. She did not see the newly born puppy that was squirming on the stairs, and she could not catch herself after she squashed it with her foot. She lost her balance, and her momentum carried her tumbling down the staircase.

At first, she cried more out of fright than pain, but her tearful face and pronounced limp softened Mr. Casey's resolve. By the time she returned with the bread and peanut butter, her leg was throbbing, and she was in great pain.

Patty carried Sue Anne to the couch and raised her leg, but as the hours passed, the pain was intensified, and the swelling increased. As a last resort, Patty turned to John and said, "Go out and try to find Momma."

"Where should I look?" the seven-year-old boy asked, surprised.

"Go to all the bars around here, but DON'T tell them who you're looking for, or why. Just look and see if you can see her."

John started out the door, and Pat warned him again, "Remember, don't say nothin' to no one."

Of course, John had no luck. He was chased from most of the bars as soon as he showed himself. After two hours, chilled to the bone, the only thing he returned home with was the tiny dead puppy that Sue Anne had stepped on.

Patty and John took turns the next day sitting with Sue Anne and searching for June. Sue Anne's pain got worse, and she alternated between sleeping and crying. On the evening of the third day, her leg had swollen and discolored horribly, and Patty announced "We got to take her to the hospital."

"How?" John asked. "How we gonna get her there?"

"I'll carry her . . . piggyback," Patty responded.

"But what about Momma? She'll kill us if she finds out."

"We got to," Patty said. "It looks like her leg is gonna explode. And it's turning black. You wait here with Karen. If Momma comes home, tell her where I went."

"Uh-uh," John demurred emphatically. "If Momma comes home, I don't want to be here when she finds out what you done. I'm coming with you."

So the issue was resolved. They walked the six blocks to the hospital. Three-year-old Karen laughing in John's arms, and Sue Anne sobbing with pain on Patty's back.

It had been a warm day, but the children were not dressed for the cold October night. Pat and John were exercising enough to keep warm, but Karen, who had been taken from the apartment in her pajamas, was shivering by the time they approached the hospital. Pat, who was beginning to struggle with her heavy burden, instructed John to run ahead to the front desk for directions. At first, the receptionist amusedly thought that John was asking to have his sister Karen admitted for her sniffles, but when she saw the older girls come through the door, she leapt into action.

She tried to take Sue Anne off Patty's back, but Patty would not let her go. In seconds, two orderlies rushed into the lobby from the emergency room but stopped short.

"Holy Jesus, Ralph, look at that leg. Go get a gurney. Quick!"

As soon as the gurney was in place, the two orderlies gently pried Sue Anne loose and placed her on the table.

As they quickly rolled her from the lobby, the three other children started to follow.

"Just a minute," the receptionist said. "I need some information. You can't go in there. Where is your mother? What's her name?"

"Working," Pat mumbled.

"What's that?"

"She's working. My mother's working . . . look lady, I got to stay with Sue Anne."

"Well, who's taking care of you?" asked the woman, ignoring Patty's demand.

"The baby-sitter . . . but she couldn't come," Patty answered, glancing nervously toward the doors through which Sue Anne had been taken.

"Where does your mother work? We've got to call her."

"I don't know," Patricia said. "Besides, if you can just give Sue Anne some medicine, we'll carry her home, and Momma won't get worried."

The receptionist got on the telephone, and a few minutes later, the children were led into a young doctor's office. He tried his hand at getting more information from Patricia, but she was determined not to expose her mother.

Finally, he told them that Sue Anne might lose her leg if she was not treated immediately, and that she could not be treated until her mother or father signed a consent form. The doctor pleaded with her for the information until he finally impressed her with the urgency to treat Sue Anne without delay.

Haltingly at first, Patricia told the doctor that they hadn't seen their mother in about a week, and their father was in prison. That was the first time she had spoken of her personal life to anyone else, and she was ashamed at that moment to admit to the kind of life they were leading. The doctor cursed violently and telephoned the police.

In moments, two uniformed policemen were hurrying toward them. "Momma was right," Patty thought. "They're gonna put us in jail, and we'll never see each other again."

The policemen were very gentle with the frightened children as they explained that Sue Anne would be taken care of in the hospital, and that Patricia, John, and Karen would spend the night together in a special home for children.

The first thing next morning, a juvenile court judge made the four children temporary wards of the state, and a guardian ad litem was empowered to authorize the dangerously belated treatment on Sue Anne's leg. Meanwhile, the other children were comfortable in the detention home, especially when the matron finally convinced them that they would not be sent to jail.

The surgeons were barely able to save Sue Anne's leg, but the accident set off a chain of events that was to have an impact on the entire family and permanently affect Patty's trusting attitude toward adults.

The sound of Sue Anne returning from her bath in the river snapped Patty back to the present. It was daylight, and Patty felt guilty for appearing to have spied on Sue Anne after her younger sister had taken such obvious pains to bathe in private.

Patty was about to explain herself from her perch on the edge of the hole when John began to stir.

"Oh, Jesus," he said, stretching, yawning, and mumbling in his half-sleep.

"What did you say?" asked Patty.

He rose to his knees, looked up at her and spit out each word angrily. "I said I feel like shit . . . I'm hungry . . . I'm thirsty . . . My stomach hurts . . . And I'm stiff all over. Now do you understand?"

Patty understood that John was not really angry, but she was disturbed by the change in him. "Don't be so grouchy," she said softly. "Why don't you get off your knees, wash your face, and get us some corn?"

John wrinkled his nose at the mention of more corn, but he crawled up the side of the hole, stretched and tested his legs, and walked down toward the river.

The conversation had aroused Karen and Charlie. When they were awake enough to realize they had been holding on to each other instead of to Patty, they pushed away and looked around in panic. Patty laughed at the scene, and Karen sprang for her waist and put her head on Patty's lap. Charlie just sat where he was, stuck his thumb in his mouth and grinned because something was obviously funny.

The third full day of their stay by the river had officially begun. *Wednesday—it had to be Wednesday*, and Patty decided that if this was going to be home they couldn't live with a permanent layer of sand and dirt covering their bodies.

"C'mon you two, let's get washed up."

Charlie waddled and Karen stumbled through the soft sand leading down to the river. The water felt good and cool. Karen emulated Patty's actions, and Charlie plopped down behind them waiting to be washed.

"Would you guys get some corn together while I get these two cleaned up?" Patty shouted to John and Sue Anne.

Patty then turned her attention to Charlie without waiting for their response. The faded T-shirt rode above his protruding belly, and the permanently brown-stained diaper hung out both sides of his baggy short pants.

"Okay, squirt, if we're gonna live out here, you'll have to go like the rest of us, and I'll be damned if I'm gonna keep yanking this diaper on and off."

If Charlie knew what she was saying, it did not register on his face. The diaper was stained beyond cleaning, and in spite of Patty's attempts to keep it rinsed, it was filthy to the point of rotting. Charlie's bottom was a mass of red bumps, and some were beginning to fester.

Patty stripped Charlie, rolled the brown diaper into a tight knot, and heaved it into the river as far as she could. By the time she finished scrubbing at his skin, he was fighting her with all his might, and as soon as his baggy pants were in place, he squirmed away and waddled quickly toward the hole where the others had gathered to chew on the raw corn.

Without the bulky diaper to help hold his pants up, the worn elastic in the old shorts proved inadequate to the task, and his pants fell to his ankles before he had taken three steps. They all laughed, and Charlie's mood changed instantly. It was time to put on another show. He pulled his shorts up to his knees, took a few steps, let them drop, and tumbled to the ground.

It was great sport, but by the time he got to the hole, he had walked out of the shorts and forgotten about them completely. "Well, Charlie, why not?" Patty said. "Let's just leave it that way. Maybe the sun will dry up that rash."

Patty casually hung the shorts on one of the lower

branches of the tree, dropped into the hole, and picked up an ear of corn.

"You're not really serious, are you?" John asked indignantly. "What if someone sees him running around like that. I mean it just ain't right."

"You're a real dummy," Sue Anne shot back. "Who do you think is gonna come out here anyway? We're HERE because nobody CAN find us!"

Now it was John's turn to be practical, but it was the kind of practicality that Patty did not want to hear. "Stay out here for what—for how long? How long do you think we can last out here? I mean it's going to get cold, and . . ."

Patty cut him off. "I don't know. We'll make it, and we'll make it on our own. It ain't gonna be like last time. It ain't *ever* gonna be like that again!"

She screamed the last few words to underscore the fact that the conversation was closed. She knew it didn't make sense, but winter seemed so far away. The sun had barely risen, and the oppressive heat was already beginning to close in like an invisible wall.

"Something's wrong with Charlie!" Patty had been staring off into space when Sue Anne's alarm interrupted her thoughts.

Charlie was only a few steps away, lying on the ground holding his stomach. When she got close to him, Patty saw and smelled the problem. Charlie had diarrhea, which in itself was not unusual, but his obvious pain and the raw corn flowing from his system alarmed her.

"No more corn for anyone," Patty ordered. "John, does your stomach still hurt?"

As she was talking, Patty picked up Charlie and carried him toward the river.

John caught up with them and whispered, "Yeah, and I got the same problem Charlie has, too."

Within several hours, it became obvious that they all shared the problem and that Patty's warning about the corn had come two days late.

It was going to be a bad day for all of them. The novelty of being free, playing in the river, and living outdoors was beginning to lose its charm. As the afternoon waned, Patty made a decision; "Tonight, John and I will go to the house and find some *real* food. The worst is almost over, and so is this rotten day."

They decided to leave before it got completely dark. Too many trips through the dry corn stalks had badly scratched Patty's skin, and she was covered with painful infections, so she selected a different route to the Wilson house. They skirted the cornfield by walking west along the riverbank until they were directly south of the farmhouse. They still had four hundred yards to travel, but the house was in sight, so they hid themselves in the clover until it was dark enough to move closer.

Patty was grateful for the moonlight, because this was new terrain for her. They headed for one of the outbuildings that she had earlier suspected to be an unused garage. By keeping the building between themselves and the house, they managed to screen their approach. Then they knelt behind the garage to regroup and discuss their plan of action.

"The garbage cans are right around the corner and down toward the front of the garage," Patty whispered to John. "I'll pick out anything we can eat, and pass it to you, then you come back here and wait while I go up to the house for water." John nodded his agreement, and they crawled forward, each carrying an empty tin.

As she turned the corner of the building, Patty became ensnared in a rabbit fence. "Shit!" she exclaimed. "I'm tangled up in something."

"It looks like a garden," John said, as he moved forward to help her extricate herself from the wire. "It is," he added. "There's some tomatoes."

Patty was skeptical about the value of more raw vegetables, so the discovery of the garden did nothing to excite her. "Let's check out the garbage first," she said, stepping over the low fence.

When they reached the garbage cans, Patty made a discovery that delighted her. Coiled at the base of the rack was a garden hose, and it was connected to a spigot at the front of the building. From now on, she would be able to draw water at a safe distance from the house.

Patty then removed the first lid and reached into the dark can, trusting her tactile senses to find something edible. There were empty cans, crumpled paper bags, newspapers, cellophane, and some unidentifiable liquids, but nothing else. The second can contained more of the same, except there were also coffee grounds and some soft solids that might have been mashed potatoes. Then her fingers closed on a familiar item, and the image of a loaf of bread flashed to her brain. She carefully extricated the package, handed it to John, and returned to the search, but there was nothing else to be had.

Patty glanced furtively at the back porch of the house as she carefully replaced the lid with both hands. Then she drew water from the garden hose to wash the slime from her fingers and fill the two tins.

As they returned through the garden, Patty stopped to pick four tomatoes, unable to determine whether they were ripe or not, and John pulled at some greens that were growing in a neat row, unearthing a handful of carrots.

Patty and John relieved their pent-up anxiety by giggling most of the way back. They were obviously pleased with their success as they retraced their steps along the riverbank and John said, "That was *really* fun!"

"Yeah," Patty laughed. "But if we don't spot that damned tree, we're gonna follow this river all the way to California, and THAT won't be so funny."

"It's right up ahead," John said. "I can see the top of it."

Patty was anxious to get some of the hard bread into the younger children in the belief that it would solidify their bowel movements, so she awakened them immediately. Sue Anne was hesitant to eat the vegetables until John assured her that they had come from the garden, and not the garbage. Then she joined the others in relishing the flavor of food that was something other than corn.

They settled in for the night with much the same contentment as they had enjoyed that first evening. But as John's music began to lull the others to sleep, Patty scratched her head and discovered a large lump that had not been there that morning. Searching the rest of her scalp, she discovered four more bumps, and not even John's music could dispel her concern.

That night Patty dreamed about the warts on her head, and she awoke scratching vigorously. Her fingers were sticky, and as the darkness faded, she saw that they were covered with blood. She ran to the river to rinse her hands and hair, but she continued to bleed for some time. She was completely devoid of her characteristic self-confidence when the problem dealt with blood, so by the time the other children were awake, she was trembling.

It was John's turn to take control and be comforting. "Heck, I got 'em, too. They don't hurt. Just leave 'em alone," he advised.

Then Sue Anne added, "I got 'em too. It's probably a rash from eating all that corn."

As soon as her scalp stopped bleeding, Patty inspected Charlie and Karen, and found the smooth warts on their heads as well.

None of the children had ever seen or heard of ticks before, but John's advice was instinctively correct: "If they don't hurt, ignore them."

Sue Anne said they gave her the creeps, and Patty had to agree, but she forced the thought from her mind when she saw that Charlie's diarrhea had not abated and that he was excreting tomato seeds along with the kernels of corn that had not yet been flushed from his system.

"We've got to find better food," she said. "Why don't you two climb the tree and see if there are any other houses around here."

It was Thursday, the beginning of their fourth full day in the wild, and Patty was beginning to understand the gravity of their plight. John and Sue Anne shouted down a running description as they climbed the tree, reporting only the tall buildings in the distance. Then they spotted the farmhouse, and finally, "Hey, there's the place where we got the hamburgers!"

"The restaurant?" Patty shouted.

"Yeah, right down the road from the farmhouse," John replied. "Not too far away."

John shimmied down the tree filled with plans to generate new food supplies. "I could walk right up to the place. Nobody'd pay attention to a kid."

Patty knew better. She simply announced that she would check out the restaurant that night, but John was determined to make his own contribution.

"No, you won't," he said. "I know where it is, and I'll go there myself. How come you never trust me?"

Patty knew he was right, but she also knew that she could not ask him to make the trip alone in the dark. "Okay," she said. "But we'll wait till morning. It's a lot quieter then, and you won't have any trouble finding your way."

The question was settled, and John enjoyed his renewed feelings of self-importance. He spent a good part of the day high in the tree mapping out every step of his route, memorizing landmarks, identifying places to hide and rest along the way.

On Friday morning, John was on his way with the first light, before the sun was visible. He ran east along the riverbank, past the spot where he and Patty had turned toward the Wilson house two nights earlier. He continued along the river for another half-mile, stopping to rest several times along the way. Then he sprinted north across the open clover field, cutting a diagonal that would take him the final four hundred yards to the highway, and he plunged into the culvert along the side of the road. He pressed himself to the ground gasping for breath, fully expecting to be discovered, but when the roaring in his head abated, there were only the early morning sounds of birds and insects to be heard.

He ventured a tentative peek over the roadbed toward the

restaurant, then dropped down quickly to interpret the images his mind had collected. He concluded that there were no immediate dangers, so he raised his head again for a more thorough inspection.

He carefully scanned the situation. The restaurant was closed; there were no cars in the parking lot; and there was no movement to be detected anywhere. John put his hands on the ground beneath his chest, took a deep breath, pushed himself up, and bolted across the highway toward the garbage cans. He was moving so fast that he almost slid past the cans in the gravel. He reached out to grab the top of one of the cans to regain his balance, and in a single move, planted his feet and tore off the lid.

The odor of spoiled food engulfed and nauseated him, and his heart sank as he peered down into the sickening conglomeration of slops that must have been baking in the heat since the previous afternoon. He slammed the lid down and leaped to the next can. The result was the same except the stench was not quite so strong.

On his fifth try, John got lucky. This must have been the last barrel to have been set out the night before, because the odor was minimal, and it contained see-through packages of dinner rolls and the burnt end cuts of several roasts. John quickly dumped the rolls from one of the bags and filled it with pieces of meat. Then he snatched two more bags of rolls, and, more like a frightened animal than a ten-year-old boy, he bolted across the road to safety.

He landed in the ditch with a loud thump, rolled over onto his stomach, and cocked his head to listen. There was nothing. He had made it! He lay there trembling with excitement as he relived every moment of his wild dash.

Before departing the scene, John wanted to have one unhurried look at the place where they had suffered so much only five days ago. He stared at the spot his father had parked the car to let the children out; he looked at the front door of the cafe and remembered the air-conditioned room; and he saw where he and the other children had sat waiting all afternoon for their parents' return. He looked at all those reminders of that terrible day, and he felt nothing but a detached contempt. He shrugged his shoulders, then rolled over to a sitting position, up to his feet, and he was on his way.

As the days passed, new routines were established, and regular chores were assigned. The children came out of their depression and began to look upon the hole near the river as their permanent home. Different parts of the area were designated for the performance of bodily functions, the storage of food and water, sleeping, and recreation, and each of the children was assigned maintenance duties.

The focus of the children's play changed from the river to the large tree. John and Sue Anne regularly climbed high enough to command the best view, but even Pat, Karen, and Charlie enjoyed looking out over the cornfield to the highway from the lower branches.

John played his harmonica every chance he got. Sometimes, he played up and down the scales without thinking; sometimes, when the others felt like singing a little parody they enjoyed, he played "The Battle Hymn of the Republic," and they joined in softly:

> Mine eyes have seen the glory
> Of the burning of the school.
> We have tortured every teacher,
> We have broken every rule.
> We have tied up all the principals
> And flushed them down the stool.
> Our gang goes marching on . . . .

The children usually giggled and stumbled their way through this song because no one but Sue Anne knew all the words. Little Charlie knew only "STOOL," which he gleefully shouted—on cue or otherwise.

But the melody that John played most often was "Edelweiss." He never tired of it. He played it to drown out the night sounds as the children settled in for the night, and he played it after returning from the nightly scavenging trips before falling off to sleep himself.

One night, Leona Wilson called her husband out to the screened porch. "Harry," she said, "what is that noise?"

"I don't hear anything unusual," he responded after a moment of silent listening.

"There's *something*," she said. "It comes and goes. Once in awhile I hear it during the daytime, too. It's kind of a whining noise. Maybe like a wounded animal. It's kind of eerie sounding."

"Shh! There it is again!" she whispered excitedly. "It seems to be coming from the cornfield."

"No, I don't hear a thing," he said. "It's probably just the corn. Everything's so dry that the slightest breeze turns every corn stalk into a flute."

Mrs. Wilson was not convinced one way or the other, but she had lived in the country long enough to be accustomed to strange noises, so she was not in the least bit frightened. In bed that evening, though, she was attentive, to say the least.

In the days and nights that followed, Leona Wilson continued to hear the strange sounds, catching short bursts as they wafted in on the breeze. After several days, she began to perceive that the broken sounds had a melodic continuity, and she understood the meaning of fear.

She knew that either she was losing her mind or something was out there conjuring eerie music. Harry good-naturedly blamed it on the drought and everyone's anxieties over potential crop losses and range fires. But Leona grew fearful of venturing outside the house and spent much of her time at her second-floor bedroom window scanning the enormous cornfield.

Harry's hearing was not as sharp as Leona's; he trusted her. On the surface, he appeared to humor her, but his loaded shotgun was always within reach.

* * *

Patty supervised her brothers and sisters tenaciously, and one of their inviolable rules was that they tell her whenever they were leaving the immediate area. On Saturday, August 15th, there was a near-disaster. It was midmorning, and John and Sue Anne had slipped off to explore the eastern boundary of the cornfield. Karen was sitting on the edge of their hand-dug hole cradling a pathetic excuse for a doll that had been fabricated for her by John and Sue Anne from cellophane and corn silk. Patty was trying to knock out the dents in a new "drinking water can" that had been unearthed. She was totally absorbed in her task when she heard a gurgling scream. She dropped the can and looked around but could only see Karen playing in the sand. Something was wrong, but she couldn't figure it out until she realized that Charlie was missing.

She jumped out of the hole and looked around frantically. Then she saw the blond head bob up about twenty yards out into the river. With a scream, she dashed across the sand and into the river—to the spot where she had last seen him. Patty dove under the water four times before she finally came up with her brother in her arms. He was unconscious. She was shaking him violently even before getting him to shore.

Pat was sure that Charlie was dead. She could hear the water sloshing in his stomach, and his eyes were closed. She knew nothing of artificial respiration, but she frantically pushed in on his swollen stomach and forced some water out. Then she held him upside down and shook him vehemently, screaming, "Charlie, Charlie, don't die . . . don't die." Before long, he started to cough and spit water, then all three of them cried and hugged one another tightly.

From that point on, she insisted that no one go anywhere alone. John, not having seen the near-drowning, screamed back that he was old enough to take care of himself, and he would go *wherever* he wanted, *whenever* he wanted. Pat reached out and slapped his face, snarling, "You'll do what I tell you." John rubbed his stinging cheek and knew the issue was closed.

* * *

Sunday, August 16th, was to be the children's last full day of living in the wild.

John took off on his regular predawn excursion to the restaurant. He now traveled with complete familiarity and assurance. He took pride in his ability to sift through the garbage in an organized manner. His nose would tell him which of the garbage cans had been in the sun too long to yield anything worth eating and which of the cans contained the food that had been thrown away after closing hours the night before.

As was his custom by now, he first lay in the ditch beside the highway to survey the scene. He had determined that there was no one in the restaurant, and he was preparing himself to cross the highway when a truck came around the curve and pulled into the rear parking lot, backing up to the small loading dock. John hugged the ground, and he saw the driver leave the cab of his truck and knock at the back door of the restaurant. No one answered. The sleepy driver scratched his head for a minute, then opened the tailgate and pulled out stacks of small white boxes, which he piled up outside the kitchen door. When he had unloaded, he wrote a note, stuffed it under one of the strings, and drove away.

John waited for the truck to disappear around the curve, then he sprinted across the highway to investigate. He was in for the most delightful surprise any ten-year-old could hope for: the truck had made the regular Sunday delivery of fresh pies and pastries. When he saw what was in those boxes, his calm assurance left him. His mind raced with excitement. *It was too good to be true! Somebody was sure to drive up and catch him!* As excited as he had been on that first trip to the restaurant, John snatched up two piles of boxes, tied together in lots of six, and holding on to the strings that bound them, he raced back across the road without a glance in either direction. He bounded into the clover field and across to the cornfield. He did not stop running until he saw Patricia peering out from the hole, then he stopped.

"What's wrong?" Patty asked, waking the others.

"Nothing. Wait till you see what I got!" He had run all the way, and he was out of breath, but the thought of the pleasure that he was about to bring the others had him giggling and gasping for air at the same time. He stood there with a broad smile on his face, waiting for them to ask what he had, and when they did, it was like Santa Claus and Thanksgiving and Birthdays all rolled into one.

John continued to laugh as the others tore open the boxes. Charlie was the first to scoop out a blob of goodies from a cream pie, and Sue Anne soon followed suit with the chocolate cake. Patty tried to bring order to the pandemonium, but there was no stopping that emotional derailment, and she finally sat back, and, laughing to herself, she opened one of the boxes and tore into a cherry pie.

When they had thoroughly gorged themselves, they lay around like bears in hibernation, moaning contentedly in their discomfort.

Then the realization finally struck Pat that they might now be one step closer to being discovered. "You know," she said thoughtfully, "when they find out about those missing cakes, they might come looking for us."

"Naw," said John. "They'll never miss them. Besides, they'd never find us."

"I don't care," Sue Anne added. "I'm tired of corn and tomatoes and hard bread." That ended their discussion, but John and Sue Anne spent an inordinate amount of time that day watching the highway from the high branches of the big tree.

By four o'clock that afternoon, the ever-present southwest breeze had died down, and there was an unusual stillness that began to unnerve the children. The birds had stopped singing, and Patty wondered whether the river was still flowing. The air seemed heavy and hot. John and Sue Anne descended the tree to join the others in the hole. They all had some strange sense of foreboding. Patty was as frightened as she had been after Charlie had almost drowned, but she didn't know why. No one said anything, but first Karen and then Charlie began to cry. When Patty asked her why, Karen sobbed, It's spooky. Something bad is going to happen."

Patty looked to the south, across the river, and she saw the heavy black clouds rolling in to the accompaniment of distant thunder. Darkness approached earlier that night because of the dense skies, and the flashes of summer lightning brought the kids to the point of panic. Anyone who knows about typical prairie thunderstorms knows that there is no such thing as a typical prairie thunderstorm. No two are alike, and no two people ever react in the same way to what happens. First, there is an eerie stillness, then the fading light takes on a greenish tint. Finally, the rain and wind strike with a furious blast. Aluminum lawn chairs are picked up by the wind and thrown against the houses, and garbage can lids fill the air like flying saucers. Motorists must pull off the road because the windshield wipers cannot compete with the massive downpouring of water, and those at home strain their eyes looking for a funnel cloud, especially when a lightning flash momentarily illuminates the horizon.

For most people, a prairie thunderstorm is both exciting and ominous, but there was only terror for the Clawson children huddled together on one side of that hole when the storm hit, experiencing the first real threat to their existence.

The rain fell in torrential proportions, and their hole began to fill with water immediately. Lightning seemed to be crashing all around them, each flash an electrical explosion that made them all scream. Patty looked at the old cottonwood directly above their hole and realized how dangerous it would be to stay there, so she grabbed Charlie and shouted to the others to start out for the house. It was difficult to climb out of that muddy hole, but they were on their way in minutes. They ran with their hands over their eyes to protect themselves against the wind and rain, and they had to shout at the top of their lungs to communicate, even though they were only a few feet apart.

Unlike the first time they had approached the house as a group, they were neither tentative nor hesitant. The bathroom light was burning as it had every night, and the children instinctively headed for that spot. The bathroom extended three feet from the rest of the house, so the children took shelter behind the protrusion, under the eaves. They were still getting wet, but they were out of the worst of it.

As their terror diminished, John began to play his harmonica softly. The soothing strains of "Edelweiss" had its usual calming effect, and as the intensity of the storm passed, the children fell asleep.

Before Patty dozed off, she reconsidered their predicament. She had earlier decided that living alone in the wilderness was not much different than living alone in an apartment in Philadelphia. She had fantasized about staying there forever, about playing in the river and the sand, and about not hearing grown-ups screaming at each other or getting drunk. Here by the river, they were free and happy. But now for the first time, she was forced to face the realities of thunderstorms, cold weather, and snow. She was saddened by the thought that their idyllic life had come to an end, because now she had to think up another plan.

They slept on the east side of the house, and Pat was the first to awaken the next morning, just before sunup. She stirred the other children, and they sleepily stumbled back to their hole next to the river. It was still partially filled with water, but Patty assured them that it would dry out as the sun came up. She told them not to worry, but SHE worried. What would they do now?

The children set about to restore the condition of the hole. Patty told John to bury the empty pastry boxes in the sand while she and Karen used the old coffee cans to bail the water from the hole. Sue Anne climbed the tree to see how much the storm had changed the face of their cornfield world.

All five of the kids were covered with mud, but each of them shared a feeling of accomplishment that came with surviving the terrible storm. Patricia took particular delight in the fact that Karen was smiling—for the first time in more than two years.

Sue Anne particularly enjoyed watching the cars go by on the highway. Her only complaint in this whole adventure was that she missed seeing people. That morning, though, she saw something that she wasn't pleased to see. Her warning was not shouted loudly, but the intensity in her voice caught everyone's attention when she said, "There's a cop just pulled in the farmyard."

Pat screamed at Charlie and Karen to get out of the hole immediately, and John stood up, not knowing what to do, but waiting for instructions from Patty.

"It was those pies . . . those damned pies," Sue Anne blurted as she climbed down from the tree. "I bet they're comin' to get us 'cause we ate those damned pies."

John said, "God, I shouldn't a-done it!"

Patty said, "It doesn't matter. We can't let them catch us. And if they DO catch us, don't no one say a thing . . . nothing at all. They can't prove we took those pies. Just don't say anything."

Patty looked around anxiously and realized that they were exposed there by the river, compared to the cornfield, where, by stepping a few feet one way or the other, they could hide themselves from anyone searching for them. "We've got to go into the corn. We've got to stay down low, and stay together. And when we stop, no one move—don't no one move an inch—just stay right where we are." With that, the children, running on tiptoes as if the sound of their small feet hitting the sand and silt would expose their presence, dashed into the cornfield. As they banged across the furrows and through the stalks, they knew that the policeman would hear every rustling leaf and cracking stalk, but they also knew that they had to get deeper into the cornfield and lie quietly.

Patty fell to her knees and signaled the others to stop and lie flat. Everyone was shaking, but no one was crying. The heat was oppressive, and the corn dust adhered to their skin along with the encrusted mud. They heard a car door slam, and they were not sure whether someone had just emerged from the police car or entered it. Assuming the worse, Sue Anne said, "Let's get out of here!"

"Shut up and stay put," Patty hissed. "Don't move!"

A few minutes later, they heard the thrashing and trampling of cornstalks that signaled someone's entry into the cornfield. The sound in the dry cornfield was distorted to the point that the children could not tell how near or far away their pursuer was, but they were more frightened than ever.

John sprang to his knees, practically sobbing, "We can't all get caught. It was me that took the pies. It was me that done it." Before Patty could calm him, John dashed north toward the highway. She jumped up and chased him through fifteen or twenty rows of corn before she was able to catch up to him and pull him down with a headlock. John was sobbing. "Shut up!" she panted. "Don't move!" But in an instant, the noise of the other children coming to join them signaled an end to their hope of remaining undetected. Even before she caught sight of them, Patty heard a woman screaming an alarm from the farmhouse.

Before long, the screaming stopped, and there was no more movement at the west end of the cornfield. The children lay still for thirty minutes. The dust and sweat and heat had combined with the corn fibers to drill a million holes into their skin, and the more they attempted to rub away their discomfort, the worse it became.

"Let's go back to the river," Sue Anne suggested.

"No," Patty said. "We'll wait till dark."

Before long the children heard the sounds of many sirens, followed by the noise of tires skidding across the gravel driveway of the farmhouse. From the sounds of car doors closing, they knew that four or five more policemen had joined the search. In a matter of minutes, they heard the group enter the western edge of the cornfield. The children hugged the ground as the noises got closer and closer. Finally, they saw one of the men cross over into the row that they were sitting in. He was big and fat, and he was wiping his face with the back of his arm. When they saw that he was carrying a shotgun, they bolted up and headed for the river.

They could hear that lady screaming again as they exited the cornfield and threw themselves into their hole near the river. The shouting and cursing of the men got louder and louder. It sounded like a herd of cattle was stampeding toward them, trampling cornstalks in its path. The children huddled closer and closer as the charging men approached.

Suddenly, there was a shotgun blast from the edge of the hole, and all five bodies jerked upward as one.

About the same time the Clawson kids had been gorging themselves on the fruits of John's Sunday morning pastry raid, Leona Wilson was fuming at her husband across the breakfast table about the fact that the sheriff had not sent someone to investigate her complaint. "I waited around here all day yesterday," she said. "I killed the whole day. It seems like they could have called if they weren't going to come."

"Well," Harry drawled, glancing up from the Sunday paper, "you know how Saturdays can be this time of year. There might have been a wreck or something. Besides," he chuckled, "I'm not too sure you convinced them about the musical prowlers. I can see why they might not have got around to it."

"Very funny, Harry. I think that's it, all right," she replied angrily. "You make me sound like an idiot—like I imagined the whole thing. You're ALWAYS doing that. They probably thought I was crazy, just like you do."

"Well, whoever it was, he's long gone now. Do you want me to call again?"

"No. Forget it. I didn't hear anything last night. I'm just aggravated about their attitude. A rapist has to be smashing down the door before that sheriff takes it serious, then you can't find him if you need him. I feel like calling my brother-in-law and seeing if the County Commission can't make the sheriff do his job."

Mrs. Wilson's mood did not improve until late afternoon, when she saw the storm clouds gathering to the south. The drought had shortened tempers throughout the farming community, and she prayed that the clouds would bring rain.

Later that afternoon the storm hit with such fury that the Wilsons soon forgot the prowlers, the noises, and their need for water and began to concern themselves with wind damage and floods. "If it's not one thing, it's another," lamented Harry. "If the damned crops don't dry up, they're drowned or blown into the next county by the goddam wind."

The storm continued for several hours. During that time, Mrs. Wilson thought she heard the strange sounds again, but Harry laughed at her. "It's just the wind," he insisted.

But she continued to catch tantalizingly brief snatches of noise that sounded like moaning . . . or sobbing, or maybe even a pipe organ. She forced herself to distinguish and identify each sound—to filter out the frenzy of the wind and rain. Eventually, the strange noises seemed to disappear, and she was almost ready to concede that it might have been her imagination after all.

When she awakened on Monday morning, though, her first thought was to look around outside the house. There was no grass immediately under the dripline of the eaves, and it was quite muddy there. Mrs. Wilson had no trouble spotting all the evidence she needed right there beneath the bathroom window. The muddy tulip bed was a quagmire of footprints.

She was frightened at first. She half-expected someone to jump out and grab her, so she stood still and yelled for her husband. Harry's responses ranged from "Goddam—you were right," to "JEEsus KEErist—what is it?" After the shock of discovery, Mrs. Wilson felt strangely calm—calmer than she had for days. She was not crazy . . . She was right all along . . . There was the proof.

This time, Harry called the sheriff without being asked, and this time, he was much more convincing. "We called two nights ago to report prowlers," he shouted angrily. "And you people promised to send someone out, but you never did. Now there are footprints all over the place, and you'd better get here quick!"

Leona was listening on the extension and added, "Commissioner Walters is my brother-in-law, and if you're not here in twenty minutes, the next call will be from HIM!"

There was this young deputy around there at that time—they used to call him "Studley." He had been in the department only a few months, and no one had even taught him yet how to use a gun. He was really a country kid, but built like a bull. He used to swagger around the courthouse with his big chest, his hips seemingly narrower than his head, and his pistol slung low and tied to his leg like a gunfighter. He was a frightening contrast to the more typical deputy sheriffs with guts hanging over their belts, whose pistols were so uncomfortable to wear that they looked like knives sticking out of their fat spare tires.

Studley was very conceited. He covered up his rural upbringing by playing the role of a big-city cop. The other deputies loved having him around because he was a perfect foil for the practical jokes. He was willing to do anything to better himself so he wouldn't have to pull duty out in the boondocks, and one time the others talked him into buying something for the forensics lab—a detective kit that had been advertised in his comic books.

Above all, Studley always looked down his nose at country people, whom he resented. He saw himself as a street-wise, big-city cop, and he felt far superior to the people who reminded him of his own background. That's the main reason the dispatchers always assigned Studley to answer calls from out in the country, and that's why Studley was assigned to investigate Harry Wilson's complaint.

It was easy to find the Wilson place because Leona Wilson

was waiting for him next to her mailbox, waving both arms to attract his attention. Typical of Studley's superior attitude, he pulled into the driveway and drove past Mrs. Wilson without stopping until he reached the house. Then he sat in his car until she came running up. When she began to tell her story, he held up his hand and interrupted her while he radioed news of his arrival to a dispatcher who could not have cared less.

Then he nodded at Mrs. Wilson to continue and stared straight ahead while she explained the eerie noises, the running water, the sobbing, the "music," and the movements outside the house. He was not a bit impressed, even when Harry asked him to come over to look at the footprints in the mud.

"Looks like kids, to me," he said. "Do you have any kids living here?"

"Of course not," Leona snapped. "Even if we did, don't you think we'd know if it was them out here last night?"

"How about neighbor kids?"

"Forget about the kids! None of the neighbors have kids. I tell you this has been going on for a long time. Someone is hiding out in that cornfield, and I want you to get him out of there!"

Studley was convinced that he was wasting his time with this hysterical woman, but he followed the clumps of mud from the house toward the cornfield. Mrs. Wilson led the way, pointing, "There's one! . . . There's another one! . . . He went in this way!"

"Please, ma'am, let me handle this. You folks go back to the house, and I'll check this out . . . Please."

Leona Wilson knew that Studley was going to need all the help he could get, and she told her husband so on the way back to the house. When they got there, she went directly upstairs to observe the deputy from her bedroom window, and Harry checked his shotgun.

Studley stood on the grass at the edge of the cornfield peering in. The stalks were almost ten feet tall, and he could see no more than twelve feet down the winding rows. The sun was already intense and had turned the wet field into a steambath. He had no desire to stroll into that jungle, but when he heard the commissioner's sister-in-law open her bedroom window to observe him, he knew he had no choice. He picked up a large stick and decided to placate her by carrying his investigation into the cornfield.

He hated every minute of it. He was hot and annoyed, and soon he was able to see no more than six or eight feet in any direction. The towering cornstalks slapped at him and cut him as he walked, and corn dust stuck to the perspiration on his face. Then he started to get nervous because, as a kid, outside Soporia, he had gotten lost in just such a cornfield. At first, he had been swinging that stick at the cornstalks just to make enough of a racket to convince the Wilsons that he was working hard, but as the old memories came back to haunt him, he suddenly was swinging and flailing the stick to keep away imaginary pursuers.

That was the noise that set the Clawson children running through the corn. Mrs. Wilson could see the cornstalks going down as they fled, and she screamed, "Over there! Over there!"

Studley froze in his tracks. He whirled around and looked up to see the screaming woman waving her arms and pointing excitedly. He cocked his head to listen, and he could hear the sound of cornstalks being trampled by some huge force. His fear turned to terror when he realized that it was impossible to determine what direction the noise was coming from or even how close it was to him. He felt that the pursued was now pursuing him, and whatever it was, it was big, it was moving fast, and it was about to pounce on him. He ran from that cornfield with far more enthusiasm than he had entered it.

When he broke out into the open, he was a mess. His face and hands were cut, his lips trembling, and he was dragging an uprooted cornstalk that was hooked around his holster. He stumbled to his car, trying to disentangle himself from the cornstalk. He was shouting for reinforcements even before he reached his radio, and he began his transmission somewhere in the middle of a garbled sentence.

The only thing that was clear to the dispatcher was that Studley was in big trouble, so without really understanding what the problem was, he flashed the code for "Officer in need of assistance," and four other sheriff's cars were rushing to the scene in seconds.

When the first of the four deputies skidded to a halt in the gravel driveway, Studley was facing the cornfield with his pistol in hand. The new arrival jumped from his car just as two others drove in with sirens screaming and lights flashing.

The first thing Lieutenant Carter said was, "Put away that piece before you shoot off your goddam toes."

With the help of the Wilsons, Studley told the story. Lieutenant Carter exploded when he realized that the "emergency" consisted of nothing more than unseen prowlers, eerie music, and a frightened deputy. His angry outburst was interrupted by the noisy approach of yet another patrol car. "Christ," he said. "Who ELSE is coming? Too bad you didn't call out the National Guard."

Carter then radioed his report to Sheriff Johnson, who had been alerted earlier to the emergency transmission. The sheriff agreed that it would probably be a waste of time, but Commissioner Walters had already called him. "You better take a look around, Bill," Sheriff Johnson instructed. "George Walters thinks that this could have something to do with the guys who murdered that woman last week."

"But, Sam, that was TWO weeks ago and fifty miles from here. They couldn't have walked this far without being seen," Carter replied.

"I know. I know. But why don't you look around anyway."

When the deputies overheard the news that they might be searching for killers, they went to their respective cars for shotguns. Carter was annoyed, but he didn't stop any of them except Studley. "You stay here with the Wilsons, and for Christ's sake, if any more deputies come out, send them back."

Lieutenant Carter gathered the remaining three deputies at the edge of the cornfield. "We'll go in about thirty rows apart. We'll walk at the same speed, and we'll keep quiet and listen. Pipe up only if you hear something out of the ordinary. And for God's sake, let's not be shooting at one another in there."

Before they had taken ten steps along their respective routes, it was obvious that it would be impossible to maintain their ranks. They were too far apart to see one another, and although they could hear noises, they couldn't tell who was making them, or where they were coming from.

Just as Lieutenant Carter shouted, "Stop! This ain't working," Mrs. Wilson started to scream from her second-floor window, "Go right! Go right! There they go!"

Without understanding why, the deputies began taking orders from her, crashing through rows of corn, cursing, shouting, stumbling, and running into one another in an undisciplined frenzy of confusion. Suddenly, their primary concern was not to be standing targets for the guns of the others. In fact, they had lost all sense of direction and were stumbling along in circles.

Suddenly, there was a shotgun blast, and all activity stopped.

Deputy Chenoweth shouted, "Here! Here! Quick!"

When the others finally found Chenoweth, he was standing at the edge of the hole almost sobbing.

The four deputies stared in disbelief and shock, completely immobilized by what they saw. There was a huge tangle of arms and legs and hair and eyes—down in the big hole—all tangled up and squirming like worms in a can. They could not tell how many there were down there, or whether they were even alive, except that the mass was moving.

Deputy Chenoweth said, as if in a daze, "When I stumbled onto them, my eyes told me I was looking at a batch of scared, dirty kids, but my head wouldn't believe it until my gun went off and they started jumping and crying."

Then Lieutenant Carter broke the spell and said, "Let's each grab a handful of kids and take them to the cars."

It was infinitely easier said than done. The children were so tangled up, squirming and grabbing for one another, that it was impossible to determine which arms and legs belonged to whose body. With shotguns in one hand and parts of children in the other, the deputies were unable to cope. Finally, the children started to bite, and the deputies threw their guns out of the hole to devote both hands to the task.

The deputies tried not to be too rough, but the kids fought, scratched, bit, and kicked like cornered wild animals.

During the melee, Charlie was shoved out of the hole. Mrs. Wilson, who had just run up to the scene, picked up the baby and shouted, "Stop! Leave them be!"

Everyone stopped and stared at one another, still taking orders from that hysterical woman. As soon as Mrs. Wilson turned and walked toward the house with the baby clinging to her neck, though, the other children scrambled out of the hole to follow.

There was a silent, single-file procession through the rows of corn. When they reached the clearing, Studley ran ahead to open one of the car doors. Without a word, Mrs. Wilson got into the front seat of the patrol car, and the other children climbed into the back seat.

Mrs. Wilson forgot the fear that she had experienced over the past several nights, but seeing the children and realizing what they must have lived through, and how close they had come to being shot, she clung to the baby and sobbed, "Oh God! Oh, God!"

PART II

THE SYSTEM

Lieutenant Carter's unmasked irritation crackled across the police radios: "What the hell's going on?" he demanded. "I told you guys that Studley would take the kids and follow me in to write up the reports, and I look back and see the damndest procession of patrol cars since President Truman came to town."

There was no response, so Carter came back in his clipped, controlled way, "Hocker . . . Chenoweth . . . Abernathy . . . how far does this convoy go? I want you people to get to your patrol positions . . . NOW!"

Carter was a tough, trim ex-Marine sergeant who was willing and able to back up his threats with action, and his commands were rarely questioned. But while Abernathy and Hocker searched desperately for the nearest turnoff, Deputy Chenoweth picked up his mike and said, "Lieutenant, this is Chins. I guess we're all as curious and upset about those kids as you are. Don't ask us to turn tail and run now. I'm still shaking from firing that shotgun. I'll be damned if I'm gonna wait and read about this thing in the newspapers tonight."

The radios went dead as they waited for Carter's explosive outburst.

Jim Carter knew that only Chenoweth could get by with that kind of honesty and directness. There was nothing phony or subtle about Chins—from the gut hanging over his belt to the unlit cigar butt forever stuck in his face. He was bright, honest, dependable, and tough, but Carter also knew that his heart was soft, so his anger quickly dissipated, and he reconsidered his order: "Maybe you're right. We'll get it done faster, and none of you will be worth a damn until we find out what this is all about, anyway."

The procession of patrol cars approached the city and drove toward the heart of the downtown area. Charlie had scrambled out of Mrs. Wilson's grasp as soon as Patty had settled herself, so the five children rode in the back seat of the second car, leaving Studley and the sobbing Mrs. Wilson alone in the front.

Patty's mind raced. It wasn't over yet. There was still a chance. If the others remembered her orders to keep their mouths shut, it could still be all right. Everything had happened so fast, it was hard to think, but Patty knew one thing for sure—*These bastards are not going to do it to us again.* They had to get away.

Chances were that John would obey, because he was the one who took the pies, but she couldn't depend on Sue Anne. If she wanted to speak up, there would be no stopping her.

The County Detention Home was an old three-story brick building. All the windows were secured by bars or institutional screens, and a chain-link fence ten feet tall surrounded the gravel yard. A run-down swing set on the north side of the building was the only thing that might have suggested the presence of children. The home was situated next to the old courthouse parking lot at the intersection of two busy streets. Most of the houses in that neighborhood were falling apart, and half of them had been abandoned.

The five patrol cars drove down the alley and through the gate at the rear of the home. Studley drove up to the building and parked close to the back door. Patty's hope for escaping evaporated as the four other cars pulled up and parked in such a way as to surround them on three sides, leaving open only a narrow lane to the door of the detention home.

Mrs. Higgins, the matron of the detention home, watched the arrival of the patrol cars from the kitchen window. She turned, wiping the soap suds from her hands, and said to the young attendant sitting at the kitchen table, "C'mon, Ernie, it looks like the sheriff has caught the James gang and the FBI's ten most-wanted criminals in a single raid."

Mrs. Higgins was an obese woman with a glass eye, who, except that she radiated warmth and kindness, would have scared children to death. She had been matron of the detention home fourteen years, and as custodian of these juvenile outcasts, she had cared for young rapists, murderers, muggers, and thousands of abused or abandoned children. She had come to learn that even the toughest of them were frightened when they came through that door. In spite of fourteen years of the system to meet the human needs of children in trouble, she remained an indomitable optimist, and she continued to care so much that even the most bitter of her wards felt and responded to the warmth of her caring.

She turned into the hall as the back door opened and Studley led the children into the home. She had been curious about the sudden arrival of five patrol cars, but she was not prepared for what she saw. She retreated a step as they walked past her into the receiving area, then she fell in behind Chins and followed them into the living room.

In the center of the room stood five of the most pathetic children Mrs. Higgins had ever seen. Filthy and tattered, they stood in a circle, surrounded by five deputies smeared with blood and mud, looking like characters in a bad comedy routine. Mrs. Higgins didn't know whether to laugh or cry. She looked from one to the other, then said, "What's all this about?"

Lieutenant Carter answered, "We don't know. We found them in a hole out by the river."

Mrs. Higgins then glared at Leona Wilson. "Are they yours?"

She was too surprised to answer, but as she shook her head, both hands came up to press against her mouth.

Carter answered for her. "No, we found them out at her place."

"Well, who are they?" Mrs. Higgins demanded. "Where are the parents?"

"You know as much as we do," Carter said.

Studley added, "They never said a word in the car. Maybe they *can't* talk."

The lieutenant glared disapprovingly at the most inept of his deputies, and the others contributed what little they knew, as if the children were incapable of comprehending what they were saying.

Patty stood with Charlie on her hip and Karen wrapped around her leg. Without moving her head, her eyes darted in surveillance of the possible escape routes, but there were none. A glance at John told her that she had been wrong about him. His face was red, his jaw muscles rippled, and he was about to confess. She caught his attention and glared menacingly through squinted eyes, *Keep your mouth shut!*

The nonverbal exchange did not escape the shrewd matron. Looking directly into Patty's eyes, she said, "Whoever you are, you're here now, whether you want to talk about it or not." Then, looking toward Lieutenant Carter, she said, "So let's get on with it."

Mrs. Higgins took charge. She turned to her aide and ordered, "Ernie, fill out five 'John Does' and call Bud Griggs while we get these kids cleaned up." Mrs. Higgins then placed one hand against Patty's back and indicated with the other that they were to go upstairs. Then she signaled Mrs. Wilson to follow.

Patty disengaged Karen from around her legs, took her hand, and walked slowly toward the staircase. About halfway up, she glanced over her shoulder to make certain the others

were behind her, and Mrs. Higgins climbed past her to assume the lead position. At the top of the stairs, the children
stopped and stared in alarm as they encountered a fearful
and unexpected sight. They did not speak, but Leona Wilson, who had not yet reached the landing, sensed that something was wrong.

When she reached the top of the stairs, she saw the cause
of their concern, and she trembled instinctively. The center
hall was flanked by four jail cells. The walls and ceiling of
each cell were solid steel, and the floor was concrete; the tiny
windows were covered with heavy steel security screens that
were sandwiched between inside and outside sets of bars.
Each cell contained nothing but a toilet and a thin mattress
on the floor. Mrs. Wilson's apprehension soon matched the
children's.

Patty suddenly understood what those movie people
meant when they talked about their blood turning cold. *So
this is what they look like. Mama had always warned us about the
cells—the place they put kids who tell on their mama. They're even
worse than she said.* Patty stared into the cells with mixed feelings. Surely they had lived in worse places, but those were
places you could get out of. Then the thought—more like an
unarticulated emotion—struck Patty that once you got behind those steel bars, inside the steel walls, it was all over. It
wasn't just a cell. It was a tomb—a place to die. John started
to cry, and Patty's self-control began to slip away.

Mrs. Higgins had walked ahead to the large bathroom
down the hall, but when she looked back and saw their
terrified expressions, her businesslike demeanor melted, and
she scurried back to comfort them. The massive woman
seemed to cradle the entire group, almost crooning as she led
them away from the cells. "Those aren't for you. You will
sleep in a big bedroom with the other children." She had no
way of knowing whether the children understood what she
was saying, but she continued, "We have to have cells for

some of the older children who try to hurt themselves or someone else."

The trance was broken, and as the procession continued, Natalie Higgins looked again at the cells and shook her head as if seeing them for the first time. Whom was she trying to convince, herself or the children? Those god-awful, ugly, ancient rooms were unsuitable even for those few children who *needed* the security of a locked room. She had tried repeatedly over the past twelve years to convince the county commissioners to convert those cells into secure holding rooms, but to no avail. She could still hear one of the pompous old sadists saying, *Every kid ought to be put in one of those cells. It would be a good lesson. Yessir, by gawd, I betcha the little bastard would think twice before getting into trouble again!*

Bud Griggs was the Director of Juvenile Court Services. He was twenty-seven years old, but his graying hair and weathered complexion added ten years to his appearance. The only thing casual about Bud Griggs was his manner of dress. He rarely wore a tie except for his weekly appearances in juvenile court. He was an outdoorsman trapped in an office job where he dissipated his pent-up energies constantly pacing his office, shouting orders through the halls instead of capitulating to the convenience of the newly installed intercom. No one ever described Griggs as diplomatic, for he was direct and abrupt with everyone except the troubled children being herded through the crowded dockets. His face was mobile and expressive, in spite of the fact that he wore a perpetual frown and looked at the world through squinted eyes. His intensity was reflected in his relationships with people, the way he threw himself into his work, and the fury with which he attacked his sparring partners in the ring.

When the phone rang that day, he had been characteristically pacing around his office dictating to his secretary. He leaned over and searched for the receiver under piles of paper strewn about the top of his desk. There was no apparent order to the chaotic welter of files, letters, and reports, but each was part of the orchestration required to care for and rehabilitate growing numbers of children, and he was completely cognizant of the content and location of every piece of information there.

The telephone came away from the disorder as if it had been ripped from asphalt. "Griggs," he barked into the mouthpiece. Ernie quickly identified himself, then nervously described the situation at the detention home. Griggs was unusually quiet as he absorbed the information, then he murmured, "Okay," and slowly replaced the receiver.

"What's wrong?" Louise asked as he stared into space.

"I don't know for sure. Get Del in here right away."

Del Howard had been Bud's boyhood friend, but he was new to the job. Judge Harrington had been insisting for a year that Bud hire an assistant, but he was more comfortable handling the extra case load than developing new relationships. He knew how frustrating it would be to try to fill an important job that carried a small salary, and the succession of misfits who had applied convinced him early on that it was not worth the effort.

Then one Monday newspaper carried the story of a great football career that had been prematurely terminated by a blind-side block, resulting in compound fractures that would stiffen Del Howard's elbow for life. Green Bay had lost the services of an all-pro linebacker, but perhaps Griggs had found his assistant.

There was more than a twinge of guilt as Bud traced his friend's whereabouts to the hospital in Chicago. As he dialed the number, he reasoned that Bud was bright, he cared about people, he spent the off-season doing volunteer work with kids, and he had made enough money at the game to afford the meager salary the county was about to offer.

Del's mother had already arrived, and when she answered the call, Bud asked, "Mama Howard? How is he?" It wasn't necessary for Griggs to identify himself, because she was as familiar with his voice as she was with her own children's.

"Hi, baby," she answered. "It's hard to tell. He's kind of groggy, but no worse than usual," she laughed.

When Del took the phone, there was again no need for formalities. "What the hell do YOU want?" he asked first.

"Nothing special. I hear there's a vacancy in Green Bay."

"Don't YOU bother to apply. Your white ass is too yellow for that job."

"Hell," said Griggs, "I don't have time to play those kiddy games. I just didn't want you coming back home as a burden on our welfare rolls, that's all."

"I sure as hell ain't gonna freeze my ass off in Green Bay selling pencils if I can come back for some home cookin' and free money."

"Can't do that, blood," Griggs said, using the term of endearment reserved for the closest of friends. "I'm gonna make an honest man out of you. I'm gonna make you my assistant and raise your station in life."

Then Del started laughing that infectious laugh of his and said, "Shit, Griggs, you never did have any class," and hung up.

"You want me?" Del asked, surprised to find his old friend seated behind his desk.

Del had been on the job for two weeks now, and it was time to throw him into the water. Bud waved the back of his hand toward an empty chair and struggled for a way to describe the problem. "Little Ernie just called over from the detention home and said that the sheriff had just brought in five kids."

"Okay, what about it?" Del asked after a moment of silence.

"We don't know who they are or where they came from. They were probably dumped, and they were living out near the Wilson place, next to the river. We don't know how long or anything else. The kids won't talk to anyone."

Griggs seemed distracted as he related the facts, and Del instinctively understood that he was having difficulty surrendering any turf by assigning the case to his new assistant.

Del Howard smiled imperceptibly and asked, "You want me to take this case?"

"Maybe so. You have a good way with children, and those kids are too scared to talk to anyone. Still . . ." Griggs mused, "This could be a tough one to cut your teeth on."

"Why don't you come with me?" Del suggested, and Griggs was out of his chair with a lurch.

When Bud reached the door, he turned to see his old friend smiling at him. "Well?" he asked.

"Hell, I still don't know whether you want me to take the case or not."

"Yeah, I do. But you're gonna need me to keep your ass out of trouble, so why don't you come along and see how it's supposed to be done."

They drove the six blocks to the detention home in minutes. As Griggs threaded his car around the five patrol cars in the parking lot, Del observed, "It looks like a goddam fire sale."

They let themselves in the back door and found that the deputies had settled into the large front room. It was the only room that looked noninstitutional, with its clean but worn overstuffed furniture, plugged-up fireplace, and carpeted floor. Most of the time, it was filled with children, but that afternoon they were all swimming at the YMCA under the supervision of volunteers from the law school.

Lieutenant Carter was sitting in the corner with a writing pad on his knee, trying to compose a report based on the observations of his fellow deputies. The others were so intent on their speculations and comparing their wounds that they did not notice the arrival of the two newcomers, so Bud and Del stood at the door and listened.

"They're retarded," said Studley. "Have to be."

"Naw, they're not retarded," Chenoweth answered.

"Have to be."

"How do you figure?" Abernathy asked with a trace of annoyance for Studley's know-it-all attitude.

"Well, they can't talk, for one thing."

"You mean they *haven't* talked. How the hell do you know they *can't* talk."

"Look, I was with them kids the most," Studley said defensively. "They was in the back seat of *my* car, not yours, not yours, and not yours," he said pointing a finger at each of the other deputies in turn. "The only thing them kids done was sit and scratch theirselves. They didn't even know what was happening, I tell you. I watched them real careful the whole trip. No way one of 'em crazy kids was gonna jump *me* from behind. I watched 'em the whole way, and them two little ones kept sniveling, and them three older ones just stared straight ahead. They *have* to be."

"Being how Studley here is a trained officer of the law," Abernathy allowed sarcastically, "let's just suppose they *are* retarded . . ."

"No, no, no," Chenoweth interrupted. "You can see it in their eyes. Those kids are as bright as new money."

"Now, wait a minute, Chins," Abernathy said solicitously. "I said just *suppose* old Studley is right."

"And they're quick as cats," Chenoweth added. "They gave us all we wanted down in that hole."

"Please, Chins," Abernathy said, "I agree with you, but just for the sake of discussion, I'd like to know how 'Inspector' Studley figures them kids survived on their own if they was retarded."

"You know," Hocker intervened, "If they *are* retarded, they could have escaped from some asylum or something. Is there one close by?"

Before anyone could respond to Hocker's otherwise reasonable suggestion, Studley stuck his neck out again. "Naw," he said broadly. "I saw a TV show. They're prob'ly what you call FEERal kids."

"What in the hell's a 'FEERal' kid?" Abernathy demanded in unabashed anger and frustration.

"They been raised in the wild by animals."

"Oh, shit," echoed Abernathy and Chenoweth in unison as

the laughter from the doorway called attention to the two Juvenile Court officers standing there enjoying the spectacle.

"That's 'feral,' " Griggs said. "But I doubt it."

The only thing that could have gotten Studley off the hook at that moment was the arrival of an outsider. And when that happened, the other deputies immediately coalesced behind Studley and his ridiculously untenable hypothesis. Only a moment before, Tom Abernathy had been driven almost to the point of violence in reaction to Studley's preposterous theory, but now he directed his sarcasm toward Bud Griggs. "Well, praise be," he said, bowing slightly with affected deference. "A man has come among us who knows all the goddamn answers. Doesn't know the facts . . . just the answers." Abernathy was warming to an appreciative audience, gesturing broadly as the others chuckled. "Well if those kids ain't whatyacallit kids . . . Whatyacallit?"

"FEERal," yelled Studley.

"Feral," corrected Griggs, wishing he hadn't.

"Whatever. If they ain't related to wild animals," he said, rolling up his sleeve, "what do you call this?" There were scratches and blood-caked teeth marks all over his forearm. "Or this?" he asked, pulling on Chenoweth's hand, forcing him to expose more teeth marks, more caked blood and mud, and bits of hanging flesh. Abernathy was so carried away with his own performance that he caught himself in mid-gesture, stopped, and leaned over to the side of Chenoweth's face and whispered loudly, "You know what, Chins? I almost convinced myself he was right," jerking a thumb toward Studley, generating laughter from the entire group.

Bud Griggs stepped further into the living room and said, "Now, if this portion of the entertainment is over, maybe we could talk about what happened and what you know about those kids."

When Lieutenant Carter's silence signaled them that he was not ready to talk, Jerry Hocker—the quiet one—surprised the others by taking the lead. Hocker was in his early thirties, known as a serious police officer, and he was liked and respected by the other deputies. Therefore, when he started the chronological recounting of events, everyone knew it was back-to-business time. The lieutenant picked up his pencil and prepared to take notes, Abernathy lowered his massive body into an easy chair with a grunt and stuck a cigarette in his mouth, and Chins unwrapped a fresh cigar to chew on. A pall settled over the group as they steeled themselves to think seriously about the children again.

The first indication that they were wrong came with Hocker's description of Studley's terror, and the way he had been waving his pistol around, with the cornstalk hooked to his holster, breathlessly describing the fearsome force that had tried to attack him in the tall corn. The group came to life again and laughingly relived the discomfort of the fat, sweating Abernathy, the mass confusion created by the screaming of Leona Wilson from her upstairs bedroom window, and the Keystone Cop reactions of the deputies in the field. They were now out of their chairs and poking one another with their elbows as they joked about Hocker hitting the ground and taking out three rows of corn when he thought Chenoweth was going to shoot him by mistake. Then they painted the imaginary picture of a thousand soldiers and National Guardsmen marching through that tall corn and getting screwed up by Mrs. Wilson's screaming, reducing their orderly ranks to a crisscrossing jumble of humanity looking more like a ragtag band attempting to perform intricate maneuvers during halftime ceremonies . . . only this time with loaded rifles.

Abernathy wheezed and coughed hysterically, Chenoweth's round face glowed with laughter, and Hocker—the instigator—never changed expressions. He continued his dry reporting in a staccato tone, but Lieutenant Carter was no longer taking notes. He just sat there and grinned quietly, waiting for them to get it out of their systems.

During the confusion, Studley ambled over to Griggs and Howard and, with his thumbs hooked over his holster belt, he leaned toward them and allowed in a confidential tone, "Shoot, them kids ain't the only crazies around here."

Griggs watched the slapstick antics of the three deputies

with growing discomfort. He knew they were masters at decompressing through humor, and he got his first disturbing insight into the high level of stress and nervous tension they were trying to avoid.

"Okay. Okay," Griggs said loudly, raising his hands in the air to bring order. "We've got to talk about the kids." As the deputies returned to their chairs, Griggs turned to Del and said, "Why don't you go upstairs and see what's happening. Just play it by ear. Don't force anything. We can talk to them later." Then he turned to Chins and said again, "Tell me about the kids."

"Well, it was really like we been joking about. The corn was so high and thick we couldn't see nothing. We could hear noises, but we couldn't tell who was making them or where they were coming from. It got real spooky, then that woman started yelling for us to go left, to go right, and we got so turned around, we didn't know left from right, and we started running into one another and chasing ourselves around with loaded shotguns in our hands. Finally, I got my bearings and headed toward the river. I didn't want to get shot at."

"Well," Chins continued with a sigh, "when I got clear of the cornfield, I could still hear that lady shouting and screaming, 'There they go, there they go,' and it was spooky as hell. I kept walking along the edge of the cornfield, but I kept turning circles as I went, and I began to imagine somebody was gonna jump out at me or come up behind me or something. Then I heard some strange noises right in front of me. It sounded like whimpering . . . real loud whimpering. So I cocked the gun and sneaked up to where the noises were coming from, and it was a huge hole, about four feet deep and six or eight feet across. I didn't realize they was kids. It was just a big pile of bodies . . . arms and legs grabbing for one another with wild eyes. I had that gun . . . pointed . . . down into the hole." Then tears came to his eyes. "It was such a shock. You can't imagine. I've been in the department since the war, and I never once fired my gun off the range. I sure as hell don't remember squeezing the trigger, and only God himself could have pointed that gun into the air, because I don't remember doing it!"

"I'm telling you, I never want to come that close again." He was gaining control of his emotions again, but not for long. "When that gun went off, all those bodies jumped a foot in the air and came down screaming and crying and grabbing for each other even tighter than before." The tears were rolling down his cheeks.

Abernathy cleared his throat and diverted attention from his friend's distress while the others looked away in discomfort, fearful that they themselves might lose control. "When we heard that blast, we all stopped in our tracks. Then someone started yelling, 'Over here. Over here,' and we all headed to the spot. It was like Chins said. They was crying and screaming, and you really had to study them to figure what they was. We all just stood there looking down into the hole, still holding our shotguns."

"That's when Lieutenant Carter ordered us to get them untangled and out of the hole," Hocker added. "But it was easier said than done. It was as if they were fighting for their lives. Finally, Mrs. Wilson came up and picked up the baby, and suddenly, it was all over."

In the course of the next hour, each deputy contributed his own observations about what had happened, and the depression of the group was finally replaced by a concern for the welfare of the five children they had manhandled back to civilization.

When Del Howard reached the top of the stairs, he reacted the way he usually did to the sight of those terrible steel and concrete cells. As if sensing some kind of physical threat to himself, his strong right arm instinctively moved to cover the massive cast on his left arm. He walked quickly and quietly through the hall toward the voices in the washroom.

As he approached, he heard Mrs. Higgins say, "Let's get these clothes off them. If we can scrape through enough dirt and mud, we might even find out if they're boys or girls." Del thought she must have been talking to herself, but then he noticed the silent Mrs. Wilson testing the temperature of the sudsy water in one of the two bathtubs.

In deference to the feelings of the two girls whose clothes were being stripped away from them, Howard ducked back around the doorway before anyone but Patty had caught a glimpse of him. He leaned against the wall in shock. His mind was trying to interpret and untangle the horrible picture his eyes had flashed. As if scanning a freeze-frame or a carved tableau, he subjected every image to careful scrutiny. Two older women, Mrs. Higgins, whom he knew, and a stranger—she couldn't possibly be a professional—seemed too upset—hair disheveled, eyes puffed up and red from crying. Then the five children—vaguely, an infant sitting on the floor looking up at the oldest girl, and next to the baby, another child, maybe five years old, also looking up at the oldest girl. Del held that image of the triad, and he knew it established the oldest girl as the leader and caretaker, so he tried to focus on her. Skinny, long dark hair hanging almost to her waist, but tangled and dirty; a flat nose and compressed lips—but pretty; and her eyes—large, brown, sad, resolute, and quick. Yes, quick. In a flash, it occurred to him that she had seen him. It had happened so quickly, but she never reacted. She was the one in control, and she would be the one to contend with. Del's image of John was clouded: probably a boy, but his shirt was off and his back to the group, modestly facing the far bathtub, beginning to unbuckle his pants. Then Del Howard shifted his attention to his image of Sue Anne: strawberry blonde, dirty, freckles under the dirt, pug nose; but her eyes seemed to be pleading. Why were they pleading? She too was looking strangely at the oldest girl as Mrs. Higgins began to lower her jeans past her knees. That's it! One leg was normal, but the other was a stick.

Howard straightened up and instinctively frisked his pockets for the cigarettes he had given up four years earlier. He closed his eyes to confirm the images he had conjured, and for the first time in memory, he was overwhelmed and confused.

Immediately after catching sight of the huge black man in the doorway, Patty sensed Sue Anne's plight and tried to maneuver herself into a position to screen the view of Sue Anne's crippled leg from the others. But Mrs. Higgins was way ahead of her. Without the slightest break in her flow of chatter, the huge matron seemed to envelop Sue Anne's frailty as she scooped her from the floor and into the sudsy water. Patty intuitively recognized it as a deftly compassionate act, and she felt a twinge of gratitude toward this prattling, fearsome-looking woman with the glass eye.

Patty followed Sue Anne into the large tub, and Mrs. Higgins crossed the room to put Karen into the tub with John. Soon after the four children were in place, the frothy white bubbles dissolved, and the water turned brown. Mrs. Higgins was washing Karen's hair and said, "I believe it would have been easier to walk you kids through the car wash." She caught John's involuntary snicker, but did not comment, storing it away as valuable corroboration of her earliest assumption that these were bright children who understood exactly what was going on around them.

Mrs. Higgins looked over to Leona Wilson, who was washing Charlie in the sink. "I thought I'd seen everything," she said softly.

"What is it?" Mrs. Wilson asked.

"Ticks . . . Their heads are full of ticks."

"The baby, too. Do you have a comb?"

"No," Mrs. Higgins responded. "We can't comb them out or pull them out. It leaves the tick's head stuck in the skin and causes infection."

"Well, I know that," Mrs. Wilson said with a trace of annoyance. "But there are so many . . ."

"You pull a tick out of the scalp, and it will bleed like hell,"

Mrs. Higgins warned. "A cigarette butt would take them out as quick as anything, but we'd burn off too much hair. Let's wait for the doctor."

The children had not yet spoken a word, but noting their expressions of alarm and the way they looked to Patty for unspoken reassurances, Mrs. Higgins again used the conversation with Mrs. Wilson to comfort them. "Dr. Cyrus Metzger has been treating ticks in these parts for so long they fairly jump out of the skin as soon as he walks into the room. He'll just rub a little lotion into this hair, and those ticks will fall out like snowflakes."

Doctor Metzger arrived as the children were drying themselves. They had managed to effect privacy in that open room by orienting themselves to separate areas: John facing one far corner, Sue Anne the other, and Patty and Karen close to the door, while Mrs. Wilson dried Charlie, and Mrs. Higgins continued to screen Sue Anne's leg.

The children then wrapped themselves in dry towels as the doctor went from one to the other. He noted that their stomachs were distended and their lips parched, but he reported to Mrs. Higgins that they were all basically healthy, but hungry and undernourished. After dealing with their ticks, he observed that they were considerably healthier than he was.

"Are there any special instructions?" Mrs. Higgins asked as they joined Del Howard in the hall.

The old country doctor reached into his storehouse of medical training and experience and said, "Yes . . . Feed them."

Del led the doctor away from the door and said softly, "The deputies think they might be retarded."

"Retarded?" Metzger said, looking over his glasses. "Those deputies were probably looking at themselves in the mirror."

"Did you find any physical reason why they haven't spoken?" Del asked.

"Yes . . . two," the doctor said with a mischievous glint. "Number one, they're scared, and number two, this woman talks too much to give anyone else a chance to say 'howdy.'"

Then he looked directly into Mrs. Higgins' good eye and said, "You go ahead and feed them, and if your cooking is as bad as I remember it, I expect you'll be hearing them say things you'll wish you hadn't!"

"Thank you, Cyrus," Mrs. Higgins exhaled with an exaggerated sigh. "You're such a comfort in my old age."

By the time Del Howard descended the stairs to report to Bud Griggs, the detention home was overrun with children returning from the YMCA pool. Fourteen children ranging in age from six to sixteen, and the noise was fearsome. Little Ernie tried to tempt them into the kitchen with promises of cookies, but most of them were drawn out of curiosity to the uniformed deputies. When Mrs. Higgins put in an appearance, however, her orders left no room for negotiation, and the children quickly assembled in the kitchen for a "family" meeting.

Mrs. Higgins passed out the cookies and informed her wards that five new children had just been admitted. She reminded the group that the custom was to go to their dormitories while the new children were being processed, and within minutes the crowd had moved from the first to the third floor of the old building. That was her way of admitting new children with a minimum of discomfort and confusion, and it had worked effectively for more than a decade.

Griggs informed the deputies that it would be best if they were not present during the initial talks with the newcomers, so they reluctantly departed. Lieutenant Carter indicated that Sheriff Baker was anxious to be briefed and would appreciate information as quickly as possible, and Chenoweth placed a hand on Griggs' forearm, saying, "Please, Bud, I need to know as soon as you do. I got a funny feeling about this one, and it's not just because I was the one who fired the shot. Can I call you at home tonight?"

"No need," Griggs said. "We'll know in a couple of hours, and I'll get it on the air."

"Yeah, but if you don't, can I still call you at home to-night?"

The sincerity and concern in the large man's voice moved Griggs, and he said, "Sure. Matter of fact, why don't you call either way?"

Griggs then joined Howard in the living room and listened to the information he had accumulated, ranging from his personal recollections and impressions to the assurances from both Mrs. Higgins and the doctor that the children were capable of speaking and had understood everything that was taking place.

Mrs. Higgins poked her head into the room and said, "They're putting on some fresh clothes, then we're going to feed them. Will you need to talk to them before that?"

"No, we can wait," Griggs said. "You go ahead."

As soon as Mrs. Higgins disappeared, Howard said, "That woman really shows me something. She knew all along that those kids understood what she was saying, but she didn't try to trip them up or trick them into speaking. The old doctor was the same way. They both said the kids were scared, and that they'd come around to talking when they felt more comfortable."

"Well, maybe," Griggs said. "But *one* of them should have said *something* by now."

"I think it's that oldest girl. She's controlling the situation, and they're not going to talk until she tells them it's okay," Howard said. "I'll tell you something else. She's tough. And if she gets the idea that we're coming on too strong, she's going to get tougher. I think you were absolutely right when you sent those deputies out . . . But I think we still have one too many here."

Griggs looked up at his old friend and new assistant and asked, "You think one of us ought to leave? . . . Which one?"

Del stared for a moment in silence, then he said softly, "That's up to you, old buddy, but I sure have a feel for that older girl. I think I know what's going through her head, and

I think she'll talk to me." Griggs did not respond, so Del continued, "Like I said, it's your decision, and I'll go along with whatever you say. And I don't want to come down too heavy after two weeks on the job. All I *am* saying is that you're going to have to give up some territory sooner or later, and if you're willing to give it up now, I feel like I can take this one off your hands—or at least start the process on my own."

Griggs thought for a moment, then said, "We'll see," just as the Clawson children started down the stairs. Mrs. Higgins came to the bottom of the stairs to direct them to the dining room, and the two men remained in the living room, out of sight. Griggs shifted his chair so that he could see them as they reached the last step. In spite of more than two hours of briefings and debriefings, they were not what he expected them to be. Freshly scrubbed and wearing clothes bleached white from many washings, they hardly looked capable of terrifying so many people and inflicting so much damage on those burly deputies. The quizzical expression on Griggs' face silently asked the question, and Howard responded with a soft laugh, "Yep, that's them."

The two men moved into the front hall and watched Patty place Charlie into the high chair at the dining room table. Then she pulled out her own chair, and the others followed suit. Their food had already been placed before them, but, hungry as they were, they sat straight-backed and quiet, and no one except Charlie touched the food until Patty gave them a nonverbal cue to do so. Then they attacked the food voraciously while Mrs. Higgins beamed her approval.

Bud Griggs viewed the proceedings with mixed feelings. In the first place, he tacitly agreed with Mrs. Higgins' homespun philosophy that kids that ate with that much gusto were going to be easy to help. He would never find it in his college texts, and his old professors would have disparaged him severely, but it always seemed to work out that way. In the second place, Del Howard's observations had been right on target: the oldest girl was calling the shots, and it was going to take a one-on-one approach to gain her confidence. And furthermore, Del had been regrettably correct when he predicted that Griggs was going to have difficulty turning this case over to him.

Griggs was characteristically abrupt. He wasted no time verbalizing his capitulation. He just took his towering assistant by the sleeve, and walking toward the front door, instructed him, "See if Mrs. Higgins can bring the girl into the front room by herself."

"I doubt that she'll leave the others," Del interrupted.

"Well, whatever," Griggs resumed impatiently. "Just be yourself. Try to find out who they are and where they came from, but don't scare them. Don't be too pushy. We might even have to give them a day or so. Just don't get impatient and lean on them," he urged, impatiently leaning on his old friend.

"I got you," smiled Del. "It's called 'Do as I say, not as I do.'"

"You're not as dumb as you look . . . sometimes," Griggs growled and headed for the back door of the detention home.

Howard grinned and walked toward the front room. Two boys were perched on the banister. "What they in fo', sh'ff?" asked the six-year-old.

"I'm not the sheriff."

"Yo' still a cop ain't ya?" asked the older boy, who appeared to be fifteen or sixteen.

"No, not exactly. I work for the Juvenile Court."

"That's just the same to me," the boy said contemptuously. "Sheeet!" Then he turned and climbed the stairs, and as the six-year-old jumped from the banister to follow, he echoed the older boy's sentiments with another, "Sheeet!"

That kind of fighting instinct thrilled Del, and he wanted to vault up the stairs to hug the two of them and urge them never to give it up. But he restrained himself and moved through the living room to wait in the tiny office.

The floor seemed to shake as Mrs. Higgins approached. He felt and heard her coming before he saw her. "They're ready," she said. "I'll slide the doors shut so you can have privacy. Just yell if you need anything."

"Thanks," he said. "But leave the doors open. It might make them feel shut in if we close them."

When Del walked into the parlor, the five children were seated on the long sofa. Patty sat at one end with Charlie on her lap and one arm around Karen. John sat next to Karen on the edge of the cushion so his feet could reach the floor. Sue Anne sat at the other end of the couch, some distance away, with one arm over the back of the cushion and the other on the armrest. She was not uncomfortable with her feet dangling, although her good leg was crossed over the other one. Del noted her independent attitude and resolved to approach her next if he failed to get through to the oldest girl.

His initial "Hello" was bright and cheerful but drew no response. He pulled up a large chair and sat directly in front of Patty. John was startled by the ease with which this huge man with one arm in a cast had rearranged the living room furniture, and he hoped the man would not find it necessary to handle him in the same manner.

"You guys have had quite an adventure, haven't you?" he asked casually.

"I bet it was fun camping out there, wasn't it?"

"How long were you out there?"

"Are these your brothers and sisters?"

Del was feeling increasingly uncomfortable with the silence. Alone in the little office, he had rehearsed countless questions leading subtly to the kinds of hard information he would have to have. His plan was to engage them in child's talk, maybe get them laughing a little, and lead them to the point that they would be telling him all about themselves without his having to ask. Now, after only the fourth question, he was panicked by the fear that he might run out of things to say, so the questions got more direct, and he felt like kicking himself for his impatience.

"Where are your parents?" seemed to make them tense.

"Where is your home?" didn't seem to matter to them.

And, "What school do you go to?" almost brought a smile to Patty's lips, as if a response of "P.S. Fourteen" would make any difference to this man.

Del asked different versions of the same questions over and over again. "Look," he pleaded, "I'm trying to help you. Why won't you even tell me your names?" He wanted to assure this stubbornly determined little girl that the worst was over and that he would care for all of them. He understood her fear, and thinking of the recent time immediately following the operation that ended his football career, he knew how alone and lost she must have felt.

But after an hour of fruitless pleading and tentative exploration, he had not detected the slightest sign of recognition from any of them, and he began to suspect that the deputies might have been right after all. Perhaps they *were* retarded. He started to phrase his questions in more simplistic terms, finally resorting to a combination of baby talk and sign language. "Can Del hold baby? Del loves baby," he babbled, rocking his upper torso and cradling his good arm.

Suddenly, the insult was more than Patty could bear. She sat up and looked him in the eyes. Her expression reflected maturity, wisdom, and strength that were inconsistent with her small frame and little-girl face. Del realized instantly that he had made a fool of himself. He stopped the rocking motion, wiped the silly expression from his face, and was beginning to withdraw his cradled arm when her anger bubbled out with her first words— "Don't feed me that shit!"

Patty's outburst so intimidated Del Howard that later in the afternoon he asked Griggs to take him off the case. He was angry at himself for handling the interview badly, and he was furious with the children for humiliating him. He had sensed he was in trouble as soon as he saw Patty's eyes suddenly light up in anger and frustration. "I just sat there, rocking back and forth, with that stupid expression on my face," he groaned. "And when those kids started laughing at me, I wanted to clobber them."

Griggs had tried to explain that it was not unusual for children coming into the detention home to refuse to talk. "We have to get them talking—about anything. We don't care what, just so they say *something*. Usually, they just cuss us out, but at least they're unstuck."

Griggs was not only trying to placate his discouraged assistant, he was telling the truth. The more such children were cajoled into talking, the more stubborn they became. It could become a game to them, and he was particularly concerned about the possible effects of five children playing the game together. They might strike a psychological contract that would make the one who spoke first the "chicken," and it could take days before the children tired of the game and opened up. "You got them talking in two hours," Griggs said. "I don't know what in hell you're so down about."

"Well," said Del, "suppose I *do* stay on the case, where do you see us going from here?"

"In the first place, I see us working together." Then, as if in response to a shadow that crossed Del's face, he added, "That's not a criticism of you. You've been right on target so far, but we always try to work in teams."

"Can I still be effective with those kids?" Del asked. "First they were mad at me, then they thought I was goofy."

"Hell, most of the people you know think you're goofy, and that hasn't hurt you yet."

Both men laughed and began the closing of notebooks and the pushing back of chairs that usually signaled the end of a meeting. This time, however, it signaled the end of a long day. As they walked toward the door, Del put his hand on his friend's arm and said earnestly, "Bud, please level with me. Do you *really* think I did a good job today?"

Griggs covered Del's hand with his own and replied with deep conviction, "You did a great job today."

"Good," he said so brightly that Griggs knew he had fallen into another trap. "Maybe we can talk about increasing my salary."

Griggs pushed Del's hand off his arm in mock disgust.

"That's what I deserve for taking you seriously. When will I learn? The truth of the matter is that I'll be lucky to keep the judge from firing you. On second thought, maybe I won't even try."

Griggs had told Del Howard that the children would be chattering away before nightfall. It was intended as an exaggeration, but he was not far wrong. Mrs. Higgins had cared for thousands of troubled children in her time, and she knew all the tricks. Foremost among her philosophies was her unshaken confidence that, among children of all ages and lifestyles, there was one irresistibly equalizing force—the kitchen stove at mealtime. She had come by that conviction honestly, for her first experience in the detention home was as a volunteer cook in 1950. The tiny kitchen was constantly packed with children savoring the odors, sampling the food, or waiting for the cookies to come from the oven. Then she would distribute them liberally with, "Here, Purse Snatcher, these are for you. And take these to the bank robber . . . Just a minute Hub Caps, you'll burn your fingers." And the children worshiped her—so much so that the matron at the time saw her as a "threat to discipline and security" and had her dismissed. Within two months, however, life at the detention home became intolerable for the matron, and she gave two days' notice of her intention to leave town.

Mrs. Higgins applied for the job, and the County Commission hired her for all the wrong qualities—they saw her as huge enough to slap the kids down when necessary, earthy enough to talk the language of the streets, and ugly enough to frighten juvenile offenders into submission.

In all of their perverted wisdom, however, the commissioners could not have selected a better person for the job. The first thing she did was to reassign the volunteer cooks to other duties. Then she had the kitchen walls knocked down to take in the space that had once been a bedroom at the rear of the house. The commissioners had been loath to spend any money on the old house to make it more livable for the children, but they agreed to remodeling the kitchen for "security reasons," for now this fearsome creature with the massive girth and glass eye would have ample room to discipline troublemakers by forcing them to assist in the preparation of meals.

Actually, Mrs. Higgins instinctively understood a concept it was to take visiting academics years to define—some kids simply enjoyed the creative aspects of cooking, especially when vying with others to perfect recipes that would elicit praise. The technique worked so well that a visiting sociologist was moved to describe it to his observing students as "A socioenvironmental therapy for juveniles with a pervasive fear of authority figures, in which the patient is placed in a milieu that fosters freedom of expression, competitiveness, and independent action, provided, however, that the supervisory personnel remain warm, friendly, and protective, and can accept hostility and aggression without rancor or punitive retaliation."

Mrs. Higgins reply was, "All I know for sure is that the kids enjoy it."

And after fourteen years, the kids were still enjoying it. Monday evenings meant chocolate-chip cookies, and John and Sue Anne stood on the fringe of the crowd as the younger children mixed the batter and spooned it onto the baking sheets, and the older children took the hot trays from the ovens to make room for the next batch.

John's deep frown attested to his profound interest in the proceedings. Mrs. Higgins nudged him and held out two warm cookies. "Here, Giggles, pass these to your sister."

John absentmindedly took them and spoke his first words. "Here, Suni," which gave Mrs. Higgins a first name and confirmed the brother-sister relationship.

Mrs. Higgins did the honors herself with the second round of cookies. "Would you like some more, Susie?"

"Susie?" Sue Anne laughed, except it came out "Thuthie."

"Isn't that what your brother called you?"

"No, he said 'Suni,' but that's a baby name. My name is Sue Anne."

"What about 'Giggles' over there? Does he have a name?"

"Who, John? Yes, he does, but don't tell Patty I told you. She told us to keep our mouths shut."

John? Sue Anne? Patty? . . . Mrs. Higgins knew she was clever when it came to extracting information, but that was *too* easy. She stepped back and bent over to look directly into the eyes of the disarmingly cute girl who spoke with a lisp and walked with a limp. Who was manipulating whom here? Sue Anne's eyes twinkled, and she suppressed a grin. Mrs. Higgins enjoyed the joke and laughed like a stevedore. "You and I are going to get along fine, chickie," she howled, hugging Sue Anne to her stomach.

The sudden outburst alerted John to trouble, and when he saw his sister disappear face-first into the huge woman's apron, he stiffened perceptibly. "Hold on, Minuteman," Mrs. Higgins roared, "I'm not going to bite her. See?" she said as she released Sue Anne, and her grinning face appeared. "Come here, Johnny Jumpup, I got something for you, too. Come over here."

John advanced hesitantly while she fished elbow deep into her huge pocket. When she found what she was looking for, she withdrew his harmonica and held it out to him. In a tender voice, she said, "I believe this is yours, John." Hearing his name on her lips, he realized the game was finally over, and when he reached out for the harmonica, he took more of her hand than was necessary, and he held tight.

That first night was traumatic for all of them. Patty, Sue Anne, and Karen were assigned to the girl's dormitory, and John and Charlie were to sleep with the boys. Patty's objections were overruled peremptorily, but as soon as Charlie was passed from Patty's arms to John's, the infant howled an appeal that was immediately sustained. They pushed two bunk beds together, but all four of them slept on the lower level so as not to lose touch with one another.

John's separation from the others was more difficult. He lay on his cot and suffered the torture of abandonment all over again. He longed for the night sounds of the river, the crickets, and the distant animals, and he ached for the reassuring presence of his sisters. The deep breathing of the other boys signaled untroubled sleep for some, but then he heard the mournful sobbing. John raised his head quietly to identify the source, and when his eyes became accustomed to the darkness, he saw the blankets trembling two beds away.

John remembered the boy because he had impressed him as tough and invulnerable. Mrs. Higgins called him "Guzzler" because he had culminated a long series of misdemeanors by attempting to shoplift a bottle of wine. He was declared incorrigible by the juvenile court and was remanded to the detention home pending psychological evaluation. He had been there for six weeks, and by Guzzler's own admission, the wine wasn't even his favorite brand. The fourteen-year-old boy had gone out of his way to establish his credentials with the younger newcomer, and John was impressed with his cavalier dismissal of the serious charges pending against him. John had admired the toughness of the boy who was now sobbing, and as the image of the compassionate woman with the scary glass eye flashed in his mind, John realized that nothing in his new world was as it seemed to be. He fell asleep that night wondering whether the penalty for stealing wine from a liquor store was the same as stealing cakes and pies from a restaurant.

Tuesday morning brought a pleasant surprise. John had waited outside the second-floor boys' dormitory for his sisters to come down for breakfast. As they descended the stairs, the tempo of his heartbeat quickened. He was genuinely happy to see them. He climbed several of the steps to greet them as Patty whispered urgently into Charlie's ear. When they met, Charlie shouted, "Ja! Ja!," and they all laughed and applauded the performance that had successfully capped more than an hour of practice. Charlie was so glad to see his brother that he reached out and allowed himself to be taken from Patty's arms for a moment.

But the real surprise awaited them in the kitchen, where the steam table offered such treats as orange juice, scrambled eggs, bacon, biscuits, and French toast. John automatically returned Charlie to his perch on Patty's hip, and she accepted him without question and seemingly without notice. He then took the tray and plate that Ernie held out to him and started down the line. Observing the way it was being done by the older residents, he scooped up a ladle of scrambled eggs and shook it onto his plate. Most of the eggs stuck to the large spoon, permitting painfully little to fall to his plate. He was disappointed, but he was hesitant to reach for more. As his questioning eyes sought Ernie's, Mrs. Higgins bellowed, "C'mon, Johnny Jumpup, you're gonna need more food than that to play that harmonica for us today."

Patty's eyes shot up at the mention of John's name, but she calmed herself by assuming a coincidental use of another of Mrs. Higgins' nicknames. John did not wait to be asked a second time. He piled more eggs on his plate before adding four strips of bacon. When he got to the French toast, his eyes asked the same question, and Mrs. Higgins gave him the same encouragement: "Go ahead, boy, if we need to, we'll build a fence around that plate to hold the food in."

Patty looked disapprovingly at her brother as he passed her on his way to the dining room. He never noticed, because his eyes were locked on the sumptuous array of foods piled high on his plate. Then Mrs. Higgins' words sent a chill through her bones: "Take some more, Patty, you're eating for two." Patty intuitively avoided acknowledging Mrs. Higgins' use of her name, but her facial expression tightened perceptibly. She went through the line without looking up but without seeing the food, either. She walked quickly toward the dining room with the sparse tray in one hand and Charlie on her other hip.

"Who told her my name?" she whispered harshly into John's ear.

"I don't know," he said indifferently. "Have you ever *seen* so much food?"

"Forget the goddam food," she hissed. "Who told her my name?"

"Maybe I did," Sue Anne said.

As Patty turned to vent her wrath on Sue Anne, Mrs. Higgins came through the door carrying another plate of food. Patty saw her and put Charlie into the high chair. "You looked like you had your hands full," Mrs. Higgins said softly. "So I brought something for the baby to eat. The eggs and biscuits are nice and soft. Do you think he can handle the bacon?" Mrs. Higgins was deliberately deferring to Patty's judgment, accepting her as the maternal authority. Patty recognized the gesture but could not bring herself to respond. She simply took the plate from Mrs. Higgins and placed it under Charlie's impatiently flailing hands.

"Let's go," Patty demanded as soon as she had finished her juice.

"Ain't finished," John muttered through a mouthful of food.

"Neither is Karen," Sue Anne said as her younger sister continued to stare at the strangers and pick at her food.

"We got to TALK," Patty insisted firmly. "Let's go outside . . . NOW."

John and Sue Anne carried the five trays into the kitchen, then joined the others near the old swing set in the front yard. Several boys were tossing a football, and one girl was swinging a hula hoop. Patty was visibly upset. "How did she find out my name?" she demanded of Sue Anne.

"She gave me some cookies last night, and it just slipped out, I guess."

"But I told you to keep your mouth shut!"

"I didn't want to," Sue Anne said stubbornly. "I wanted to talk to someone, and she's a nice lady."

"She found my harmonica," John added. "And she asked me to play later."

"And did she ask you if you were the one who stole the pies?" asked Patty spitefully.

"No," John answered balefully. "I don't think she knows about the pies."

"Bull! . . . That's why we're here, dummy. And as soon as they find out which one stole the pies, then they'll know who to put in jail, and I won't let that happen, because as soon as they find out which one to lock up, they'll split up the rest of us." Tears came to Patty's eyes as she articulated a possibility too terrible to contemplate.

John's head was bowed, and he mumbled, "It's my fault. I'm sorry."

Sue Anne could not contain herself. "What are you guys blubbering about? This place is neat. We just won't tell them who took the pies, and we can live here forever while they're trying to figure it out."

"No," Patty decided. "We gotta find a way to escape."

That brought a forcefully negative reaction from John and Sue Anne. "How we gonna climb that fence?" Sue Anne asked. "It's higher than the second-floor window."

"And it could have electricity in it," John added. "And these places usually have guards with rifles . . . somewhere," he said, scanning the perimeter of the fence and the roof of the building.

"I warn you," Patty said with intense deliberation, "if we don't find a way to escape, they're gonna split us up, just like Mama always said." The appearance of Ernie broke up the conference. "Mom Higgins wants you to come into the house," he told Patty.

"She ain't *my* mom."

"Well, she wants you anyway."

As the five of them started toward the house, Ernie asked, "Would you guys like to shoot some baskets?"

"I better not," John said hesitantly.

"I will!" squealed Sue Anne.

"You don't even know how," John laughed.

"Let's both show her how," Ernie suggested, accomplishing the task he had been assigned.

Mrs. Higgins met the three children at the front door and led them to the living room, where Bud Griggs and Del Howard were waiting. Mrs. Higgins had briefed them on the information she had elicited, her positive personal impressions of them, and her conclusion that they were runaways. "Why else," she had said, "would they want to keep their names a secret?"

"Patty, you remember Mr. Howard from yesterday. This is Mr. Griggs. They both work for the Juvenile Court, and they want to talk to you." Patty was unresponsive. Charlie shifted on her hip to look at the two men, and Karen maintained her hold on Patty's hand. "Would you like me to take the baby? It looks like he might be ready for a nap." Patty twisted her hip sharply to move Charlie out of the matron's reach, and the older woman looked to the two men for direction.

"That's okay, Mrs. Higgins," Griggs said. "We'd like the three of them to stay. Would you like to have a seat, Patty?" motioning to an empty chair. The girl did not move or acknowledge the invitation.

"Patty, our job is to help you any way we can," Griggs said softly. "But before we can help you, we will need some help from you. You will have to trust us." Griggs had intended to carry the investigation much further, but at the mention of "trust" he perceived a slight sneer on the girl's lips, so after a seemingly interminable pause of thirty seconds, he slapped his knees, rose, and said, "We'll be around if you need us. See you later."

Patty emerged from the house and shaded her eyes to look for John and Sue Anne. She descended the front porch and walked toward the corner of the building. Her pace quickened almost to the point of jogging when she saw that her brother and sister were standing on the basketball court talking to a policeman, but she came to an abrupt stop when she heard Sue Anne's laughter and saw John push the officer playfully. "C'mere, Patty," Sue Anne yelled. "This man has a funny name. He says his name is 'Chins' because his face is so fat," she laughed.

As Patty, Charlie, and Karen joined the group, John

brought her up to date on their conversation. "Chins was one of them who caught us yesterday."

"I'm not sure who caught who," laughed Chins, massaging his bandaged hand.

"Yeah, him and his friends got all bunged up rassling with us," John reported proudly. "He says they got teeth marks all over their bodies. He wanted to know if we spitted up any extra fingers last night." Then, more seriously, he asked, "Are you the one that shot at us?"

"I pulled the trigger, but I wasn't shootin' at you. It's like I was starting to tell you. There you all was, wallerin' around down the bottom of that hole, when what should fly outta that tree but a terrible six-fanged googily bird . . . trying to decide which one of you he was going to eat first. It's a good thing for you I scared him off."

Sue Anne giggled and said, "Mr. Chins, you're crazy."

Chins had clearly won over John and Sue Anne, but Patty remained aloof. "Well, m'am," he said—wondering why in the world he would call this eleven or twelve-year-old girl "m'am," except she seemed so much older—"I was just feelin' bad about what happened yesterday, and I wanted to stop by and see that you was all okay. I'll see you again, real soon."

"He was really funny. Do you know what he said, Patty?" Sue Anne asked.

"No, and I don't care, either," Patty snapped as she turned away from the group and toward the house. "Charlie's ready for his nap. Let's go."

There was some hesitation on Sue Anne's part, then she said, "I think I'll stay here for a while."

Patty stopped and turned to glare at her sister. She was about to remind her that they had agreed to stay together when John said, "Maybe I'll stay outside, too." As Patty walked to the house with Charlie in her arms and Karen in tow, she was disturbed by the emptiness that came with the loss of control. She was assailed by other new and unexplainable feelings, too, but that would have to wait until she had some quiet time to sort things out.

* * *

Charlie fell asleep immediately, but Patty had to pull the shades down over the south windows before the dormitory was dark enough for Karen to drop off. Patty sat on the side of Karen's cot and rubbed her back gently until sleep came. In the process, Patty tried to cope with some of the unexpected and unwanted feelings that were creeping into her consciousness. She had made up her mind never to like or trust grown-ups again, but after less than twenty-four hours in the detention home, her resolve was starting to slip. The images of four people paraded through her mind: Mrs. Higgins—*she doesn't talk like a grown-up, and all the kids seem to like her . . . and she didn't try to take Charlie away from me*; that huge colored man from last night—*any other cop would have squashed me, but he looked confused . . . like he wanted to cry, instead*; that man from this morning—*he didn't push on me . . . he said he would wait until I was ready to talk to him*; and that Chins—*Sue Anne liked him a lot, and she is not easy to fool . . .* and John, *he seemed to like kidding around with a man.* By that time, she was casually pacing the floor, and the thought of John and Sue Anne made her look through the window for them in the yard below.

Sue Anne was easy to spot. She was jumping rope on the basketball court with four other girls, and her limp was hardly noticeable. Her face was flushed from the heat of the sun, but Patty also recognized an exhilaration there that she hadn't seen in a long time.

John was more difficult to find. He was sitting against the fence playing his harmonica for a group that included Mrs. Higgins. The matron was standing there with her arms over the shoulders of children on each side of her, and it was impossible to tell what they were looking at. Then, obviously at the conclusion of a medley, the group responded with enthusiastic laughter and applause. Patty was able to see John only after Mrs. Higgins moved in and leaned over to hug him in appreciation and approval. His face beamed.

Patty came away from the window musing over the unexpected turn of events. Sue Anne and John were obviously happy . . . Those grown-ups who seemed to be trying so hard—could they be trusted? . . . Was escaping still a realistic alternative, or should she explore other ways of keeping the family together?

Patty's perception of the changes that were taking place was further corroborated at lunchtime. She waited in the front hall for the family to reassemble, but Sue Anne came through the front door chattering with three older girls and walked past her without noticing, and John came through the door laughing and pushing two new friends with no more than, "Oh, hi, Patty."

After a quick repast of sandwiches and soup, John and Sue Anne hurried from the house with their respective groups of friends, and this time it was Patty who was the last to leave the table. "I'll be right back, Karen," she said as she gathered their trays and carried them into the kitchen.

Mrs. Higgins was pouring herself a cup of coffee when she saw Patty. "What's wrong, dear? You look sad."

Patty shrugged her shoulders and turned to leave.

"Why don't we talk?" the matron asked.

Patty looked back and mumbled, "Karen and Charlie are out here," no longer caring about preserving any remnants of anonymity.

"Well, I'll join *you*, then," and they moved to the dining room together.

They sat on the same side of the table, with Charlie's high chair separating them. "John and Sue Anne seem to be adjusting very nicely," Mrs. Higgins commented without expecting a response. "When I think of the changes that have taken place in them since yesterday . . . ," she sighed, "it's hard to believe they're the same children." There was a long silence. "What about you, Patty? When you came in yesterday, you were so mad your eyes were spitting darts. Now you seem sad. What's wrong?"

Mrs. Higgins then answered her own question. "I think I know what's wrong. When you kids decided to run away from home, you agreed to stay together, and now you think your brother and sister don't love you anymore."

Patty looked up sharply and blurted, "We didn't . . . "

Mrs. Higgins knew that her remark would seem to be a clumsy attempt to extract information, and that was the domain of Bud Griggs, so she backtracked immediately. "You ought to try to make friends so you don't feel so alone. What about hopscotch . . . No, you're right. She's too young . . . What about mumblety-peg? No, you're right. She's too much of a tomboy."

There was a trace of humor in Patty's eyes as she looked directly at Mrs. Higgins because the older woman was doing all the talking, as if they were carrying on a two-sided argument.

"You're absolutely right," Mrs. Higgins continued. "They're either too young for you or too old for Karen and Charlie." Then, with her index finger to her pursed lips, she said abstractly, "Absolutely right . . . Karen and Charlie, is that right at least?"

This time, Patty did not suppress her reaction, and as she giggled, she nodded her head affirmatively.

Seeing Patty open up that way, Mrs. Higgins was struck with the contrasting images of a young girl and a mature woman. She had never thought of Patty as a mature woman until that instant when she saw a glimmer of the little girl in her come out. She wondered what had happened in her life to accelerate the aging process, but she understood now that it must have been terrible, and any of the other children in the detention home would be too young to develop a friendship with Patty.

"There's only one more thing, dear. Mr. Griggs will be coming in to say hello in a little while, and I want you to know that you can trust him. Whatever you've done, or whatever has happened, he can help you."

Griggs and Howard found Patty combing Karen's hair on the front porch. Griggs sat down next to her, and Del went off to the basketball court to be with the boys. "Don't let me interrupt," Bud suggested spuriously. "I can only stay a few minutes, but I wanted to bring something for the children." Three years earlier, Griggs had started to accumulate used toys, games, dolls, and comic books for the younger children coming through the juvenile court system. Sometimes they were used to occupy the youngster's time while awaiting disposition of a case and returned the same day a little worse for wear. Other times, such as this, the items were offered as permanent gifts. The collection had been started and maintained with the best of intentions, but Bud's first secretary, who used to store the playthings in a large cardboard box that had originally held packaged toilet paper, dubbed the collection the "bribe box," and the name stuck. Before leaving the office that afternoon, Bud had offhandedly pulled out a shabby little doll for Karen and a scratched metal top for Charlie, fully intending that the gifts might elicit enough information to justify the uncomplimentary name that had been given to the collection.

"This is for Charlie," Griggs said, pulling the large metal top from the paper sack. He placed the base of the toy on the porch and pumped down on the lever, causing the brightly colored cylinder to spin to the accompaniment of tinny musical sounds.

Charlie stared indifferently, but Patty was delighted, and after she demonstrated the technique to him several times, her enthusiasm was transmitted, and he was entranced with the effect he was able to achieve on his own. Karen joined in the excitement, instructing Charlie in better and better ways to operate the lively little toy. That was the first time Griggs had seen Karen display any kind of emotion.

"Oh, yes, there's something else down here," he said, reaching into the bag. "And . . . let's see . . . it has a girl's name on it. It looks like the name 'Karen.' Now who could that be, Patty? Is there a little girl around here with that name?" Patty was not looking at Bud. She was smiling at Karen as her little sister's face lit up and bubbled, "Me. That's me. I'm Karen."

Her reaction was so immediate and enthusiastic that Bud was suddenly hesitant to take a chance on disappointing her with a secondhand rag doll. He regretted having made such a big production over the thing and tried to mitigate her expectations. "I'm afraid it's not really all that much. It's . . . I mean I wasn't sure . . ." Karen never heard a word. She threw herself across Bud's lap and tore the bag open in her frenzy to disclose its contents. When she saw the doll, her eyes opened wide, and she gasped in surprise and pleasure. She held it at arm's length for a moment, then clasped it tightly to her face, trembling with happiness.

Griggs profoundly regretted that the material value of the gift did not justify the enjoyment with which it was received, and he was ashamed of his motives for giving it. He was uncharacteristically flustered, and fearing that Patty might have seen through his charade, he stammered, "It's nothing, really. Just something to help pass the time." Patty was grinning, but he couldn't tell whether she was sharing the happiness of her siblings or laughing at him.

Bud struggled for control and managed a confident smile. "I'm glad they like their presents," he said. "I gotta go now, but I'll see you after supper." He stood and signaled Howard that he was ready to leave. Del trotted over and smiled down at the children as he bounded up the stairs and followed Griggs through the house and out to the parking lot.

"Well, what did you find out?" he asked the pensive Griggs.

"I found out that Charlie likes tops and Karen likes dolls, that's what I found out."

"Yeah, I noticed that. What else?"

"When we get back to the office, we're gonna burn that old crap in the bribe box and get all new stuff. It's a crime to be giving kids junk like that to play with." They approached the courthouse, but Griggs turned south instead. "I'm not ready for the office. Let's go work out."

Del's exercises were limited to sit-ups and light therapy for his injured arm, so he was particularly fascinated by the furious pace being set by his old friend. Because no sparring partners were available on short notice, Griggs attacked the speed bag, skipped a rope that whirred through space in a blur, then pounded the heavy bag until his breath came only in great, laboring gasps, and his arms refused any longer to respond.

It was not until the two men sat in the steam room that Griggs shared his frustration. "I made the worst mistake possible. I underestimated the whole situation. How old can she be—twelve, at the most?" Howard nodded his agreement. "I figured, a skinny little dirty kid, dumb enough to get them all eaten alive by ticks—she's coming from nowhere. But there's a lot more to it. This is a complicated son of a bitch, and I can't get a handle on it."

"Well, we can forget about that retarded stuff, right?" Del asked.

"That's for *damned* sure. I might have had my doubts about that little girl, but not after she jumped all over me for that doll."

"What about Higgins' theory that they're runners?"

"I don't think so. For one thing, they're not from around here, or they would have known about ticks, and they speak with an Eastern accent—somewhere between Chicago and New York. If they don't open up soon, I'll bring in a linguistics man from the university to analyze their speech patterns. So if they were runaways, they had to have traveled between six hundred and fourteen hundred miles, and that's out of the question. Most of all, there've been no reports, and it seems to me that *someone* would have noticed five kids missing from home."

"Then either something happened to their parents or they were abandoned."

"My gut feeling is that they were dumped," said Griggs. "But I can't figure why they're so scared to talk about it. And I can't figure Patty. It's almost as if she's the mother—and a damned good one, too."

* * *

Griggs was sitting in the living room when the children finished supper. Patty surprised him by opening the conversation. She walked into the room with the ubiquitous youngsters and said, "Karen says to thank you for the doll . . . Charlie, too."

"Come in, Patty. Have a seat." He was still hesitant to push her directly for information, fearing that he would lose hard-won ground, so he decided to use an indirect approach. "Patty, this is your second day here. Do you understand what's happening? Do you have any questions?"

"Yeah. Why are you keeping us here?" she asked. "When can we get out?"

"We have to keep you here until we find out all about you. We can't let you go until we know where you belong. I told you this morning that we would need your help." Patty stared in silence, and Bud asked softly, "Will you help us find your parents?"

"No," she said shaking her head and struggling with Charlie. "I can't do that."

Griggs thought about her response and concluded that she was literally correct—Patty was incapable of helping to find her parents—probably because she had no idea where they were.

Charlie grew more restless and almost unmanageable, so Griggs decided to terminate the conversation. "I'll see you again tomorrow. Maybe we can talk better when Charlie and Karen are taking their naps."

"Okay," she promised.

Griggs was pleased with the results of his efforts. Patty had responded directly on three occasions, and he was satisfied that the entire story would unfold the next day.

On Wednesday morning, Patty was still undecided about divulging any information to Bud Griggs. Perhaps Sue Anne was right, and they would remain together in the detention home for as long as it took the cops to get the information they needed. On the other hand, maybe they would get tired of asking and split them up just to get rid of them. Patty devised alternate scenarios and decided to be extremely cautious about sharing the truth with Bud Griggs.

She caught a glimpse of Griggs right after breakfast, and she grew apprehensive about saying the wrong thing, wishing he would just leave her alone. But he seemed more interested in talking to that boy they called "Guzzler." Somewhere close to noon, she saw him again, but this time he was bringing a new boy into the home, and all the children had to go outside during the processing, so perhaps he didn't notice her. She wondered if Howard or Griggs had been talking to Sue Anne and John instead, but that was not the case, either. After lunch, Patty had Sue Anne sit with Karen and Charlie during their afternoon nap, and she made herself conspicuously available, but Griggs again avoided her. By suppertime, Patty had come full circle, for she spent the rest of the day trying to attract Griggs' attention. She had awakened that morning determined not to disclose any information, and by the end of the day she was searching for someone who would listen to her.

Griggs and Howard had agreed to spend Wednesday gathering as much information as they could about the five children. Griggs was certain that Patty would be ready to talk that evening, especially if the two men avoided her all day, and he wanted to have as much corroborative data as possible prior to the interrogation. Such intelligence was often useful in prodding memories or goading further disclosures.

Information sheets were tacked to the bulletin board in Mrs. Higgins' office, each one titled with the name of one of the children, followed by lists of specific pieces of information to be discovered and written in: surname, age, place of birth, residence, education, interests, hobbies, names and occupations of parents, and so forth. The assistance of every professional coming into the home that day was enlisted. Each was instructed to be circumspect and avoid the appearances of gathering direct information. Much of it was teased from their young friends. Data were painstakingly accumulated and recorded, and the information sheets began to flesh out the life histories of five children. The crime lab uncovered several important pieces of evidence. Technicians were able to reinstate the faded label on Karen's dress and found it had been sold by a store in Philadelphia; John's harmonica was an excellent quality house brand that had been manufactured in nearby Downington, Pennsylvania; and most important, the T-shirt John had been wearing when found was standard issue in federal prisons, and it bore the faded stencil, "Clawson, Thomas Calvin," a name that the FBI was already researching.

By nightfall, Griggs had the information he needed to proceed. Patty had started asking about him, and he knew she was ready to talk. He had not understood how desperately she *needed* to talk until he found her alone in the living room, thumbing aimlessly through a magazine. "Can we talk now?" he asked gently.

She looked up slowly, and for the first time tears came to her eyes. She nodded her head, and Griggs understood that she wanted to be an eleven-year-old girl for a moment—not a mother. He slid the ancient pocket doors together to close off the living room, then he dragged up a straight-backed wooden chair and straddled it directly opposite her. He reached over to the arm of the couch and lightly covered her hand with his own. "It's all right. Take your time."

"Well, I don't know for sure what you want me to talk about."

"Start wherever you are most comfortable."

"Okay, but I finally figured out today that you don't care about the pies and cakes, do you?"

"What pies and cakes?" he asked with a confused expression.

"Never mind," she said. "We all took some pies and stuff from outside that restaurant, and at first, that's why we thought we were arrested."

Griggs laughed, "No, no. We don't care about that. I need to know more about where you came from, and if your family is worried about you."

Patty thought for a long time, then she said, "No, they're not worried . . . They're not even coming back. I knew they wouldn't. I just didn't want any more trouble in case they did."

"Who isn't coming back, Patty?" It was important to make her say the words and have her face the psychological realities.

"We used to live in Philadelphia, but we were moving to California because Daddy got in trouble again."

"What kind of trouble, Patty?"

"I don't know, but we knew something bad was going to happen."

"You said that he got in trouble 'again.' What kind of trouble was he in before?"

She looked away and decided to withhold the information concerning her father's imprisonment, but Bud's next question alerted her to the fact that he knew a lot already. "Your father was in prison, wasn't he, Patty?"

"Yes, he was in prison. He got out a few months ago, and, like I said, we knew something bad was going to happen."

"How did you know that?"

"Just the way Momma was acting. She was gone a lot."

"Was that unusual for her?"

"While Daddy was in jail, she was gone a long time. Then Daddy said, 'We're getting out of this town,' and right after we left Philadelphia, we ran out of money, and us kids had to beg for food and money from the preachers."

Griggs was aware that Patty had just covered untold years in two sentences, but he decided to let her get it all out before going back to fill in the details.

"Momma and Daddy began to yell a lot, and I had to keep the kids quiet. I knew something was funny when they stopped at the restaurant and told us to buy hamburgers. They said it was Karen's birthday present. We got the hamburgers and came outside, and they were gone."

"Gone?"

"The car was gone." Patty's narrative pace slowed, and her eyes filled with tears. "We waited until it got dark, but they never came back."

After a moment of silence, Griggs asked, "How long did you wait?"

Patty's voice turned resolute, with a trace of anger. "I don't know. But I knew they'd never come back. We sat on the curb. I don't know why we waited. I knew the second we walked out the door we'd never see them again. I guess I just didn't know how to tell the kids . . . Sue Anne figured it out pretty quick, but John wouldn't believe it, even when we finally told him."

They sat in silence again.

"What did you do then?"

"Charlie was crying, and it was starting to get dark. We didn't know what to do, so we started walking down the highway. The kids kept looking for the car. They kept asking would we find Mom and Dad. I told them to shut up—we'd never find Mom and Dad again! Then they all started to cry and wouldn't walk no more. We didn't have no place to go, anyhow."

"Then what happened?"

"There was this cornfield, so we went in there to get out of sight and ate the cold hamburgers."

"How long ago was this?"

"I don't know."

"Well, you must have some idea," Griggs pushed. "How many days was it before they found you? Was it two days . . . three?"

"No. A lot longer than that."

"You mentioned Karen's birthday. Was it really her birthday when you went in for the hamburgers?"

"Yes, because Momma talked about it the day before."

"Do you know Karen's birth date?"

"Of course," Patty answered indignantly. "August ninth."

Griggs calculated rapidly, then said, "That can't be right. That was more than two weeks before they found you."

"That's about right."

"My God, are you telling me that you lived out there for more than *two weeks?*" he asked incredulously. "Where did you stay? What did you do?"

"Next morning, we dug a hole down by the river."

"What did you eat?" Griggs was getting caught up in the story, eager to hear every detail.

"At first, we found some corn and tomatoes and things. Then we took stuff from the garbage cans, then . . . I already told you about the pies from the restaurant. We figured that's how you found out about us in the first place."

Griggs repeated his earlier assurances with a wave of his hand and encouraged her to proceed.

"The worst time was when it rained, and we had to go up to the farmhouse and sleep under the window with the light on. That was really scary."

"But, Patty, you're a smart girl. Why didn't you ask for help? People will *always* help children."

The expression Del Howard had seen that first afternoon returned to her face—as if she were about to say again, "Don't feed me that shit." Instead, she shook her head vigorously.

"Grown-ups *don't* help kids. One time, when Momma was gone a long time, Sue Anne hurt her leg, and they took us away and put us in separate places. All we got now is each other, and I don't want 'helping people' to take that, too."

Griggs was mesmerized by the transition in her face and voice. Having started the interview as an anxious and frightened little girl, she was concluding it with the wisdom of a Solomon and the determination of a Joan of Arc. "You were afraid the grown-ups would separate you again?" Griggs asked. After another moment of thought, he added, "It doesn't *have* to happen that way."

"Why not?" she asked warily.

"Because I won't *let* it happen."

Patty stood up, walked a few paces away from him, then turned around, and pointing her finger, she demanded, "You promise?"

Griggs knew better to make such a promise. He knew that the possibility of finding a foster home large enough for five children was remote. But he also understood how important it was to this little girl, so with all the confidence he could muster, he said it. "I promise."

Bud Griggs called a debriefing meeting in his office on Thursday morning. Del Howard was there, and so was Lieutenant Carter and Sheriff Johnson. Chins Chenoweth made himself conveniently available, but Griggs had to decline in the interests of protocol, and he promised to talk with Chins before noon. Griggs was able to relate the facts in no more than ten minutes, then he spent an equal amount of time sharing his observations and conjectures.

None of them had realized the dimensions of the problem, and Del was staggered. ". . . Fifteen days," he said in an awed tone. ". . . Leaving five kids in a strange town more than a thousand miles from home. I'd love to be locked up in a room with those animals."

The sheriff's mind was elsewhere. "How about the papers? That young reporter contacted me on Tuesday morning, but I stalled her. Did she call you, yet?"

Griggs nodded his head. "Several times. She saw the possibility of a big story. The wire service guy told her to check out the parents and see if they had been killed, or kidnapped, or something juicy. I doubt they'll be interested in a simple case of abandonment."

"SIMPLE?" Del bellowed. "What the hell's so simple about leaving five kids to die?" He glared at the others, and, seeing no reaction in their faces, he asked, "What are you going to do about the parents? How're you going to find them? Can we put out an all-points bulletin?"

Sheriff Johnson lowered his head and looked over his glasses at Griggs in disgust. Griggs shrugged his shoulders in return, and the observant Del Howard said, "What the hell's THAT for?"

Griggs responded, "Sorry, Del." Then to the sheriff, sarcastically, "Sam, why don't you explain to Del how thrilled

the law enforcement world is going to get when we ask every
cop between here and California to drop everything and
search for two runaway parents?"

The sheriff snickered.

Del pounded the top of the desk and shouted, "We're not
talking about runaway parents, we're talking about two bastards and what they've done to their five babies."

The sheriff rose from his chair saying, "I don't know how
to tell you this, rookie, but the police between here and California would be a lot more interested in this case if those people had stolen the hamburgers instead of dropping those
kids." Sheriff Johnson nodded toward the door and spoke to
Lieutenant Carter, "Let's go, Jim. We better get out of here
so Griggs can start school," and the two men left

Del was overwhelmed with shock and surprise. "Does that
mean we don't do anything?" he demanded.

"Of course not. We'll run a tracer on the parents, ask the
Philadelphia boys to check out the neighbors, and see if anyone has a forwarding address. If we luck out, we'll pick them
up in California, if that's where they are."

"That sounds thin to me," Howard observed in a skeptical
tone.

"No shit! This jailbird has probably skipped out on credi-
tors, old cronies, one pissed-off parole officer, and maybe
even the police. I wouldn't bet your Confederate money that
there's any trail to follow in Philadelphia."

"Then that's not enough," Del objected.

Griggs felt his anger rising. "What I'm trying to tell you is
that I don't give a shit about those parents. Suppose we bust
our asses and do happen to catch them? They'll just promise
to be good folks, take the kids back, listen to a short lecture,
head down the road, and do something worse to them."

The two men studied each other in anger. "I didn't come
here to work with you so I could diddle myself," Del said res-
olutely. "If you want me to stay, you'd better do what the
man said and open school."

"Okay . . . good." Griggs had been pacing the room and

stopped to lay the palm of his hand against the chalkboard, tapping his fingers on the sparse inventory of facts he had scribbled earlier. "The first thing we need to do is sort through this mess."

"First, we have to decide whether to accept the girl's story. At this point, we have nothing else to go on except what she told us."

Del disagreed. "We've got the label on the girl's dress that puts them in Philadelphia; and John was wearing his old man's prison T-shirt."

"Yeah, but you can pick up that crap in any surplus store. I have to brief Judge Harrington in a half hour, and he's going to want to be sure that we've covered every possibility."

"For instance?" Del asked.

Griggs' impatience came through again. "For instance, he'll ask how I know she's not feeding me a line of crap. He'll ask if I'm sure she's not a psychotic kid who's snatched one or more of the other kids from a good home in the next county."

"Come on, that's stupid, and you know it," Del chi. l.

"Look, old buddy, this is your first neglect case. I've kept you on the vandalism and misdemeanor stuff for the past two weeks because I didn't want to scare you off. That's pretty predictable stuff. You decide whether the kid's sociopathic, or has an identity problem, or is rebelling against authority, or whatever the hell else, you send him and his parents for some counseling, and you're finished until the next time. In just about every case, though, there is at least one parent who's trying to help the kid."

Griggs walked to his desk and picked up some folders. "In abuse and neglect cases, that element is missing. The parents are not trying to help the kid, they're the ones trying to destroy him. The whole system gets so screwed up *nothing* is predictable, and you can't take anything for granted."

"I agree with you," Griggs continued. "I don't think Patty was lying to me, but neither were these kids lying," and he tossed the folders into Del's lap. "Open the top one," he instructed. "That was a four-year-old girl that I sat up with until three o'clock in the morning, until she died of the beating her old man gave her." There were several photographs in the file. The first showed a vivacious and smiling girl at her fourth birthday party. The second was a picture of the same girl taken soon after being admitted to the hospital. Her eyes were swollen shut, her nose was broken, and her lips were battered and puffed to three times their normal size. Her face was completely discolored with a sickening array of reds, purples, and blues. The third picture showed the child dressed out and made up . . . lying in her casket. Del Howard began to understand his friend's rage.

"But you know what?" Griggs asked rhetorically, "Sometimes it's even tougher on the kids who don't die. Take a look at that next file. That's a thirteen-year-old girl who first came to us for help after her father raped her . . . And the next one is an eight-year-old boy who had his ear pulled off by his father." Griggs paused to let the facts sink in, then he dropped the bomb. "Both those kids are behind bars."

Del was again skeptical. "Behind bars? You don't mean literally?"

Griggs fought to control his response. "I mean . . . those kids came to us for help . . . and the system screwed them over worse than ever. They were bounced from detention home to foster home, and back and forth, over and over again, until there was no place left but the reform school . . . and that's where they are right now."

"You're saying that those kids were not delinquents?" Del asked.

"Not even status offenders."

"And they are in the state reform school?"

"Now you got it," Griggs said sarcastically. "If the parents don't want a kid or can't take care of him, we have to try foster placement. But when a kid runs out of foster homes to go to, there's no place else except reform school."

"Could that happen to the Clawson kids?" Del asked, adding, "If that's their real name."

What makes these kids any different? Griggs thought to himself. But he shrugged and didn't say it, because he felt that Del had had enough of an education for one day.

Immediately after Bud Griggs had left her on Wednesday evening, Patty bounded up the stairs to confer with John and Sue Anne. They had agreed to meet outside the third-floor dormitory, and they were sitting in the hall when Patty arrived. "Everything's gonna be all right," she enthused. "He promised not to split us up, and he said not to worry about stealing the pies."

Bud Griggs entered the detention home through the back door that afternoon and asked Mrs. Higgins if he could use her office to speak to Patty again. Ernie and Beth were dispatched to find her, and within minutes she descended the stairs holding Charlie on her hip. Karen was holding her shirttail with one hand and her doll with the other. The air-conditioned house was filled with the noisy activities of children escaping the afternoon heat, so Bud suggested, "Let's get out of this confusion." He led them toward the tiny office, and when they reached the door, he said, "It might be better if we talked by ourselves. Can we leave the children out here? Beth will keep an eye on them."

Karen agreed to sit in the hall with Charlie, but the top half of the office door had to be kept open. Griggs agreed to the arrangement. "We may not be able to hear ourselves, but at least we'll be out of the traffic."

Once seated, he said, "I've just met with Judge Harrington, and he has set the hearing for one week from today—next Thursday, and I need a lot more information for my report."

Patty asked, "Why do we have to go to court? Are they gonna find us guilty . . . or something?"

Bud laughed and shook his head. "No, they won't find you guilty. It's just a formality. The judge needs to have you all in the room before he can tell the welfare people to start looking for a home for the five of you."

Patty wrinkled her nose and frowned. "Do we get to pick?"

"Pick what?" asked Griggs, not sure what her question meant.

Patty spread her hands and answered, "The foster parents. Do we get to pick our foster parents?"

Griggs was once again confronted by his own inadequacy. It first struck him as a preposterous suggestion, but suddenly the clear and simple rationale became obvious. What better way could there be to match foster parents and children? He hesitated for a moment before saying, "No, I don't think it works that way," and it occurred to him that he had never really thought much about foster homes, how they work, or how foster parents were selected. That had always been the province of the welfare people, and he had somehow managed to survive mistakenly believing that it was no concern of his.

"I guess we'll just get whoever comes up next on the list, huh?"

Griggs did not answer, because he knew Patty didn't expect him to. He studied her as she stared blankly through the upper half of the door, and he wondered what it must really be like to be an eleven-year-old child waiting to be assigned new parents, wondering whether they would honestly care for you.

The little girl never ceased to amaze him. Staring at her and trying to digest the profound implications of what she had said, he realized that he had been watching cases grind through the process for more than five years without once facing up to these essential issues and fears.

He was lost in his thoughts, but Patty was becoming restless and bored. "What else do you want to know?" she asked.

She had put him in a pensive mood, and it was difficult to shake. Her offer to answer his questions bespoke her new-found trust. In spite of her horrendous experiences with adults, she was manifesting her resiliency and her capacity to trust yet another adult. Logically, Griggs should have felt elated, because that was precisely the goal he had been striving for. But at that moment, her trust in him represented a responsibility that was to become a heavy burden. Griggs shook himself from his reverie. "Let me see, I guess I need to know a lot more about your mother and father, but first I'd like to know more about you."

At that moment, Karen's face appeared on the ledge of the lower door. "Patty, can we go out to the swing with Sue Anne?"

Patty seemed surprised at Karen's willingness to leave her, and her voice seemed uncertain when she answered, "Sure. Is Sue Anne there?"

"Boo!" Sue Anne giggled as she poked her head around the corner. "Me and Beth will take them outside."

"Okay," Patty agreed dubiously. "I'll be right here if they want me."

Griggs was pleased. "That's a good sign," he announced, but Patty didn't answer, so he changed the subject. "Tell me what it was like when you were a little girl."

Patty thought for a moment, a faint smile on her lips. "I remember when John and Sue Anne were little. Momma was gone a lot, like I said. She would always tell me, 'You're the oldest. It's your job to take care of your brother and sister.' The grocery man and the butcher used to call me 'little mother,' and I used to fix frankfurters, and tuna fish, and cereal, and stuff like that."

"Did you take care of the children yourself? Weren't there any friends to help?"

"Oh, yes. I remember Mrs. Gargiulio. She stayed with us when Momma went to the hospital to get Suni, but mostly I took care of them myself. Momma used to say that if anyone found out she was gone, the police would take us all and put us in separate jails."

"Who took care of the other children when you went to school?"

A shadow crossed her face, and Griggs knew he had touched a tender subject. "Tell me about your school, Patty."

The story of Patty's formal schooling began in 1959. Sue Anne was a happy and alert two-year-old, and John was

learning to help Patty manage the household. The neighborhood merchants had warmed to Patty immediately, and she
loved it when they called her "little mother." In January,
1959, they lavished her with special treats to celebrate her
sixth birthday. Most of them asked when she would be starting school, but Patty hadn't given it any thought.

As Patty began to reflect on the prospect of going to
school, however, her interest grew. She had been so involved
with the raising of her brother and sister that she had only a
cardboard image of what it meant to go to school, so she decided to learn more about it. To begin with, she ventured two
blocks north to stand near the corner and watch children on
their way to school. Some looked younger than she, and all
were dressed nicely. Under their long winter coats, Patty
noted that the girls wore bright dresses and matching socks.
Above all, there was a camaraderie that went with the pushing, shoving, teasing, and laughing, none of which was familiar to Patty. She thought how well Sue Anne would fit into
that sort of thing, but doubted her own ability to do so.

At three o'clock in the afternoon, she returned to the same
corner and concluded that school couldn't have been so bad,
for those same children were still laughing and running on
their way home. If anything, they seemed more excited and
energetic than they had that morning.

The next step was to follow the children all the way to the
school building, and when she witnessed the same scene of
gleeful confusion repeated a hundred times over in that
crowded yard, she made up her mind that that was where
she wanted to be, and she resolved to talk to her mother as
soon as possible.

Patty waited patiently for the right moment. June had not
left the apartment for more than a week, but it was difficult
for Patty to ask for something for herself. When she perceived the time to be right, Patty was circumspect. "Momma,
Mr. Gordon, the butcher, and Mr. and Mrs. Gerber asked
me when I am going to start school."

"You don't start school till you're six," June grumbled.

"But I *was* six. Don't you remember?"

"Oh, yeah," June murmured, lost in her thoughts. Then, as if forcing herself to seriously respond to her daughter's request, she asked, "You wouldn't want to be away from the kids all day, would you?"

Patty stared blankly.

"That's what would happen, you know. You'd leave here in the morning before anyone was awake, and you'd get back late at night, and with homework and all, you'd never even get to talk to John and Sue Anne anymore. They'd forget all about you, and someone else would have to take care of them."

Patty already had a clear understanding of the time demands, and she wondered why her mother was distorting the picture.

Then June sighed loudly and gave her the answer. "Besides," she said sadly, "you're old enough to know . . . we're gonna have another baby."

Patty was pleased, especially for Sue Anne, who would now, in Patty's mind, have a playmate. "When are we getting the baby?" she asked.

"In August," June answered. "And you would be starting school right when I need you the most. I think you'll have to wait another year."

Karen was born on August 9th. June was beyond caring that there was no way of determining who the father was, but she was pleasantly surprised when her welfare checks were increased. As soon as she could hit the streets again to supplement her income, things would be pretty good.

In early November, when Patty was almost seven years old, a truant officer climbed the stairs of the old tenement and knocked on the Clawson door. Patty was wary because they never had visitors, and no man in the neighborhood ever wore a suit except to funerals and weddings. "Is your mother home?" he asked when Patty opened the door a crack.

"No, she had to go out for something," Patty lied, knowing

that June was asleep, and knowing also that if this man was one of her mother's "friends," June would not want him to see her looking so bad.

"What is your name?" the man asked.

"Patricia Clawson," came the guarded reply.

"Do people call you Patty?"

"I like Patricia," she said, sensing formalities might be in order.

The man then asked how old she was and why she wasn't in school that day, when June's rasping shout commanded, "Goddammit, Patty, tell him we don't want any, and shut the door."

"I gotta go," Patty said and closed the door.

Two hours later, the same man returned but this time there was also a uniformed policeman and a social worker. The policeman gained entrance for the group, then left them to discuss the school issue with June and Patty.

The social worker walked Patty through the enrollment process the following morning, then she and Patty spent several hours shopping for school clothes.

In spite of the fact that Patty was more than two months late starting school, she quickly caught up with her classmates. Patty enjoyed being a little girl in a first-grade environment. She wasn't very good at playing games, and she regretted her exclusion from the teasing and pushing that, for the other children, was a part of walking to school and waiting for the bell to ring.

Her official records indicated a highly developed superego, a strong desire to please her teachers, an inability to make friends, an unmistakable maturity, and a poor attendance record—for the joys of being a seven-year-old first-grader took second place to the demands of surrogate motherhood.

Patty's narrative was sketchy, but Griggs had no trouble fleshing out the facts. "John started school the next year," she said, then laughed, "but he didn't get no new clothes, because the social worker didn't *make* him start school."

"With both you and John in school, did your mother stay home more to take care of the children?" Griggs asked.

"Yeah, well, she did sometimes," Patty answered hesitantly. "But she was dipping in and out of bars, and sometimes she wouldn't come home for a long time."

Griggs interrupted, "What do you mean by 'a long time'? Do you mean overnight?"

"Yeah, like sometimes she was gone overnight. Sometimes she was gone all week."

Griggs was almost indignant. "Who took care of the kids?"

"I did mostly, I guess. Like John and I would switch off going to school so one of us could stay home and take care of Karen and Sue Anne. If we missed a whole bunch, the school got shook up and sent the big TRU after us."

Griggs had never heard the term. "The big T-R-U?"

Patty became annoyed with the repeated interruptions and answered curtly, "Yeah, you know, that guy who comes around checking if kids don't go to school."

Griggs smiled in recognition of the term, then said, "Patty, we'll have time to talk tonight, but if you're not too tired right now, I'd like to hear more about the time Sue Anne got hurt and you were sent to different foster homes. You started to tell me about that last night, remember?"

Her face clouded as she thought for a moment. Then she stood up and announced, "I better check on Charlie and Karen."

Griggs watched her walk from the room and sat making notes to himself for five minutes. Then the realization struck him that there were eighteen other cases demanding his immediate attention in that building alone. Without moving from his chair, he bellowed for Ernie and instructed the young aide to bring Tommy Jackson to the office.

"Who?" Ernie asked.

"Tommy Jackson . . . GUZZLER," he clarified. "And tell Mr. Howard I want to see him, too."

John and Guzzler had become good friends. At first, John had avoided the older boy because he was embarrassed about having seen him cry himself to sleep that first night. But Guzzler's daytime facade was impenetrable, and John took great comfort in his bland assurances and grandiose schemes. When Ernie found them in the yard, Guzzler was regaling John with fantasies of his indestructibility. "Mr. Griggs wants you in the office right away," Ernie interrupted, and whatever vicarious strength John had gathered evaporated when he saw the color drain from Guzzler's face.

"Come in, Tommy. You know Mr. Howard, don't you?" The boy nodded nervously, and Griggs tried to calm him. "You've been here six weeks now, and it looks like they'll be ready for you tomorrow morning at the Diagnostic and Reception Center."

"What are they gonna do to me?" he asked tremulously.

"There's nothing to be scared of, son. They're going to give you a medical examination, then they'll give you some written tests, and a psychologist will talk to you. You should be there three or four days, at the most."

"Then what's gonna happen to me?"

"Mr. Howard and I will talk to Judge Harrington, and he'll decide where would be the best place to send you. It might be the State Hospital, it might be to the Boys' Industrial School, it could be to a foster home, and it's even possible that he might send you home again."

"That'd be good. My mom would like that . . . if I could go home, I mean."

"We'll see, pal. I can't make any promises."

The boy understood the interview was over, and he knew he was expected to leave, but he hesitated. "Mr. Griggs, I never did nothing *really* bad. I mean, no worse than a lot of other guys. I mean, I never *hurt* nobody, you know?"

"I know that, Tommy, and so does Judge Harrington. But you've been in trouble with the law for seven or eight years now, and you're only fourteen. We don't want to punish you. We just want to find out what's wrong with you and try to help you straighten up."

The boy turned to leave, but stopped at the door to look back at Griggs and Howard. There were tears in his eyes, and when he spoke, his voice cracked. "Ask the judge not to do nothing bad to me, willya?"

The boy left the room, and Griggs spoke softly to Del Howard, "I'd appreciate it if you could take him up there tomorrow." Howard looked up and nodded silently.

Patty put the children to sleep and found Griggs waiting for her in the living room. She seemed younger. The unique opportunity of talking to someone about her life had had a purgative effect on her, but it had quite the opposite effect on the bedraggled Bud Griggs. She was no longer reluctant to respond to his earlier question, but Griggs nevertheless phrased it differently. "Do you remember when it was that you all went to the foster homes?"

She thought for a moment, then said, "Well, Charlie wasn't there yet, and Sue Anne was like in the first grade, and Karen was still kinda like a baby . . . so I guess it would be about two years ago."

"Was your father at home then?"

Patty looked up and answered with a half-laugh, "No, he wasn't at home. The first time I saw my dad that I can remember was only a couple of months ago, when he got out of prison."

Griggs sat there trying to figure how this could fit in with the fact that there were four children younger than Patty, but as he was about to ask the question, it dawned on him that this worldly eleven-year-old girl was laughing at him again. He decided that it made no difference where they came from—they were there now.

"Well, anyway," she continued, "it was one of those times that Mom was gone a long time, and Sue Anne fell down these steps going up to our place. She hurt her leg, but none of us knew what to do for her, and we couldn't find our mom anywhere."

Patty stared into space, and her voice softened to the point that he could hardly hear what she was saying. She looked up abruptly, shook her head as if to clear it, and continued in a normal voice. "It got real bad. Sue Anne slept all the time, and we couldn't wake her up. And when she *did* wake up, she would cry and scream until she went to sleep again. Her leg got real big and purple, and she was hot and red all over."

This time Griggs did not interrupt and gave her time to collect her thoughts before continuing. "I told John we had to take her to the hospital, so John and me got Suni on my back, and John carried Karen. The hospital was like only six blocks away, so we got there real quick. And these doctors and nurses and everybody started fussing all over the place, and the next thing I know, this lady started talking to me about where did we come from, and where was Momma, and where was Daddy, and all this other stuff.

"Then the cops showed up and took us to a house like this," Patty said, waving her arm. "There were a lot of kids, just like here, and two days later, they split us up and put us in different houses and told us we would live there until our momma could take care of us again." Her recollection of the separation was obviously traumatic for Patty, and as she thought about them taking Karen from her arms and John shuffling out with his head down, she cried openly.

Griggs said softly, "Why don't you tell me what it was like for you in the foster home. How did you get along with the parents?"

Pat sat up and looked at him. Tears began to fill her eyes. "Well, it wasn't like they weren't good people. I know they were good people. Their name was . . . I don't remember."

Then, because she didn't remember, she thought it might help if she described them. "She was big and fat, and he sat around most of the time working crossword puzzles. I don't know how old they were, but everybody said what fine people they were.

"My social worker told me that if I would go partway, then they would go partway, and we would get along fine. They prayed a lot and we went to church a lot. And whenever I did anything dirty or bad, we would all pray some more.

"And like the time I dropped my first 'M-F' on her, man, she got all red, and her blood things stuck out on her face and neck, and I thought she was gonna bust her girdle! And that was the time she didn't think I was really talking to God the way I should talk to God, so she put me in a closet so I could have more quiet, and I could talk to God better, and maybe He could help me with my problem."

She stopped talking, looked down at her lap, and began to fidget with her fingers. He could hear wrenching sobs coming up from her stomach.

She looked up and wiped her eyes with the back of her hand. "Do you know what? I didn't even know 'M-F' was a dirty word. And I didn't even know me, and people like me, were dirty until I went into that place. It wasn't like they were bad people, and I really tried what that social worker said I should do, but you know what, it was like we were still ten miles apart after we had both gone partway."

For the first time, Bud Griggs began to understand Pat's determination to keep the family together. He remembered what she had said in their first conversation: "At least we got each other."

He suddenly wanted to change the subject, but Pat continued to describe the foster homes the other children had been placed in. "John had a good one. He liked the people. They were older and didn't work any more, and they did things together. John didn't even want to come home when we got everybody picked up about three months later, and momma came after us. That's where he learned how to play the harmonica and sing neat songs and stuff like that. 'Cause those people that he was with did all those things. He kept talking about them all the time, until one day I just told him to shut up! I didn't want to hear about them no more. I didn't want to talk about them no more."

Griggs asked, "What happened to Sue Anne?"

"Well, it wasn't like going into a foster home like John and me or Karen, because Sue Anne kept going in and out of the hospital, and they kept having operations and stuff like that. And she would go into places for a little bit at a time."

Then Griggs asked, "Do you know anything about what happened to Karen?"

Patty compressed her lips and shook her head quickly. "No, I don't know what happened to Karen. Before they took her away, she was happy and laughed all the time, just like Charlie, but when she came home again, she didn't talk, and she didn't smile any more. But I don't know what happened to Karen."

Griggs knew it was past time to conclude the interview. "I have to write a report of all this for Judge Harrington. If you don't mind, I'd like to talk with Sue Anne and John for a little bit, too."

"Sure," she responded. "You want me to get them?"

"No, I'll find them tomorrow morning. It's no big deal, I just want to see how they're getting along."

"Those two could get along in a peanut butter factory," Patty quipped as she rose to leave. "Especially Sue Anne."

Griggs remembered their stories of existing on nothing but peanut butter for so long that they could no longer stand the thought of it, so he put his hand on her shoulder and laughed, understanding that to Patty, a peanut butter factory would have to be a vile and dreadful place.

Griggs emerged from the air-conditioned detention home on Friday morning and stood in the bright sun, scanning the yard for the children. John and Guzzler were leaning against the cyclone fence talking with Del Howard and a boy who had been admitted the night before. Sue Anne was with a group of girls jumping rope, and Karen and Charlie were huddled nearby with Deputy Chenoweth, who had brought a metal dump truck for Charlie, and he was demonstrating the proper way to raise its bed.

Patty, who was no longer alarmed to see the uniformed

deputy playing with her brothers and sisters, observed from a distance. Chins had become a fixture since that first day, and his interest in the Clawson children was genuine. He had already endeared himself to them, and he alone seemed capable of bringing Karen out of her shell. She exulted in grabbing for his bandaged hand and having him recoil in feigned terror. Patty grinned as she overheard Chins exclaim, "I tell you, Karen, the doctor took your tooth out of my hand right after you bit me. It's not there anymore," attempting to hold the giggling girl at bay with his good hand and work the dump truck with the other.

Griggs watched Patty and marveled at the transformation that had taken place in so short a time. Then he looked at the others and told himself that they were too involved in their own activities to interrupt them, so he returned to Mrs. Higgins' office and called the welfare department to find out which social worker had been assigned to the case.

George Matthews, the prissy and bookish director of social welfare, refused to come to the phone, but Griggs could hear him instructing Marge Hackett, his secretary, that Nancy Sloan had been assigned to the case and would be in touch with him soon. Griggs reacted negatively to so inexperienced a social work supervisor being assigned to a tough case like this because he knew it would take a wily and experienced professional to find a foster home large enough for five children. He also knew it would take special kinds of foster parents to deal successfully with the diverse problems and personalities the Clawson family would bring, but he did not verbalize his objections because George Matthews disliked and disapproved of him, and Griggs realized that it would be fruitless to complain. Instead, Griggs affected a saccharin tone and said, "Okay, Margie, just tell that pinch-nosed, fairy-assed boss of yours that I appreciate him taking the time to talk with me . . . and to stuff it."

"Yes, sir," she said with a conspiratorial giggle, "I'll pass along that recommendation."

* * *

That was Friday, August 28th, and Griggs spent the morning laboring over the final predisposition report that would be required at the court hearing on Tuesday. The close relationship that he was developing with the Clawsons was making it difficult for Griggs to be objective. The clinical language of the judicial process didn't seem to fit at all. The court records would portray Patricia as "a female caucasian, 11 years of age, with no visible infirmities." That didn't do justice to the slim, pretty girl with freckles ranging across her nose from one cheek to the other; whose long, dark, straight hair fell across the left side of her face whenever she bowed her head; a serious little girl who was at once a child and a mother, a provider and protector; a youngster who was stubborn and determined on the one hand, yet fearful and self-doubting on the other; but most of all, an innocent in the truest sense of the word who had been subjected to the cruelest pain that can be inflicted on a young girl in need of love. How was it possible to introduce a description of these qualities into the judicial process?

And what about John, thought Griggs—the boy who savored all the joys of boyhood—running barefoot through clover fields, playing the harmonica, making friends, telling jokes, laughing—all those good things except one—he was somehow not good enough or worth enough to be wanted by his own parents.

And Griggs pictured the others. Sue Anne, who would walk with a limp for the rest of her life because there had been no one to care when she broke her leg. And Karen, who rarely smiled any more, who was so terrified of being abandoned again that she clung to her older sister constantly.

It was impossible for Griggs to describe these small human beings as though they were unidentified cadavers that had washed up on a deserted beach, yet it was equally impossible to articulate his deep feelings toward them. He spent the entire morning sifting through his emotions, but he could not bring himself to write that report. The right words wouldn't come.

"Knock knock," said Del Howard from the doorway.

Griggs had been staring vacantly into the blank wall with his face propped up in both hands. The sound of his friend's voice startled him, and he was immediately embarrassed.

"You okay?"

"Yeah, I was thinking about the Clawson report. It has to be just right, and it's giving me fits."

"Sorry to disturb you, but I'm getting ready to deliver Guzzler to the Reception and Diagnostic Center, and I thought I'd see if you still wanted me to handle it myself."

"No problem," Griggs replied. "Just have the admissions officer countersign the transmittal order and bring the receipt back to me. If you have any problems, just call. I'll be here for an hour or so."

Howard then ventured closer to Griggs and said softly, "The kid's still pretty scared. I think he'd feel a lot better if you could talk to him for a minute."

"Sure, bring him in."

"It might be better if you came out. Higgins is stuffing his pockets with cookies right now, and if we don't get moving, we'll be late."

When the two men walked into the kitchen, however, Mrs. Higgins was no longer concerned with the cookies. The enormous woman stood in the middle of the room with her arms around the sobbing boy, trying to comfort him and stem her own tears. "You been here almost two months, now, Tommy boy. Longer than any of the others. It's time you move on and get taken care of. Nobody's gonna hurt you. They're just gonna help you, you'll see."

Griggs moved in and gripped the boy's shoulder with just enough pressure to separate him from Mrs. Higgins. As he turned from the matron's embrace, he dropped his eyes to conceal his tears, but the sobbing continued. "She's right, Tom. I've already explained that they're just going to do some tests to help you get straightened away."

"The cells," the boy sobbed, looking up into Griggs' face. "That place has regular jail cells. Why can't I stay here while ·

they take their tests? I don't want them to lock me in a cell. Please Mr. Griggs," he pleaded, "tell . . . tell the judge I don't want them to lock me in a cell."

"You got it all wrong, Tom. It's not like the adult prison. This place isn't too bad at all. You'll be in a cell, but it'll be like a bedroom. And the door will be locked only at night. The rest of the day you can play basketball, or Ping-Pong, or just read or listen to the radio in the rec room. Besides, you'll only be there four or five days."

"Will I be all by myself?" the boy continued. "I mean, will I have a . . . a roommate?"

"No question about that. That place is pretty busy."

Tom was relieved to learn that he would have company in his cell, but one thought still troubled him. "Will I be with another *kid*? I mean, I heard that those older men do things to kids in jail, and I sure don't want to be with one of them."

"For the last time, son," Griggs assured him firmly, "you are *not* going to the adult prison. You are going to the *Juvenile* Center. There will not be any adult prisoners except maybe for a couple of trustees who are working there." Griggs then nodded to Del Jackson to take over, and Tom gave Mrs. Higgins one last hug before picking up his bag and following Del to the rear door.

Griggs stood on the back porch and watched the car swing through the gate of the cyclone fence. As he turned to re-enter the detention home, he caught sight of John near the corner of the house, somberly watching his friend's departure. Griggs decided it was not the time for a conversation, so he left John to his own thoughts. He resolved to apply himself to the predisposition report on the Clawson children without further procrastination, but when he passed through the kitchen he was glad to see Deputy Chenoweth sitting at the table while Mrs. Higgins poured his coffee.

"Hey, Bud," he said, "you got a minute?"

"Sure, Chins. Let me grab a cup, and I'll join you."

The big man seemed troubled. "Patty tells me that you have decided to keep the five of them together. That right?"

Griggs looked into the eyes of the older man and said, "I'm gonna try, Chins. I'm gonna give it the best shot I can."

"Do you have a place picked out yet?"

"No, that's social welfare's job," Griggs responded.

Chenoweth was persistent. "Then how do you know you can find a place big enough to keep them all together?"

Griggs got defensive. "Hell, Chins, finding a big enough house is only half the problem. The real trick will be finding the right foster parents. Patty is already a mother to those kids, you know. We gotta find foster parents who'll be able to deal with that and not come down too hard on them."

"You know, Bud," Chenoweth said thoughtfully, removing his unlit cigar, "that's kind of what I wanted to talk to you about." He hesitated for a moment, then continued, "I live out there in that big house all by myself." He seemed embarrassed. "The kids and I get along real good, and I know they like me. Now I *know* most people can't see me taking care of kids, but I've always liked kids, and you know, with Patty being like the mother and all, I was thinking maybe they could move in to my place and live with me." Chins seemed relieved to have it out, and he leaned back and waited for Bud's reaction.

Griggs was genuinely touched, and he searched for a diplomatic response.

"I can see you don't think much of the idea," Chins observed.

"Not at all," Griggs blurted. "I think it's a *great* idea. It just caught me off guard a little."

Chins sat forward. "Then you think it'll work?"

"Well, that's really out of my hands. You know the welfare people are in charge of finding and approving foster placements, and . . ."

"Hell, we don't need those bastards," Chins interrupted. "I'm not asking for county money to take care of those kids. I just want to keep them together and keep them with me. I don't need their money. I got enough put aside to make it without them."

"It's not the money, Chins. I'm just not sure how they'd react to placing the kids in a foster home without two foster parents—a man *and* a woman."

"Yeah, I thought of that," Chins said dejectedly, ramming the cigar back into his mouth. "How about if I adopted them? Can I do that?"

"We'd have the same problem, Chins. Social welfare wouldn't approve an adoption to an unmarried man. But I'll talk to them. Nancy Sloan is the caseworker, and maybe she can convince her boss, but Matthews lives strictly by the rules." The two men sat quietly for several minutes, then Griggs voiced his thoughts. "You know, the more I think about it, the more sense it makes. I'm only thinking out loud, mind you, but where else would we find someone with a large enough house who's willing to take in five youngsters? Of course, you'd need some help."

"My sister lives right next door," Chenoweth blurted. "She would help out, and her oldest daughter's seventeen. And Mrs. Martinez—she comes in every afternoon to clean up and start supper—five days a week. I know she'd be willing to spend more time." Chenoweth was excited as the alternatives unfolded.

"Let's work on it," Griggs suggested. "I'll talk to Judge Harrington, and maybe he can get to George Matthews. It might make sense, especially if it means not splitting them up."

Chenoweth snatched for his cigar in alarm. "That would kill them, Bud. Especially Patty. That would kill her if we split those kids up."

"I know, and it wouldn't even make . . ."

"Mr. Griggs, come quick," Ernie shouted from the door. "Mr. Howard's on the phone, and he said it's an emergency."

The urgency was not lost on Bud Griggs. He bolted from the table and was across the room before Ernie could get out of his way. Griggs untangled himself and grabbed for the telephone without losing stride. "What is it," he barked into the mouthpiece.

"Something's gone haywire," Howard reported. "The receptionist stopped me at the door, and I asked to see the admissions officer, just like you said. Then she took the papers and signed them herself and gave me the pink copy. I told her I needed to see the admissions officer, but she said he was gone, and it wouldn't make any difference anyway, because Tommy would not be admitted to the Reception and Diagnostic Center until there was room for him—maybe four or five days."

"What're they gonna do with him till then?"

"She said they'd ship him over to the penitentiary with the others."

"What others?" Griggs demanded.

"There must be fifteen kids in here—from all over the state. They're shipping them all to the penitentiary until there's room for them here. Guzzler's about to come unglued. What do you want me to do?"

"You tell them to jam it," Griggs shouted. "Just get him back here to the detention home, and we'll turn him over to them when they've got room for him."

"That's the problem," Howard replied. "We've *already* turned him over to them. When I told the woman that I'd take him back with me, she laughed and said he was the property of the Bureau of Institutions now, and I wouldn't be taking him anywhere."

Griggs' mind raced, but his voice was controlled when he finally spoke. "You listen to me. I am *ordering* you to grab that kid and get him out of there, even if you have to knock down the door to do it. You understand?"

"I understand, but are you sure?"

"I'm sure, goddammit. Just get that kid out of there!"

"Okay, but I'm gonna be traveling pretty fast," Del said, obviously pleased to be in action again, "so get that back gate unlocked for us."

Griggs held the receiver to his ear with one hand and disconnected the line with the other. He explained the situation to Chenoweth and Higgins as he dialed Judge Harrington's

number. "Put the judge on," he said into the phone, then to
Ernie, "get the back gate opened for Mr. Howard. He'll be
here in a couple of minutes.

"Judge? We got a problem. Can I see you right away?"

Judge Harrington's office was a different world. The book-
lined walls and thick blue carpet absorbed and muffled the
sounds within, and the heavy oak doors shut out the clamor
from the marbled halls. Next to the judge himself, Bud
Griggs was the chief officer of the juvenile court, so he was
no stranger to the room. Nonetheless, the effect of walking
into that office never changed for Griggs. It exuded the gentle intimacy of a small chapel and cushioned sounds like the
fallen needles of a dense pine forest. The room itself
personified the gentle warmth and maturity of the man who
worked there.

Wilbur Harrington was a man in his middle fifties who had
spent more than half his professional life as presiding judge
of the Juvenile Court. Because of his calm demeanor, his
family and friends were calling him "Judge" long before he
thought of attending law school. His presence inevitably
soothed the concerns of tortured parents and calmed the
frightened children caught up in the juvenile justice system.
When he was initially appointed to the court, seventeen years
earlier, his colleagues predicted a brief and agonizing tenure
for the man whose compassion was boundless. But they had
not accounted for the strength and resiliency that was to carry him through a litany of human suffering and abuses un-
matched in the criminal justice system.

The soothing influences of both the place and the man
combined to calm Griggs' anger, and when he conveyed the
story of Tommy Jackson, it was done without the urgency
that had possessed him earlier. Griggs dwelled on the boy's
fear of being committed to the adult prison, but he was factu-
al and to the point. The growing fire in the judge's eyes belied his placidity, and Griggs knew there was no need to elaborate.

"That woman was correct, Bud. The boy became the property of the Department of Institutions the moment she countersigned the transmittal order. Your jurisdiction was terminated at that moment, and your subsequent actions were unlawful. The commissioner may be obliged to initiate a formal complaint against you and your deputy."

"I hear you, Judge, but no kid is safe in the penitentiary, and you know it."

Judge Harrington ignored Griggs' remark and said, as if to himself, "As I remember this boy, the psychiatric report indicated no serious pathology."

"Hell, Judge, this kid actually cries himself to sleep every night, begging for his mother to come and take him home," Griggs interrupted. "He's a pussycat."

"As I recall, he's about fourteen years old, and he's been in and out of the police station for six or eight years."

"Yeah, but petty stuff—truancy, shoplifting, broke a car window once . . . crap like that. But he's still got damned good stuff in him." There was a moment of silence, then Griggs added, "I tell you, I trust Mrs. Higgins and that young Clawson boy, and they both like this kid."

Judge Harrington looked up sharply at the mention of John Clawson, but rather than divert the conversation to another of his pressing concerns, he forced himself back to the case at hand. "Tell me about his parents. What are they really like?"

"Good people," Griggs replied. "He works at the feed and grain store, and she used to work part-time at the school cafeteria, but she quit not long ago, hoping we'd send Tommy home again."

"How many other children are there?"

"Four . . . two sets of twins. The problem really started when the youngest kids were born . . . eight years ago. The shrink thought that might have had something to do with the way the kid started acting up."

"Bud, it sounds to me as though you want me to send this boy back home." Griggs said nothing, so the judge continued, "If that's the case, what makes you think this time will be any better than all the others? We put him in detention because we felt he was getting ready to hurt himself or someone else. Has that situation changed in your mind?"

Griggs nodded broadly. "Mainly, when we put that kid behind the fence, they *all* found out that we meant business. Both parents have been cooperating with the caseworker, and Mrs. Higgins says that Guzzler—that's what she calls him—is one of the best kids she's ever had there."

"This is very troublesome for me, Bud. I did not have this boy committed to detention to teach anyone a lesson or to show them that 'we meant business.' I ordered him committed because I was convinced he needed help, and nothing you have said here has changed my mind."

Griggs slumped back dejectedly, because the judge's words made it clear that Guzzler would soon find himself behind bars again.

"This is an extremely serious matter," Judge Harrington continued sternly. "Right after you telephoned this afternoon, I received a call from the deputy commissioner of institutions. Helen said he was upset and demanded to speak to me immediately, but I sensed it might have something to do with your call, so I didn't speak to him."

Griggs stared up at the ceiling without responding.

The judge slammed the desk with his fist in a rare display of anger. "Dammit, Bud, you don't seem to appreciate the fact that this amounts to a jailbreak, and you and Howard are accessories."

At that moment, the buzzer sounded, and Judge Harrington picked up the telephone and listened for a moment before thanking his secretary. One of the lights on the phone was flashing impatiently as the judge informed Griggs, "We can forget about the deputy commissioner. The commissioner himself is on my line right now." He jabbed a finger down on the flashing light and said, "Hello, Arthur, what can I do for you?"

The judge cringed and held the telephone away from his

head to relieve the pressure on his ear and to share the indignant shouting with Griggs. When the clamor on the other end subsided, Judge Harrington spoke again. "Now, Arthur, I don't think you have the entire story . . . No, Arthur, that's madness. Of course I will not issue a bench warrant for my own probation officers . . . If you will just calm down for a moment, I'm sure I can explain it to your satisfaction." The judge listened for a moment longer, glowering at Griggs the entire time.

Judge Harrington's face flushed, and Griggs correctly guessed that the commissioner had gone one step too far. When the judge finally spoke, his voice was firm and cold. "Now you listen to me, Mr. Commissioner. The fact is that Thomas was indeed scheduled to be transferred to the Reception and Diagnostic Center, but his progress at the detention home was so remarkable that I accepted the recommendation that he be paroled to the custody of his parents. I signed the amended order several hours ago and failed to notify Mr. Griggs. As soon as he found out about it, he rescinded Mr. Howard's instructions and ordered him to return the boy to my office."

There was a momentary pause, then he continued, "That's right, I have ordered Mr. Griggs to bring Mr. and Mrs. Jackson to my office immediately." The judge emphasized the statement and glared at Griggs in such a way as to make it clear that he was to go and do just that. As Griggs reached the door, he heard Judge Harrington assure the commissioner, "That's correct, Arthur, I'm certain Mr. Griggs is already on his way to the Jackson house." When the judge saw that Griggs was looking at him from the door with a wide grin on his face, he said, "Arthur, you can take my word for it, if they are not all here within the hour, Mr. Griggs will rue the day he was born." Then, as Griggs disappeared through the open door, he heard, "And I would be surprised if Mr. Howard isn't IN MY OFFICE with the boy in TEN MINUTES."

The hastily called meetings came off as scheduled. Howard

responded quickly to Bud's radio call and delivered Guzzler while Griggs went after the boy's parents. The judge spoke privately to the youngster for almost an hour, finally assuring himself that he was indeed doing the right thing. Then there followed a tearful reunion with the parents and another long session that concluded with the three Jacksons leaving the office in a mutual embrace, assuring Judge Harrington and Bud Griggs that they had seen the last of the Jacksons in Juvenile Court.

Griggs and Howard tried to slip out with the Jacksons, but the judge's gentle touch restrained them. His smile lasted only until the door closed, then he turned to them coldly and said in a matter-of-fact way, "Gentlemen, perhaps we are out of danger, but if so, we were extremely fortunate. Above all, I want it understood that today's events were a once-in-a-lifetime mistake, and that they will not be repeated." Then, looking at Del Howard, he asked, "Is that understood?"

"No, sir . . . Ah, I mean, yes, sir . . . Er, Judge, you asked three questions. Which is the one you're asking about?" Del looked around in desperate confusion, but saw only amusement in Griggs' eyes, so he turned back to Judge Harrington and stammered, "What I mean, Judge, is yes, it was a mistake; no, it won't be repeated; and yes, I understand."

Griggs clapped enthusiastically but stopped when he saw that Judge Harrington was not amused.

"I've never seen the old man pissed before," Del observed in the car.

"And you still haven't," Griggs assured him. "He wasn't pissed at all. As a matter of fact, he was having a good time at our expense. If anything, he was sticking it into the commissioner, not us."

Del thought about the situation while Griggs drove the short distance to the detention home. As they approached the gate, Del asked, "What'll we tell the kids? They must know something has been happening."

"You can bet your outhouse on that," Griggs said. "News

travels faster on the inmate network than it does on TV, and I don't care whether it's adult felons in the penitentiary or runaway kids in detention, *there's no faster communications known to man.*"

Howard chuckled as Griggs delivered the end of his statement in imitation of W.C. Fields. "You'll never change," he laughed. "You've got more crap in you than Kelley's goat."

"Is that what you think, oh loyal minion?" Griggs asked as they swung through the gate and drove up to the rear of the building through a phalanx of grinning children. "If you don't believe me, dummy, just look at those silly faces."

"I'll be goddammed," Howard laughed spontaneously, precipitating more pushing and giggling among the children. Before Griggs brought the car to a complete stop, Howard rolled down the window with his good hand and asked in his best tough-guy voice, "Hey, you, what's so funny?"

A pimply-faced fifteen-year-old girl snickered at him and said, "Nothin' . . . 'cept you, maybe."

The car stopped, and Howard reached through the window and playfully grabbed John's arm. "And you, boy, what're *you* laughing about. You think I'm funny, too?"

"Naw," said John grinning. "We heard about Guzzler."

"Guzzler?" Del asked in mock chagrin. "You laughing about pore ole Guzzler? What's so funny about chopping up that pore little boy and feeding his pathetic little carcass to the monkeys out at the zoo?"

"Aw, you didn't do that to Guzzler," John said derisively.

"Yes, we did," Howard responded emphatically, "and we would have done the same thing to you, but you're too scrawny. That's why Mrs. Higgins was feeding him all those cookies. By the way, have you had *your* cookies today?"

"Bull!" John said with finality. "Guzzler went home with his mother, and you know it."

Del released his grip on John's arm, rolled up the window, and looked at Griggs in amazement. "How in the goddam hell is that possible?"

Griggs responded haughtily as he opened his door to get

out of the car, "Next time, don't question the wisdom of your superiors."

Griggs spent several minutes with the Clawson children, informing them that Nancy Sloan had been assigned to supervise their case, and that she might be around to talk to them over the weekend. Patty seemed confused and a little alarmed at the thought of a new outsider coming into their lives, but Griggs assured her that Miss Sloan's job was to find them a new home to move into right after the hearing next Tuesday. At that point, Patty asked for more assurances about the hearing, so Griggs explained it again. As he was about to leave, it occurred to him that John had seemed distracted and thoughtful, so he asked if John had understood what he had said.

It was obvious from John's response that he was preoccupied with something else. "Mr. Griggs," he asked timidly, ". . . that thing that happened to Guzzler . . . you know, going to jail and all . . . will that happen to me, too?"

Griggs rarely showed his emotions, and he almost never touched the children, but John's question moved him to reach out for the boy and encircle his shoulders. "No, John," he answered softly, looking down at the boy. "That won't happen to you."

John tossed and turned in his bed that night as he wrestled with many conflicting emotions. The dormitory seemed deserted and hollow, although Guzzler's old bunk was the only one empty. And the absence of his friend's nightly sobbing made the room seem unnaturally quiet, although the darkness was filled with the sleeping sounds of nine other boys. John was happy for Guzzler's good fortune, but a twinge of envy went through him as he thought of the boy sleeping comfortably in his own home with a mother and father who cared.

John thought back to his first night in the detention home and how strange and frightening it had all seemed then. It suddenly occurred to him that several of the children who had been living there when he arrived were now gone. It took the loss of a close friend to bring him to the realization that the home was a place where children arrived and departed continually, where change was a way of life.

He laughed to himself when he recalled his first walk through the breakfast buffet. He had been so uncertain then, afraid that he might be scolded for taking too much food. Now after five days, he was an "old-timer," and it made him feel worldly and important to walk through the food line with confidence and assurance in the presence of other frightened newcomers.

His thoughts became disjointed as he began to drift off to sleep. Suddenly there was an eruption in the hall outside the boys' dormitory. Men were shouting as the unmistakable sounds of a struggle filled the night. Then there was the dreaded report of steel against steel, and John knew that someone had been thrown into one of the cells. Ten pairs of feet hit the floor at the same time as the boys rolled out of their bunks and raced to the door for a closer look.

As they gathered behind the closed door, they instinctively positioned themselves in an hierarchical order. Among every group of inmates, the development of a pecking order is a way of life, and it was not different among these children. Mrs. Higgins had worked tirelessly to mitigate the usual consequences of that kind of ordering, and as a result the physical and homosexual abuses that are so common in such institutions were indeed rare for that particular detention home. Nevertheless, the stronger children rose to positions of leadership and supremacy to which certain privileges accrued. No leader was expected to take second place in the chow line, for instance, and every child knew to wait his turn at the YMCA pool. Mrs. Higgins knew of the existence of this subclassing of her wards, but the genius of the woman was to permit it to exist in a controlled environment. She was able to identify the current leader without ever being told, and she accorded proper recognition by designating that person as the "chief itch and rub," which in her home carried with it responsibilities as well as privileges.

Vito Falcone was the current chief itch and rub, and on this particular occasion, the muscular seventeen-year-old was accorded the place closest to the dormitory door. The other boys parted for him as he sauntered forward and quietly gripped the doorknob. He looked out over the others imperiously to command complete silence, then he turned the knob gently and cracked the door. The light from the hall knifed through the darkness of the dormitory, and Vito placed an unblinking eye against the opening. Two of his minor chieftains kneeled at the door to catch a glimpse at the proceedings, but the others, with their heads turned sideways, had to settle for what little they could overhear.

The angry murmurings of the three arresting officers wafted down the hall. "The goddam sonofabitch tore my shirt." . . . "Where's my hat?" . . . "I hope you rot in there, you little black bastard."

Then the loud recriminations of Mrs. Higgins filled the air, but her abuse was directed at the city policemen rather than the panting boy in the cell. The three boys at the door could hear her climbing the stairs shouting, "I hope you apes are satisfied. You woke up half the goddam town." Then she reached the top of the landing and looked into the cell. She saw a fourteen-year-old boy whose face was covered with perspiration and blood, gasping for breath, his eyes glaring with insolence and hatred.

"Oh, beautiful," she exclaimed in disgust. "Why didn't you break both his legs while you were at it?"

"Kiss my ass, Higgins," one of the officers barked.

"Stuff it, junior," the huge woman spat back at the youngest of the policemen. "You guys on the graveyard shift may know about prostitutes and pimps, but this is a *kid*, and the judge is gonna want to know how come he's beat up so badly."

"Let's all calm down," suggested the oldest of the three policemen. His stripes identified him as a sergeant. "This kid was breaking into vending machines at the laundromat in Parkhurst Village. He tore up the candy machine first, then he broke into the cigarette machine. I think he cut himself on the glass."

"Well, let's just take a look," she said, reaching for the key to unlock the cell door.

"Careful," Sergeant Coombs warned.

Mrs. Higgins shot a look of contempt and pulled open the steel door. The boy retreated to a corner of the cell and coiled like a wounded animal. "Let me have a look, boy. This won't hurt." Then she took his face in her hands and turned it upward toward the dim light. The tenseness drained from his body immediately as she turned his face from side to side to survey the damage. "What about this knot on his forehead?" she demanded. "Did one of those candy bars jump out of the machine and clobber him?"

"He resisted arrest," the younger officer said defensively. Then, as if reading from his police primer, he continued, "I took whatever action was necessary to subdue him and abate the threat."

"Phoo!" Mrs. Higgins said disdainfully. "After you've read Chapter Two, we'll talk about it." Then she looked directly into the boy's eyes and said, "Let's go down the hall and get you cleaned up a little."

The crowd behind the door froze as Mrs. Higgins led her newest charge down the hall toward the bathroom, chattering soothingly to him the entire way. Without the slightest pause in her patter, she reached for the knob of the dormitory door and said curtly, "Go back to sleep," as she pulled it shut, almost catching Vito's nose in the process.

It was a rumpled and sleepy-eyed Bud Griggs who arrived at the detention home a half hour later. He climbed the steps to join Sergeant Coombs in the kitchen.

"I sent the others back on patrol," the sergeant said over a cup of steaming coffee. "Do you need them tonight?"

"I don't think so," Griggs answered, reaching for a coffee

cup. "What have we got?" referring to the boy in the cell up-stairs.

The policeman pushed a manila envelope containing the youngster's confiscated possessions, and flipped open his tiny, worn notebook. "Eurastus Thompson," he intoned, "age fourteen, Negro, breaking and entering, malicious mis-chief, resisting arrest, assaulting a law officer . . ."

"Okay, okay," Griggs interrupted, "just tell me what hap-pened for right now."

Jerry Coombs slouched imperceptibly, as if signaling an end to the formalities. "This is a strange one, Bud. It's almost as if this kid *wanted* to be caught. A young couple from the college were in the laundromat when he walked in a little be-fore midnight. Just as cool as you please, he takes off his shoe and breaks the glass on the candy machine. Then he sits there and eats a couple of candy bars."

"What did the couple do?" Griggs asked.

"Nothing, at first. They just minded their own business, kind of keeping an eye on the kid." Coombs paused to sip at his coffee as Mrs. Higgins entered the room and walked to the table. "Then the kid walks over to the cigarette ma-chine—one shoe on and one shoe in his hand—looks over at the couple, and knocks out that glass, too. That's when the husband went to the phone and called the station. Pete and Doug were cruising the neighborhood, so they got to the laundromat in no time flat."

"How did they catch up with the boy?" Griggs asked. "That was good police work."

"That's just it," Coombs answered in a bemused tone. "The squad car rolled up with flasher, sirens, and the whole works. The husband said he could hear it three blocks away, but when Pete and Doug came through the front door, the kid was still there—standing near the side door. Doug or-dered him to freeze, and the kid jumped out into the alley and ran like hell."

"Sounds like he wasn't too eager to escape, was he?" Griggs observed.

"That's what it sounds like, but that little bastard ran like a scared rabbit. Then, when Doug finally caught up with him, he fought like a maniac. Finally, the kid pulled out this knife, and Doug gave him the nightstick across the head. When I got there, they had the kid spread-eagled on the ground, and they were emptying his pockets."

Mrs. Higgins picked up the long jackknife that Sergeant Coombs had shaken from the manila envelope, and she felt a twinge of guilt for accusing the young policeman of needless brutality. She was compassionate enough to realize that he must have been as frightened as its young owner.

Coombs understood her feelings and nodded. Then he finished his report. "We took the kid back for the couple to identify, and we brought him here and told the dispatcher to call you. That's it."

"How much did he get from the vending machines?" Griggs asked.

"That's the hell of it," Coombs exclaimed. "He never got anywhere near the coin box, and he never touched the cigarettes after he broke the goddammed glass. Just a couple of candy bars . . . that's all he went after, and that's all he got."

"Well, tomorrow's another day," Griggs said wearily. "I'll get back to you then." He moved forward as if to rise, but sat back. "Oh, one more thing, have you checked for prior arrests, yet?"

"Are you joking?" Coombs laughed. "We're strictly 'uptown' these days. That new computer gave us a complete rundown before we ever got here. This one has no priors, but he's from a bad bunch. He's got one older brother in the penitentiary, and there's another one . . . Lennie, I think . . . in the Boys' Industrial School for vandalism, shoplifting, and you name it."

"Lennie Thompson," Griggs mused, trying to recall.

"I remember him," Mrs. Higgins said. "We used to call him 'Bigfoot'."

"That's right," Griggs concurred, "a tall gangly kid . . . used to play basketball."

"He still does," Mrs. Higgins offered. "I hear he's the captain of the BIS team."

"Whatever," Sergeant Coombs said with finality. "It's a bad bunch, and if this kid has no record, it's only because he was never caught!"

Griggs was too familiar with that attitude to attempt a rejoinder, so he simply rose from his chair, stretched his arms, and complained, "I just wish someone would teach these kids to confine their fun and games to weekdays—preferably from nine to five. I haven't had a weekend off since Christmas."

The following morning, John waited outside the boys' dormitory for his sisters to come down from the third floor. He was eager to share the news of last night's excitement with them, but he was disappointed to learn that they were already aware of everything that had happened, up to and including the kitchen conversation. It was his turn to be surprised by the efficiency of the inmate grapevine. '

Sue Anne, Karen, and John hurried past the locked cell, too frightened to look in on the caged prisoner. Only Patty, with Charlie on her hip, had the courage to look at him, and the sight of the glaring boy in the corner of the cell, completely engulfed by steel and concrete and darkness, almost brought her to tears. She stood silently for a moment, then asked quietly, "You okay?"

The boy seemed surprised that she should care enough to ask. He simply shrugged his shoulders and turned away.

John was waiting for his sister halfway down the stairs. "Are you *crazy*, Patty?" he demanded. "What did he say? . . . What did he look like?"

Patty was too moved to respond. She simply walked past her brother and proceeded to the kitchen. John followed closely, bombarding her with questions. Patty finally stopped and said to him, "He's just a kid, and I think he's scared . . . just like we were."

"*Were?*" John demanded. "Don't say 'were' . . . Man, I'd

crap my pants if they locked me up in that cell. I'm *still* scared of that."

"I know," Patty responded thoughtfully. "How can they do that to people?"

The conversation throughout breakfast centered on the new arrival. The younger children chattered nervously, because no one had been locked away in the time that any of them had lived at the detention home, but the older boys and girls maintained facades of indifference. Most of them were facing similar commitments to reform schools, so their psychological defenses interpreted incarceration as no big deal.

To Patty and John, however, the specter of imprisonment was too frightening to dwell on, so neither of them had much of an appetite for breakfast. Soon after seating himself at the table, John carried his laden tray back into the kitchen and asked, "Mrs. Higgins, could I take this upstairs? I hardly touched the food."

"You know there's no food allowed in the dormitory, John," Mrs. Higgins said sternly. "It brings on roaches and mice. You know that."

"No," he corrected her immediately, "I mean to that new kid."

"Oh," she brightened, "I'll tell you what, Johnny Jumpup, let's fix him a fresh tray and take it up together."

"You'll go with me?" he asked. "What's he like?"

"He looks like a nice boy to me," she reassured him, "and you can be his first friend. I think he'll like that."

Together they selected an assortment of scrambled eggs, bacon, sausage, toast, and pancakes, topped off by milk and orange juice. As the mound of food swelled, John, titillated by the prospect of confronting an imprisoned desperado, giggled with excitement, commenting that there was enough food to feed an entire gang.

"Coming from you, that's quite a statement," Mrs. Higgins laughed. "I'll tell you something, J.J., most of my guests don't exactly come to me with full stomachs. I remember the first morning you walked through this line. I thought your eyes were going to fall out of your face and roll around the floor like little brown marbles."

Mrs. Higgins laughed prodigiously while John blushed. "Yeah, I was really dumb, then."

"Oh, shut up," she said, playfully ruffling his hair. "Let's get this food upstairs before that boy eats his way through the bars."

"Let me have that," John said, taking the tray from Mrs. Higgins. "If he sees me carrying his tray, maybe he won't be scared of me." Mrs. Higgins looked at the nervous boy and broke into an uncontrollable laughter that was so intense that she had to sit down to catch her breath. "C'mon," John pleaded, "this stuff is getting cold."

Mrs. Higgins led the way wiping tears from her eyes and shaking her head in disbelief. Every few steps, she would look back at him and start giggling anew. John was pleased with himself for precipitating that reaction from her, but he was not quite sure how he had done it. As they climbed the steps, however, his confidence waned, and he suggested, "Maybe you ought to take this in to him . . . give him more time to get used to me."

"Good idea," she said with an understanding grin.

"Oh, by the way, what's his name?" John asked.

"Shoot," she exclaimed, handing the tray back to him. "You know how bad I am with names." She fished in her deep pocket saying, "Erasmus . . . no . . . Eurasia . . . no, that's not it, either." Then she found what she was looking for, and her hand emerged clutching an index card. "Eurastus Thompson," she read slowly. "I gotta remember that. Yoor-Ass-Tuss, Yoor-Ass-Tuss, Yoor-Ass-Tuss," she repeated to herself as she climbed the stairs. When they reached the cell, she balanced the tray in one hand and unlocked the door with the other, practicing the name under her breath. "Yoor-Ass-Tuss . . . Yoor-Ass-Tuss . . ." Then she noted that the bruise on the boy's forehead had swelled to the size of a golf ball, and she said, "C'mon over here, Bump, and have some breakfast."

"What you call me?" the boy demanded.

"'Bump,' I called you 'Bump.' I hope you don't mind. It just popped out."

"I don't mind," he said with a hint of a smile. "It sure better'n 'Rastus.'" Then his eyes beheld the heaping tray of food, and his bright face erupted into a dazzling smile. "Matter of fact, I *likes* it . . . yeah . . . Bump . . . that's me." Mrs. Higgins happily crumpled the note card and let it fall into her seemingly bottomless pocket. For the remainder of his brief life, the boy completely disassociated himself from the name born out of slavery, and Eurastus Cassius Thompson thereafter answered only to "Bump."

When John saw Bump's face light up with that infectious smile, he gravitated closer, as if mesmerized, and his fears of both the boy and the cell completely evaporated. In the magic of the moment, Mrs. Higgins had forgotten about John, so when she backed into him, she was startled. Then she recalled her purpose and quickly recovered. "Bump, this is Johnny Jumpup . . . J.J. for short. He helped me with your breakfast tray."

"You cook this food?" Bump asked incredulously.

"Well, no," John stammered. "I just sorta . . . well, you know . . . not exactly *cooked* it, just sorta piled it up on the tray."

"It *good!*" Bump enthused through a mouthful of scrambled eggs.

John's heart immediately opened to the older boy. Gone was the menacing demeanor of the past six hours, and in its place surfaced the most likable person John had ever known.

Mrs. Higgins watched Bump wolf his food with enormous satisfaction. Fearful that he might run out of food before he ran out of appetite, she turned to John in feigned alarm. "J.J.!" she exclaimed, "I believe we forgot the toast."

"I'll get it," he cried excitedly, and he bolted from the cell, descending the stairs three at a time. When he reached the bottom and turned toward the kitchen, he collided with Bud Griggs.

"Whoa, outlaw," Bud laughed as he reached to keep John from falling. "How's Bump this morning?"

John yelled, "GREAT!" and maneuvered past Bud to continue his run. Then he pulled himself up and turned questioningly toward Griggs. John had witnessed Bump's private "christening" only moments earlier.

"How did you know . . . ?" Then, as if accepting the futility of questioning the grapevine, he mumbled, "Oh, shit. Never mind."

Griggs laughed at John's obvious distress and turned to flash a victory sign to the grinning Mickey Maloney, who had followed John and Mrs. Higgins to the cell, and who, at seven years of age, had already learned the value of instant communications along the inmate network.

Griggs fully expected the new prisoner to be easier to deal with after one of Mrs. Higgins' famous breakfasts, but he was not prepared for the change that had taken place. Only several hours earlier, the boy had resembled a night creature that had been bloodied, beaten, and caged, but not subdued. He remembered the fierce eyes, snarling lips, bared teeth, and tensely muscled body coiled fearsomely in the darkened corner of the cell. What he found that morning, though, was a brightly smiling fourteen-year-old, laughing with John and applauding the younger boy's harmonica renditions with gleeful foot-stomping appreciation.

He suddenly felt silly about talking to the boy behind the protection of steel bars, so he suggested, "Why don't we go downstairs?" Then, as if to mitigate the harshness of the security that had been imposed, he added, "John knows where the office is. I'll be down in a few minutes."

The story that Bump related to Griggs that morning was a

familiar one to the juvenile probation officer. Bump had never known his father, and his mother had been an alcoholic for as long as the boy could recall. His oldest brother had been in the penitentiary for so long that Bump barely remembered him, but it was a different story with Lennie, who had been committed to the Boys' Industrial School two years earlier. Lennie had learned to write there, and his letters described a happy existence of three meals a day, very little classroom schooling, and a great deal of time for sports of every description. To Bump, a fourteen-year-old, high-spirited boy who was being forced into the stewardship of his three younger brothers and sisters, his older brother's life behind bars seemed idyllic.

About a week earlier, Bump's mother had left home and never returned. There was no food in the house, and the younger children cried incessantly. One of their neighbors, Mrs. Miller, gave them some food, but no one in the black neighborhood would consider reporting the situation to the authorities. Finally, Bump accepted the only alternative open to him, and he left the three youngsters on Mrs. Miller's front porch and walked across town searching for a crime to commit.

"Me and Lennie can be together again," he explained. "Them babies—they weren't no *real* kin nohow. At least Lennie and me, we had the same papa. Besides, Mrs. Miller can take care of 'em better'n me. All the kids on the block goes to Mrs. Miller for help when they's in trouble. She like ev'ybody's mama."

Del Howard edged quietly into the office with the informality that came with Saturday morning, and when Bump saw the black man, he looked at Griggs suspiciously. "What *he* doin' heah? He goin' take me back? I don' wanna go back. I wants to go where *Lennie* is."

"No," Griggs said, "Mr. Howard is not going to take you back. Nobody's going to make you go back there if we can't find your mother, but we'll have to try to find your brother and sisters and make sure they're all right."

"I tole you," the boy said with annoyance, "Mama Miller done took *care* of them."

Griggs then left the office and directed Mrs. Higgins to start the intake process and get Bump settled into the dormitory as quickly as possible. He and Del Howard then retreated to the deserted kitchen to discuss their next steps.

"Social welfare is going to have to check into that family situation," Griggs said, "but we ought to try to find those kids as soon as we can." Griggs had no illusions of finding them, because he understood that the blacks in Shanty Town, as the black area was called, resisted interference from the outside community. He also knew that the black neighborhood was dotted with certain older women who held the subculture together—women who cared for runaways, found homes for abandoned children, and harbored fugitives from the white man's police. Mrs. Miller was apparently one of those women who made up the latent power base of the black community, and if she was as effective as others Griggs had known, the younger Thompson children had already been parceled out beyond the reach of outside authorities.

Howard was obviously uncomfortable. His own family had settled into an integrated lower-class neighborhood, and he was raised with Italians, Poles, and Mexicans, never relating to the residents of Shanty Town. His parents, hard working and adept at the black-white game, were accepted by the whites as "good people," and their instincts compelled them to patronize the establishment so that their own children might survive and prosper within the white ethic.

Their values were uncomplicated. They simply followed the rules and gratefully accepted their rewards. They thought of themselves as "colored," and rejected the lawlessness of the "no-'count niggers" from across the tracks as rigidly as any redneck in the county.

But Del Howard emerged from adolescence in a period of expanding social awareness. He had been educated in integrated schools, attended the state university, and succeeded in professional athletics, but he was beginning to realize that all of his accomplishments had been earned within the white man's milieu, and often for the white man's gratification.

The year was 1964, and now he was part of the entrenched establishment, yet inexorably drawn by guilt toward that part of his heritage he had been taught to disclaim. As a result, he was emotionally attuned to neither culture, and he was increasingly torn between enforcing the laws of the majority and supporting the struggle of his minority brothers who had come, in turn, to disown his kind.

When Del Howard ventured into Shanty Town in search of Mrs. Miller that day, he entered an alien and hostile world, and he felt unprotected, vulnerable, and ashamed. He inquired door to door, but the people were cold and uncommunicative. As a last resort, he wandered into a noisy pool hall to ask directions, but all activity came to a halt as every eye in the room seemed to focus angrily on him. He surveyed the belligerent faces one by one, fully prepared for battle. Then his eyes lighted on an incongruously smiling face from out of his past.

He stared intently, trying to remember. "Cornelius?" he asked tentatively. "Is that you, Dude?"

The man responded with a burst of throaty laughter and came forward with his arms outstretched, exclaiming to the onlookers, "Hey, he *remembers* . . . My man remembers . . . How 'bout that!" The two men embraced, imprisoning Del's cast between their bodies, and the noise level in the room erupted with the resumption of normal activities.

"My God, how many years has it been?" Del asked above the din, holding his friend at arm's length.

"Who knows? One year's the same as the other," he laughed, "but you ain't laid eyes on the old Dude since The Man busted me on the field that day. Then you went off up the yellow brick road, and I spent time bustin' rocks."

A smallish man with a mischievous glint approached the two and bowed with affected elegance, " 'Scuse my boldness . . . *Cornelius* . . . but is you *IN* the game, or is you out?"

Dude conjured a menacing tone and replied loudly, "Don't you lay that 'Cornelius' jive on me, my man, or I'll stuff that cue stick into your nigger mouth sideways."

The intruder danced away impishly, and Dude led Del Howard to the bar, calling for two beers. "I heard you was in the neighborhood, man, and I know what you want."

"The Thompson kids?" Del asked.

Dude nodded his head.

"Mrs. Miller?" Del persisted.

"Thas right, man . . . the whole scam. Everything's cool, so you can forget it."

"But you don't understand, Dude. I gotta pick up those kids and make sure they're okay."

The friendliness vanished from Dude's face, and harsh reality returned. "You don't *PICK UP* no one down here. You unnerstand?" Then he drained his glass in a single motion and slammed it to the bar to punctuate the finality of his statement. He narrowed his eyes and said ominously, "We take care of our own."

"I understand . . . and I won't interfere," Del said. "But I also want to learn, if it's not too late for me."

Dude's expression softened as he examined the troubled face of his boyhood friend. He understood what Howard was asking for. "Let's just say for now that Mamä Miller takes care of things like that. Them kids is okay, so forget it."

"That's good enough for me, Dude. Thanks."

Weekends in any detention home are generally depressing and lonely, and Sunday morning is the worst of all. The usual buzz of activity comes to a complete halt as probation officers, social workers, and policemen spend the day at home. It is usually a sad day for the children, for little is left to occupy their time except to contemplate their own sad lives and the bleak prospects that lie before them.

This Sunday was different. Throughout the week, the officers who had struggled to remove the Clawson children from the cornfield returned to see them on any pretense.

That first morning after bringing them in, Chenoweth returned out of genuine concern for the children, but the others were motivated primarily by morbid curiosity. They soon discovered, however, that the wild animals they had dragged into captivity were warm and courageous children, and their admiration for them grew as the personal relationships developed.

Karen started it when she inadvertently bumped into Chenoweth's heavily bandaged hand. Caught unaware, Chins recoiled with the shock of the pain, and Deputies Hocker and Abernathy laughingly pleaded with Karen to show mercy. Karen was frightened at first, thinking she had done something bad, but it soon turned into a game between the children and the deputies, and the resulting laughter and giggling became a way for all of them to relate. Even little Charlie had fat Abernathy hopping around on one leg on the pretext of protecting his injured shin in the broadest comedy spectacle of all.

Mrs. Higgins was laughing to herself about the antics of the deputies and the children when her first cup of Sunday morning coffee was interrupted by the surreptitious appearance of Chenoweth and Hocker attempting to sneak six dozen hot doughnuts through the back door of the detention home. Chins was surprised to find her in the kitchen so early in the morning and seemed embarrassed to be caught in his good deed.

Mrs. Higgins was well aware of his wish to take the Clawson children into his life as their foster parent, so when Chins attempted to stammer an apology for disrupting the Sunday morning menu with seventy-two doughnuts, she said, "Relax. I know how you feel. It *has* been fun watching those kids blossom out, hasn't it?"

The doughnuts never reached the dining room table. The children soon flocked around, and there were twenty pairs of hands reaching for them before the boxes could be opened by the laughing deputies.

As she watched the Clawson children vying and giggling

with the others, Mrs. Higgins was intrigued by the transition that had taken place in so short a time. Only six days earlier, they had been hunted as wild animals, and for two days after that, they behaved like recluses in the detention home. She tried to isolate the reason for the transition, and she decided it had begun the moment Griggs assured Patty that they would not be separated.

Irrespective of the reason, it was a beautiful thing to observe.

Deputy Hocker extracted himself from the maelstrom surrounding Chenoweth and his doughnuts and sidestepped his way toward Higgins and her coffeepot. Laughing at the spectacle of the huge man clenching an unlit cigar between his teeth, trying to hold the last box of doughnuts above the grasping hands of the children, Hocker, the usually quiet analyst, began to interpret the dynamics of the scene.

"It's interesting how kids react to mob psychology," he said. "Sometimes they revert to their basic values, and sometimes they assimilate the values of the group." It sounded a little deep for Mrs. Higgins, so she did not encourage him to continue. "For instance, look how Vito and Esther look out for themselves. Whatever they can't grab from Chins, they take from the smaller kids. To them, it's like a deadly serious game; they're not having a bit of fun, are they?"

Mrs. Higgins looked at the two older children and saw that he was correct. "What does that mean to you, professor?"

"I don't know," Hocker replied. "By way of contrast, though, look at the Clawson children. Patty takes turns holding Charlie and Karen so they can reach the doughnuts. She's getting a big kick out of the whole thing, and I doubt she's even gotten one for herself yet. Sue Anne's managing real well for herself, and John and that new kid . . . Bump . . . are helping each other."

Hocker sipped his coffee thoughtfully and murmured, "Interesting. I'm not sure what it means, but I think those Clawson kids are psychologically well put together."

Then Hocker sneaked a sidelong glance at the matron.

"You know, Higgins, those five kids support one another just right. I'll just bet you they don't even *need* a father and a mother. I think they would do real well living with a single father, don't you?"

Mrs. Higgins answered his question with a laugh. "You guys have been pimping for Chins all week long. You can save your breath, because I don't have squat to say on where they will be placed."

"I didn't think I was so obvious," he chuckled. "Maybe you're just getting smarter."

"Either way," she said, "Chins gets my vote."

After the game, Patty was out of breath and flushed with excitement. She retreated to the front porch to fix Karen's hair while Charlie played in the sand with his dump truck. Sue Anne came bounding out of the house with three boys and ran with them to the basketball court. Patty stopped looking for John when she heard the harmonica music coming from the living room. Patty was still concerned about her brother, so she let her mind free-associate around him while she teased icing from Karen's hair.

John had spent his Saturday trying to teach Bump to play the harmonica, but the older boy was more interested in hearing John play, so they searched for a complementary instrument for Bump. He tried blowing into empty bottles, rattling spoons, and humming through a comb wrapped in tissue paper, but nothing worked quite like beating out the rhythm with his hands. Once the decision was made, they walked from room to room testing the resonance of the walls, the floors, and the large metal pots. When they finally tried the living room coffee table, they knew they were ready to form a band.

They spent the entire morning perfecting three numbers. When it became apparent that they might reach the level of tolerability, Mrs. Higgins formulated a plan. "Listen up," she said at lunch. "We used to have amateur night around here on the first Sunday of the month. How 'bout if John and Bump play for us tonight?"

"This ain't the first Sunday," Vito grumbled.

"Right," Mrs. Higgins agreed, "but if we wait that long, those two might not be amateurs any more. "

The children laughed, and Bump beamed and squirmed excitedly, but John flushed with embarrassment. He did not care about playing around the others as part of the background noise, but the prospect of performing for an assembled group terrified him. Bump enthusiastically jabbed him with his elbows, but John shook his head vigorously.

Vito Falcone weighed the idea as a potential threat to his leadership, and he was about to reject the suggestion instinctively, until he took note of John's reluctance. Instead, he seized the opportunity to exert his supremacy. "They'll *do it*," he announced. "Not too long, though, just till 'Gunsmoke' comes on."

"What'll we *do*?" John pleaded. "We don't know enough songs or nothing," he whined as his mind went blank.

"I'll fix up a place for you to practice," Vito announced imperiously. "You guys," he barked to two of the other boys, "clean up your dishes and carry that coffee table upstairs."

"Good idea," Mrs. Higgins concurred. "They can practice in private."

Vito beamed as if the idea had been his all along. "Yeah, that's what I figured."

John was miserable, and the expression on his face reflected it. He had been taught to play the harmonica by the foster father to whom he had been assigned while Sue Anne was in the hospital. Mr. Dean had been an older man with a fondness for country music, so John's initial repertoire had been limited to "Streets of Laredo," "Wabash Cannonball," and "Big Rock Candy Mountain." The first song John had learned on his own quickly became his favorite, but he doubted that the other children would be thrilled with "Edelweiss" for long. To add to his consternation, John had mastered his craft during that blissful period when folk music briefly prevailed over rock 'n' roll, and the radio stations filled his mind with the likes of "Blowing in the Wind,"

"Green Green," and "If I Had a Hammer." But this was 1964, and the Beatles had successfully usurped the lilting music of the folk movement with their frenetic and cacophonous "Liverpool sound," and the disc jockeys now plugged such strange titles as "Twist and Shout," "A Hard Day's Night," and "I Want to Hold Your Hand," none of which seemed within his musical range.

As he walked dejectedly toward his forced rehearsal, Chins reached for his shoulder. "Why so sad, pal?"

John shrugged and moaned, ". . . I just don't know the songs."

"Oh, come on," Chins teased. "I hear you playing all the time. And when you were out there in the cornfield, you and your harmonica scared the britches off old Mrs. Wilson every night. What'ya mean you don't know any songs?"

"Yeah, but those are *old* songs," the boy responded dejectedly. "I never tried any rock 'n' roll and stuff like that."

"Thank the Lord," Chins laughed encouragingly. "Now I *know* I'm coming to hear you." Chins saw that he had done nothing to bolster the boy's confidence, so he suggested, "Look, you play the 'Edelweiss' real good. You can start the show and end it with that one, and just plug in a few others in between. It'll be great!"

John slumped dejectedly in the abandoned dormitory when Bump burst into the room humming a lively popular tune to accompany his own version of a go-go dance. "Cheer up, man. There's lots of songs to play." Bump then switched on Mrs. Higgins' radio and scanned the dial for a music station. The discordant sounds were pushing John deeper into his funk when a disk jockey introduced "the runaway favorite of 1964"—"Hello, Dolly." Bump whipped out his handkerchief to imitate Louis Armstrong's style and swayed with the music as he mimed the words.

The melody sparked a familiar chord in John's memory. "Hey," he shouted, sitting up on his bed. "I *know* that one." And indeed he did, because it had been one of Mr. Dean's favorites, except he had taught the melody to John as the "Sunflower Song." The boy snatched for his harmonica and accompanied Satchmo's rendition flawlessly. At the conclusion, Bump whooped with pleasure, and the faint smile on John's lips suggested there might be some hope.

Vito Falcone assumed the duties of master of ceremonies without being asked. Standing in front of the closed living room doors, he turned to his audience in the dining room and intoned like a circus announcer, "LAAADEEEZ AND GENTULMENN . . ." Then, reverting to his own frame of reference, he continued, "Amateur night will *now come to order.*"

"Should we *all rise?*" Esther giggled impertinently.

Vito had prepared an elegant introduction designed to underscore his own primacy, but when stage fright blanked the words from his mind, he said meekly, "Let's get this thing started."

The pocket doors slid open magically to reveal the two musicians. Mrs. Higgins and Chins erupted in loud applause to put them at ease, and most of the children followed their example, but Patty and Sue Anne were too nervous to move. Bump acknowledged the applause with a huge smile and jumped up from behind his table to take a deep bow just as the flustered John rushed into the first song.

"Hey?" Bump complained as a look of surprise replaced the smile, and he quickly dropped to the floor to pick up the rhythm on the table. The audience laughed, and John's "Edelweiss" almost defied recognition as Bump struggled to catch up with him. Several bars into his opening number, John swung tentatively into some of the old songs that had been revived among young people in 1963. The first one sounded only vaguely like "Red Sails in the Sunset," and Mrs. Higgins exchanged a worried glance with Chins as Patty covered her face in despair.

But then the lightness in John's stomach and legs began to dissipate, and the medley continued with stronger renditions of "Till Then" and "Deep Purple." His confidence grew by the time he reached the final song of the set, and he moved effortlessly into a lively rendition of "Hey, Good Lookin'," which they concluded with the spontaneous approval of their audience. Patty's face beamed with pride.

As soon as the applause settled, Bump came forward and announced, "Lak ah was *suppose* to say befoe, them wuz the 'golden oldies.' Now we goin' play some *folk* songs." He resumed his position on the floor and introduced the next set with a virtuoso coffee table solo. John joined in at what must have been precisely the right moment, if one were to judge from Bump's sudden smile, and the two launched into sensitive renditions of "If I Had a Hammer, " "I'm Just a Country Boy," "Blowing in the Wind," and the imported Australian favorite, "Tie Me Kangaroo Down, Sport," concluding both the medley and the program with a sweet and moving "Edelweiss." The transitions from one song to the next had been smooth and confident, and both boys glowed warmly as the children in the dining room jumped in applause and the adults shouted, "More! . . . More!"

But Vito realized that things had gotten out of hand, so he cut off the applause by marching to the television set and announcing, "Time for 'Gunsmoke.'"

One of the girls loudly complained, "No, it's not. It's too early. Besides, it's just another rerun."

She was right. As the sound level rose, the room was filled with groans because it was only the news—anathema to all children. This time, however, it was different. The announcer's voice was filled with so much emotion as he described the first registration of Negroes into the white elementary schools of Biloxi, Mississippi, that the children stood transfixed. The historic event had been accomplished without violence, and as the strains of "We Shall Overcome" emanated from the crowd of observers in Biloxi, Bump picked up the rhythm on the coffee table, at the rapid rate of sixteen beats to each bar and the rat-a-tat-tat from the living room moved several of the children to join in the song. Then John picked up the sad melody on the harmonica as some sang the words and others stood in mute respect.

Tears came to the eyes of Patty, Chins, and Mrs. Higgins as "We Shall Overcome" assumed a new meaning for each of the incarcerated children.

When the song ended, there was no applause. Everyone seemed drained of emotion. Finally, Mrs. Higgins cleared her throat and called for attention. "Every amateur night has to end with a prize," she said quietly, "and this one is no exception. I practically had to clean out the basement, but I finally found something that I think is appropriate." Then she stooped to retrieve a set of bongo drums from behind her chair. "I make this presentation to Mr. Bump Thompson in the name of the county in the hope of saving my poor coffee table and keeping his fingerprints off the walls."

Bump's mouth fell open in surprise, and he stood rooted in place.

"C'mon, Bumper, this is yours," Mrs. Higgins urged.

A path opened for him as he shuffled forward in shock. Then the other children closed ranks behind him as he approached her. "I hope you enjoy it," she said, handing him the twin bongos.

Bump accepted the prize tenderly, handling the drums with profound love and awe. His fingertips gently traced the bright silver bands and caressed the taut drumheads. Bump was speechless. He turned wordlessly and retraced his steps toward John without seeing the other children around him.

John's face was awash with tears as he moved forward and embraced his friend with a wrenching sob.

Bump remained in shock for several hours, gingerly testing his drums for fear of breaking through the skins. When he finally came out of it, though, the speed of his hands flying back and forth across the drums was matched only by the pace of his chatter as he planned next Sunday's performance. Then, an hour before bedtime, Bump became thoughtful and uncommunicative once more, so John spent some time with his brother and sisters, reliving the successful performance.

John entered the darkened dormitory and slipped into his bunk as quietly as possible. He lay quietly for a moment then leaned toward the next bed and whispered, "Bump? You asleep?"

"Naw," came the hoarsely whispered reply. "Cain't sleep nohow."

John rolled out of bed and knelt on the floor. "This was a fun day, huh?"

"Yeah."

"Where did you put your bongos?"

"You jokin'? They rat *heah*," Bump said, lifting his covers to display the drums.

"Oh," John said, trying not to sound surprised. "Is there enough room in your bed?"

"If not, man, I gonna sleep on the floor." John giggled, and Bump continued, "No one never gave me nuthin' befoe. Ah likes this place." Then, after a moment of silence, Bump added, "J.J.? You de bestest fren' ah evah had."

"Me, too, Bump . . . Good night."

The only thing on Bud Griggs' mind that Monday morning was to contact Nancy Sloan. Her boss, George Matthews, had sarcastically reassured Bud that she would be calling, but she had made no attempt to get in touch with him or to interview the Clawson children. He dialed her number and asked for her.

"I'm sorry, Mr. Griggs," her secretary said, "but Miss Sloan is in conference right now. May I have her return your call?"

"Please do," he said with annoyance, ". . . and remind her that the Clawson hearing is set for tomorrow."

Griggs slammed the phone down and was talking to himself angrily when Del Howard walked into the office. Griggs continued talking, except he spoke loudly enough for Del to hear. "She hasn't even taken the trouble to meet those kids. I don't like the smell of this at all."

"Fine, thank you," Del said. "And how was *your* weekend?"
"Shitty, if you must know."
"That's nice," Del responded with affected sweetness.
"Now, whose smell don't you like?"
"Goddam, you're thickheaded for a college boy. You
couldn't find your ass in a telephone booth with a flashlight
without my help."
"Yeah, well, you just keep your hands off my ass," Del
laughed.
"It's that goddam social welfare," Bud explained. "Nancy
Sloan is supposed to be the casework supervisor for the
Clawson kids, but she can't assign a caseworker until she in-
terviews the kids, and she hasn't taken the trouble to inter-
view the kids yet, and it's been a goddam week." Then, in a
voice loud enough to carry to the outer office, he shouted,
"And where in hell's my goddam coffee?"
The unseen secretary responded in a pleasant and
unruffled tone, "In the goddam coffee pot, down the goddam hall, where it will goddam stay until you go get it."
"That's just what I need on a Monday morning—more
shit!" Bud complained.
"Yeah, it's too bad we can't all be like you."
"As soon as you're finished with the Amos 'n' Andy routine, we can make believe this is an office and you can ask me
how come I had to work all day yesterday while my assistant
enjoyed himself at the ball game."
"In the first place," Del responded, "it was too hot to enjoy
myself at the game, and in the second place, I know why you
worked all day yesterday."
Bud's mind flashed ahead to prepare the next quip, but
Del turned serious. "You worked all day yesterday because
you're worried about those kids, and you haven't been able to
think of anything else for a week."
Griggs stopped his pacing and flopped down in a chair.
"You're right, Del. We've *gotta* keep those kids together, and
I'm not getting any cooperation from social welfare. They're

putting the squeeze on me. Maybe I ought to try to find them a home myself."

Just as he seemed ready to accept defeat, Griggs lurched from the chair and resumed his pacing, gesturing rapidly with his hands as he spoke. "It's that pissant Matthews. He assigned that dumb broad to the case just to screw things up. She doesn't know her ass from third base."

"If you say that often enough, you'll start believing it," Howard said. "You used to say that Nancy Sloan was the brightest supervisor up there."

"Yeah, but that's because Matthews hates her guts, so I figured she must not be all bad. I guess I'm worried because she's too new. She's bright, all right, but she doesn't know her way around yet. Finding the right foster parents will be tough enough, but locating parents with a house big enough for five kids is gonna be a miracle. It's gonna take someone with the skills of a cat burglar and the instincts of a con man."

"Maybe you're . . . maybe you ought to find the home yourself."

"Very funny. I don't know what put you in such a good mood this morning, but as long as you are so bright and alert, maybe you ought to take over the follow-up on Bump Thompson."

"Anything special?" Del asked.

Griggs nodded. "I talked to that young cop last night. What's his name?" Griggs asked himself as he flipped open a file. "Crimmins . . . Doug Crimmins. The one Bump pulled the knife on."

"The kid never flipped the blade, did he?"

"No. I tried to explain to Crimmins that Bump just wanted to go to jail to be with his brother, but it didn't wash. I told him the kid wouldn't have opened the knife to use it, but he wasn't listening."

"What did he say?"

"He figures he would have been cut if he hadn't clobbered the kid in time."

"What do you want me to do?" Del asked.

"Just talk to him and see if he'll drop the deadly weapons charge . . . Maybe even soften up his report a little." Del turned to leave, and Griggs said, "Let me know if you have any problems, and I'll try to get to the judge."

Howard stopped at the door and said, "You got company."

"Who?"

"Me," a deep voice responded as Chins Abernathy, dressed in civilian clothes, appeared in the doorway and walked to a chair without waiting to be invited.

"Chins, I've known you for ten years," Griggs said, "and in all that time I've never seen you out of uniform or without one of those rotten cigars stuck in your face. Now look at you. You look downright naked."

The huge man shifted uncomfortably in the chair and searched through his bulging pockets for a cigar. He came out with two, one of which was mangled and shredded from many hours of chomping. He returned the fresh cigar to his breast pocket and jammed the old one between his teeth. "That better?" he asked.

Griggs noted the ill-fitting, coffee-stained sports jacket, the baggy pants, and the shirt collar that pointed north, and he laughed, "Not hardly, you big slob."

Chins puckered his mouth in mock disgust. "Well, that's too bad," he said, "'cause this is as good as it's gonna get. These are my *courting* clothes."

"Your *what*?" Griggs asked incredulously.

"You heard me," Chins said. "I got to thinking about what you said the other day . . . You know . . . about me needing to be married before I could take the Clawson kids in with me."

"I never said any such thing," Griggs protested indignantly. "You must have had a hot doughnut stuck in your ear."

"Well, you didn't say that *exactly*," Chins agreed, "but you did say that social welfare would never place kids in a foster home with only one parent. Right?"

"Well, yes," Griggs admitted grudgingly, "I might have said something like that. So what?"

"Well, I've been dating Rosie Cunningham . . . Do you know Rosie? Out at the diner?"

Griggs nodded.

"Anyway, I've been dating Rosie since right after her husband died."

"Her third husband, right?"

"Her fourth," Chins answered meekly. "Anyway, we get along real good, and we've been thinking about getting married for six months now."

"Chins," Griggs interrupted, "that woman has already been through four husbands and killed off three of them."

"Two."

"All right, two then. Do you seriously want to marry her just to make a home for the Clawsons?"

"No, no," Chins protested loudly. "That's only *part* of it. Like I said, we've been planning to do it for a long time now. We get along real good. This might speed it up a little, that's all."

"You're crazy, do you know that? For one thing, we need to find a home right now! Like this week. Even if you and Rosie got married *today*, it would still take two months to qualify you as foster parents."

"It would?" Chins asked in chagrin.

"Of course it would," Griggs responded emphatically. "They don't parcel kids out like stray dogs. It takes time." Chins looked as though he had been punched in the stomach, and Bud knew he should have been more diplomatic. "Look," he said gently, "this doesn't need to change any plans you and Rosie might have made, does it?"

"Rosie?" Chins blurted, "Who the hell needs Rosie?" Hauling himself from the chair, he looked down at Griggs and said, "Actually, she wasn't too crazy about the idea, either. That's how I got this coffee stain on my jacket."

* * *

Griggs spent the rest of the morning completing the Clawsons' predisposition report, and at noon, he had a sandwich brought in rather than take a chance on missing Nancy Sloan's call. He was obsessed about the seeming indifference of the people at social welfare, and he grew angrier as the hours passed. By three o'clock, he was completely exasperated, and he shouted to his secretary, "Tina, get her on the goddam phone."

"Her who?"

"Nancy Sloan, goddammit."

Tina's smiling face appeared in the doorway. "I'll do better than that. I'll have her in your office—live—in three seconds."

"What? . . . Is she out there?"

Tina nodded, pleased with herself, and Griggs came out from behind his desk shouting, "About goddam time!"

Then he heard Nancy's laugh. "Maybe I ought to toss a piece of raw meat in on the floor to calm him down."

"Dammit, Sloan, where have you been? You were supposed to return my call five hours ago."

"Sorry, Bud. I didn't know it was urgent." The glint of humor in her eyes indicated she was enjoying Griggs' outrage. She was more comfortable dealing with his acting-out behavior than she was coping with George Matthews' quiet disapproval and contempt. Matthews disliked her because she had been appointed to his department over his objections, and he was determined to vindicate his judgment by overloading her and her social workers with the toughest cases that came in.

"Really, Bud, I'm sorry. I would have returned your call, but we have had one emergency after another. I am supervising three caseworkers, and between us we have a total of forty-two foster placements. This morning alone, we've had demands to remove eight foster children immediately. And we had two runaways over the weekend."

Griggs forgot his anger. "So you're saying that ten out of

forty-two of your foster children are being kicked out of their homes today?"

Nancy nodded her head. "Two of them were placed only last week. Most of the others have been in a dozen homes in the past two years."

"Can you find new placements for all of them?"

"I think so," Nancy responded. "All except the two runners. They are in custody right now, but we'll have to put them in the detention home until they cool off."

"I don't know where in the hell you'd put them," Griggs said. "They're completely full right now."

"I know, but we're getting ready to move two of the boys. Vito Falcone has been assigned to the Industrial School, and the Thompson boy will go to the Reception and Diagnostic Center as soon as possible."

"Bump?" Griggs asked. "I'd like to hold off on him. He's got this crazy idea that he wants to go to the Industrial School to be with his older brother, but that's not exactly a boarding school, is it? I mean, it's not a hotel where people can check in and out at will . . ."

Nancy shook her head. "But he's not exactly a paying guest, either. He earned his ticket when he pulled that knife on the arresting officer."

"I know all about that. Del is trying to straighten that up right now. I sent him out to talk Crimmins into giving him a break."

"Good luck," Nancy said sarcastically. "I talked with Officer Crimmins this morning, and there was no doubt in his mind. He wants the boy put away."

"Well, you can do me a big favor by holding off for a couple of days. I'm sure we can work it out. And we'll make room for the others, too." Bud waited for her reaction as he walked toward his desk. Nancy said nothing, so he assumed the matter was settled. "Listen," he said, "I called you about the Clawson hearing. It's set for tomorrow, and no social worker has interviewed them yet. Who's going on the case?"

"I am."

"You? I was hoping . . . I mean I thought maybe Vera . . . or Ted . . . you know, one of the old-timers might have more luck. You know, more contacts."

"You're absolutely right," Nancy agreed. "But our dear friend, and my beloved boss, ordered me to take this one myself. He heard you were personally interested in this case, so he probably figured I could screw it up worse than anyone."

Griggs cursed George Matthews mentally, but he tried to keep his disappointment from showing. "What about tomorrow?"

"I can't possibly be ready for the hearing, Bud. I have to ask for a week's postponement."

"Impossible," he declared with finality, shaking his head. "The kids are all primed, we're all set, and besides, the judge would NEVER stand for it . . . NEVER."

"I just came from Judge Harrington's office," she said sweetly, "and he thought it was a great idea."

Griggs was about to erupt with indignation over the gall of the woman who presumed to go over his head. The judge would never have approved a postponement if Griggs had spoken to him first. Then he read her laughing eyes, and he knew that Nancy was well aware of that fact. She made up her mind to have the case postponed, and she knew exactly how to neutralize Griggs to get what she wanted. Stripped of his defenses, and left with no alternatives, he said, "Good idea. We can use the extra week."

Nancy, who relished beating Griggs at his own game of tactics, made her next move in sugar-coated tones. "That's really nice, Bud. I'm *so* glad you approve."

Griggs reappraised her on the spot and grinned, "I think you'll do fine."

Patty was relieved to hear about the postponement. She and her family had adjusted comfortably into the routine of the detention home, and the uncertainty of the changes that would take place when they moved out were unsettling to her.

Meanwhile, life inside the fence went on as usual. The presence of the two younger children—Karen and Charlie—at first surprised the new arrivals, but even the hardest among them, especially the girls, soon warmed to them and "adopted" the youngsters as their own brother and sister. Mrs. Higgins noted with pleasure that Karen and Charlie served as transitional identifiers for new girls, who often refused to communicate with anyone else for the first few days. And she was also pleased that Patty was beginning to relax enough to permit the other girls to assume some of the custodial responsibilities of the youngsters. Although Patty always observed from the fringe, she allowed the other girls to help with the bathing, toothbrushing, and dressing chores.

As the week progressed, John and Bump perfected their musical routines. They were convinced that Sunday night's performance would be the best ever offered at the detention home.

Early in the week, seven-year-old Mickey Maloney was taken to his new foster home by his caseworker. Before he left, Vito Falcone took him aside for some fatherly advice. "Just do what they say, and don't give them no shit," he said, "and maybe they'll keep you. And call them 'mom' and 'dad.' They like that stuff."

Mickey was bubbling over with excitement, and he was determined to please his new parents in every way possible, but three days later, he was back. "They wanted me so's I could play with their kid," he said tearfully. "But the kid wouldn't share or nothing, so they told me I had to leave."

Vito was taken out the following day, but there were no illusions about his coming back. He was sent to the children's prison, which was euphemistically known as the "Industrial School." One of Vito's lieutenants, Checkmate Hawkins, ascended to the leadership, so there was no change in unwritten regulations among the young inmates.

Friday morning found John and Bump sitting back to back in the bright sunshine. Both boys loved the outdoors, and earlier in the week, John had asked Bump why he would want to be locked away in the Industrial School. "Shoot," Bump reasoned, "dey's got sunshine dere, too. It just got stripes on it. 'Sides, y'all's fambly's together. All's ah got's Lennie, and he dere."

By Friday morning, however, Bump's attitude began to change. He and John had grown closer and closer, and they enthused about the prospects of forming their own band. They shared their plans, their fantasies, and their laughter, and they shared a common dream that Bump might somehow be placed with the Clawsons in the same foster home. To Bump, the once-longed-for confinement in the Industrial School came to symbolize the threat of separation from the only friend he had ever known.

That afternoon, they took Bump to prison.

The task of removing children from the detention home usually fell to social workers, but two angry policemen showed up to transport Bump that Friday. Griggs and Howard had spent the entire week trying to convince Officer Crimmins to drop the charges of assault with a deadly weapon, and they were beginning to make progress with him. Then, on Thursday, a highway patrolman stopped a car full of teenagers for a routine speeding violation, and the patrolman was shot dead as he approached the car.

Bump was no longer seen as just a misguided child. He was suddenly a potential cop-killer, and the relatively light security of the detention home was deemed inadequate. In a highly charged atmosphere of passionate retribution, the charges against the boy were upgraded to include felonious assault and attempted murder of a law enforcement officer. Judge Harrington's Juvenile Court no longer had jurisdiction in the case, and the Criminal Division of the District Court ordered Bump's removal to the County jail.

Neither Griggs nor Howard had been forewarned about the direction the case had taken, so neither was present when the boy was removed from the detention home. Mrs. Higgins called Griggs as soon as the policemen arrived, but in the few minutes it took the two men to rush to the home, Bump was already gone. He was permitted no time to pack his personal belongings, and not a moment to say good-bye to his friend.

The whole thing happened with such speed and efficiency that neither boy had a chance to do anything but be terrified. Griggs and Howard found John trembling and ashen, sitting on Bump's bed, staring into space. When Griggs touched his shoulder, the boy collapsed into uncontrollable sobbing.

Mrs. Higgins took charge of packing Bump's pitifully few belongings, and Del Howard was given the job of delivering them. An hour later, Del returned to the home with only the bongo drums. "They won't let him have this," he mumbled disconsolately, dropping it on a kitchen chair.

Patty had tried to comfort John as he slowly brought himself under control. She searched his face carefully for the signs of extreme stress she had detected at the beginning and end of their cornfield experience. She feared he might crack then, and now her fear returned. She wished he would have continued to cry and get it all out. Instead, he sat transfixed in the kitchen, the color drained from his blank face. He stared at the small twin drums and picked them up while the images of his friend flashed through his mind. He traced the tips of his fingers along the silver bands as Bump had done. He was torn between destroying the drums with his bare hands or carrying them up to the dormitory. Instead, he placed the drums on the table and walked out of the room.

It was almost dark by the time Griggs finished his verbal report to Judge Harrington. Nancy Sloan and Del Howard were also present. The judge was incensed. He called the county attorney and the criminal court judge who had collaborated on preparing and signing the order for Bump's removal, and their stories were the same—a highway patrolman had been murdered, leaving behind two children and a wife who was seven months' pregnant. The murderer was a sixteen-year-old boy who shot down the officer for no reason and without warning, and the community was outraged about the coddling of juvenile offenders, so people like Bump Thompson would be made to understand the consequences of their crimes. Furthermore, if they were old enough to use weapons, they were old enough to be treated like adults and not like children.

The judge was exhausted. He said, "Miss Sloan, I asked you to be here because, at this moment, you are the only one among us who will have access to young Thompson. For the present, he is irretrievably outside the reach of anyone from the Juvenile Court. Nonetheless, I want you to see the boy and give him a message from me."

Then he looked at Griggs and said, "Bud, I want you to deliver the same message to the Clawson boy."

The judge leaned back and shifted his gaze from one to the other. "I want you to tell those boys that I will do everything humanly possible to correct this travesty. I will take this matter to the attorney general, and if necessary directly to Governor Parkhurst." Then the weary judge leaned forward and sighed, "Above all, tell them both not to lose hope."

The Saturday morning ritual for Bud and Del was to have coffee in the informal atmosphere of the truck stop diner. When Griggs arrived, he found Del reading the sports pages and grumbling over the baseball situation. "Can you believe those Cardinals?" he asked in disgust. "Nine games in back of the Phillies!"

"Big deal," Griggs grumbled.

"Well, it is to me," Howard protested. "This will be the first autumn I won't be banging around in a football uniform, and I was promised World Series tickets by the league office. But I'll be damned if I'm gonna go all the way to Philadelphia or Baltimore just for a baseball game."

"Maybe it's not too late for the Cardinals," Griggs offered.

"You kidding?" Howard responded disgustedly. "This is

already September sixth and they're nine games out. Impossible!"

"Don't get pissed off at me, dummy. I've done *my* part. I taught Bob Gibson how to pitch, and Ken Boyer and Tim McCarver everything they know about hitting. Now they're on their own," Griggs said brushing the palms of his hands together to illustrate his point.

"Now what else shall we talk about?" Griggs asked, leaning forward. "Politics? . . . Let's see . . . Bobby Kennedy is gonna run for the Senate. How about world affairs? I see where the Turks are raising hell with the Greeks again. Isn't that interesting?"

"How about chemical warfare," Howard injected. "I see you got some new stains on your shirt."

"Oh, damn," Griggs responded, looking down at his chest. "I must have grabbed one of Chins' shirts by mistake." Then he looked up and said, ". . . Speaking of which . . ."

"I know, I know, we've got work to do."

Griggs agreed but said, "Nancy Sloan is going to spend the morning with the Clawson kids, so let's go to the gym."

Nancy Sloan lost no time getting acquainted with the children. As usual, Patty took the lead but had a difficult time containing Sue Anne. John was still despondent over Bump's departure, and his bloodshot eyes testified to a sleepless and tearful night. Nancy gave a brief description of her role in the case, which was primarily to find them foster parents, then to work with them after they left the detention home.

Patty asked questions about the court hearing, and Nancy answered in the same way Bud Griggs had. She described Judge Harrington as a kind man who liked children and wanted them to have happy lives. She explained that Judge Harrington would have to declare them "wards of the court" in order to make it legally possible for the social workers to place them in foster care.

Sue Anne wanted Nancy to be sure to find a home with a basketball goal, and she asked that there be lots of other children in the neighborhood. Nancy laughed but jotted down her requests. John refused to be drawn out on his likes and dislikes and restricted his responses to head signals and shoulder shrugs.

The clothes worn by the children were clean but shoddy hand-me-downs from Mrs. Higgins' storehouse of donated and discarded garments. County regulations provided for the purchase of two complete sets of clothes for any child about to be placed into a foster home for the first time, so Nancy cheerfully suggested, "Why don't we go out this afternoon and buy you all some new clothes?"

"What do you mean?" Patty said suspiciously.

"There are some very nice department stores downtown, and we can pick out some nice clothes for all of you. You want to look nice for the hearing, don't you?"

"You don't know our sizes," Patty said hesitantly.

"I don't have to know," Nancy assured her. "You can just try things on till you find something you like."

Patty brightened. "You mean, you'd take us with you."

"Of course."

"Downtown?"

"We'll leave right after lunch," Nancy said. "Maybe Mr. Griggs can take John to the men's shop, and the rest of us will go off on our own. Boys don't have much patience with that sort of thing, do they?"

The question was directed at John, but Patty responded, "I don't know, we never bought new clothes."

Nancy stared in disbelief and berated herself for her own insensitivity, but recovered quickly. "Then we're *all* in for an exciting afternoon," she enthused.

The group assembled as scheduled and departed the detention home in two cars. Patty was filled with a new exhilaration as they passed through the gate, and she gazed at the disappearing fence through the back window of the car with a growing sense of freedom and joy. For her, the prospect of shopping for new clothes was secondary to the relief of deliverance. Sue Anne squirmed on her seat with the pleasure of a new adventure, but, with her capacity for finding happiness anywhere, the awareness of being free did not seem to matter. Beth Carruthers, one of Nancy's social workers, sat in the front seat and provided a running commentary as they passed the city's landmarks.

Griggs drove the second car, and Del Howard joined John in the back seat. Both men tried unsuccessfully to raise the boy's spirits. "Judge Harrington told me to tell you that he would get it all straightened out," Bud assured John. "I wouldn't be surprised if Bump was back right after Labor Day."

"When's that? " John asked quietly.

"This is Saturday. Labor Day is Monday. I wouldn't be surprised if he was back on Tuesday . . . maybe he'll be there when you get back from the hearing."

"I doubt it."

"'Don't lose hope.' That's what the judge said. He even promised to talk to the governor."

Griggs tried to sound optimistic, but it was difficult, because he knew better than anyone else that it was virtually impossible to alter a child's course within the bureaucracy once he was swallowed by the system. His spirits sank even lower as he thought of Maria Guittirrez. Eight years earlier, in 1956, she had been living up in Omaha with her four children, ranging in age from five to twelve years old. Her husband had been injured in a construction accident, and they were trying to make ends meet on workmen's compensation. A social worker was called in to investigate the truancy of the oldest girl, and when she arrived at the Guittirrez house, she found the two youngest children playing on the curb, near the traffic, so she surmised that there was "inadequate supervision." When she entered the home, the arrival of a government official frightened the parents and moved them to reach out and embrace their children protectively. The social worker identified this instinctive reaction as evidence of ". . . unnatural physical and emotional relationships," and the four children were removed from the home without so much as a court order.

They tried to fight back in every way they could, but without the money to hire a lawyer and pay for court costs, they faced an uphill battle. By the time Manny Guittirrez died two years later, not one of the children had yet been returned. Maria held down two jobs and took in washing and ironing to save enough money to bring her children home.

Carmen, the oldest girl, was finally released in 1959, after more than three years of imprisonment in reform school, and young Manny was released four months later. They all dedicated themselves to working and saving their money, but the terrible part of it was that they were unable to locate the two youngest children. There seemed to be no official record of their existence.

In 1961, Carmen, who was seventeen years old, married a young brickmason, and the groom joined the crusade to find his wife's brother and sister. In 1962, the family located Theresa in a mental institution in Missouri, where she had been locked away for five years. The case gained national attention when it was learned that the doctors there had repeatedly certified Theresa as sane, but no one had any idea by that time about where to send her next or how she had ever come into the state in the first place.

Griggs met Maria Guittirrez for the first time in 1963. She made the three-hundred-mile trip from Omaha to follow up a report that an unidentified boy had been placed by the Juvenile Court three years earlier. She spoke of her five-year-old Antonio as though he had been snatched away from her the day before, when in fact it had happened seven years earlier, and her baby, wherever he was, was now approaching adolescence.

Maria Guittirrez never found her son. Griggs assumed that Antonio had been adopted out, and that the usual practice of sealing the court records served to cover his trail forever. The case was a living reminder to Griggs of the complexities of extricating a child caught up in the maze of our juvenile justice system, and he intuitively accepted the probability that none of them would ever see Bump Thompson again.

Griggs tried to shake his depression with another bland assurance: "Don't worry, tiger, Judge Harrington promised . . ."

"Yeah," John murmured dully, ". . . and my mom promised to take me to California."

The two men remained silent because there was no way to respond. John had obviously accepted the inevitability of losing his parents and his best friend. Perhaps it was appropriate for them to build from there. Del covered John's knee with his huge hand and said firmly, "Maybe you're right, pal. I don't necessarily think so, but maybe you are. You're the man in your family, and it's up to you to help your brother and sisters start a new life. Can you accept that responsibility?"

John fidgeted for a moment, recalling how it had fallen on *him* to clear the way into the cornfield that first night, and how *he* had torn up the cornstalks to make room for the others to sit and eat their cold hamburgers; he thought of the other ways in which they had depended on him . . . the daily jaunts to the garbage racks at the diner, unearthing the drinking cans, and climbing to the highest levels of the tree to survey the highway.

The ten-year-old boy sat up straight and responded simply, "Okay," closing the door on any further self-pity.

If John's enthusiasm began to grow with the purchase of his new clothes, it positively exploded with the presentation of his first three ice cream sodas. It was another first in his life, and the two men basked in the gratification of suggesting it. Griggs was particularly expansive. "This is Labor Day weekend. Do you know what folks do on Labor Day weekend?"

"What?" John asked.

"They go on picnics, that's what. How long has it been since you've been on an old-fashioned picnic?"

John juggled a chunk of ice cream on his tongue to keep

the cold away from his teeth and muttered, "Ain't never been on a picnic."

"That settles it," Griggs announced with a slam on the table. "We'll do it tomorrow!"

Del lounged in his chair with a vacuous grin until Griggs' stare made it clear that he was about to lose another Sunday to the cause. "Whoa," he demurred, "I gave away my baseball tickets so's I could watch the Packers on TV tomorrow."

"No problem," Griggs said confidently. "What time's the game?"

"One o'clock."

"Bring a radio."

"Aw, Bud," Del complained.

Griggs ignored him. "You get the cold drinks and cookies, and *I'll* get the fried chicken . . . just so you don't accuse me of getting ethnic with you."

Del laughed in resignation, and the matter was resolved.

The plan called for Bud to collect the children before driving over to pick up Del. They were waiting on the back porch for him, and all were dressed in their new blue jeans and cardigans. They rushed to the car to greet him, and when they lifted the backrest to climb into the back seat, Griggs suggested, "Some can sit up front."

It turned out that none of them had ever ridden in the front seat of a car before, so the decision was easy—they all sat in front. The ubiquitous Chins grinned widely as he helped them pile in. As soon as the four older children were in place, Chins passed Charlie through the open window to Patty, and he waved them off with a flourish.

Confusion was written all over Del's face when he surveyed the tangled mass of humanity on the front seat. No one moved to permit him to enter the two-door vehicle, so he placed both hands above the window on the driver's side, leaned over, and peered directly into Bud's face. "Am I supposed to get *in* this car, or *on* it?"

Bud grinned, "We must have decided you'd be more comfortable in back. Let me out, and you can climb in this way."

As they drove away, pedestrians stared at the spectacle of six people in the front seat and a lone passenger in the back, but it was a crazy day, and they were already having a good time.

The two men decided to have lunch in the city park and then introduce the children to the wonders of the local zoo. The kids chased everything from dogs to bumblebees during lunch, and their uninhibited joy was infectious. They devoured the chicken and practically inhaled the cookies. Griggs had packed a jar of peanut butter as an emergency backup, in case they ran out of food, but when the kids saw it, their unanimous response was "YUCK," recalling the three months they had survived exclusively on that particular staple. Del and Bud joined their laughter when John and Sue Anne animatedly related the story.

By three o'clock that afternoon, they were ready to tour the zoo. They started with the monkey house, then proceeded to the great cat house. The younger children seemed to thrill at every new discovery except the live snakes that slithered around their glass cages in search of food. Laughing at the expression on Karen's face, Del asked what she thought about the snakes. She said, "YUCK . . . reminds me of peanut butter."

Their day at the zoo ended, as promised, with a ride on the miniature railroad. There wasn't room for all of them on the train, so Patty volunteered to remain behind with Griggs and gave Dell the dubious honor of squeezing into the narrow seat and accompanying the others. There was no hint of reluctance on Karen's part to leave Patty, and she raced with the other children to the train as soon as it pulled into the station. Del lumbered behind with Charlie bouncing excitedly in his arms.

As Patty and Griggs stood on the platform waving goodbye to the others, a simple thing happened to him that was ultimately to change his life: Patty reached up and placed her hand in his. It was like a butterfly lighting on his sleeve—he was afraid to move a muscle for fear it might fly off. Neither of them said a word until the noisy group returned.

Patty remained silent on the trip home, and Griggs asked her what was wrong. She said, "Bud, everything was fun except seeing the animals in cages. They looked sad—like they wanted to be out, but there was no one to help them."

When Tuesday morning arrived, one of the young attendants from the detention home helped Chins to pack the children into the back seat of his patrol car for the ride to their hearing at the county courthouse. Mrs. Higgins had helped them to select their most attractive outfits for the event, and she promised to have milk and cookies for them when they returned. If she could have foreseen the events of the next two hours, she probably would never have let them go at all.

The waiting room outside the Juvenile Court was crowded with parents and children of every description. There were whites, blacks, Indians, and Mexicans; they wore white patent leather shoes, open sandals, and workboots; a few had the look of affluence, but most were obviously poor. They shared a common apprehension about what might take place when their turn came to appear in court.

Del Howard led the Clawson children to a bench immediately outside the courtroom. Charlie sat on Patricia's lap, and Karen was on her right, sitting with her legs drawn up under her. John and Sue Anne showed an animated interest in the people who were milling around the area. Chins paced nervously in the background like an expectant father.

Bud and Del had done such a thorough job of convincing the children that there was nothing to worry about—that this thing had to be done so that Nancy could begin to find them a new home—that they were very comfortable. In fact, they looked more like disinterested spectators who had wandered in off the street to observe this procession of troubled people.

Griggs walked out of the courtroom with the parents and child who were the principals involved in the second of his three cases for the day. He was explaining what had happened during the proceedings, and he was attempting to schedule an appointment with them and their probation officer.

As he walked by, Patty reached out to touch his leg. He turned and looked down at her, and she flashed a radiant smile. He noted again how pretty she really was. She had a new dress, and her hair was curled. He stared a moment, then said, "Boy, do you look pretty!"

Then he looked at the other kids, all of whom were scrubbed and wearing new clothes. "You *all* look pretty . . . Well, not you and Charlie," he said to John, "but you two look handsome." Charlie giggled and clapped his hands. The other children smiled and fidgeted in their seats, obviously pleased but unnerved by this unaccustomed attention and flattery.

Griggs then turned to conclude his conversation with the parents and child whom he had just led from the courtroom.

He walked them to the door and returned to the Clawson children trying to look cheerful. "Well, I guess it's our turn." He motioned toward the door. "Why don't you all come in, and I'll show you where to sit."

The courtroom was wood-paneled and had high ceilings. The spectators' section consisted of four rows of benches separated from the counsel tables by a mahogany railing. The judge was dressed in a dark suit, and he was seated on an elevated platform, behind a large desk.

Judge Harrington was busy writing his dispositions, not paying any attention to the people entering the courtroom.

Seated at the counsel table was the court-appointed guardian ad litem, whose job it was to represent the interests of all children brought before the Juvenile Court. A confusion of case folders was spread across the table in front of him, and he was leaning back tiredly, with his hands folded across his stomach. His only introduction to the Clawson case had been a two-minute summary that Griggs had given him prior to the reading of the docket that morning.

Nancy Sloan and Griggs entered the courtroom, and Griggs approached the bench as Nancy took her place in the visitors' section, opposite the children.

Judge Harrington dropped his pen, looked up, and said, "Okay, gentlemen, what's next?"

"Your honor," Griggs said, "this is the case of the five Clawson children found in the cornfield a few weeks ago."

Judge Harrington interrupted him with a short wave of his hand. "Oh, yes," he said, as he searched for a file buried on his desk.

The judge looked past Griggs, towards Nancy, and said, "Miss Sloan, have there been any further developments since we talked yesterday?"

She shook her head.

Griggs was puzzled by the disclosure that Judge Harrington had discussed the case without him, and he wondered why the meeting might have been so important as to conduct it on the Labor Day holiday.

As soon as the judge had familiarized himself with the file, Griggs proceeded with the formal presentation of his findings and recommendations. "Your honor, Case six four nine one four seven involved five minors who were abandoned by their . . ."

The judge interrupted, "I am aware of the facts in this case, Bud. Let's proceed informally." Addressing himself to Nancy, he said, "It was my understanding yesterday that you were going to talk to the chief social worker concerning the placement of these children. Is he present?"

Nancy rose, and as the judge beckoned her and the guardian ad litem to the bench, Griggs was disturbed by the realization that he had lost control. Things had happened, and negotiations had obviously taken place without him and without firsthand knowledge of the kids' needs.

As the group formed around the bench, the judge said, "I see no reason to formalize these proceedings. The parents abandoned the children several weeks ago, and, as far as we know, have not been heard from since. It is simply a matter of beginning the process of severing parental rights so that the state may take custody of the children and provide funding for appropriate placements. It is also my understanding that Miss Sloan and her staff have worked through the night to obtain foster home placements."

Bud's alarm turned to panic as the word "placements" echoed through his head. "What's happening?" he thought. "This is all wrong." He opened his mouth to speak, but nothing came out.

"Harry," the judge said, "as guardian ad litem, do you see any reason why we should not proceed in this way at this time?"

"No, your honor," he said mechanically and indifferently.

Griggs heard himself saying stridently, "I can. What do you mean by 'placements'? You mean 'placement.'" The desperation in his voice immobilized the group, and they all turned and stared at him.

Patty sensed his anxiety and scooted forward on the bench as if to decipher the muffled conversations among the adults in front of the room.

The urgency in Bud's voice was rising. "Your Honor, you don't understand. The children are to be placed in the *same* home."

"But that's not possible, Bud."

"But I *promised*. I'm sure there must be a way. Just give me some time. I'm sure I can find a way."

His alarm was clearly transmitted to Patty, even though she could not hear the words. She turned her head rapidly from one side to the other as if looking for friendly reassurances. There were none.

"Miss Sloan, is this a new development?" the judge asked.

"I'm sorry, Your Honor, I don't know what he's talking about. We don't have a foster home licensed to care for five children."

"Bud?" the judge asked.

His mind was a blank. He did not understand what they were talking about. "Judge, there seems to be some confusion here. Can I have a few minutes alone with you?"

"Good idea. In my chambers."

As they were leaving the courtroom, the judge turned and said to Nancy, "Miss Sloan, this might be an opportune time for you to talk to the children. They look anxious."

Nancy turned from the bench and walked toward the children. She leaned on the railing and began to explain the situation in a quiet voice.

Meanwhile, in the adjoining room, Griggs could not contain his annoyance with the judge, and he asked, "What the hell is going on?"

Looking confused, the judge asked, "What do you mean?"

Griggs said excitedly, "They're going to take those kids away."

"Of course they are. What did you expect?"

"No. I mean *separately*. They're going to split them up—send them to different homes."

"Of course they are. You're acting crazy."

"But I promised . . . I promised."

"Promised what?"

"That they would stay together."

"You *what*? Why in the world would you do such a dumb thing?"

Griggs was infuriated. "Don't you listen? Didn't you read my reports? Why do you think they half-starved themselves in that damned cornfield for two weeks?"

Then, reaching out and grabbing his lapel, Griggs shouted, "Because 'helping' people like you and that snooty bitch split them up once before. And Patty knew it would happen again. And she told me so. She told me, 'All we have left is each other.'"

The judge put his hand on Bud's wrist. He was sympathetic, but said firmly, "Listen. It's out of our hands. We don't operate the foster homes. The state does. We're out of it. We were out of it the second we realized that the parents weren't coming back. Our job was to keep their bodies warm and dry until the state took over. Period! As soon as I sign that order, it's official."

Griggs shouted, "I don't care what the stinking system is! I don't care who pays for what! Aren't we here to help children? Aren't we . . ."

A piercing scream from the next room interrupted his outburst, and they rushed into the courtroom. They could hear the sobbing children, but could not see them because they were surrounded by Nancy Sloan and four other social workers who had been called in to escort the children to their separate foster homes.

Griggs stood frozen in the doorway. He was unable to speak. He was unable to think. Then, from the cluster of children and social workers, Patty made her way across the room and stood in front of him trembling. Her face was smeared with tears, and her hair was disheveled. She was drained of all emotion. Barely capable of standing, she sobbed, "You promised."

Griggs couldn't say a word.

Nancy put her hands on Patty's shoulders to steady her, but Patty suddenly lashed out at her with her fist. Nancy was caught off balance and fell, and the bailiff threw his arms around Patty to restrain her. Her teeth were bared, and she continued to struggle violently.

Finally, the bailiff threw her up on his shoulder and started out of the courtroom. Before they turned the corner, the hysterical girl shouted at Griggs for the last time: "You promised! You lying bastard! You promised!"

PART III

THE QUEST

The Clawson children were taken from the courtroom and hustled into separate cars waiting to take them to their respective foster homes. Patty was curled up and sobbing in the corner of Nancy Sloan's front seat as the car pulled away from the courthouse parking lot.

"Patty," she pleaded, "we didn't want this to happen any more than you did. There was no choice. You're no more than a child yourself . . . we can't let you grow up being a mother to four other children."

In the past two years, Nancy had been a part of some bad scenes pulling children away from parents and siblings from each other, but none could compare to the wrenching sobs and total pain etched in the face of this eleven-year-old girl. Nancy knew that Patty wasn't listening to her, but she found the silence intolerable. "Later on, when you all get settled, I'm sure you'll see your brothers and sisters again." That sounded patronizing, and Nancy regretted saying it.

She searched her mind for something else to talk about. "You're going to a nice foster home, and you'll have a pretty room all to yourself," she prattled. "You'll even go to school. I know how much you used to like school."

As Nancy chattered, Patty began to assess her predicament silently. *They think it's all over, but it's not. They won't get away with this.* She made a conscious decision to get hold of herself, hide her true feelings, play their stupid game, and wait for the opportune moment to escape.

The car came to a stop. "Here it is, Patty. Don't you think it's a beautiful home? I know you're going to like it here." Nancy walked around and opened the passenger door. "C'mon Patty. The Palmers are lovely people, and they're anxious to meet you."

Patty emerged from the car noting the many windows and doors in the large house that would provide an opportunity for immediate escape. She knew instinctively that she would have to move quickly and find her brothers and sisters before they got too spread out. *I'll find them. I'll find them all. When I do, I won't listen to anyone else. Big people lie! They lie to make you behave and not run away . . . then they say they're sorry.*

Everything had happened so fast. Her whole world had been turned upside down after she had been carried to the parking lot and saw her brothers and sisters being driven away in separate cars, their white and frightened faces framed in the windows of the departing vehicles. But that was then and now was now, and the resilient and determined youngster wiped her eyes, straightened her hair, and resolved to play the simple little girl who was going to accept these strangers as parents and this house as home.

They walked to the front door without speaking. The yard of the two-story white colonial was carpeted by thick grass broken only by patches of flower beds strategically located for maximum effect. From the fenced side yard, a small dog yapped at their approach, its tail wagging and its nose wedged between the pickets for a better view of the visitors.

A plump, gray-haired, middle-aged woman answered the door. "Hello, Mrs. Palmer, I'd like you to meet Patty Clawson."

"Hello, Patricia," the woman said reaching for the girl's hand with a nervous smile. "I hope you will be happy here."

Nancy misinterpreted Patty's tentative grin as an indication that there might still be some hope. They stepped into the front hall and Nancy touched Patty's shoulder to direct the girl into the living room. Patty flinched and pulled away from contact and walked directly to a chair in the front room.

Mrs. Palmer hovered at the entrance to the room until Nancy was seated. "Before we get started, would anyone like something cool to drink?"

"That would be nice," Nancy said.

"I have iced tea or Coke. Which would you prefer?"

Patty shrugged her shoulders indifferently, and Nancy answered, "Whichever is easier."

Nancy wanted to say something to Patty before Mrs. Palmer returned, but she didn't know what to say or how to say it. This had been the most difficult placement she had ever made because she had committed the cardinal sin of becoming emotionally involved with the little girl sitting near her with the stony face. Nancy Sloan believed that what she was doing was in the child's best interest, but she was at a loss to put it into words that the girl would accept.

"Patty, I know you're very uncomfortable right now . . . so am I," Nancy said softly. "Would you like to go upstairs and spend some time alone? Maybe you'll feel more like talking after you've had a chance to sort things through for yourself."

Patty sat up and looked at Nancy for the first time. "Yes, I think I'd like to do that," she said.

The cold drinks arrived as the two were about to leave the living room. "Mrs. Palmer, Patty has had a difficult morning, and I think she would feel better if she spent a little time alone in her room," Nancy explained.

The lady stood there holding her tray of drinks, a confused expression on her face. Then she smiled and said, "Certainly. Would you like to take a drink with you, Patricia?"

Patty reached out and took a Coke from the tray. "Thank you," she said, and followed Nancy Sloan upstairs.

"It's a beautiful room, isn't it, Patty?"

Patty took a deep breath, knowing the game did not have to last much longer. "Yes, it's very nice."

"You get yourself comfortable," Nancy said, "and I'll be back in an hour or so with your things."

The Coke was good, and Patty sipped it thoughtfully, looking around the room with one purpose in mind. It would be impossible to walk back down the stairs and out the front door without being observed. She walked to the only window in the room and discovered that it looked out over the concrete patio, twelve feet below. If she could somehow escape through that window, she would have the advantage of a one-hour head start.

The window was partially opened, so it was no problem for her to raise it high enough to crawl through. She unhooked the screen, but the frame was painted shut. If she kicked it out, it would make too much noise. She surveyed the small, pleasantly furnished bedroom and walked to the vanity to examine the comb and brush set. She returned to the window and attacked the wire screen with the sharp handle of the brush, managing to gouge a hole in it large enough to accommodate her entire hand. She grasped the torn screen and pulled until the hole was large enough for her body.

Patty did not think about the height. She simply crawled through the opening backward, held on to the window sill and lowered her body to full length. Then she kicked against the side of the building and dropped. Her dress flew up around her face as she fell, and she lost her balance. It seemed to her that someone must have taken the ground away, but when she finally landed, her backside stung and her feet ached sharply.

She rolled over on the ground and came up sprinting. At first, her left ankle simply burned, but when she had run through the alley for two blocks, she stopped to catch her breath and noted that there was already some swelling.

She was generally aware of the direction from which she

and Nancy had come, but she cursed herself for not having been more observant. She struck out on a straight line for the downtown area, walking to avoid being conspicuous. Her ankle throbbed painfully, but Patty told herself that most injuries healed themselves if you left them alone long enough. She thought of Sue Anne's leg and realized there were obvious exceptions, but for now, she would have to tolerate the pain and hope it wasn't a serious injury.

Her primary objective was to get away. Finding her brothers and sisters would have to come later.

Nancy Sloan thought it might be a nice gesture if Mrs. Palmer checked on Patty and asked if there was anything the girl needed. She heard the older woman knock at Patty's door. There was no response. Mrs. Palmer knocked again. Nancy rose from her chair and was already climbing the steps when she heard Mrs. Palmer open the door and exclaim, "Oh, my God, what has she done?"

Nancy was there in an instant, and she was not really surprised to see the empty room and torn screen. She walked slowly to the open window and said, "She's run away. I'm sorry this had to happen."

Her first reaction was to look through the window and survey the alley in both directions, but there was no movement. Then she glanced at her watch and realized that Patty had come to the room more than forty-five minutes ago. While she and Mrs. Palmer were discussing everything from Patty's past history to the care and feeding of adolescents, the girl had gained enough time to cover a considerable distance.

"I'm afraid she's had a pretty good head start. I want you to call the police and give them her description," Nancy said. "I'll start driving around. The sooner we get on this, the better chance we have of finding her."

She walked quickly from the room with Mrs. Palmer in close pursuit. "But I don't understand. What did she . . . ? Did I do something wrong?"

Nancy stopped at the top of the staircase and looked at Mrs. Palmer. The woman was more confused than ever. Patty was to have been their first foster child. Their own three children were grown and gone, and the Palmers decided to share their large house with someone who could take the place of their missing children. It suddenly occurred to Nancy that this nice woman was no more prepared to care for the needs of Patty Clawson than Patty was to adjust to her middle-class expectations.

"Please believe me, Mrs. Palmer, you did nothing wrong. All the wrongs happened before you ever met Patty Clawson." Nancy then turned and descended the stairs with all the speed she could muster.

As she stopped to negotiate the ornate knob on the front door, Mrs. Palmer shouted from the top of the stairs, "When you find her, you won't bring her back here, will you? I'm not sure we're quite ready for this."

Nancy stopped just long enough to respond, "I'll have to call you about that later."

She drove around the block three times, then expanded the parameters of the circle. In the two years she had worked for social welfare, Nancy Sloan had become an expert on runaways from foster homes. She knew that driving in a pattern of expanding circles produced the best results, but she also knew that the odds of finding a runner diminished dramatically after two hours.

Nancy expected very little help from the police. After receiving Mrs. Palmer's call, the name of Patricia Clawson would be added to their runaway list, but there was little probability that the police patrols would search in earnest for a runaway foster child. For one thing, it was too common an occurrence. Lieutenant Gamble had once admonished her, "Lady, if we dropped everything else to search for one of the kids you keep losing, there wouldn't be time for anything else."

As she searched, Nancy kept looking at her watch, and as the minutes passed, the odds of finding Patty grew longer. At four o'clock, she called her office and advised her assistant, Claudia Wexler, that enough time had elapsed to list Patty officially as a runaway.

At seven-thirty, Nancy decided to give up and go home. The sun was setting, but the evening was unusually warm for September 8th. *At least she won't be cold, wherever she is,* Nancy thought, and she could only imagine what might be going through the mind of that desperate little child/woman.

Nancy continued to search for Patty during every spare minute of her busy schedule. She enlisted Chins' support on that first night. He was at first bitter and accusatory, but his personal indignation evaporated when he learned that Patty was in trouble. He soon came to accept the fact that Nancy had been blameless in the Clawson affair and that her concern for the children was as sincere as his own. Chins spoke with Abernathy, Hocker, and Lieutenant Carter, and he later assured Nancy that if Patty was wandering around out in the county, they would find her.

The first place Nancy had searched that Wednesday morning was the Wilson farm, thinking that Patty might have returned to their hole next to the river. She knew that runaways usually returned to familiar territory, but this time it was a wasted trip. The corn had been cut, and she had a clear line of vision all the way from the highway to the row of trees along the river.

With the protective cover now gone, Nancy held little hope that Patty would be in the area, but she alerted Mrs. Wilson to the possibility that she might be. Mrs. Wilson promised to be vigilant and said that she would place some "decent food" near the garbage cans at regular intervals, "just in case."

Nancy retired early that Friday evening, planning to spend the entire weekend searching for Patty. Three days and three nights had passed, and she had no idea about where to look. Her troubled sleep was interrupted just before midnight by a telephone call from a night watchman at her office.

"This is Ralph Hughes, night security, down at the State Office Building. I've got a girl here who says she's your niece."

Nancy shook her head to make sure she wasn't dreaming,

threw off the covers, and sat on the edge of the bed. "A who? What are you talking about? Who is this?"

Mr. Hughes sighed deeply and started again. "I have a young girl—skinny—kind of run-down looking. She claims she's your niece. I caught her in your office tearing things up, and I thought I better call you, Miss Sloan. I was gonna call the police, but she claims she fell asleep on your couch and got locked in and was looking for your key to get out."

"Oh, my God," Nancy exclaimed as the pieces began to fall into place.

"Sounds fishy to me, Miss Sloan, but I thought I'd call you first."

"You did exactly right, Mr. Hughes," Nancy said in a calm and authoritarian voice that belied her excitement. "Just hold her there, and do not call the police. I'll be down in fifteen minutes."

"Yes, m'am."

"And be sure someone opens the door for me downstairs."

There was a pause before Mr. Hughes acknowledged his instructions. "Okay, Miss Sloan, but this is all kind of crazy. I don't understand."

"Yes, I know," Nancy said. "I'll explain when I get there. Goodbye."

Patty sat on the edge of the big chair behind Nancy's desk staring daggers at the old man who was leaning against the door frame talking into his walkie-talkie. "Hank, there's gonna be a lady by the name of Miss Sloan comin' down to the front door in about fifteen minutes. You be there to open it for her."

There was a garbled question from the other end that Hughes somehow managed to decipher through the static. "Hell, I don't know what's going on. I'll tell you later, after I find out. All we can do is wait."

Patty had grown accustomed to waiting. She had tracked down the location of Nancy's office with the patience of an experienced hunter. She remembered Nancy saying that her office was close to the courthouse, so Patty started there. To the east of the courthouse lay the State Capitol, which fronted on fifteen acres of manicured lawns that extended all the way to the business district. Patty walked through the Capitol Building but found it largely deserted. The areas north and south of the Capitol were given over to business and light industry, so she discounted those and concentrated on the cluster of buildings immediately west of the courthouse.

Patty positioned herself as inconspicuously as possible in front of the State Printer's Building, planning to screen the crowds of employees entering and leaving the four buildings across the street. She realized quickly that her chances of spotting Nancy were small, because there were perhaps two thousand people scurrying into and out of the buildings, each of which had at least four sets of doors.

During business hours, when pedestrian traffic diminished, Patty walked through the enormous parking lots looking for Nancy's car, but that yielded no results because there were no lots specifically designated for state employees, and the thousands of parking spaces in the area were privately owned and available for long or short-term rentals to everyone from public and private employees to casual shoppers.

Patty shifted her attention from one building to the next, but by the end of the second full day of searching, she was no closer to finding Nancy's office. Every evening she returned to the university campus to spend the night in the Student Union.

Patty's escape on Tuesday had taken her through a section of the city that was completely unfamiliar to her, but she instinctively sought the anonymity of crowded places, and as she limped along the streets, she began to blend with the growing traffic patterns of students which led her first to the campus, then to the Student Union. Inside the building, she discovered a secluded reading area that was furnished with plush carpets, drapes, and overstuffed furniture. She slept safely and comfortably behind one of the couches and managed to find a selection of foods in the kitchen, where the bread drawers were unlocked and canned fruits and vegetables were stored on open shelves.

Patty's vigil was again unrewarded on Friday morning, but at noon, she saw a familiar face in the crowd. An alarm went off in her brain that sent her scurrying to safety as she tried to place the woman in her memory. Her primary frame of reference was the detention home, so she tried to recall the faces of the parents, visitors, and social workers who visited constantly. *That's it,* her mind screamed, *social workers . . . Mickey Maloney's social worker.* Having made the association, Patty began to relax, but another thought came to her mind—*Nancy is a social worker!* In the few seconds that it had taken Patty to process the information, the woman had walked only to the corner, and Patty spotted her waiting for the traffic light to change. The young girl followed the woman several blocks to Macy's, then to the lunch counter at Woolworth's. In less than an hour, the woman led Patty directly to the largest of the four office buildings, where she disappeared into a waiting elevator.

Patty was surprised to see an information desk in the lobby. She walked to the counter and spoke to the young woman. "My mother told me to meet her in Miss Sloan's office. Is that in this building?"

The receptionist ran her finger down a worn sheet and asked, "What's her first name?"

"I don't know," Patty lied. "I think she's a social worker."

"Yes, that would be Nancy Sloan. She's in room nine fourteen."

"Is that the ninth floor?"

"That's right."

"In this building?"

"Just take that elevator."

That was easy, she thought as she walked from the counter. Three days of unsuccessful sleuthing, and all she had to do to find Nancy's office was to walk up and ask. It occurred to Patty that the bold approach might be best.

She took the elevator to the seventh floor, inspected the

rooms, and formulated her plan. At four-thirty that afternoon, she returned to the seventh floor, entered the ladies'
room, and locked herself into one of the stalls; then she sat
on the stool and raised her feet to avoid detection. When the
noises in the halls abated, she made herself comfortable and
waited for darkness.

It was nearly nine o'clock when she ventured from the ladies' room and walked up the stairs to the ninth floor. She
cracked open the heavy metal door but closed it quickly
when the sounds of vacuum cleaners and custodial personnel
reached her. Two hours later, she slipped through the door
and found herself in the middle of an enormous room filled
to capacity with rows of desks and filing cabinets. This was
the central office for all social work personnel, and the rooms
lining the periphery were numbered clearly.

Patty entered 914 and headed directly to the file cabinet
that would contain the addresses of her brothers and sisters.
The information *had* to be there, because, if it wasn't, she
knew no other places to look. Patty's heart sank when the top
drawer refused to open. She depressed the trigger inside the
handle and pulled again with all her strength. That's when
she saw the lock in the top corner of the cabinet.

She spent the next twenty minutes searching through the
office for a hidden key, but it was nowhere to be found. Finally, she took the heavy letter opener from the top of
Nancy's desk and tried to force the drawer open. The im-
provised tool bent and twisted, but the drawer refused to
budge, so, in frustration and anger, the girl kicked and beat
on the metal cabinet. That momentary loss of control was
enough to alert Ralph Hughes to her presence, and when the
night watchman flipped on the office lights, he found the
young girl pulling furiously on the handle of the file drawer.

When Nancy arrived at the office, she found Patty curled
up in her swivel chair, staring out at the lights of the city. "Hi,
Patty," she said, walking around the desk for a better look at
the girl. She was shocked by her appearance. There were
dark rings under both eyes, her hair was matted and dull,

her skin was covered with dirt, and her new dress hung like a torn and filthy rag.

Nancy Sloan sat on the corner of the desk and asked, "Where in the world have you been, Patty? We've been worried to death about you."

Patty kicked at the radiator and swung the chair away from the woman. Nancy's frustration and pain welled up, and it came out in anger. She twisted the chair around in a violent motion and snarled, "Don't you turn your back on me!"

Patty stared blankly at the protruding jaw and pointing finger and appeared totally unmoved by the little outburst. Nancy felt ridiculous as it occurred to her that temper tantrums did not impress Patty Clawson, and that, when it came to anger and violence, this little girl had survived in a league that the Nancy Sloans of the world didn't even comprehend.

Nancy decided that a personal relationship with the girl had to be developed in some other way. "C'mon, Patty, you're coming home with me tonight."

Ralph Hughes was standing in the outer office when Nancy and Patty passed him. "Hey, lady, I gotta put something in my report. This is breaking and entering here."

Nancy sighed and spoke in a soft, confidential tone. "This is a touchy case, officer. I would appreciate it if you would just say that you found a little girl in my office looking for something."

Nancy started to turn, but he reached out and said, "Yeah, but what?"

Nancy wanted to answer from the depth of her own guilt, "For some compassion and understanding," but instead she said, "For her brothers and sisters."

It had rained earlier in the evening, and water was still standing on the streets, glistening in the glare of the headlights. The cool air blowing in through the car window brought the first touch of fall, signaling an end to a miserably hot and dry summer. The whole effect might have been exhilarating if Nancy had been anywhere but in the company of that small blob of gloom sitting next to her. For the past three days, she had been consumed with apprehension for the well-being of the girl, but now the worst was over.

Nancy tried again to open some line of communications with the youngster. "I am taking you home with me instead of to the detention home because the regulations say that when a child has run away from foster placement, Mrs. Higgins is required to place that child in lockup for at least twenty-four hours, and I didn't want that to happen."

There was no response or change of expression. Patty continued to stare straight ahead, and Nancy wondered whether the inevitable had already occurred. Every child has a breaking point, and her catatonic stare was frightening.

"Patty, I want you to talk to me. I don't have any magic answers, and I am not going to make any promises I can't keep, but I can tell you right now that running away from foster homes and trying to find your brothers and sisters on your own is not going to work."

Nancy detected a derisive reaction in the set of Patty's face, so she assumed the girl could hear what she was saying and decided to prepare Patty for the worst. "If you keep running, we will have to put you where you *can't* run away, and you don't need that. You're old enough to realize that running away and getting locked up is not going to solve your problems."

Nancy continued her monologue until they reached her apartment building. She was tempted to hurry around and open Patty's door to discourage the girl from getting away again, but she was too tired to play the game and too frustrated to believe that she could keep the girl from running if and when she made up her mind to do so. "Come on, Patty. Let's go in and get cleaned up and go to bed."

Patty opened the door and followed, and for the remainder of the evening, she did what she was told, reacting like a robot incapable of responding to anything but commands. Nancy drew a warm sudsy bath and laid out a fresh flannel nightgown for the girl. When Patty emerged from the bath, Nancy said, "Why don't you sit down and have that sandwich and milk?" The question came out more like an order, and Patty did as she was told.

Nancy gave up her own bedroom to Patty and slept on the livingroom couch. Just before turning out the light, Nancy wondered whether Patty would still be there in the morning. Then she planned her next moves. She had already broken the first rule by not taking Patty to the mandatory lockup, and George Matthews would skin her alive in the morning. Matthews was a full-blooded bureaucrat who lived by the rules and took pride in his professional distance. He never got emotionally involved with others, and he could shuffle kids around faster than anyone on record.

She knew he would be in the office on Saturday morning, and she guessed that he would already have heard about Patty's return, in which case he would first reprimand Nancy, then threaten Patty, and finally, order Nancy to deliver the girl to a new foster home selected by himself.

Nancy slept longer than she intended. Her first thought was to rush into the bedroom to check on Patty, but she forced herself to be casual—strolling into the room in search of her slippers. She was relieved to find the girl lying in bed and said, "Jump up, sleepy, and we'll go out for some breakfast."

Sitting across from the silent child in the pancake house, Nancy tried once again to break through the barrier. "We're going to have to go down to the office this morning and decide what to do with you, but I hate to drag you in there looking like you've just walked through the Chicago fire. Let's stop off and get you some new clothes."

It was a beautiful morning. The rain had washed everything clean, and the cool air lingered from the night before. Nancy found a parking spot directly in front of the department store and accepted it as a good omen.

Inside the store, Patty showed no interest in the new clothes, so Nancy selected a coordinated sweater and slacks outfit for her and directed the girl to the fitting room. Nancy positioned herself so as to observe the entrance to the fitting room at all times and selected several other outfits while she waited. She enjoyed clothes, and time passed quickly for her when she was on one of her shopping sprees.

Before long, her preoccupation with materials and color combinations was disrupted by a chilling thought—*Patty was taking too long.* She tossed the clothes she had gathered on top of one of the racks and ran to the fitting room, but all she found was an open window and a tattered dress on the floor.

George Matthews ordered Nancy to sit silently while he finished reading the report of the night watchman. Her mind jumped randomly from one unconnected thought to another—she should have called Griggs and Chins last night to tell them she had found Patty—maybe it was just as well they were still searching for her, because now she was gone again. Then she caught the glare from Matthews' jacket, and it occurred to her that he had three suits—one black, one gray, and one dark brown—and they were all made of the same kind of shiny material. The man was always immaculately dressed and was absolutely wrinkle-proof. He always wore a white shirt, and his dark hair was short and never out of place. His rimless glasses rested primly on his pointed nose and seemed to be the perfect style for his thin, pale face.

Unlike the other workers in Matthews' department, Nancy was not afraid of his angry outbursts. She knew she had violated policy, and she knew she was about to be severely reprimanded, so she psychologically defended herself the best way she knew how—by wondering whether the man ever removed his jacket and tie before making love with his wife. The ludicrous spectacle had intruded itself without warning, and she tried to stifle a grin.

"Miss Sloan, only a maniac would find something humorous about this situation." Matthews squared his shoulders and prepared to chew on the one person in his department that he enjoyed chewing on most. Nancy Sloan had been thrust upon him because of a college degree and political influence, and he resented her for both. She could not be trusted to follow the rules that were necessary for the tidy operation of his department, and the lame story she had just told was a perfect example of why those rules had to be enforced. "In the first place, if you had followed regulations and placed that child in lockup, we would have her this morning. Who authorized you to take her home with you? Who authorized you to buy her clothes?"

Nancy understood that the questions were rhetorical and that the worst thing she could do was to interrupt Matthews once he had developed this head of steam. He continued to rave for several minutes, then concluded with, "I warn you, the county does not pay your salary for a cheap imitation of Florence Nightingale. The next time that girl is taken into custody, your responsibility will be strictly limited to delivering her directly to lockup. I, and only I, shall decide where she goes from there."

Having delivered his remonstration with imperious severity, Matthews was satisfied he had put the woman in her proper place. Then he leaned forward and glared as menacingly as he could, almost defying her to respond, "Are there any questions?"

"Yes," she said glumly, "does this mean the department won't reimburse me for Patty's breakfast?"

Nancy would like to have stayed to see the conclusion of Matthews' apoplectic reaction to her question, but she had some important loose ends to tie up. On her way out of his office she signaled Claudia Wexler to join her. The stout woman in the tent dress followed Nancy into her office.

"I want you to call the foster parents of the other Clawson children and tell them that Patty is on the loose and trying to find them," Nancy said.

Claudia peered over her old-fashioned horn-rimmed glasses and asked, "How does she expect to do that?"

Nancy stared at her assistant and said, "I don't know. You have been involved with the other children, but you don't know Patty." Nancy turned to look out at the city and continued, "There is an angry determination in that girl that's unbelievable."

"I know," Claudia said. "I saw her in the courtroom. It was scary."

"That kid is going to get her brothers and sisters back or die trying," Nancy said, ". . . and I'm not using that idiom carelessly." Then, as if to shake herself from her gloomy forecast, Nancy returned to business. "When you call the foster parents, don't get them all worked up. Just have them call us if they see or hear from Patty. Meanwhile," she continued, "I'll return this call to Bud Griggs."

Nancy was unable to reach Griggs by noon, which was Saturday quitting time, so she assumed it wasn't too important. All the way home, though, she wondered about his call. He had refused to speak to her since the hearing, and in spite of the fact that she had not known of his promise to Patty before that day, she felt guilty. It was a stupid thing for Bud to do—not even telling the judge about it—but it was the kind of stupid thing she herself might have done.

She was so deep in thought as she entered the hallway and approached the door of her apartment that the sight of Bud Griggs sitting on the stairs startled her. She jumped back and dropped her keys.

"Sorry," he said.

"That's okay," she said breathlessly. "I guess I'm just a little jumpy." The color was gone from Griggs' face, and his lips were tightly compressed. "I need to see John," he said stiffly.

"John? . . . Why?"

"I need to talk to him."

"Come in, Bud. We can talk about it inside."

"I don't want to come in, and I don't want to talk about it." His voice was brittle, and he seemed to be trembling.

"You know how Matthews feels about you seeing any of the children. Did you speak to him about this?" Nancy asked.

"He threatened to have me arrested if I tried to see any of them," Griggs said without emotion.

"I know," she added, "and he made it perfectly clear to me

that he would arrest anyone who helped you, too." She looked at the floor and shook her head vigorously. "I can't do it, Bud. I can't tell you where he is. You could blow this whole thing . . ."

"Bump is dead," he interrupted.

"What?"

"Bump Thompson is dead."

"Oh, my God," she sobbed, covering her mouth with her hand. "How did it happen?"

"They claim it was suicide."

"Bump? . . . That's ridiculous!" she said indignantly, remembering the smiling face of the fourteen-year-old boy who celebrated every minute of life.

"That's what they say . . . hanged himself."

"Oh, no. I can't believe that. How did it happen?" Nancy stammered incredulously.

"They were so pissed off because they said he had tried to kill a cop that they kept him in solitary confinement for six days. Then they put him into the tank on Thursday, and he was raped at least four times." Nancy's legs got shaky, so, with her back pressed against the wall, she slid down to sit on the bottom step.

Griggs continued the horror story. "The word is that the kid screamed and fought, but no one came to help until it was all over. Then one of the guards came back and said, 'You're not so tough now, are you, black boy?' " Griggs was beginning to lose control, so he concluded the report quickly. "The following night—last night—they did the same thing to him, and he pulled the plug about three o'clock this morning."

The two sat in silent grief before Nancy murmured, "I can't believe it. I can't believe it."

Then Griggs dealt the final blow. "I picked up his clothes at the morgue this morning, and I found these in his pocket." He held out his hand and in his palm were four broken teeth.

Nancy stared in horror and started to tremble violently, but she did not break. Griggs took the keys from her, opened the door, and helped her into the apartment. He guided her to a kitchen chair and gave her a drink of water. Then he sat back and waited for her to recover. When he finally spoke, it was softly, trying to reason with her. "Bump and John were like brothers. This could destroy him."

Nancy began to breathe more normally, and the stiffness in her muscles began to dissolve. She stood and walked a few steps into the living room to test her legs and sort things out in her mind. When she returned to the kitchen area, her decision was made.

"All right," she said. "Bump is dead . . . but the Clawsons are alive . . . and they *need* us. Whether they know it or not, you and I are all they have right now." Nancy paused to study Bud's face for a positive reaction, but he was anticipating her next statement, and anger began to show in his face. "If I tell you where to find John," she continued, "you will go to him . . . the foster parents will call Matthews, as they have been told to do . . . and you and I will both lose our jobs."

Griggs slammed his fist to the table and said angrily, "I don't give a good goddam about . . ."

It was Nancy's turn to shout, "I know, I know, but what happens to the Clawsons when we're gone?"

Griggs could not comprehend her reasons for denying him the information, and he knew it would be impossible to bully her, so he tried a compromise. "Look, I don't have to know where he is. You can pick him up and meet me someplace."

Nancy was now resolute and completely in control. "No, Bud. We can't take the chance. I'll talk to John and try to make him understand. Dr. Sylvester and I will arrange for whatever psychological support is indicated."

Griggs was furious, but he did not erupt. He pushed his chair away and stood over her menacingly. "I'll find out some other way," he said coldly. "I thought there might still be a shred of human decency in you."

* * *

When Patty ran from the department store, she melted quickly into the crowds of Saturday shoppers. The natural instinct for a fugitive on the run is to follow a downhill course, and Patty did precisely that. Eight blocks from the department store, the character of the buildings began to change. Like her old neighborhood, there were small shops and bars on the street level, with run-down apartments on the upper floors. As she approached the railroad yards that bordered the river, the rows of condemned tenements and empty warehouses pervaded.

Patty had found her milieu. It wasn't a big city like Philadelphia, but it was big enough for her to fade into the environment and function without being noticed, especially in a neighborhood like this. She began to feel good again, and as she walked slowly through the area, her mind returned to the plan she had begun to formulate during the night.

She would retrieve the children one at a time. Karen and Charlie would have to be the last, because they would require her full-time attention, and she couldn't care for them and search for the others at the same time. John and Sue Anne would require no care and could help Patty find the others. Besides, John and Sue Anne would be the easiest to find. Last night, Nancy had said that they were about to start school, so all Patty had to do was to check out all the schools in town. Simple.

They would need a safe place to stay until they were all together and ready to leave the city. That's why Patty was so pleased to find the run-down neighborhood she was in. If it was anything like the slums where she grew up, there would be lots of abandoned apartment buildings. One of John's favorite games in Philadelphia used to be climbing fire escapes and inspecting vacant apartments, and now she was ready to do the same.

After forty minutes of wandering around, Patty found what she was looking for. Directly beneath the bridge there was a row of three-story brownstones whose shattered windows assured Patty that they were uninhabited. The store windows on the ground floor were completely boarded, and the doors leading upstairs had been barred shut and locked. In the back, however, the metal fire escapes ran up the outside of the building.

Patty stacked boxes against the building to reach the ladder, then she scrambled up to select her new home. She peered through the broken windows of the second-story apartment and discovered that the plaster was hanging dangerously from the ceilings, and the floors were covered with decaying trash probably tossed from ground level by children testing their marksmanship. She climbed to the top floor and found the rooms more to her liking, so she entered through the window for a closer inspection. There was broken glass on the floor, and the place was covered with dust and dirt blown in through the opening.

When she walked into the next room, she knew she would have to look no further. It had been a small bedroom, and the window was intact, so there was little dust to contend with. There was a torn and filthy mattress on the floor, but it reeked with the sour odor of urine, so Patty screwed up her face and dragged it from the room, then she returned and forced open the window to air the place out.

Nancy had hoped to spend Saturday afternoon catching up on some of the sleep Patty had caused her to miss, but the visit from Bud Griggs made that impossible. Instead, Nancy called Bob Sylvester, the department psychologist who had last worked with John Clawson, to discuss the potential impact of Bump's death on John, and whether they should tell him immediately. Dr. Sylvester settled the matter by ordering her not to break the news to John until the boy's foster home situation stabilized.

Nancy's appearance that afternoon would not have won any awards for beauty. Her bloodshot eyes and pallid complexion confirmed her inability to function on three hours' sleep; and as a result of indulging her nervous habit of pulling at her curls in moments of stress, her hair resembled an electrically charged frizz. That's how she looked when she answered Claudia Wexler's knock.

The short, stout woman surveyed her supervisor from head to foot and asked sarcastically, "How is it possible for you to look so pretty all the time? If you look this good on Saturday afternoon, I'll bet it would be worth the trip to see you when you wake up in the morning."

Nancy smiled and stepped aside as Claudia entered. "Thank you, thank you," she said. "I don't know why you're being so sweet. Either you want to borrow my car for the weekend or you're softening me up for some bad news."

Claudia sat on the sofa and sighed, "I'll tell you this much—I don't need another car."

Nancy flopped into her favorite chair and said, "Somehow I didn't think so. What's wrong?"

Claudia opened her files, spread them on her expansive lap, and pulled her glasses down to the reading position at the end of her nose as she began her report. "I got in touch with all the foster parents to tell them about Patty, and the— ah—well, I don't see their name—anyway, the people who took John—when I called them, the foster mother answered the phone and said that it didn't matter whether Patty was trying to find John or not, because he wouldn't be staying there much longer anyway."

Nancy's lips compressed, and she asked, "Why not?"

"Well, I don't know the whole story. All she said was that their five-year-old son didn't like John. John didn't do anything wrong. But the kid apparently got to the point where he wouldn't eat dinner with the family until John agreed to eat by himself in the kitchen."

Nancy slammed the flat of her hand on the armrest. "How can people be so cruel! What idiots! What did you say to her?"

Claudia waited until she had Nancy's attention. "I just said I would find another home for John, and she said, 'Fine,' and hung up."

Nancy rose and paced the floor. "Where in the world do

we find these people? I didn't know it was possible to turn over so many rocks in one county." She looked to Claudia for a response, but she was busy shuffling through her folders. "I have a strong feeling you're not through. You want to continue?"

"The Flahertys—they took in Karen—they said she was safe, and they weren't concerned about Patty."

"Well, hoorah for them," Nancy exclaimed.

"But then they asked me why we hadn't told them that Karen was retarded."

Nancy slumped in her chair and pulled at the strands of hair pinched between her thumb and index finger as she digested Claudia's report. "And what about Sue Anne and Charlie?" she asked cautiously.

Claudia's face brightened. "Charlie seems to be doing fine. The young couple that took him ask a lot of dumb questions—even for first-time foster-parents—and they are constantly on my ass about one thing or another, but they certainly seem interested in him."

"One out of three isn't much to cheer about," Nancy said glumly. "What about Sue Anne?"

"Sue Anne went with the Potters, and the jury is still out."

Nancy tapped the side of her nose with her index finger, trying to jog her memory. "The Potters . . . the Potters . . . aren't they the ones we talked about a couple of months ago in our team meeting? They keep foster children for about two months, and everything goes great until things suddenly blow up?"

"Yep, that's them."

"Why in the world did we place Sue Anne with the Potters?"

"If you will remember, we decided to give them one more try and keep a close eye on them to see what's going wrong."

Nancy shook her head. "I really didn't know those were the people we placed Sue Anne with. I mean, how many kids do they have to screw up before we write those people off?"

Claudia tried to calm Nancy's anger. "Look," she said appeasingly. "In the first place, we don't have enough foster homes, and in the second place, the Potters have done nothing specific that we know is wrong. We figured that Sue Anne is the kind of kid who can get along with anyone, so we thought we would use her on this one last try."

"I can't believe that logic," Nancy cried angrily. "We take a kid who isn't screwed up yet, and we put her in a home with a record of screwing up kids, then mix the two together to find out how long it takes for one of them to explode. That's crazy!"

Claudia Wexler had been a social worker longer than anyone else in the department. She had survived countless directors, supervisors, and coworkers because she had the ability to be selectively stupid and block out negative events that threatened to intrude on her cheery little world. She was gregarious, but she was also efficient and pragmatic, and Nancy had come to like her in spite of her faults.

In typical fashion, Claudia chose to retreat from battle rather than argue the logic of the situation. She closed her files and stood up. "Nancy," she said, "don't let them get to you like this, or you won't last any longer than the others."

Too weary to argue the point, Nancy said simply, "Keep me up to date, Claudia."

In another part of the city, Patty Clawson was ready to venture out and survey her new neighborhood more closely. She flipped the hook on the fire escape ladder, and it rattled all the way to the ground. It occurred to her that she would be able to pull the ladder up after her in the evenings, just like the *Swiss Family Robinson.*

Four blocks from home, she entered the commercial district, and the first department store she happened across was Montgomery Ward, so she joined the crowds of weekend shoppers ferreting out post-Labor Day bargains. She strolled through the store with no particular purpose in mind, but when she wandered into the sporting goods department, a display of sleeping bags caught her eye, and she was suddenly attracted to the possibility of providing for some of her creature comforts.

She threaded her way through the congestion and selected a thick sleeping bag that was plush enough to serve as a mattress in her spartan room. Recalling the lesson she had learned searching for Nancy's office, *the direct approach is best*, she bundled it under her arm and re-entered the stream of traffic in the aisle leading to the exit.

Patty struggled with her self-recriminations the entire way. Other than the pies and a few candy bars that she and Sue Anne used to pick up at the larger grocery stores, she had never before stolen anything. She tried to tell herself that things were going to change now. She had been robbed of the only thing she treasured—her family—and from now on she would do whatever she had to do to survive. For her, there would be no rules until her brothers and sisters were returned.

But her determination waned as she neared the exit. She remained resolute about her license to strike back at will, but she considered the consequences of being apprehended for shoplifting, and her gait slowed. She meandered into the hardware department, then over to cameras before deciding that the risk was too great.

She scanned the overhead signs to reorientate herself to the sporting goods department, and she retraced her steps to the sleeping bag display. As she re-entered the area, a busy sales clerk bumped into her and said, "Sorry, may I help you, miss?"

"I need to return this sleeping bag," Patty said noncommittally.

"Do you want a refund or an exchange?"

"Well, I don't know," she said hesitantly, confused by this unexpected turn of events.

"What's wrong with it?" the clerk asked pleasantly, influenced by her new outfit and neat appearance.

"My mother got the wrong color."

"If you want a refund, you'll have to take your receipt to

customer service, but if you want to exchange it, I can take care of it right here."

"I don't have the receipt. My mother has it in the car. She told me to hurry."

Patty's facial expression betrayed her confusion and anxiety, but the clerk mistook it for despair, so he ignored the demands of his other customers and focused on helping her before she started crying. He relieved her of the bag and lead her to the display. "Here's a nice red one," he offered.

"Can I have that?" she asked excitedly.

"No problem at all," he said magnanimously. "They're the same price, so we'll just put this one back on the shelf and wrap the red one for you."

"You don't have to do that," she said, more anxious than ever to be gone.

"I'd better," he said. "I wouldn't want you to get stopped on the way out."

Me neither, she silently agreed.

Patty's mood was especially buoyant on Sunday. That afternoon, she would walk to the university and scavenge a sumptuous meal at the Student Union, and the next day she would call all the elementary schools in town to locate John and Sue Anne. If all went according to plan, the three oldest Clawsons would be reunited by the next afternoon.

She climbed the steps to the Union cafeteria and walked directly to the head of the serving line, where she picked up a clean plate and a selection of eating utensils. Then she strolled toward the west wall, where a long conveyor belt carried dirty dishes into the kitchen. She positioned herself behind a screen that had been set up at the point where the conveyor entered the work area of the kitchen.

The diners deposited their dirty dishes on the belt at any point along its forty-foot length, and Patty selected untouched delicacies as they trundled past her. She had become an old hand at the routine, and she executed the task calmly and confidently.

Patty filled her plate and found a table. She dined on a meal that included roast turkey, salami, pickles, and bread, but she wished someone would have deposited a dessert that was not to his liking. Then she spotted a cheerleader type coed with an undiminished strawberry shortcake headed for the conveyor belt. Patty jumped up and hurried to her position behind the screen watching the dessert advance toward her. She reached out for the jiggling mound of whipped cream and strawberries, delighted with her good fortune, when her luck changed.

"What are you doing there, kid?"

The startled girl jumped, dropping the dish back onto the conveyor belt, and turned to see the scowling face of a middle-aged man wearing a blue blazer with a coat-of-arms on the pocket that identified him as an employee.

"Nothing . . . I'm not doing nothing," she blurted.

"What are you doing behind the screen?" the man persisted.

"Nothing . . . I'm just messing around."

"That's no place to mess around," he scolded. "Get out of there."

Patty sidestepped the man and walked directly from the cafeteria and out to the street. As her nerves settled, she asked herself, *What did I do? That's what I get for eating other people's garbage!* Patty felt humiliated, but the worst part of it was that she would have to find another source of food.

Patty returned to the Student Union on Monday, but this time she was there to use the courtesy telephone. The receptionist had shown her how to find the school listings in the Yellow Pages, so she made her first call.

"Hillcrest," came the rapid response after the second ring.

"Pardon me?" Patty asked.

"This is Hillcrest Elementary School."

"Oh, yeah . . . I have two . . . friends who go to school there, I think. Anyway, I'm trying to find them, and could you tell me if they go to school there?"

"I'm sorry, but we don't have the student enrollment lists yet."

Patty failed to grasp the full impact of the statement, so she said again, "I need to find my two friends, and all I need to know is if they are in school there."

The secretary became impatient. *"I said,* we do not have the names of the students yet. Registration ended last Friday, and we won't have a list of students until the end of the week."

"This is *important,"* Patty pleaded. "Maybe you know them . . . John Clawson and Sue Anne Clawson."

"I'm sorry, but you'll have to check back on Friday. Good-bye."

Patty was too confused to be discouraged, but after receiving the same response from four more schools, she finally got the message, and the disappointment was traumatic. Alone in her room that night, she permitted herself the luxury of crying.

Nancy's week was going from bad to worse. Her insolence toward George Matthews was not overlooked, and he went out of his way to make her life miserable, fully intending to push her beyond her capacity and force her out of the department. He overloaded her with work, then harangued her throughout the day to make it impossible for her to get it done. She found that her most productive time was early in the morning, so she began arriving at seven A.M.

On Thursday morning, she had a shock that transcended several dimensions. In the first place, when she reached the office, she was surprised to find that George Matthews was already there. He was searching through a file drawer in the central office when he looked up at her, smiled in his self-satisfied way, and said, "Good morning, Miss Sloan . . . beautiful day, don't you think?"

She stared at him in mute surprise, then suspicion, because it occurred to her that she had just driven across town in a thunderstorm. Nancy stepped past him cautiously, wary of his strange behavior, and backed toward her office, keeping him in view the entire way.

"Ah, Miss Sloan," he purred, "I believe Miss Wexler has some interesting news for you."

Matthews' bizarre behavior puzzled Nancy, but the sudden appearance of Claudia Wexler put her at ease. "I need to talk to you," Claudia said softly.

"So I gather. Come on in."

Nancy hung her raincoat and umbrella on her clothes tree, and before she turned back, Claudia said, "They caught Patty last night."

Nancy walked to her chair without saying anything, afraid to ask the question. "Is she all right?"

"Still stubborn as a mule," the stout woman laughed, ". . . a very *skinny* mule, but by my standards, who isn't."

Nancy's relief was reflected in the flash of her smile. "Get serious, you turkey. Are you sure she's all right?"

"I'm absolutely certain. She looks like the wrath of God, but she's a tough cookie."

"You *saw* her?" Nancy asked in confusion. The smile dissolved and a frown appeared as she verbalized her thoughts. "If they caught her last night, the police would have checked their runaway list. Why didn't they call *me?*"

Claudia shifted uncomfortably, searching for a response.

"When did you find out about this? Where is she now?"

"Mr. Matthews called me last night and told me to go down to the city jail for a positive identification."

"The *jail?* Dammit, why didn't he call *me?*"

"Now, before I tell you what's going on, I want you to promise to hear me out, then count to ten before you do anything."

"Please get on with the story, Claudia, and don't play games."

"All right. She was shoplifting some food, and the store manager caught her. He had noticed her several times before, and he was suspicious because of the way she looked— wild hair, dirty clothes—but he didn't actually catch her till last night." Claudia chuckled nervously, "A girl after my own heart . . . she was loaded down with Twinkies."

"Okay," Nancy said impatiently, ". . . so they catch a runaway kid copping some food. What's the big deal? She should have been brought to the detention home, not the city jail. And dammit, why wasn't I called?"

"That's what I'm trying to explain," Claudia responded. "After the episode with Patty last weekend, Matthews notified the police that they were to call him—not you—if and when she was apprehended." Nancy was about to interrupt, but Claudia stopped her. "Wait . . . there's more. Matthews signed a criminal complaint charging her with breaking and entering, willful destruction of state property, escape from lawful custody, and flight to avoid prosecution."

"Whew!" Nancy exclaimed. "That's quite a rap sheet for an eleven-year-old girl, isn't it? No wonder they clapped her into the city jail," she said sarcastically. "I'm surprised they didn't haul her directly to the penitentiary."

"It's worse than that." Claudia's jolly round face contorted in misery. "Three days ago, Matthews personally made all arrangements—papers and all—to have Patty committed to the State Hospital, for a complete evaluation, as soon as they caught up with her."

"That's impossible!" Nancy scoffed. "The children's wards are backlogged for eighteen months. There's no way *anyone* could get a child committed in three days."

Claudia looked at the floor and murmured, "She's not going to the children's hospital . . . she's going to the security ward of the *adult* hospital."

Nancy leaned back and stared incredulously. When George Matthews appeared in the doorway, he said, "I trust you have been brought up to date."

"When do I see her?" Nancy asked wearily.

Matthews' tone was jaunty. "You don't. I have taken over as supervisor of this case, and Miss Wexler will report directly to me. You are to have no further contact with the girl. Is that understood?"

"I understand only that you are punishing this girl to get

back at me, and I understand how much you would like to see me resign," Nancy said with cold and measured precision. "But I'm not going to make it that easy for you. I am going to stay, and I shall make certain that you are held accountable for every child you've destroyed."

Patty sat on a wooden chair in Lieutenant Chamberland's office. She was disgusted with herself for getting caught. For days, she had successfully slipped packages of cheese and some candy bars under her sweater, but cupcakes and Twinkies were too bulky to hide. She sat there in the police station reviewing the mistakes she had made and making plans to correct them next time, because she was certain to be on the streets again very shortly.

Soon after arriving at the police station, Officer Gillis checked the runaway list and matched her with the description on file. As soon as he called her by name, Patty answered his questions, and he began to reconstruct her background. Soon the light came on, and he said, "Hey, I remember that case. Was that you in the cornfield? No kidding." Then he called Lieutenant Chamberland in to hear the story, and several other patrolmen drifted over as Patty became a curiosity item.

As the story unfolded, Patty won their sympathy and respect. Lieutenant Chamberland invited the group to move to his office, where they would be more comfortable. When he heard enough, Chamberland called George Matthews, who was overjoyed with the news of Patty's capture.

"I'm calling mainly about this commitment order," Chamberland said. "We've been talking to the girl for over an hour, and it seems to me that she's got a helluva beef."

"What's your point, lieutenant?"

"Well, my point is that the hospital is a pretty drastic step." He was trying to be vague to avoid alarming Patty, but he was having difficulty expressing his concerns. "Would you object to us taking her to the detention home?"

"Lieutenant," Matthews said in exasperation, "is the commitment order in proper form?"

"As far as I can tell."

"Good. Then your instructions are clear. I shall send a Miss Wexler to make a positive identification, then I expect you people to transport the girl to the State Hospital, as ordered."

"Just a minute, Mr. Matthews. Can you hold on for a minute? I need to get to another phone." Chamberland's face was flushed with anger as he walked quickly to the adjoining office.

Patty could hear the lieutenant shouting and cursing into the telephone, then she heard him slam the phone down and make several more calls. Officer Gillis leaned over and spoke quietly, "Patty, I don't know what's going on, but we have orders to take you to the State Hospital for an . . ."

Gillis was interrupted by the reappearance of Lieutenant Chamberland. "You better go," he said to Gillis. "There's nothing we can do about it."

Patty sat alone in the back seat of the patrol car, staring at the gray-brown predawn landscape. This was the first time she noticed that the leaves were changing colors and the grass was turning brown. She began to wonder how cold it would get in this part of the country. Running in the wintertime would be uncomfortable, and she would have to plan ahead for that contingency.

Forty-five minutes out of the city, the car began to slow down, and Patty could see the large four- and five-story cream-colored brick buildings set on the expansive grounds of the State Hospital. Most of the massive buildings looked old and worn, and some of the windows had bars on them.

Patty thought it was a scary place, but she would stay only long enough to get some food and rest before running again. This would be only a temporary detour, she thought, as she scanned the beautiful grounds unblemished by guard towers or fences.

The patrol car stopped in front of the main building, and the three occupants emerged and walked up a long flight of concrete steps to the front door. Gillis pressed a button, then identified himself by slipping papers through a metal slit in the door. They entered a small room with a steel door at the far end. As soon as the outside door closed, the inner door swung open, and the three walked toward the nurse who waited inside.

They entered a reception area that served as the hub for five long hallways leading from it. The ceilings were high, and the hallways reminded Patty of long tunnels with screened-in lights evenly spaced down the center. Patty felt three inches tall as she stood and gaped at the bigness of the place. The gray floors were made of concrete, buffed shiny and slick with countless layers of wax. The walls were also of concrete, painted institutional yellow, broken only by the placement of solid steel doors at eight-foot intervals down both sides of each tunnel.

The place combined the odor of medicine with the rancid stench of the urine-stained mattress that Patty had dragged from her room five days earlier. She tried to assimilate the sensory images that were bombarding her, but when the groans and cries emanating from behind the steel doors and echoing down the halls reached her, she knew where she was, and she ducked and tried to run between the legs of the patrolmen standing behind her. Each one grabbed an arm, urging her to be calm. She struggled for a few minutes, then went completely limp, sobbing one more time about grown-ups who lie. "You told me this was a hospital! This ain't no hospital—it's a *prison.*" Then she struggled and twisted, screaming, "A prison! This is a prison!" Patty tried to say more, but the wrenching sobs coming from the pit of her stomach muffled and distorted her words.

A middle-aged woman wearing a crisp white smock over her two-piece suit walked into the reception area and spoke to the two policemen. "Why don't you gentlemen bring her into my office."

They had to carry her the length of the room, then they guided her forcibly into the small office. Officer Gillis caught his partner's eye and wrinkled his nose in distaste for the job they had been assigned. This was not the first time they had taken a minor to the adult security ward of the State Hospital, but the others had been totally different. They had all been raging maniacs, completely incoherent, and older than this little girl who knew exactly what she was doing, and why.

"M'am," Gillis panted, "I don't know what this girl's doing here, but I want you to know that we spent an hour this morning trying to rescind the commitment order. We talked to her the whole time, and she doesn't need this kind of treatment," gesturing toward the long hall.

The woman spoke directly to Patty, although the communication was obviously intended for the recalcitrant policemen as well. "Patricia, this is a hospital, and this area is for patients who try to hurt themselves or someone else. It might look bad to you, but we try to take good care of our patients." Then she motioned toward the nurse and said, "Mrs. Skelton will complete the intake forms and will answer any questions you might have."

The smaller woman took the doctor's place behind the desk. The gray-haired nurse was as formidable as the doctor who preceded her. She was very much in control of the situation, but there was less aloofness about her. She spoke directly to Officer Gillis. "I know how you men must feel. My husband is with the Sheriff's Department, so I can appreciate how difficult this is for you."

She sighed and leaned back in her chair when it appeared that the two men would not leave until something was resolved. "We received word four days ago that Patty would be brought to our section as soon as she was picked up. We were led to believe that she was violent and needed the structure provided by one of our security rooms."

The two men looked at each other in disbelief, so Nurse Skelton elaborated, "According to Mr. Matthews' verbal report and written affidavit, Patty initially attacked five deputy sheriffs, ran away from a foster home, escaped from custody, and vandalized state property." She let that information sink in, then continued, "But whether the reports are accurate or not is not the issue here. The simple fact is that I have been ordered to take this girl and place her in a security room."

She looked at Patty, but continued to speak to the police-men. "Gentlemen, this is never a happy situation, but I promise you we will make her as comfortable as possible and get her out of here as soon as we can."

Her final remark seemed to register with Patty, so Nurse Skelton spoke directly to her. "We have been told to place you here because you are a habitual runaway and in need of psychological evaluation. We have a children's hospital, but it is not secure, and it is full."

Patty had managed to bring her sobbing under control, but her hands continued to twist and writhe in her lap.

"You will not have to stay here very long," the nurse as-sured her, "and as soon as the doctors have completed the evaluation, you will be placed somewhere else." Then, as if to provide the policemen with final assurances, she said to them, "When we discovered we would be dealing with an eleven-year-old girl, we fixed up the security room closest to the office to make her more comfortable."

Gilli_ said, "M'am, if you'll buzz that door for us, we'll get out of here. I still don't know what's going on, but I sure feel better about it after talking to you."

The nurse gave Patty a pill. "This will help you sleep. I know you'll feel better when you wake up."

As she took the pill, Patty again looked around the barren room. It was eight feet long and four feet wide, and cream-colored paint covered the steel walls. The only window was six inches wide, three feet long, and covered with institution-al screen. The glass in the window was frosted.

"Patty, I'm going to leave your door open, but I must warn you, if you are ever found outside this room unattended, we will have to lock the door. The only way out of this building is through the front door, and it would be impossible for any-one to go through that door unless someone else was there to activate the release."

The pill began to take effect immediately, and Patty ac-cepted the fact that whether the door was open or not, this was a cell, and not a room, and the chance of escaping through those double doors in front was absolutely zero. Nurse Skelton covered Patty with the sheet and blanket as her half-sleep filled her mind with the images of her brothers and sisters playing near the riverbank. It was the sound of John playing "Edelweiss" that finally lulled her into deep sleep.

"Okay, Sleeping Beauty, it's time to wake up. Your Prince Charming has arrived." The voice was loud, crisp, and filled with warmth and laughter.

Patty's head bobbed up from the pillow, but she was unable to place herself in time and space. Her mind seemed spaced out and blank. She threw off the covers, raised up on her elbows, and shook her head violently in a panicky attempt to clear her thoughts. She saw the steel walls and the long narrow window, and the pieces began to fall into place. Then the groans and cries and odors assailed her, and her reorientation was complete.

Patty slumped back into the mattress, and she lay there unable to move. Then she felt the weight of a body sitting on the edge of her bed and opened her eyes and saw the smiling face of a huge black man dressed completely in white. His massive shoulders seemed to stretch the seams on his jacket to the breaking point. His smile was warm and his voice like deep velvet. The after-effects of the sedative wrapped her in a fog, and the sound of his voice gave her the pleasant sensation of floating in a syrupy substance. She began to smile and surrendered herself to the exquisite sensation.

Then the huge black hand came toward her shoulder and began shaking her back into a world she wanted no part of. "Hi, Patty, my name's Jake. Are you awake?" That was followed by a delightfully sonorous laugh. "What about that? I'm a poet and didn't know it." Then, in a musical beat, he chanted, "My name's Jake. Are you awake?"

Patty came out of her trance, laughing at the infectious geniality of the newcomer, but as the fog cleared from her brain, she remembered again, and there was nothing to smile about. She flipped over and faced the wall. All she wanted was to be left alone. What she felt could not be shared with anyone else.

But Jake obviously had other ideas. He placed the palm of his hand gently on her back and said soothingly, "Princess, there's NO way I can pretend to know how you're feeling right now. I can't even comprehend how alone and frightened you must be in this place. But I want you to trust me, because old Jake is going to help you to live through it like a human being."

Jake tugged gently on her shoulder and turned her toward him. Her eyes were filled with anger, hatred, and resentment, and his were large brown pools of love and compassion. "There's a lot of craziness inside and outside of this place, most of which has nothing to do with the patients. Your being here is part of that craziness, but I can't do anything about that. All I can do is promise to help you be as safe and comfortable as possible."

Patty tried to block out the words, but the sentiment enveloped her and wrapped her in a special kind of security blanket. While Jake Clemmer sat staring at the frightened child, trying to find the words to ease her pain and let her know that he cared, her psychological defenses abjured the magical words of adults—*Trust me,* he had said . . . *I promise*—the usual grown-up lies.

At fifty-four years of age, Jake Clemmer was not a typical aide at the State Hospital. His official title was chief aide of the security ward. Psychiatric aides were at the bottom of the professional pecking order, but they were the people who kept the institution functioning humanely, often providing patients with their only regular contact with the outside world.

On most wards, they were the people who made sure the bodies were clean, warm, and well fed, but the security ward aides enjoyed a special status. Their patients were dangerous, and most were perceived to be hopeless cases, but Jake Clemmer had spent nineteen years proving they were wrong in just enough cases to earn a reputation and respect.

Jake had been a gandy dancer for the Union Pacific Railroad for more than twenty years. He had always taken pride in every aspect of his work, from competing in the old-time handcar races to pounding spikes more efficiently than anyone else on the line. There seemed to be no physical limitations on the potential accomplishments of his massively muscled body, but when he was thirty-five years old, a rookie lost control of his hammer, and the full impact of the twelve-pound sledge was absorbed by Jake's right knee, ending his career with a stiff leg and a slight limp.

Jake applied for janitorial work at the State Hospital because that was one of the few state agencies hiring blacks at that time. He was turned down on the spot, but the senior resident of the security section perceived his physical strength and gentle temperament as an ideal combination to cope with the peculiar problems of the security ward.

There were forty-two raving, dangerous maniacs storehoused in four-by-eight cells, and the wary aides were unwilling to do anything but shove food through the small hatch in the locked door. The doctor was convinced that some of them could benefit from treatment if physical control could be exerted over the patients during the initial stages, so he explained his problem to Jake and conducted him on a memorable tour.

The cells and the patients in them were filthy and gruesome. Jake watched them through the observation slots cut into the steel doors at eye level. He saw men and women of all ages tearing at their food like vicious animals, smearing feces on their faces and walls, lying on mattresses stained with the urine of countless hundreds of nights, devoid of human emotions, and completely removed from all human interaction.

Jake's strength and courage took him into the cells where he cajoled or restrained the patients long enough for the doctors to administer medication for the first time. The program was an immediate success, and the other security aides were required either to emulate Jake's techniques or find other employment, so it befell him to train the aides who decided to remain and to recruit replacements for those who left. Two months after Jake Clemmer had been refused a janitorial job, he was appointed chief aide of security ward.

Jake and his staff continued to deal with the acting-out problems of some of the most dangerously disturbed people in the state, but every once in a while they ran into a situation like the one now lying on the bed. There were no rules for such cases, and they had to trust their own intuition.

Jake's intuition told him to be gentle and patient. He had been studying Patty's file since it had arrived with the original commitment order three days earlier. He worked his way methodically through the file, and as the pathetic injustices became clear to him, Jake hoped the girl might escape capture.

"Patty, I know most of your story, but I honestly don't know why you're here, except that you continually run away, and some people are afraid. I know you are angry because they separated you from your brothers and sisters after they said they wouldn't, and you've probably made up your mind to get them back all by yourself."

Jake sat quietly to let the words sink in, then he continued, "You're here for an evaluation, and I want to be sure you know exactly what an evaluation is. I'll tell you straight out what an evaluation is . . . they want to find out if you're crazy. Now, you can continue playing games if you want to, but if you don't talk to the doctor, the psychologist, or the social worker—if you don't tell them how you feel and just keep it inside—they won't be able to evaluate you, and you will stay right here until they do."

Jake rose to his feet, and the bed sprung back to its original position, bouncing Patty like a cork on a pond. He wanted to pick her up and comfort her, but he knew that the time to reach out was when the patient wanted and needed it. He knew he would have to restrain himself until Patty reached out to him, and it hurt him to realize that she was a long way from reaching out to an adult once more.

* * *

Patty would never forget that first night. The stark appearance of the steel walls and narrow window was gruesome, but not nearly as frightening as the shrieks and moans emanating from the locked cells. The barren cells and the empty halls created an echo effect that magnified the tragic horror, and Patty almost wished that they had locked her in for her own protection.

The next day, Patty stood at the entrance to her cell and watched people going and coming through the front door. The system was foolproof. In order to activate the locks, one person needed to press a buzzer while another, twenty feet away, inserted a key into the door lock.

Patty decided that Jake Clemmer's advice had been straight. She would try to hold herself together long enough to pass whatever tests she had to pass. Intellectually, she realized it was just a matter of time, and she would have to be patient. Emotionally, however, the temptation to lose hope and give up was overwhelming.

On the fifth day, one of the patients broke free from two aides attempting to administer medication. They had left the cell door open, and the patient ran down the hall screaming and clawing at the air. Patty jumped from her bed in alarm when the patient came to a sliding stop in front of her open door.

Patty couldn't tell whether it was a man or a woman. Its hair was white and wild, sticking up in all directions. Its eyes were set deep in a wrinkled, pasty face and twitched back and forth erratically. The creature tilted its head to one side and gaped open-mouthed and drooling into Patty's room just as the aides arrived to take control.

The young girl did not have time to be frightened while the incident was unfolding, but when it was over, she cried hysterically. Someone came in and tried to comfort her, but she kept pushing him away until he gave up and left.

When she stopped crying, she stared hypnotically at a small seam in the ceiling, and something strange happened. Everything began to fade, much like that first afternoon when she experienced the aftereffects of the sedative. As the fog enveloped her, it was no longer necessary to think, to hurt, to fear, or to know how totally alone she really was.

Two hours later, Jake Clemmer appeared in the doorway with a broad smile on his face and her dinner tray in his hands. There was a napkin draped over one arm, and he was about to portray a waiter preparing to bestow elaborate services upon his favorite customer, hoping to elicit a little laugh that might break through the impregnable shield Patty had drawn around herself. He stepped into the room with a flourish, but she did not laugh. She was totally unaware of his presence.

Her open-eyed, blank stare sent chills up Jake's back, because he knew what it signified. The catatonia was a very real warning that Patty's psyche had absorbed all the emotional trauma it could handle, and the breaker switch in her brain was turning off further outside disruptions. It was a comfortable sensation for the girl to blank out the outside world, but she failed to realize that she was not totally in control, and that the overload of emotional trauma needed a healthy outlet.

Jake moved quickly to place the tray on the floor and sit beside her on the bed. He grasped one of her hands and slapped it lightly but briskly, calling, "Patty, Patty, snap out of it. Wake up!" Then he vigorously massaged her arms until she came out of her trance and forced herself to a sitting position.

Jake had tried to be permissive and solicitous toward Patty for the past five days, but he realized he had done the wrong thing. "Eat your dinner," he said firmly. "Then put your shoes on. We're going for a long walk." The following day, Patty was put on a regular schedule of walks, exercise in the gym, television, and soft drinks in the canteen, and there was no recurrence of catatonic episodes.

Jake redoubled his efforts to have the evaluation process

begin. He had been trained to help bring the mentally ill back to normality, but in this case, the process was moving in reverse: a perfectly normal child was being driven toward insanity.

Jake's confrontation with the chief psychiatrist brought no results because the case load was too great for the limited staff. He pleaded for Jake's understanding saying, "There simply aren't enough hours in the day," so Jake decided to extend the day, and he stated his concerns to three people who would listen, and they agreed to work with Patty on their own time.

The evaluation started the following morning at ten. "Hello, Patty, my name is Miss Lockhardt, and I am a social worker. Do you know what a social worker is?"

She might as well have asked Mickey Mantle if he knew what a baseball was. Patty had been surrounded by social workers all her life. If they deigned to mark the right box with their magic pens, the check came in for food and clothes once a month; not enough to fill a stomach or cover a body, but enough to stay alive. It was a social worker whom June Clawson had to snow to get the kids back the first time they were separated, and it was a social worker who had arranged for other social workers to take her brothers and sisters away from the courthouse in separate cars. Patty indeed knew what social workers were—the poor man's deity.

"Yes, m'am, I know what a social worker is." She took a deep breath and looked away. She could never lie like her mother could, but if there was ever a time to be good at it, it was now. They called it an "evaluation," but she called it a test. If she flunked, they would keep her locked up forever.

"Patty, I want you to relax and just talk to me. I want you to tell me how you feel and what you want."

Patty knew from her own experiences with social workers that she would have to strike just the right balance. If she were too sweet, she would be labeled phony; if she were completely honest, they would know she would never give up her search. Expressing herself carefully, Patty spent the next two hours confessing a need to be with her brothers and sisters. She would like to have conjured some tears for proper emphasis, but that was beyond her volition. All in all, Patty was quite satisfied with her performance.

The session ended with Miss Lockhardt's promise to come back the next day.

Jake Clemmer waited anxiously for the appearance of Bernice Lockhardt. He sat at the rear of the cafeteria with two cups of steaming black coffee. She appeared at noon, precisely on schedule. Bernice was tall and thin, with light brown hair that was long and stringy. Her face was bony and devoid of makeup, and she wore a wrinkled pantsuit with a gray trim that had once been white. She was probably attractive, but the entire picture was of a woman who was not concerned about appearances.

Bernice was one of the few professionals who could function well with the patients on Jake's ward, and Jake held her as a friend and esteemed professional. He had asked that she head up the evaluation team that would include a psychiatrist, Dr. Berea, and a psychologist, Dr. Kadiak.

"Well, what do you think?" he asked eagerly.

She grinned at her friend and shook her head. "Jake, you know it's too soon. Kadiak will complete the psychological testing by five o'clock, then Berea will have to conduct at least three interviews."

"Yeah, yeah," he said impatiently. "So much for the shrink games, now what do you *think?*" He looked around to be certain no one else was within listening range, then he persisted, "Come on, Bernice, I really want to know what you think of that girl."

She reached into her massive leather bag and fumbled for a cigarette. "One thing I found out was that you didn't tell me all you knew about her, did you?"

"I told you all I knew," he said indignantly. "She has hardly said a word to me. How did I mislead you?"

"You said she was bright, attractive, has been through hell, and has been given the shaft, all of which I agree with, but you didn't tell me how close she is to the edge—*Bonkersville.*"

That was one of her favorite slangisms, and the shadow that crossed Jake's face expressed his disapproval. She laughed and said, "Sorry, I know you hate me to be so technical."

"Bernice," he said seriously, "I feel like we're in a race with disaster. Don't let me down."

She reached over and placed her hand on his forearm. "Jake, this is going to take some time. Patty spent two hours this morning laying the sincere and righteous act on me. It may take her a month to open up. Meanwhile, the best thing you and your people can do is keep her busy."

"Don't you worry about that," he smiled. "You get her head screwed down tight, and we'll keep her bouncing like a Ping-Pong ball."

With the new schedule of walks, workouts, canteen breaks, and occasional movies in the gym, Patty began to relax. The interviews with Miss Lockhardt and the doctors got easier as the days passed. She never came to trust them, but she felt they were not trying to trap her, so she followed Jake's repeated advice and tried to be as honest as possible without confirming that she would run again the moment she was free.

"What kind of name is Jake?" Patty asked in one of her more relaxed moments. "I never heard of it before."

"Well, I'll tell you, little lady," he said, preparing to launch into another of his inexhaustible string of anecdotes, "my real name is 'John,' just like your brother's, but they called me 'Jack.' I ran away from home to work in a carnival when I was not much older than you are right now. Oh my," he sighed, "those were fun days, but the people started calling me 'Blackjack,' and I didn't know whether I was a bottle of whiskey or a card game." Patty giggled without knowing why, except that his face had broken into a huge smile.

"A couple of years later, I lied about my age and went to work for the railroad, and I told them my name was 'Jake,' because I hated that 'Blackjack' nickname. Then they used to say, 'Everything's Jake,' which meant 'good,' and I liked that, so I decided to keep that name." Then, satisfied with the story, he sat back and concluded, "And that's how I came to be known as 'Jake.'"

Suddenly, it was over. Five weeks after that nightmarish morning when she was dragged into the security ward, the final evaluation was completed, and read as follows:

> Patricia J. Clawson is an 11-year-old girl, referred to the security ward of our hospital by the State Department of Social Welfare, Children's Division. The initial request for placement came from Mr. George Matthews, Director, Children's Division, and acting supervisor of the Clawson case.
>
> As indicated in the initial case history material, Patricia is the oldest of five children abandoned by their parents approximately ten weeks ago.
>
> We have found her to have above average intelligence and high maturity level due largely to the parental role she was forced to assume.
>
> She is obviously depressed and anxious, which we find to be a healthy, normal reaction to the abnormal situation she is presently experiencing. There is *no* evidence of pathology or neurotic behavior. Patricia's primary anxiety is due to the separation from her brothers and sisters. She feels responsible for their care, and unless they are reunited, we find it most probable that she will continue to elope from any placement made.
>
> We therefore recommend that Patricia and her siblings be placed in one foster home. We realize how difficult it will be to find an appropriate environment for five children, but we cannot overemphasize the importance of reuniting this family. The emotional and physical trauma and the resulting dam-

age that has been experienced will be compounded by long separation.

The treatment team strongly recommends that in the future, children not be referred to the adult security ward of our hospital.

Submitted by:

Bernice K. Lockhardt, MSW
Treatment Team Leader

Bernard J. Kadiak, Ph.D.
Psychologist

Nathan W. Berea, M.D.
Psychiatrist

George Matthews was famous for two distinctly different types of temper tantrums. The most common was the cold, clasped-hands, clipped-speech, insulting type in which he camouflaged his hostility behind his usual exterior of self-control until it was too late for his target to retreat. The day he received the report from the State Hospital, however, he regressed to another kind of tantrum replete with the waving of his arms as he paced, the bulging of his blood vessels in his neck as he raged, and the spasmodic disruptions of his speech as he screamed.

"J-J-Just l-l-look at that re-report," he stammered hysterically. "Have y-you ever seen such a ridic-ridic-ridiculous recommendation?"

Claudia Wexler shifted uncomfortably in her chair and figeted under the angry outbursts and pointing finger of George Matthews. "It *looks* like any other evaluation report from the State Hospital," she said timidly.

Matthews looked at her in scathing disgust and came around the desk to snatch the paper from her hand. The

move caught her by surprise, and she flinched, thinking that
he had finally dropped all inhibitions and was about to break
her face.

"'N-N-No evidence of p-p-pathological or n-neurotic behavior,'" he shrieked, reading from the report. He looked at
Claudia's blank face, and his upper lip twitched involuntarily
as he wondered if the fat simpleton had any idea how deva-
statingly hostile the report really was.

He finally concluded he was wasting his time, so he ordered her to leave. He needed private time to think through
the implications of this latest attack on his authority. His
mind flitted randomly through the accusatory connotations
of every paragraph as Claudia set a new record for extricating herself from the deep chair and scurrying from the
office.

When he was finally able to bring himself under control,
Matthews pondered a particular aspect of the report upon
which he would contrive appropriate requital. The most
offensive section was the recommendation pertaining to reuniting the children in a single foster home. This was a direct
attack on his own judgment and the decision of the Juvenile
Court. There was a more effective method of curtailing the
girl's determination to find them—he would order the children relocated into foster homes throughout the state, separated by hundreds of miles. He would place the oldest girl in
the rural northwestern corner of the state, 245 miles away,
and when—not if—but when she ran from that placement,
she would find herself behind bars in the State Reformatory.

With that issue resolved in his mind, he began to fume
over the uncomplimentary closure of the document
. . . "Submitted by . . ." Every other report from the State
Hospital closed with, "Respectfully submitted." They would
respect him again after he showed them how wrong they had
been. By law, he had the power to dispose of the case as he
saw fit, without regard to their recommendations, and, by
God, he would show them how to do it.

*   *   *

If the definition of "depression" is anger turned inward, then Bud Griggs spent the three months following the Clawson hearing in a state of profound depression. He remained angry with himself and every other member of the cast who had participated in the destruction of five children. Most of all, he was infuriated with the inexorable system that had permitted it to happen. He was so preoccupied with finding new ways to project his own guilt that the echoes of Patty's screams—"You promised! . . . you promised!"—had all but faded from his mind.

He found himself attending strictly to the administrative aspects of his job, completely avoiding any personal contact with the children who continued to parade through the Juvenile Court. His duties made it impossible to avoid Judge Harrington, but he could not forgive the judge for the part he played, in spite of the fact that Griggs knew him to be a wise and compassionate jurist.

Judge Harrington was attempting to discuss the upcoming docket one day in early December, but Griggs' attention seemed to be elsewhere, so the judge decided it was time to bring the matter to a head. "Come on, Bud," he scolded, "get with it! You're not thinking. We've got some tough cases tomorrow, and if I'm going to make some decent decisions, I need to know what's happening."

Even though Bud thought the Clawson case was all but forgotten, the "decent decisions" remark brought it roaring back from the unconscious. "Shit, Judge, we don't make decent decisions—we process bodies. The hell with who they are or what they need—just get them in and get them out. Run them through the turnstile, then wash our hands of the whole mess!"

The judge sat back and actually seemed relieved. "Good," he said. "Now we can finally get this out on the table." His voice was calm, but Bud could see the hurt in his face as he leaned forward and clenched his hands tightly on top of the desk. "You have been obsessive about the Clawson case for two months, and you are convinced that you were betrayed.

What makes you think that you're some kind of a god that has all the right answers? What makes you so sure that keeping those kids together was even the *right* thing to do?"

The firmness in his voice kept Bud from interrupting, and he continued, "Patricia had been both father and mother to those children for several years. You know damned well that she would not have allowed any foster parents to take control. I know that I don't have all the answers, either, but the fact is that *I* had to make the decision, and in my best judgment, Patricia deserved a chance to be an eleven-year-old girl again, and the other children needed to have adult models to grow up with."

There was a moment of silence, then he continued, "In this business, we can never be sure that we have done the right thing. All we can hope for is to arrive at the right decision based upon all the information we can gather. I felt then, and I feel now that you were too close to the situation to be objective. In any case, we have to go on. Too many other children are depending on us."

The judge's rationale seemed to help both of them live with the injustice and bury the pain that Bud had a powerful need to bury. Within a week, Bud was almost his old self. He supervised the probation officers but refused to involve himself intimately in any of their cases. Then the call came from Nancy Sloan. He had not seen or heard from her since that day in her apartment when he had begged to see John Clawson. He had no desire to resurrect those memories again.

"I need to talk to you," she said.

"I'd rather not. We don't have anything to say."

"You're wrong, Bud. This is about the Clawson case."

"All the more reason for me to stay out of it. Matthews threatened to have me arrested when I tried to locate those kids, so you can kiss off. I'm out of it."

Five minutes after he hung up on her, Judge Harrington called. "Bud," he said, "Nancy Sloan just called . . . I thought the mourning period was over."

"It is, Judge. I just don't want to dig up the bodies again."

"I think you'd better," he said. "It wasn't easy for her to call, but she needs your help. I told her to be in your office in an hour."

Bud had mixed feelings, but could not deny the excitement that was building within, and he was glad the judge had overruled his petulant reaction to Nancy's call.

Nancy arrived ten minutes late and found Bud pacing the floor. She was clearly nervous about the situation and started by apologizing for the traffic problem, the parking problem, and any and all past misunderstandings. Bud cut her off as gently as he could and asked her to tell him what was on her mind. Her anxiety changed to pain, and he wished he had followed his original instincts and stayed out of it.

"It's Patty," she said quietly. "It's bad—it's very bad."

Griggs came out of his chair in alarm. "What happened to her," he demanded.

Nancy fought to hold back the tears, and said, "Patty has been committed to the Girls' Reform School."

The color drained from Griggs' face, and he flopped back into his chair. "Tell me the whole story," he said wearily. "Start from the beginning, and don't leave anything out."

Nancy related the events of the past few months as quickly and precisely as possible—the bailiff holding Patty as she watched her brothers and sisters being taken away from the courthouse in separate cars, her flight from the foster home, the ransacking of Nancy's office and her subsequent escape, and Patty's commitment to the security ward of the State Hospital.

As Bud listened, he cursed under his breath and clenched his fists but remained silent.

Nancy's voice took on a new determination. "Matthews was livid when he read the evaluation report from the State Hospital. We waited until he cooled off, then we begged him to follow the recommendations of the treatment team, but he felt he was being pushed into a corner, so, like any true paranoid, he came out swinging. Besides, I think he had his mind already made up.

"He was like a crazy man, Bud. He shouted that no juvenile delinquent was going to tell him how to run his department, so instead of bringing the kids together, he shipped her off to the western part of the state—almost two hundred and fifty miles away. She stayed in that foster home only long enough to break in her new shoes and learn her geography—about a week—then she took off with a large jar of peanut butter and the family road maps."

Griggs was filled with fear and pride for the girl, and this new example of her indomitable spunk elicited a short chuckle from him.

Nancy looked at him and nodded quickly in agreement. "Well, they picked her up three days later, and she had already traveled a hundred and twenty miles in a straight line back here. The local sheriff reviewed the latest list of runaways and contacted us immediately. Matthews took the call and later called the judge out there, but we don't know for sure what they said. All I know is that he was happier than he had been in months, and he asked me to drive out to Wilbur County the next morning to make a positive identification.

"The judge was one of those part-time judges, and he called the hearing for the same day so he could get out and finish his fall plowing. Patty was charged with being a habitual runaway and beyond parental control. I argued that she could not be adjudicated beyond parental control, because the state had severed all parental rights three months earlier.

"He called me 'girlie,' and sentenced Patty to an indeterminate sentence at the Girls' Reformatory."

Griggs was too shocked and angry to speak, so he tried to picture the little girl locked up in a cell at the reform school. Then his mind went blank, and into the void came the image of Patty that day at the zoo when she said:

Everything was fun except seeing the animals in cages. They looked sad—like they wanted to be out, but there was no one to help them.

Nancy's voice began to tremble as she concluded her report. "I begged Patty to cooperate just a little. I told her that everyone else would go a mile if she would only go an inch. I pleaded with her to tell the judge that she would stay in the next foster home. I told her that the judge would change his order if she would only promise. She refused to say a word until I got up to leave her cell. Then do you know what she said, Bud?"

Nancy began to sob uncontrollably. "She said . . . 'My teacher once told me . . . that even the *meanest* slave owners . . . tried to keep families together.'"

Griggs spent most of that evening repeating Nancy's story to Judge Harrington, and he decided to have Bud take a trip to the Girls' Reform School in Belton. Even though she was officially a ward of the state, she was now under the jurisdiction of the Division of Institutional Management, which gave them the right to get involved again.

When he left the judge's house, Griggs was convinced that they had done the right thing, but as he drove home, it occurred to him that none of them had asked *why* he was going to make the trip. What was the purpose? Two days after her arrival, Patty had attempted an escape from the reformatory and had been locked up in maximum security ever since. What good could possibly come out of his sitting down and talking with Patty in a lockup cell? Was the purpose to assure her that they still cared. He was sure it was too late for that. *Suppose she asks me about her brothers and sisters? Can I tell her that John has already been thrown out of one foster home, that Karen was sitting on a bed wasting away with a broken doll in her arms, and that Charlie and Sue Anne were in foster homes with three hundred miles separating them?*

As Griggs drove over the 250 miles of flat farmland the following morning, he had plenty of time to fantasize about what he would find and what he would do. He stared out at the December landscape spotted with complacent cows grazing on the brown grass. The plowed fields were black and rich, separated by ugly hedgerow windbreaks. The summer had been so hot and dry that the fall colors had never materialized, and the November browns limply deteriorated into December gray, which fit his mood perfectly.

The question that kept nagging at him was, "What is the purpose of this visit?" Somehow, there was a missing thread—a latent agenda that refused to surface into the conscious level. There seemed to be something they were all thinking, but not saying, but it evaded him, so he began to free associate and fantasize about the trip. *What would the lockup section of the Girls' Reform School look like?* Griggs had been in juvenile jails that were ancient relics of many decades, and he had been in some that were stainless steel, glass, and marble, but both had one thing in common: even with cells crowded with inmates, they were like tombs, devoid of normal activity, seemingly uninhabited by human beings as sounds of the clanging of steel-on-steel echoed off the walls, the bars, and the hard-surfaced floors.

And who were the children behind those bars? Many would not yet be in their teens; some were there on serious charges, and some for no charges at all; most were tough-talking—all were helpless. Recalling the statistics, Griggs knew that fewer than ten percent of the children in jail had committed a crime against the person, and seventeen percent more had stolen property, as often as not food or clothing. He knew also that one out of every three children had been placed behind bars because their parents did not want them and the state needed to furnish them with a safe place to live. *A SAFE PLACE.*

A safe place . . . Griggs thought about Herman . . . God, that was a long time ago. He hadn't thought about him for five years. Herman's mother and father divorced and moved to different states. Herman loved them both so much he used to run from one to the other. He was finally locked away in Texas as an ungovernable juvenile and habitual runaway. When he tried to escape from the juvenile prison farm, he was run down by the dogs and placed in solitary confinement until his mind snapped permanently. He was fourteen, and he had been given a "safe place."

ESTELLA . . . that name jumped into his mind. She had been arrested and paroled twice for breaking into the same grocery store for food she couldn't afford. The third time she was caught, the court labeled her "hopeless" and sentenced her to a year in the juvenile corrections institution. She had Patricia's spunk. She told the judge, "I'm *glad* to go. At least I'll be warm this winter." She was fifteen when they found a "safe place" for her. Unfortunately for her, though, there was no room in the juvenile reformatory, so Estella was placed in the women's jail, where she was gang-raped the first night. After six months, she said, "I figure they're giving me clean clothes and good food, and I'm only getting raped once every couple of weeks. What I got to complain about?"

The sudden chill that went up Griggs' spine was not caused by the brisk December air. *PATRICIA. Is it possible to save her?* He fantasized about smuggling her out of jail under his loose-fitting raincoat, putting her in the car, and running all over the state picking up her brothers and sisters. We would head for the border, drinking pop and laughing and giggling about peanut butter and cramming that lovable and huge Del Howard into the kiddie train at the zoo.

Griggs laughed to himself as he envisioned the ridiculous scene, but a relief came over him that had not been there for a long time. What was so funny about it? Was it really that ridiculous? The scenario was outrageously stupid, but the thought made sense. *Why can't we build a home especially for these children?*

Others were doing it. They had been doing it in the SOS Villages since the end of World War II to care for the war orphans in Europe. Little villages in the middle of larger towns, where abandoned and orphaned kids grew up in houses, and stayed together as families, and went to public schools, and participated in community activities, and grew up to be normal citizens. But not someone else's home, and not someone else's food. *Their own.* Homes built and maintained only because there were little people who needed them. *Why not?*

Bud Griggs realized then that the hidden agenda was surfacing, and also that he was driving a state car at ninety-seven miles an hour. In his excitement, he almost drove past the reform school. As he searched for the visitors' entrance, he concluded only that he would not share this new hope with Patty until it was a certainty.

When those steel doors closed behind him, he was in another world of shiny marble floors, cream-colored tile walls, and metal doors with tiny windows covered with bars and heavy mesh.

Griggs was led to the lockup section by a uniformed matron who said very little. It was not his first time in a juvenile jail by a long shot, but the sounds and smells got to him as much as they ever did. Behind one steel door, a tiny voice was sobbing, "Momma . . . Momma," and behind another a young girl was vomiting.

When they reached Patty's cell, the matron unlocked the door and said, "You have a visitor. Mr. Griggs has come to see you." There was no answer, but he entered, happy to be insulated from the sounds and odors of the corridor. Griggs felt a sense of relief as the door closed behind him . . . until he saw what he had walked into.

Patty's cell was a six-by-eight-foot room with cement block walls and concrete floors and ceiling. The door was solid steel, and the small frosted glass window was covered with bars. There was a three-inch-thick mattress on the floor of the cell, and a dry commode immediately next to her mattress. The toilet was a rusty-looking green color, and there was no running water—just a large sewer pipe to sit on to perform bodily functions. The odors emanating from the commode permeated the tiny cell.

Patty was sitting in the fetal position on the floor, on top of the thin, bare mattress. She seemed catatonic, staring vacantly into space without uttering a sound. Griggs didn't remember what he said or even how he said it, but it didn't make much difference, because he was sure she wasn't listening. It seemed incredible that this eleven-year-old girl was suffering these shattering indignities only because her mother and father had driven off and left her that day at the hamburger stand. As he prattled on about one thing or another, the images flooded his mind again—Patty carrying Sue Anne through the streets of Philadelphia to the hospital—Patty running across the sand and plunging into the river to pull Charlie from the deep water—her radiant smile that day outside the courtroom when he blurted, "How PRETTY you look."

Griggs turned his face away from her to hide his tears, and he reached for the door when she said her first words . . . "How are the kids?"

He was crying openly when he finally turned to her and said, "I don't know, but I'll find out."

Griggs banged on the door of Patty's cell until the matron unlocked the massive door to let him out. He followed her down the same corridor, but this time he was too lost in his own thoughts to hear the cries of the caged children or to smell the odors of that terrible place.

As he stepped through the final set of doors, the sunlight and the noises of the outside world startled him back to a different reality. He wondered if it were possible to explain to anyone else the pain he had just witnessed. Was it possible for any group or individual with any semblance of sanity to see what he had just seen and say they were doing the right thing? It was insanity—total—unbelievable insanity—but to call it names didn't change the facts or lighten the load of his anger and depression.

In his mind, Griggs could still see Patty Clawson huddled in her cell, curled up as if she would hibernate until her next opportunity to run. And RUN she would. He had no illusions about that. She would run until someone listened to her plea, or until she died of the hurt within.

The visit had lasted for what seemed like three or four hours, but when he got back to his car, Griggs realized that he had been there no more than fifteen minutes. Patty had said only four words—"How are the kids?" But those four words represented a bridge of monumental proportions. She was still tuned in and focused solidly on her priorities. She was doing her part to hold on to reality. Now it was up to the rest of them to help her before she let go.

On the way back, he continued to think about the development of youth homes for the Clawson children and others like them, but this time the fantasy was different. This time Griggs *knew* it would happen, and any son of a bitch who stood in his way would be hurt.

Griggs arrived home to find that Del had let himself into the apartment and was waiting for him. Griggs immediately called Nancy Sloan to report on his visit with Patty, and she and Del heard it all at the same time. He told Nancy he wanted her to be at his staff meeting at nine o'clock in the morning. She said she couldn't be there because of a meeting with George Matthews, but Griggs told her to call in sick and be in his office. He hung up the phone without waiting for her reply.

The judge and Griggs alternately ran those staff meetings, but the following morning, without any verbal communication, it was obvious that this one was going to belong to Griggs. There were four full-time probation officers, the judge, Nancy, Del, and a group of law students who worked for them on a part-time basis. Griggs told them what he had seen, heard, and smelled the day before. He told them about the crying children and the innocent faces devoid of hope, and he told them it was time for them to get off their asses and do something about it.

There was going to be an alternative for those children, and the people at that meeting were going to make it happen! There was only one objective: to create a residential facility in the community with trained, professional surrogate parents who would provide an environment that would permit these unwanted children to grow up like normal human beings—an environment where children would receive the same basic structure and love that any human needs to grow up in a complicated society.

The first task was to gather facts and information. Alicia, the little rich girl of the staff, took responsibility for researching every group home and halfway house concept in existence. She was ordered to assimilate every piece of available information as quickly as possible.

Once the existing models were screened and adapted to suit their own needs, there would have to be money to build or renovate houses, to staff them, and to run them. Del and his law students were assigned the job of researching the possibilities of subcontracting with the state for the care of dependent children on a continuing basis. They knew how much money the state was paying to keep these children locked up, and they decided that they could provide better care out in the community for half that amount.

The judge had been cautious in the beginning, but as each new group formed, he volunteered to work with it, each one sounding better and more interesting than the last. He was like a kid in a chocolate factory.

The need to develop community awareness was the next item on the agenda, and Griggs told his staff that he would accept any kind of speaking engagement he was offered. He had made a practice of declining invitations to speak, assuming they were a waste of time, but not any more. He said the next time three people gathered around a mailbox to pass the time of day, he wanted to be there to tell them about Patty, and John, and Herman, and Estella; and about that jailed child crying for her momma, and the dry commodes where kids had to crap into open pipes, then live and eat and sleep with the stench; about the thin, bare mattresses on the floors and the smell of urine everywhere; and about the gang-rapes and the way such places took innocent kids and destroyed them or turned them out as hardened criminals. And then he wanted to tell them about their dream.

Oh, yes, and the judge volunteered to help him.

Nancy Sloan was given the job of tracing the Clawson kids

and giving regular reports on them. She was jeopardizing her job by doing so, but the judge volunteered to intercede if it became necessary. They agreed on a schedule of after-hours briefing sessions, and their first meeting broke up with a humorous comparison of their plan to a covert operation of the CIA.

Nancy's first report on the children came two weeks after that first staff meeting. It was short and to the point. Other people were now supervising those cases, but Nancy had been able to review the files after business hours. As Claudia had told her earlier, John had been moved from his initial foster home placement within eight days of the court hearing. His foster parents had never before taken another child, and they were totally unprepared for the reaction of their own five-year-old boy to a stranger moving into their home and competing for attention. After the first forty-eight hours, the five-year-old refused to eat at the same table with John and would say things like, "He doesn't talk right, and he isn't a part of us."

John was indifferent. As a matter of fact, there was little that John cared about. The report from his school indicated that John was not doing his work and was unresponsive to the other children. Del looked over at Griggs, and they both thought of John playing his harmonica for the pleasure of twenty children in the detention home—and John running two miles laden with boxes of pies and cakes he had taken from the restaurant.

Nancy went on to say that John's teacher thought the work might ·be too difficult for him and that he ought to be de-moted, even though he was already older and taller than any other child in the class. The principal agreed, and without any testing or evaluation, John was placed in a lower class.

John spent most of his time in his room, but little Willie continued to whine about the stranger in his house, so the foster parents notified the Welfare Department that they wanted John out immediately.

About that time, Patty had been still prowling the streets looking for her brothers and sisters, so Welfare thought it best to remove John from the city. The caseworker drove him more than two hundred miles to his next placement, and when they arrived, the whole family, which included six-year-old twins, was there to greet him. John put down his suitcase, walked over to the boys, and said, in a voice loud enough for all to hear, "Go fuck yourselves!"

The whole group broke out with applause and laughter, and Del shouted to Nancy, "Tell us again about that part where John is *indifferent.*"

Nancy concluded her report on John by saying that the social worker then put her hands on John's shoulders, turned him toward the car, picked up his suitcase, and left without another word. She said that John sat next to her on the front seat and smiled to himself all the way back to town. The next day, he was placed with an older couple with no children.

Sue Anne was placed with a couple named Potter, because she was the easiest of the children to get along with. The Potters' were on probation because they had lost five of their previous six children within the first three weeks of placement. Even though they talked a good game, the children coming out of the home said they hated it. No specific charges had been lodged against the foster parents, so Matthews decided, over Nancy's strenuous objections, to use Sue Anne as another test case.

Nancy indicated that the Potters' reports had been positive, but Sue Anne's school grades were falling drastically. Nancy recommended Sue Anne's removal on two separate occasions, but she was overruled by George Matthews both times.

As Nancy had told Griggs earlier, Karen's foster parents perceived her as an extremely stupid child, probably brain-damaged or retarded, but they were delighted by the fact that Karen was no trouble at all. She spent all of her time in her room, sitting on her bed, sucking her thumb, and holding the rag doll. They had attempted to enroll her in the first grade, but the school officials determined that she was totally unresponsive, and there was no reason to continue the effort.

The caseworker recommended that Karen be referred to the Children's Division of the State Hospital for a complete psychological and neurological evaluation, but the foster parents did not want to risk losing so complacent a child. Nonetheless, Karen's name was placed on the waiting list, and all agreed that there would be no purpose in sending her to school while the evaluation was pending, so everyone was happy.

Alicia started to cry, but Nancy said, "Cheer up. This is about to get better."

Charlie had been placed with a young couple, Tom and Alice Parks. They were twenty-four years old and had been told that it would not be possible for them to have children of their own. They had originally thought about adopting, but they read an article about the number of children in need of foster homes.

Their first shock came when they learned they would be restricted to a two-year license. In other words, they were to select a two-year age span they were willing to work with, and older or younger children would not be assigned to them.

Tom Parks had asked, "What happens if we take in a four-year-old and keep him for two years? Does that mean we have to give him up?"

He was told that he would have to apply for another license, but that it was probable that the child would be reassigned.

"But what if we don't want to let him go?" he persisted. "Suppose the child is happy with us, and we are happy with him? In fact, suppose we love the child?"

That's when Mr. Parks received his second surprise. He was told that the first rule of foster parenting is to avoid developing emotional attachments.

"But that's crazy," he said. "These children, more than any others, *need* love."

"Mr. Parks, we advise against it for your own protection."

Tom had been reluctant to become a foster parent in the first place, and he left the orientation session more opposed than ever, but Alice talked him into giving it a try.

For the first two days, Charlie would have nothing to do with either of them. They tried to get close to him, but decided that they would have to let him come around when he felt comfortable doing so. Tom and Alice Parks were gentle and loving people, and it didn't take Charlie long to figure that out.

Nancy reported that Charlie was flourishing "beyond belief," and the Parks had already inquired about instituting adoption procedures.

At the conclusion of Nancy's report, everyone stood and talked animatedly among themselves. Griggs drifted from group to group especially pleased that Nancy's report had ended on such a positive note. More than that, with the introduction of Tom and Alice Parks into the scheme of things, he felt that one more part of their group home puzzle had fallen into place.

The judge and Bud Griggs hit the banquet circuit for all they were worth. Alicia's research staff had been augmented by volunteers from the local college, and they were never at a loss to quote statistics or actual cases from all over the country. Their data were derived from FBI reports, court records, personal interviews, and current literature. They were loaded for bear.

They usually quoted the prevailing position of leading penologists that only twenty percent of the children in state correctional institutions needed to be there, and that dependent/neglected children make up more than sixty percent of the inmate population. After that, the supply of anecdotal material was inexhaustible.

They told about children sitting in their darkened cells with fecal matter smeared on their faces. They reported the tear-gassing of children in solitary confinement, and how the skin peeled from their bodies in sheets; and they described the plight of a fifteen-year-old girl who was forced to terminate her pregnancy into a slop bucket in her cell, then dump the four-month-old fetus down the toilet the next morning.

After a while, the word spread that their speeches were too graphic for luncheon meetings, but community interest was growing. The judge sobered up a gathering of "good old boys" at a football homecoming celebration by describing the solitary cells for children in an adjoining state:

> The cells are approximately six by eight feet in size, and they are furnished only with a thin mattress and a metal bucket for body wastes. The floors, walls, and ceilings are solid steel, and there are no windows. The steel doors are three inches thick, and the food trays are slid through a narrow slit near the floor. Only the insects survive. The urine-stained mattresses attest to the occupancy of hundreds of previous children. One forty-watt bulb burns constantly high on the ceiling of the dark cell, beyond the reach of children driven to suicide, and there is nothing to occupy their time.

At a Christmas banquet, Griggs told the story of a young widower who had grabbed his eight-year-old son by the ear in a fit of anger and frustration, violently pushing and pulling the boy around the room until he tore his ear off. The audiences were shocked to hear that the father was sentenced to only three years in a medium-security prison, while the son was committed to the state reformatory for the remainder of his childhood years because no foster parents wanted a kid with only one ear.

They had horror stories for all occasions, any group, and every time of the year, and every one of them was true. Valentine's Day came around, and they told about the twelve-year-old inmate who was given twenty-four days in solitary for writing "I love you" to a female instructor.

But they sometimes made "tactical errors." Like the time the judge spoke about the twelve-year-old inmate in Ohio who died for the lack of an attending doctor or nurse because there were no registered Democrats in the district who were willing to take the job. The judge didn't know that the local Democratic leader was in the audience, but he sure as hell heard about it in a hurry.

Speaking at a local convention, Griggs once eloquently described his findings that juvenile correctional officials were dedicated to maintaining high prison census levels in order to justify capital investments and guard against the possible loss of jobs among institutional personnel. He noticed that the audience consisted of burly men wearing crew cuts and white socks, and it was obvious that they were becoming more hostile by the minute. What he failed to realize, until it was too late, was that he was speaking to the spring meeting of the Tri-State Correctional Officers' Guild. The applause from that group approached the level of one hand clapping.

As the seasons changed, they talked to Indians, Chicanos, blacks, and whites; they talked to Jaycees, the Chamber of Commerce, and the union leaders; they talked to Christians, Jews, and Moslems, and the response was uniformly overwhelming.

Or so it seemed at the time.

Everyone agreed that something had to be done to keep innocent children out of prison, and the prospect of creating special homes for them was especially appealing. They had the community in the palms of their hands. Del and his law students had figured a way to compel the state to pay the cost of caring for the children who were placed in the homes; they had assimilated enough information to develop their own youth home model and to understand the staffing patterns and operational processes; and the money was coming in in the form of cash and pledges. They were way ahead of schedule. All that remained was for them to select the house and move in.

That's all.

That was simple enough. They selected a large home in a nice neighborhood, and all that happened was that their bandwagon promptly came unglued. Suddenly, all the people who had wanted desperately to do something for the imprisoned children came to the realization that whatever it was that would be done might possibly be done in their own neighborhood. When the residents organized against the project, Griggs said, "The hell with them. If they don't want us, we'll go somewhere else."

So they selected another house. Two weeks later, they were saying, "And the hell with them, too!"

It became painfully obvious that the youth home was wanted by the community at large, yet rejected by its component parts. Everyone wanted it in someone else's neighborhood. In the face of that opposition, they decided to schedule the entire summer for property acquisition, and the new deadline for opening the first home was set for Christmas, 1965.

The group was dejected, but there was no thought of slowing down. A few of the volunteers stopped coming to meetings, the requests for speeches slowed a little, and contributions fell off, but none of the people who had known the Clawson children lost their dedication and commitment.

Nancy was now reporting on a monthly basis, but none of them looked forward to it. In May, 1965, she told the group that John was about to be transferred to his fourth foster home in the past eight months, and an official recommendation was being drafted that he be sent to the State Hospital for treatment of profound depression. Nancy then indicated that John had almost been committed to the State Reformatory for Boys following the failure of his last foster home placement, and Del erupted, "Damn! We don't need any more of these goddammed reports of the kids. It doesn't help!" He then walked out of the room, but he returned in a minute with a cup of coffee, sat down, and apologized to the group.

Nancy continued with her report. Sue Anne had finally run away from the Potter home, and they had decided not to place any more children there, in spite of the fact that Sue Anne's eight months had set a longevity record for that foster family.

Karen was still on the waiting list for her psychological and neurological workup at the State Hospital.

There was no change in Patty's situation, either. They had let her out of lockup for a few days, and damned if she didn't try to ride out of the reform school inside a broken piano.

When it came time to report on Charlie's progress, Nancy deferred to Tom Parks. Griggs had long since decided that Tom and Alice would be their group home parents. It took some persuading, because Tom was a young architect who was struggling with the question of whether he could be a good full-time architect and care for eight to ten children at the same time. It was because of his deep love for little Charlie that he finally committed himself to reuniting the rest of the family. From that time on, Tom and Alice took turns attending the staff meetings, and both participated enthusiastically in the training program they had set up for them.

Everyone looked forward to Charlie's progress reports. Alice had told the group about Charlie's birthday party back in March and how both sets of grandparents had finally agreed to travel in to meet the two year old. It was love at first sight for them, too. Charlie called both grandfathers "Pappoo," and his name for Alice's mother was "Ying Yang," something that Tom was blamed for.

Anyway, to hear Tom tell it, Charlie was the smartest, the cutest, the greatest, and he could already catch and throw like Willie Mays, run like Glen Cunningham, and talk like Winston Churchill.

Tom concluded his report sadly by telling us that the adoption had fallen through because of legal complications. With tears forming in his eyes, Tom looked directly at Griggs and said, "Don't give up. We will have Charlie only one more year. If you quit now, we'll lose him for sure."

Tom's emotional appeal inspired them anew. There was never any thought of giving up, but the fact that someone close to the group might have thought so created a new commitment in each of them.

The first thing they decided was that the judge and Griggs

276 KENT HAYES AND ALEX LAZZARINO

had sufficiently saturated the community with speeches. They would now be more selective about public appearances, and they would spend more time preparing the chosen community to accept the group home. In addition, the staff would begin to redefine the projected model by visiting other versions of youth homes and halfway houses around the country.

As an outgrowth of their rekindled enthusiasm, the staff pointed themselves toward moving the kids into the home by Christmas. Alicia, who grew up thinking that everyone in the world celebrated Christmas on the Riviera, was the most vocal about it. "We'll all go caroling," she said. "All of us and the five kids. Then we'll go back to the house for hot chocolate and trim the tree together. Won't that be exciting for them?"

Del suggested that if the Clawson kids got half as excited as Alicia was, there wouldn't be an empty bathroom in town.

They located a third home that would suit their needs. This time they selected a house in a depressed area of town, thinking that the poor and oppressed people of the neighborhood—especially the minorities who lived there—would be the first to commiserate with the plight of the children.

The group left nothing to chance. They did a community survey and found no major problems. Griggs and Howard developed an educational program for those few who had stated their objections, and they managed to change some of their minds. It began to look as though the move might take place by Thanksgiving rather than Christmas, but that's before they heard of a fellow named Ethan Spotted Deer.

Ethan Spotted Deer was a full-blooded Cherokee from the neighborhood they had selected who thought that they were trying to dump something all over the poor people of the community. He had a chip on his shoulder that looked more like a giant redwood, and when Alice and Griggs went to visit him, he was totally intractable. When Alice called him "Mr. Deer," he accused her of making fun of his name and Native American heritage. When Griggs called him "Ethan," he accused him of having no respect and ordered them to leave.

Ethan Spotted Deer undertook a personal pilgrimage to scuttle the plans for a youth home in his neighborhood. For two solid weeks, he went from house to house warning one and all about the dope addicts, prostitutes, and jailbirds that they planned to bring into a single house. Foreboding the contagious effect on their own children and the declining property values that would result, he secured signatures from more than ninety percent of the residents in opposition to the plan. Griggs turned out the entire staff to counteract his campaign, but in the final survey they were able to secure no more than thirty-two percent of the necessary approvals.

The group that gathered in Griggs' office that night was totally disheartened. For the first time since he had visited Patty in jail, Griggs began to have doubts about pulling this thing off. At first, they had set their sights on one of the best neighborhoods in town, and ten months later they had just been thrown out of the slums. In addition, they were only halfway to the $70,000 goal, and the money had stopped coming in.

Griggs was ready to play out his last card.

He had arranged to speak before a meeting of the Women's League on August 9, 1965. This was one of the most influential groups in the community, since it was made up of politically active women, most of whom were the wives and daughters of the most powerful business leaders. He had had no more expectation from this speech than any of the others. When he accepted the invitation, he had assumed that they would have been in the process of preparing a home for the children in the poor section of town, and this would give him a nice opportunity to update one uninvolved segment of the populace with great things that were being done by another segment.

But now the message would be changed. There was no construction going on, and Griggs wanted these women to know why. He threw away the prepared text and started by saying:

Today is the first anniversary of an event that was simultaneously tragic and inspirational. One year ago today—possibly to the very minute—two parents abandoned their five children on the outskirts of this city. You all know the story by now. These children fended for themselves in the wild for sixteen days because they were afraid of being caught up and separated.

When they were found, I assured them there would be *some* place in this community where they could live and grow up *together*. All they wanted was to be a family and to be hugged and patted on the shoulder from time to time. But that was too much to ask for us.

We responded by tearing them from one another and placing them in separate homes. And when that wasn't enough to kill their spirit, we scattered them all over this great state. And when they continued in their efforts to come together again, we began locking them away in jails and mental hospitals. And those who weren't locked away were moved from foster home to foster home, keeping their belongings in paper bags to be ready for the next move.

Our dream was to reunite these children . . . but we have failed. The candle that we burn before the altar of "property values" has set fire to their last hope to live and grow up as normal children.

Griggs stopped talking and walked off the platform and through the side door. There was no applause. The women just stared quietly into space.

He was back in his office only a few minutes when he received a call from Nellie Ruppert, president of the Women's League. She said, "Bud, what do you need?"

He asked her what she meant.

She said, "There was a unanimous resolution to do *whatever* is necessary to build that home."

Griggs was speechless and incredulous. He couldn't believe his ears, and after a moment of silence, he said, "We need another thirty-five thousand dollars right away, and we need a large house."

Mrs. Ruppert said, "That sounds easy. Can you meet me at the boardroom of the bank tomorrow morning? I'll tell my husband to set it up."

When she hung up the phone, Griggs wanted to shout and scream and jump, but he couldn't even cry. Alicia took care of that when he informed the staff. Del did his part, too.

The next morning, the judge and Griggs were sitting across the table from the most powerful and affluent people in the county. There was no need to give a speech because Nellie had already done a lot of talking. Nellie and several of the other women took over, the men listened, and the two men from the Juvenile Court answered questions.

The remaining thirty-five thousand dollars was so unimportant to them that they waved it off impatiently. When they asked if Griggs had identified suitable housing, he told them about the first selection they had made in the good neighborhood.

Connie Towers said, "I know that house, and it would be ideal. It has seven or eight bedrooms, a living room, and enough space in the dining room and kitchen to be converted into a huge family kitchen area. It would be perfect."

The judge then told them about the problem of community resistance, and how they could not operate a group home there unless seventy-five percent of the neighbors within a three-hundred-foot radius agreed to it.

Marvin Ruppert then said, "Judge, I've been trying to read between the lines of what you've been saying, and I think I hear you telling us that if we could somehow move those kids into that house without anyone else knowing about it, it would be a lot tougher for the neighbors to move them out of there. Is that right?"

"You've got good ears, Marvin, but how could we get the place renovated and furnished without anyone knowing about it?"

"Suppose," Ruppert continued, "one of us buys the house in his own name, gets the renovation work done, then turns it over to you people at some point in the future—after the kids are in and the neighbors stop fighting it?"

"That might work," Griggs said to the judge, trying to encourage an affirmative response from him.

"And the contracts for the purchase and renovation would be in his name?" the judge asked. "Who would be willing to do that?"

Nellie then said with a broad grin, "Either it will be me and *this* Mr. Ruppert or it will be me and the *next* Mr. Ruppert!"

After so many months of clawing and scratching, it seemed impossible that so much could have been accomplished so quickly. Marvin and Nellie Ruppert purchased the house through his bank, and Griggs signed a note on the corporation for the purchase price.

Marvin Ruppert designated Griggs as his agent to contract for the massive renovation that would be required, and he made all the arrangements. It was the middle of October before all the papers were signed, and Griggs made the contractor swear in blood that the renovation would be completed before Christmas. But not only did the renovation need to be completed before Christmas—it had to be done in such a way as to meet the state codes for group living. The contractor thought Griggs was absolutely mad when he described the big red "EXIT" signs he wanted over all the outside doors. The contractor even went to Mr. Ruppert to be sure that he knew what kind of a crazy person he had authorized to oversee the renovation of his house.

The contractor's sense of aesthetics had been so badly offended that the work began to slow down. He seemed to grab at any excuse to do other things. First, there was a truckers' strike in Wyoming, then there was a frost in Pennsylvania. Finally, Griggs had no choice but to let him in on the secret. When Griggs had told him and his foreman about the children who would be moving into the house and why,

the foreman said, "Boss, I don't know about you but I ain't
about to be the chickenshit that doesn't get this house done
on time!" They both laughed and went back to work with
fresh determination.

Their dream was no longer a hope. It was a simple fact
that they would have the kids in the home and everything
would be set by Christmas Eve.

Griggs called the League office and talked to Ramona
Stiles, who was chairing the furniture committee. He told her
that they had to have the furniture ready to be moved into
the house a week before Christmas. She organized her committee so effectively that the furniture was ready for delivery
on December 15th. With no place to store it, the women of
the League volunteered their garages and basements. Then
they got together during the evenings and on weekends to
make drapes to Alice Parks' specifications. Together they
bought utensils, appliances, and the thousand other things
that were needed for a large family moving into a new house.

The staff and the Women's League volunteers met regularly to coordinate what was going on, but those were giant
giggle sessions. Everyone was so giddy with pleasure that
they looked like impish elves preparing to push Santa off his
sled at thirty-thousand feet. It was impossible for those wom-
en to have shopped for their own family Christmas presents,
but they have often said over the years since then that Christmas had never before meant so much to them.

The strategy with the State Department of Child Welfare
was relatively simple. With the help of the judge and a few
well-placed telephone calls, Griggs was going to blackmail
them into making sure the kids would be transferred into the
group home at just the right moment. None of the children
knew about the Christmas surprise they were preparing for
them.

During the first week in December, the judge called
George Matthews and asked if he had found a home large

enough to accommodate the Clawson children. He said, "No, we haven't. We don't have any foster homes for five children. I'm certainly sorry," he said smugly, with a hint of sarcasm, "but you know and I know that if we did have, I would place the Clawson children there."

The judge said he understood the predicament the director of social welfare was in and that he was also sure that if Matthews had places to put these children, he would do so.

"As I have indicated," Matthews said impatiently, "if a home were available, I would place the Clawsons there."

The conversation was taped by the judge.

There were very few rules or standards designed for group homes at that time, but what rules there were they followed to the letter. Griggs and Howard went to each agency separately: the State Department of Child Welfare, the Fire Marshal, the Health Department, and others. The agencies one by one approved the facility. The nice part about a bureaucracy, they decided, was that its own disorientation can sometimes be useful.

Four days before Christmas, the house was completed, and the judge made his telephone call. Del and Griggs were sitting in the office listening to the conversation. It was almost as if they had spent their lives inventing a new rocket and were sitting there waiting to find out whether the rocket would or would not blast off, but they had everything set and there was no way it could backfire.

The judge called George Matthews and announced that he had found a place for all of the Clawson children. The director of social welfare hemmed and hawed and said he didn't know that they had any new openings for five children in any of *their* foster homes.

The judge informed him that a group home was being opened and had been approved by all the appropriate agencies and that he was going to order the placement of the Clawson children there.

The director of social welfare said, "No, you have no right

to do that—they're under *my* jurisdiction, and I'll place them where I think they should be."

The judge said, "Don't you remember when I asked about whether or not you had a place for the five Clawson children and you said . . ." and then he proceeded to play the tape of his previous conversation with the director.

After the tape was completed and Matthews had listened to the personal assurances he had given, there was a long, dead pause on the phone. He then said, "Please stay in your office a few minutes—I need to check with one of the supervisors and find out what the present status is—I will call you back."

They sat. They all sat in the judge's office for an hour and a half. Once in a while, they'd try to make small talk or try to think of a new strategy in case something went wrong, but none of them really believed that anything could go wrong.

Matthews finally called back. "Judge, I see two major problems getting these children back together in the same home." By this time, the judge was beginning to lose patience.

"And where in the hell did you find these hurdles?"

"Now wait a minute, Judge—there's no reason to get excited. I have two very realistic problems. The first one is that the smallest child . . ." The judge began to smile. "The problem is the smallest child is in a home where he is flourishing. The people love him and I could not take that child away from those people." Matthews' tone was self-righteous.

"If that's the problem you're worried about, forget it, because the group home we're talking about will be run by the people who now have the smallest child," the judge said pleasantly. He was actually chuckling as he talked.

Because the judge was holding the phone in such a way that Bud and Del could hear the conversation, they could hear the director of social welfare laughing along with the judge as he said, "Judge, it sounds as though you and your people have done your homework, but there is still another problem." Matthews sounded confident. "Two of the children are no longer under my jurisdiction. Patty, as you well

know, is at the State Reform School for Girls, and John is in
the State Hospital."

This time it was their turn to be quiet. Apparently Nancy
had not been informed, and, as a result, they didn't know
that John was already out of their reach.

They had counted on the fact that they would have to deal
with the issue of getting Pat out of the Girls' Reform School,
but they assumed also that after the judge explained the situation to the superintendent, he would release her. All of the
children placed in that facility were there under indeterminate sentences and could be released at the discretion of the
superintendent. But they were not prepared to get John out
of the State Hospital.

The judge shook his head as if to clear it and sat back. "Mr.
Matthews, I'll call you back." He hung up the phone and
said, "You just as well handle this one—my being a judge
isn't going to help one way or the other. You need to trace
down what section John's in, talk to the physician working
with his case, and if you need any help from me, let me
know. When we know what John's status is, I'll call the superintendent of the Girls' Reform School."

Griggs and Howard left the judge's office and at first
thought they would call the State Hospital, but somehow the
urgency of the situation demanded more direct contact than
that. It took them forty-five minutes to find the doctor in
charge of John's case. His diagnosis was short and simple:
John Clawson was depressed, and over the last two months
had definitely shown suicidal tendencies. He was at present
on a secure ward and watched constantly.

They sat the doctor down and explained from the beginning what had happened and how, and that they were in a
position to get the children back together. He agreed generally that the child should be back with his family, but he was
personally not going to take the responsibility of releasing a
potentially suicidal child.

After twenty minutes of pleading, it was agreed that a
week-long trial period was reasonable, if they would take the

necessary precautions. John could be picked up at the State Hospital and the doctor would prepare the appropriate releases for Tuesday, December 24th.

They had four of the five children, and they assumed the fifth was a matter of form.

After the judge had explained the situation to the superintendent, he said, "You know me, Judge, and under normal circumstances I couldn't agree with you more—that child should be reunited with her brothers and sisters—but if you've read the papers lately, you know I've had a few problems here with the girls. And as you also know, Judge, the Governor gave me this job with the specific request that I keep the roof on this goddammed place. Well, your little girl, Patricia, has not been the most cooperative kid in the place. Every time I let her out of the lockup, she tries to run away. Now, after she has done this three times, and I turn around and release her to you, how the hell do you expect me to keep discipline?"

The judge started to speak, but the superintendent interrupted angrily, "No, you know the law. It's up to *me* when I release this kid. Those sentences are indeterminate sentences you guys make and it's my decision, and you couldn't get this kid out of here by Christmas Eve if you were the Governor."

The phone was slammed at the other end, and the judge slowly put his phone back in the cradle and looked up at the two men standing next to their chairs. "I guess it's going to take some more time. I'm sorry, but I don't see a way out." The judge came out from behind the desk. "We can't get all hung up about this Christmas deadline and blow it because we want to live out some kind of happy Christmastime fantasy. We'll get her out so that she can be with the rest of her family, but it may not happen before Christmas."

He went on as if to convince himself, and then asked, "Well, do you see a way?" as he looked at Griggs. Del was smiling and said, "He told us how to get her out."

The judge sat back down and looked up with a frown on his face and said, "What do you mean?"

Del said, "I mean just what I said—he told us. Didn't you hear what he said—well, let's *see* whether or not the Governor himself can't get her out!"

The judge looked over at Griggs, lifted the palms of his hands, and shrugged his shoulders. "What are we going to do?"

Griggs said, "You mean before or after you call the Governor?"

They all laughed as the judge picked up the phone and told his secretary to dial the Governor. He didn't get the Governor—he got the Governor's secretary, who told him that he was at present on his way home from Washington. He would arrive at approximately six P.M. and would have just enough time to change his clothes before his annual Christmas party and would, the next morning at five-thirty A.M., leave for his annual vacation, which would last approximately two weeks.

The judge hung up the phone and reported what the secretary had said. "Gentlemen, I'm not one to say 'uncle' very fast, you know, but in this case I don't see how we can possibly get the Governor to intercede."

Griggs and Howard exchanged glances, and Del said, "I've never been to a Governor's Christmas party before, have you?"

Judge Harrington frowned and said, "You guys are out of your minds. Do you realize that you're putting my political career on the line? It's all well and good for you to discuss the possibility of crashing the Governor's Christmas party, but there's something about the dignity of the bench that prevents me from relenting to such an urge." Then he said with a grin, "But I *could* use a drink. Let's go see what the Governor is serving!"

Since none of them were experienced party crashers, the plan was simple. They would drive up and park at the Governor's mansion, walk up to the door, smile at anyone who might be standing there, and walk in.

The plan worked beautifully all the way up to the front door. The highway patrolman standing there was extremely cordial as he asked for their invitations. Since they didn't have invitations, they tried to explain what they were doing as two other patrolmen ushered them back through the front door.

Out in the cold again, Del solved the problem. "I'm not sure you gentlemen will be able to handle the indignity involved in my plan, but I think it's our only chance."

They looked at him and said, "Okay, what's your plan?"

He said, "Someone in there has to be serving drinks and handing out goodies on the little silver trays. They may be concerned about who's walking in the front door as a guest, but my guess is they're not terribly concerned who's walking in the back door to serve the goodies."

The judge said, "I think I have reached my limit," and he and Griggs headed for the car to wait.

Del was absolutely right. He walked in the back door, and being tall and black and good-looking, obviously was a ready-made server for a Governor's Christmas party.

Someone handed Del a white jacket and a silver tray, and he proceeded straight to the front door, depositing his jacket and tray on the way. He walked up to the highway patrolman who had earlier kept them out and announced, "Governor Parkhurst wants to see Judge Harrington and Mr. Griggs as soon as they arrive."

The patrolman knew immediately that he was in big trouble, so he trotted out to the parking lot and found them. The judge and Griggs were never quite sure what was happening until they were led past the smirking Del into the Governor's mansion.

The patrolman led them directly to the Governor and announced, "I found Judge Harrington, sir."

Governor Parkhurst looked up and said, "Oh?"

The judge jumped right in. "Governor, I must speak to you for three minutes on a matter of utmost importance. It is an emergency."

It took them ten minutes to tell the story, and the Governor shook his head in disbelief. "What does it take to preserve human dignity?" he asked. "Are you telling me that you three had to break into my house as servants to tell me that we have practically destroyed a family of children? What is wrong with our system?"

The Governor picked up the phone and found the superintendent at his own Christmas party. "Theodore, those people who want to get Patricia Clawson out of your particular institution are sitting in my den right now. They crashed my Christmas party to tell me that you're an ass, and quite frankly, I believe them. I want Patricia Clawson released to them. Do you understand that!"

He understood.

The pickup tasks were assigned. It was agreed that they would try to get the kids into the house without telling them what was going to happen, and let their first contact with one another have more meaning. The hardest job was going to be to pick up Patty and bring her 250 miles without telling her that she was finally going to get her wish. That was Bud's job.

Alicia and Del picked up Sue Anne; the judge went to the State Hospital to pick up John; and the president of the League picked up Karen. Each child was brought directly to a bedroom without seeing the others.

Griggs had left the night before to be in Belton early, knowing that the other children would be in the house by noon on Christmas Eve. Patty was taken directly from lockup. She looked like a haggard little old lady. Her eyes were sunken, her hair was dull and stringy, and her shoulders drooped.

It suddenly dawned on Griggs that Patty had been in the reformatory for more than a year.

The moment Griggs saw her walking down the hall, he wanted to tell her all about what was going to happen, but he resisted, knowing that that moment belonged to her and her brothers and sisters. The trip back was quiet. Her only comment was, "I don't know where you're taking me, but I want to tell you now that wherever it is, I'm going to run away, and I won't stop until I get my brothers and sisters back."

Griggs said, "I understand, Patty—I really do understand."

When they entered the house, they saw Del, the judge, and Mrs. Ruppert sitting in the living room as Tom and Alice Parks appeared in the front hall. Patty looked at the judge and said, "YOU!"

There was an awkward moment of silence when the judge stood up and took a few steps toward her.

Patty recoiled and demanded, "What's going on?"

No one answered. The plan had been simple. The children were to be brought in and taken to their separate rooms without being told what was happening. As soon as they were all in place, they would be called out and let whatever happened happen.

But before anyone could speak a word, a new sound floated down from one of the upstairs bedrooms. John was playing "Edelweiss."

Patty was stunned. She looked up, and her lips began to quiver. The tears began to flow as she bounded up the stairs. Doors began to bang open, and screams of delight filled the house.

Charlie, who was almost four years old, came running out of the kitchen screaming, "I bet that was my sister . . . I bet that was my sister!" and he scrambled up the stairs and dove into the pile of children hugging and jumping on one another in the hall.